AMBUSH

Aisling came to a small clearing. Wind Dancer, who'd been scouting ahead, appeared, his mind-picture sharp: Horses! Men who waited! Aisling halted, drawing power to cloak herself. She studied the waiting men. Two of them, nondescript, one was perhaps in his forties, the other younger, maybe by ten or fifteen years.

She extended a trace of mind-touch, and both came alert. That was odd. Those who had no Gift could not detect the touch when done so lightly. But their hands had dropped to swords as they looked about. She let her glamour fall and stepped in the clearing, where she could be seen. Then she spoke quietly.

"I seek those who wait at a gate?"

One bowed. "Lady, we wait for one who comes seeking."

"In Summer the lawleaves feed many birds, " Aisling said slowly.

He grinned happily. "And in Winter, berries are few, and the lost die."

Aisling nodded. "Quite true, *but not the words I need to hear!*"

Sword at the ready, she attacked, swinging the keen blade in dazzling circles. Moving into battle positions, both men involuntarily watched the sword. She trilled a battle shout, raised the sword as if to leap in, and struck savagely with her mind . . .

"Adventure, mystery, intrigue, humor, romance. Norton and McConchie serve them up with style. This dynamic duo has created a courageous and conflicted heroine and a supporting cast that's every bit as facinating as the main players. Keep it up, ladies! Your fans love it."

—*Starlog* on *Beast Master's Circus*

TOR BOOKS BY ANDRE NORTON

The Crystal Gryphon
Dare to Go A-Hunting
Flight in Yiktor
Forerunner
Forerunner: The Second Venture
Here Abide Monsters
Moon Called
Moon Mirror
The Prince Commands
Ralestone Luck
Stand and Deliver
Wheel of Stars
Wizards' Worlds
Wraiths of Time

Grandmasters' Choice (Editor)
The Jekyll Legacy (with Robert Bloch)
Gryphon's Eyrie (with A. C. Crispin)
Songsmith (with A. C. Crispin)
Caroline (with Enid Cushing)
Firehand (with P. M. Griffin)
Redline the Stars (with P. M. Griffin)
Sneeze on Sunday
  (with Grace Allen Hogarth)
House of Shadows (with Phyllis Miller)
Empire of the Eagle
  (with Susan Shwartz)
Imperial Lady (with Susan Shwartz)
The Duke's Ballad (with Lyn
  McConchie)
Three Hands for Scorpio

CAROLUS REX
  (with Rosemary Edghill)
The Shadow of Albion
Leopard in Exile

BEAST MASTER
  (with Lyn McConchie)
Beast Master's Ark
Beast Master's Circus

THE GATES TO WITCH WORLD
  (omnibus) Including:
Witch World
Web of the Witch World
Year of the Unicorn

LOST LANDS OF WITCH WORLD
  (omnibus) Including:
Three Against the Witch World
Warlock of the Witch World
Sorceress of the Witch World

THE WITCH WORLD
  (Editor)
Four from the Witch World
Tales from the Witch World 1
Tales from the Witch World 2
Tales from the Witch World 3

WITCH WORLD: THE TURNING
I Storms of Victory
  (with P. M. Griffin)
II Flight of Vengeance
  (with P. M. Griffin &
  Mary Schaub)
III On Wings of Magic
  (with Patricia Mathews &
  Sasha Miller)

MAGIC IN ITHKAR
  (Editor, with Robert Adams
  4 Volumes)

THE SOLAR QUEEN
  (with Sherwood Smith)
Derelict for Trade
A Mind for Trade

THE TIME TRADERS
  (with Sherwood Smith)
Echoes in Time
Atlantis Endgame

THE OAK, YEW, ASH,
  AND ROWAN CYCLE
To the King a Daughter
Knight or Knave
A Crown Disowned
Dragon Blade

THE HALFBLOOD CHRONICLES
  (with Mercedes Lackey)
The Elvenbane
Elvenblood
Elvenborn

THE DUKE'S BALLAD

ANDRE NORTON AND LYN McCONCHIE

TOR®
fantasy

A TOM DOHERTY ASSOCIATES BOOK

NEW YORK

This is a work of fiction. All the characters and events portrayed in this book are either products of the author's imagination or are used fictitiously.

THE DUKE'S BALLAD

Edited by James R. Frenkel

A Tor Book
Published by Tom Doherty Associates, LLC
175 Fifth Avenue
New York, NY 10010

www.tor.com

Tor® is a registered trademark of Tom Doherty Associates, LLC.

ISBN 0-765-34552-8
EAN 978-0-765-34552-3

First edition: January 2005
First mass market edition: November 2005

Printed in the United States of America

0 9 8 7 6 5 4 3 2 1

To the Canadian contingent of my friends:

To Garth Spencer, Bill Dodds, and Rodney Leighton.

And to Jo McCarthy, in New Zealand, who loves the Witch World.

Live Long and Prosper.

—L. McC.

ACKNOWLEDGMENTS

*T*o Jim Frenkel, the Tor editor who was stuck with my inability to spell or punctuate once again, and to the copy editor at Tor who coped with similar problems. Both of them did their best, and any errors remaining are almost certainly attributable to me.

To writer friends Sharman Horwood, Janrae Frank, and Rod Marsden, who made supportive speeches whenever I flagged.

And to Andre as always, who allowed me to play in her own original brilliantly imagined backyard.

Littera scripta manet.

— L. McC.

The Duke's Ballad

I

$\mathcal{T}$he girl sat mesmerized by fear in the big chair. She would have been a good-looking woman of some eighteen summers were it not for the fear that lit her face. Kirion, sorcerer to the duke of Kars, eyed her with mock sadness.

"Silly child. You won't be able to move until I release you from my spell. Silly twice over to reject the duke of Kars quite so firmly. You annoyed him, you know. He isn't used to not getting something he wants. But he'll have you to spend time with. You'll be besotted, infatuated, and before all the court too."

The captive gasped defiantly, and Kirion snickered. "No, no. You will, I assure you." He ignored the girl after that as he gathered his ingredients. Kirion laid out a pentacle and spoke the rolling incantations while watching his victim closely. At some stage in the proceedings the girl lost consciousness. Kirion finished and spoke softly.

"The duke is waiting. Will you sleep all day when your love looks for you?"

The blue eyes seemed blank, but behind them a trapped spirit struggled for freedom. It failed. The girl looked at Kirion for a moment, then her face lit adoringly. "My lord wants me. Where is he? I must go to him at once."

"You must go to your beloved?" Kirion prompted.

"Yes, of course. I must go to the duke. I love him and he loves me. We shall not be parted."

Kirion politely opened the door from his tower in the oldest part of the duchy palace. "Do not allow me to keep you then." He watched as the girl trotted off in search of the man who had demanded her affections.

Shastro should be careful, Kirion thought. The duke had ordered his sorcerer to change the mind of a would-be lover a few too many times of late. The court was beginning to mutter. There'd been no problems when it was young women of the Old Race. Kars city didn't care what happened to them, not as long as it wasn't too blatant.

But with Shastro turning his attentions to the girls about the court, the daughters of merchants and lesser nobles, instead of the young women partly or wholly of the Old Race, not all appreciated the honor. The girl who'd just departed had been of a minor noble family. Duke Shastro of the Duchy of Kars had desired her. She'd rejected him in no uncertain fashion, and Shastro had come running to his tame sorcerer to demand that the object of his desires desire him in turn—and at once.

Kirion had obliged, but it took power. Since he'd learned the way of stealing it from others who had it, he could do many things, but all such magical thefts leeched the power. Kirion remembered how his sister, Aisling, had escaped him, and he cursed. If only he'd been able to get his hands on her. Of the three of them, him, his younger brother, Keelan, and his sister, Aisling, it was she who had the widest, deepest powers.

She'd escaped him though. Despite much searching, he had not been able to find her—until now. Last night he'd used blood to spark another mind-search. The result had been interesting. Where she was he did not know, but he knew she was about to return. She was filled with power that could be stolen, drained, and her body cast aside to Kirion's greater glory. His mouth curved in a hungry smile.

He'd wait. It was said that all things came in time to those who waited with patience.

*A*isling squealed, catching the ball tossed to her as her eyes lit with laughter. She tossed it back, and the graceful Krogan girl caught it neatly.

Aisling sighed softly. "I'll miss it here."

"Then why leave?"

"I'm homesick," Aisling said simply. "I've been here three years. I love this place, but I miss Aiskeep." The Krogan girl nodded.

"I too have yearned for my home water. I have much yet to learn, so I will stay." She turned away, the ball held absently in one hand as she slipped into the nearby stream and lay full length. Aisling smiled at her and walked toward a small rise. Atop it she stared down along the landscape lying before her.

She liked Escore. She liked her teachers and those she had met in Estcarp. But Aiskeep called more strongly each season as she remembered what the seasons were like in the great gray keep where she'd been born. She missed her grandparents and her brother. She missed her friends in Karsten. And most of all, she worried about her elder brother, Kirion, and what evil he might now have learned.

Three years back she'd fled to keep Kirion from draining her gift for his own sorcery, and to prevent his crony Ruart from marrying her against her will. Ruart had died in his pursuit of Aisling, struck down by a man whose fiancée he had murdered some years ago. Only Kirion remained as a danger. Unless, she added ruefully to herself, you added half of the Karsten population. Her country was still taking seriously the admonition "Thou shalt not suffer a witch to live."

She gazed down the valley again. It had been so warmly welcoming, so kind and generous to a lonely half-breed from an enemy land. Its residents had not cared that half of her was from the new race that had taken over much of Karsten. The other half was of their ancient blood; that had been enough. Yet kind as they had been, their land was not her home.

A lithe form bounded up the hill and sat smirking at her through slitted eyes. She dropped to sit beside him as the big cat nudged her. She looked down . . . into understanding eyes. A picture formed in her mind of the high walls of Aiskeep with Shosho, her furred companion's mother, standing by the door. Behind Shosho stood Aisling's grandparents and her brother, Keelan. Then through the scene came longing, heart-hunger. The amber eyes that held hers blinked, and the scene was gone, but the question remained. She reached out, and he climbed into her lap. He was overly conscious of feline dignity and rarely did this, but at the moment they were alone.

She held him, his warm massive purring weight. She spoke into one furred ear as homesickness flared within her.

"Yes. I've worked so hard these three years since Neevor found us. Now Hilarion says I've learned much of what can be taught. The rest is practice. I'll never be an adept, but I'm a much better healer." Her hand went up to touch the pendant hidden in her bodice, then slipped down to grasp the hilt of the sheathed dagger at her waist.

"I had these and other gifts, and he has trained me well, I believe. I have added much to my store of knowledge. But it is time, Wind Dancer. Time I returned home." She hugged her friend. "And you. You are homesick too!" His yowl was emphatic agreement; she laughed. "Then we leave in a week, my brother-in-fur who dances with the breeze. But I'll have to sew a larger carrysack for you before we go."

Her hand smoothed soft fur. Wind Dancer had grown in three years. He'd been only eighteen months when they had risked their lives to cross the mountains to freedom here. He'd always given promise of being a big cat. In the years since, that promise had been fulfilled. Now he was knee-high to Aisling, some thirty-five pounds of bone and muscle. His claws and strength could bring down one of the small hill deer without difficulty. Though *small* was a relative term as they stood three feet at the shoulder.

Through the last years he'd often been away from her, hunting, roaming, enjoying life in a new land, always returning to see that she was well, to renew their ties and stalk about the valley as if he ruled there. Aisling hugged him, asking the question all who knew him asked sooner or later.

"Your mother, who *did* she find in the hills in Karsten?" Wind Dancer purred, slitting his eyes mysteriously. She laughed again. If he knew, he wasn't telling.

Together they strolled down the rise. When they reached her dwelling and she'd finished preparing the evening meal, Aisling ate alone save for Wind Dancer, and when she was done and the scraps and dishes cleared, she lay down to sleep. For the past two nights she'd not slept well, the unmade decision to leave or stay keeping her from true sleep. Her choice made, now she could sleep. She did so, feeling the warmth of Wind Dancer, who was cuddled into one hip.

She slid into the dream unawares. There was a tower, a sickly red and black, with the colors flaring and smoking together. She drifted down to enter and saw Kirion. She stepped back in disgust at what he did. She could have left, but instead she felt warning pulse within her. She was here for a purpose; she stayed.

Over the next hour she learned much. Time had not stood still with her brother while she'd been gone. Kirion had found books of sorcery; he'd had gifts from his blood even as she. Males, wholly or partly of the Old Race, could not normally access what powers might lurk in their bloodlines. But Kirion had had a greater desire for power than most. To aid that he'd turned to sorcery and blood magic. That she had known. It was why he'd hunted her through the mountains three years gone.

Now, somehow, he'd learned of her decision to return. He would seek her again. In her sleep she frowned. She could avoid him by staying here. But why should she allow her brother to dictate her life? She'd seen what he did. How he pandered to the appetites of a man not fit to rule Kars. Besides, the need to return, to see her home once more, flared up like a physical ache. There was a tugging, a demand that she obey. She would go home. Let Kirion beware if he stood in her way. She was not the small sister he'd once frightened.

With bright morning she remembered the dream and all she had seen. Remembered too her decision to do something about Kirion's evil, as if it thrust its way to the forefront of her mind, commanding her attention. But was it simply that she hated Kirion for his cruelty and her mind played tricks? Or had she true-dreamed? She went to Hilarion.

"Adept," her voice was formal, warning that she asked advice of the power, not the man alone. "I have dreamed."

His voice was equally formal, though warm to this favorite student. "Tell me your dream." She told. When she was silent again, he considered. He'd heard about Kirion when Aisling first arrived. Later, certain others who visited the city of Kars had talked as well. Kirion was evil. Not born but made that way by his own will. In evil he saw power not obtainable from other paths. His influence over the weak and lecherous ruler of Karsten was powerful. Kirion had raised the man to be duke, but his continued assistance and encouragement of the duke's appetites and fears were dangerous both to Karsten and to all of the Old Blood still there as well as to those who had fled elsewhere.

He nodded to Aisling. "Go. I will think on this and seek further knowledge. Return at sun high." She left in silence as Hilarion turned to his books. He was ready when Aisling returned. He placed a chair for her, offered wine, and waited until she was comfortable. Then he began.

"It was a true-dreaming, my pupil. A warning that you would do well to heed. Kirion grows in power; and as he does so, he turns his eyes toward Estcarp. He plans raids on the borders to net himself captives from whom he may wring more power. But that is not what he will say to Shastro. He plans to enrage the duke against the witches there once more. Shastro knows that his people have begun to complain about his ways with the sons and daughters of the court. Kirion will see that Shastro is 'paid' in girls and youths taken in the raids. Thus both ruler and ruled will be pleased with events."

"Estcarp won't," Aisling said dryly.

"No, nor will the Valley of the Green Silences here in Escore. I see the dream as a warning to you. Kirion is your brother. The power sets a sister against him. A geas is laid upon you. The choice is always yours, but that is my reading."

She bowed her head as she thought. Then her gaze rose to meet gentle eyes. "It is my choice and I choose. I will go back to Karsten as I planned. I'll see my family, find out all I can on the way and from them. But what should I do after that? How do I stop Kirion?"

Hilarion spread his hands. "I do not know. I can see little. Only that this task is for you and that you will not return to us I think." She flinched. "No, I do not foresee your death, more likely another choice. What I do see is that this task is important to us all. In time to come it may be a foundation stone."

Aisling sat silently for several minutes. It sounded like a heavy burden, but then Kirion was adept at imposing burdens on others. She nodded at last. "Yes. Well, if I'm going I'd better pack." She stood, and Hilarion touched her arm affectionately.

"Renthans will take you to the pass. Someone will meet you on the other side with mounts." Aisling gasped. So, Escore did have spies in Karsten. She'd suspected it.

Hilarion eyed her with mild amusement. It did no harm to confirm the girl would not be quite alone if she went up against that brother of hers. The knowledge that one's back was shielded often strengthened the sword arm. He looked after her as she trotted down the valley toward her home of the past three years.

No, he had not seen her death, but then he had not seen she would live either. He'd seen nothing beyond the choice she would make: she would return and face the man she had once fled. But her choice had been no choice, in a way; a geas now bound her. True-dream had called her, and Aisling would answer. Either way she would be gone from the valley. He'd hear of her, but she'd not return. He sighed, then shrugged. In a war one accepted such things. And a hawk trained must always in the end be freed to fly.

At her shelter Aisling was packing with the dubious assistance of Wind Dancer. He was enjoying driving her to exasperation by removing objects almost as fast as she placed them in saddlebags. When she rounded on him at last in genuine annoyance he padded backward to stand looking up at her. Wind Dancer gave a long thoughtful stare, first at the bags, then at Aisling. The emotion sent then might best be described as a large question mark.

Aisling collapsed on her bed. "I don't know why I'm so upset," she told the big cat. Well, in a way she did, she thought as he bounced into her lap and settled down, purring. Her hands slid over the thick plush fur, the motion and feeling calming her as always. Of course she wanted to go home again. Aiskeep called to her. Aiskeep, grandmother, grandfather, Keelan, her brother, old Hannion, the retired master-at-arms, his nephew Harron, who now held the job. Her friends on the Aiskeep garths.

She'd left them all for fear of Kirion and his plots when her elder brother had turned to black sorcery. Three years ago she'd been a bone fought over by two snarling dogs: Kirion, who wanted to leech her power and leave her dead or mindless, and his comrade Ruart, who wanted her for other reasons but whose destruction of her would have been as sure, if slower.

She'd made an almost lethal trip through the mountains to find sanctuary. Here in Escore she'd found training for her powers. Here she'd found peace, and the learning she'd begun to crave. Wind

Dancer, kit to her brother's cat, Shosho, had accompanied her. And in the end only his determination had brought them alive from the mountains.

A ripple of emotion seared through her. She smiled down and understood. Of course she was torn. She was going back to the place and people she loved most in all the world. But she returned too, to the man she hated and feared most, to face him in sorcerous combat if need be. Joy and fear battled. Most annoying, she *had to* go, and she resented the geas laid on her. She fought against the order that she must leave her peaceful life to return to strife.

Her fingers riffled automatically through Wind Dancer's fur as she thought. There was always a choice. She could fight to stay. But if she stayed would not Kirion's evil go unchecked? But then if she fought him, what said he could not win? Then the lands would be poorer by other things she could have done had she not died. She sat among half-packed saddlebags as the day slowly waned to dusk.

In those hours she reviewed her life: her training here and all the paths she could see of possible choices made. When she rose at first dark she was so stiff she could barely stand. She stretched, her brain exhausted but calm. Wind Dancer leaped lightly from her lap and patted her with a large paw. His mind sent a desire for food to eat, sweet milk to drink.

Laughing, Aisling ran to the kitchen and fed him, returned with food and drink for herself, lit the single globe with a flick of her mind, and resumed her packing. With the stuffed saddlebags lying ready she ate, drank, then moved to lie full length on the bed. Hilarion had told the truth. Sister was set against brother on the gaming board.

She smiled as she relaxed. Yet in few games was only one piece against another. There were many. She would have Aiskeep, and old Geavon and his kin at Gerith Keep. Kirion had injured many as had his puppet duke. The victims who'd survived and those who loved them would aid her if given the opportunity. Against her she

had Kirion and Shastro: black sorcery and the lord duke of Kars—
powerful opponents.

But something fierce within her rose to fight that. They were
powerful, yes. But with the teaching she'd been given here, she
would be no easy morsel. She damped the emotion swiftly. She must
be cunning, cautious. She must undermine slowly and with care. If
her brother and the duke were seen to fail once or twice, more would
rise against them. Kirion would spend strength watching those, and
that use of strength would weaken him further. Beside her, Wind
Dancer purred approval.

Aisling snuggled into her blankets. In the morning they would
ride. She would have left the cat behind; it could be dangerous for
him, but he'd have none of it. He was returning too, and that was his
decision to make. She put out an arm and cuddled him closer, hearing
and feeling the soft rumbling purr. It wouldn't be home without him.

*M*any days' travel away Kirion sat watching his newest
puppet dance for the duke. Shastro had been delighted.
Kirion was only tired, and irritated at the loss of so much power
merely to provide another toy. He wouldn't mind so much if Shastro didn't use up his playthings so quickly, but this one would last a
week, maybe a month, two at most. Then she'd be discarded, and
the duke's eyes would light on another to be coaxed—or coerced—
to the ducal bed.

It was becoming a nuisance. He could use potions to lesson
Shastro's lusts, but without a blurring of the duke's mind as well it
would be obvious to his victim what had been done. Shastro would
rise in the kind of fury only a weak man can produce. Kirion had
seen that once. He had no wish to have it turned on himself. Not
that he could be harmed, of course, but he'd have to defend himself.
That would drive Shastro to use everything at his command.

Kirion bit back a snarl. He'd survive if that happened and the duke wouldn't, but then he'd have lost his figurehead. Lost too his tower at the palace, and his position. To take power openly was to risk too much—his own skin for a start. As long as Shastro ruled, the people blamed any excesses on the duke. Kirion was careful to counsel moderation now and again, always within earshot of others of the court. He had a name as a powerful sorcerer but one who obeyed the duke and tried to temper some of the ruler's ways.

No one liked the duke's sorcerer much. But they didn't really notice him either. And that was how Kirion wanted it. He could recall his grandmother's tales of the Horning, how her family had been slaughtered. The then duke had been set against those of the Old Race and Blood. Kirion did not desire too many to talk about his abilities, just in case. He stood and unobtrusively strolled to the door.

Back in his tower he found his scrying bowl, filled it with water, summoned stolen power, and scried again to receive the same answer: Aisling was returning. From where or when he could not discover, but she was coming home. He called, and a man cringed as he made his way through the door.

Kirion eyed the man's humble posture. The man was a competent enough steward, a satisfactory and most amusing servant although the fool knew it not. Kirion kept the man befogged in a series of dreams, paid him nothing, allowed him barely enough to eat, and permitted him to live. It was a useful system for one who was a sorcerer.

"Varnar, you will send out spies. They will watch Gerith Keep and Aiskeep, three men to each place. Each keep must be watched at all times. They are to look for a young woman, or a boy who could be the woman in disguise. If they miss her I'll have them for my tower."

Varnar shivered. "Yes, my Lord."

"They are to watch continually. If the quarry appears one of them must ride to tell me. The other two are to remain on watch. If she leaves, one man is to follow her while the other returns to tell me. Is that understood? Repeat the instructions." Varnar did so. "Good. Also you will post three men by a small abandoned garth in the hills. I'll give you a map for them. They're to make camp there. If the woman comes they are to seize her if possible and bring her to me. But only if they are sure they can take her uninjured."

His face twisted into a terrifying scowl. "Make certain they understand. If she is injured, if they *dare* to lay hands on her for anything but to restrain her, I shall visit torments unspeakable upon them. I must have her . . . *undamaged*." He invested the last word with a ferocious significance that his servant completely understood.

"They shall be told, Lord." Varnar bowed his way out and ran to find Kirion's spies. Gods help the poor young lady whoever she might be. Varnar knew only too well what such a command meant. He saw the men ride out and reported that to his lord before being dismissed. He crept from the sorcerer's presence to be alone in his own quarters. He hated his master with every fiber of his being, but something held him here. Perhaps the dreams he dreamed. Apart from which it was unsafe to cross Kirion; those who did so died in ways it was not good to recall.

He ate and slept then, wrapped in two threadbare blankets on a bare chill stone floor. He dreamed of the past. He had once slept on finest wool between linen sheets. In that time so long behind other events that the memories grew dim, he'd once given orders, shared his hall with one whose eyes smiled love. There'd been scampering footsteps, a small girl's voice. But he must forget all of that. If he remembered, Kirion would read it, and that was dangerous.

In his study Kirion did read and smiled, a slow vicious smirk that lit his face with a look that would have disturbed even Shastro. Kirion's little experiment was starting to work. Dreams, memories, life were illusions, and he was a master illusionist. Let Varnar learn that. After all, one must amuse oneself, or what was power for?

II

――――◇――――

*A*isling lifted heavy saddlebags. Beside her Wind Dancer bounced in excitement as she picked up his carrysack and tossed it over one shoulder. She exited her shelter to find a renthan named Teelar waiting. The intelligent, deerlike mount eyed her and the excited cat, then mind-sent to Wind Dancer.

"Small friend, remember your claws."

Wind Dancer made an indignant sound. Aisling smiled. "Teelar, don't worry. He'll be riding on *my* back not yours." She tossed the bags over his back and knelt to tuck Wind Dancer into the carrysack. With him secure she lifted it, fitting the straps over her shoulders and fastening the waist strap. Wind Dancer peered out over her shoulder, resting one large paw against the side of her neck.

Aisling mounted, wondering briefly if any would come to bid her farewell. It felt lonely to leave, to know that she was unlikely ever to see the valley or even Escore again. It would ease the feeling if . . .

Teelar turned the bend toward the valley's rune-guarded exit and halted just beyond the glowing rune signs. Before him were Krogan, adepts, people from the valley, and a flittering of Flannan. Hilarion stepped out from the group.

"We are come to farewell you, my student. It is only fitting that you know you leave friends here." He saw her face widen in one of her joyous smiles. He would miss the girl. She soaked up learning as

Krogan soaked up water after too long on land. Aisling whirled from friend to friend, hugging, talking, accepting small gifts and fitting them into her saddlebags. At last, after more hugging, her friends began to drift back into the valley. Other renthans appeared, and Hilarion and three guards swung up onto their respective mounts. Aisling looked a question.

"We ride with you," the adept said briefly. He signaled and the small group started. They rode quietly, senses alert. The Valley of the Green Silences was in a sense headquarters for the Light. This close, few of the Dark would dare to venture, but it did no harm to be wary. Farther on toward the mountains the Dark had strongholds that had to be passed, and to alert them too soon was folly.

They rode through a long day. Nothing of moment occurred, but even the mere riding was tiring as they had to stay alert. At nightfall they made camp in a safe haven. The guards lit a small fire, preparing food while Wind Dancer lay motionless watching the flames, his eyes half-shut. Hilarion took his pupil aside. His face was grave as he handed her a small pouch. She opened it and gave a small gasp.

"A witch jewel. But Hilarion, I was never taught to use this. You said—" He raised a hand to silence her.

"I said you had no need of a witch jewel when you had your pendant. That is true." He smiled slowly. "Nor if you could examine this would you find the usual qualities of a jewel. It is a trap. I prepared it in company with those others of us who feel you should have all the aid we can give you. It is keyed to you. Not the reverse. If it is destroyed it will cause you no pain nor any distress."

"What if another attempts to probe it?"

Hilarion looked calm. "Then it will backlash with great ferocity. It will react with power proportionate to the other's. The stronger he is, the greater the backlash, but also, as I say, it is keyed to you. If you feel you have no other hope, then there is a command you may give. It will then release all its power. You will die, but also everything within several yards of you will be completely destroyed as well." He lowered his voice.

"The command is . . ." the sound vibrated softly in the air. "But the word is only half. You must also say this in your mind, directing the thought at the jewel before you speak the word. That keys it to be ready. The moment the word is spoken aloud the power will strike. It matters not if several days have elapsed. It is keyed, and it will strike then when you say the word."

He looked at her. "I emphasize, it is not a witch jewel. It is a trap designed to appear as a jewel. I made it as an experiment. Because of its properties it could not be used by Estcarp witches. The keying is too close to their own jewels. But your pendant is different. To use one is not to trigger the other. I would suggest that you wear the witch jewel openly if the time comes when you are beset, but hide the pendant within your clothing. Let any who come against you believe that the jewel is your focus. That way they will direct any attack against it, and you will be free to use the pendant. As for the pendant, I have questions about it."

Aisling nodded. "What questions, Adept?"

"You said that you knew nothing of the pendant's origins. That it came down from your grandmother. But what of her, what do you know of her kin, her clan, her family?"

Aisling spread her hands. "She was of the Old Blood. Pure, so it was said. I remember my parents speaking once. Some tale about the line having blood other than human, too. Or a different race." Hilarian seemed to become more interested. "I know so little, only that it was given before the Horning to Larian, my grandmother's brother. When the Horning came he gave it to my grandmother for safekeeping. Before that, it was held as a bride gift to be given to the new wife of each heir in turn."

"Were there any customs?"

"None that I know, save that it was only to be given the morning after the wedding."

He blinked. "Now that is interesting. It was to be given only when the giver could be sure the receiver no longer had power to use it fully."

"I never thought of it like that."

"No." He thought a moment. "You use it as a focus to reach your own power. Have you ever tried to reach power within the pendant?"

"No, not on purpose, but . . ." her voice faded as she remembered. Kirion and Ruart had sent servants. She'd been kidnapped from Gerith Keep, struck down, drugged, taken to her brother and his lecherous crony. They'd quarreled as to who should use her, and while they gambled to decide, she'd been locked several levels down in Ruart's dungeons.

She explained. "I'd found a metal strip and picked the locks, but at the ground level the door had been barred from the other side as well. I raised the bar by the power of my mind alone." She could still recall that effort, and now she was remembering something she had forgotten from that time.

"I didn't have the pendant then, but I'd seen it when I worked with Grandmother. I think I called the shape of it. I used it to focus." Her eyes blanked as she remembered the strain of lifting the bar, her exhaustion afterward. "It was only when I could really see it in my mind that I was able to lift the bar. Is that important?"

Hilarion reached out and touched the chain on which the pendant hung. His fingers drew it into view. "The work is very old, from before the departure of your people to Estcarp. It was adept-made. I think its purpose was to improve what little power was left to the woman of the house after her wedding. But with the loss of most of her gift she could not truly bond to it, only use it.

Hilarion nodded. "Your grandmother must have become one with it as a child. It seems that the small gift she had did not lessen with her marriage. And yet she was able to pass the pendant to you, which indicates it is more powerful than it appears. It has power of a kind strange to me, and I dare not probe too deeply. I have no wish to damage it." His eyes met hers. "But, Aisling, if you are about to lose the battle and even the witch jewel has failed you, call on this."

"What about my dagger?"

"A pretty thing and useful. It too is old and made by the same hand I think. Did your grandmother ever use it?"

"No. She was given it by Larian too, but she laid it away once she was in Aiskeep." Aisling smiled. "I'm the first to wear them both. How could it be from the same place, Hilarion? They came from different sides of the family." Her teacher had a strange look on his face, the look of one who knows there is something he has forgotten and strives fruitlessly to remember. He shrugged at last.

"I once heard something I can not recall. Not that it is likely to matter. As to your question, both sides of your family carried some blood of the Old Race. Maybe once they were kin. But let us go to sit by the fire and eat before we sleep. We will ride long again tomorrow."

That they did and for another day more in a cautious circling around places where evil lurked. But close to the mountains they could swing wide no further. Hilarion went ahead and returned at a steady trot.

"Come with me, Aisling. There is a place here that should be cleansed, but there is danger." He frowned. "If we do this, then we will alert others. They will come hunting, and they must not find you." He thought briefly. "We shall wait tonight. In the morning we shall destroy this thing, and you shall ride at once for the river pass. We will remain. If hunters come seeking us then we shall ride openly in another direction. Let them follow us while you travel the pass in safety."

Aisling would have objected. She was no soft-handed lady to leave friends fighting behind her and ride on. But a look at Hilarion's stern face convinced her he meant what he said. Nor did he think the less of her. She was to ride now, so that she might fight a different battle. She bowed her head in acceptance. From the fire came an imperative yowl and a mind-sending. There was food and warmth here. Why did his human stand in the chill dark unfed? Both people laughed and walked back to the fire.

Dawn came soon enough. It was late spring and the days were lengthening. They rode, passing a small village just beginning to stir. Hilarian ignored it; they had no need for supplies as yet, and he wanted no questions as to who they were or where they rode. This place of the Dark was new. It was therefore even more important that it be destroyed. He glanced away to the left where from afar the trees of the mosswomen's forest could be seen.

The stream that circled the forest was a way into Karsten. Aisling would not have to scale mountains on this trip. The river pass was rarely used. There was only a brief time in the year when it was safe, and the whole area on the Karsten side was almost empty of people. There had always been few garths or keeps there. With the Horning most of those had been destroyed, and of the new Karsten breed, none had chosen to settle again. Teelar would take the pass at a steady trudge.

Once on the Karsten side Aisling would have to travel on foot with Wind Dancer. Farther along the trail Hilarion's man or men would be waiting for her with a mount. But right now they had to dispose of the new site that had been settled by dangerous nonhuman forces. The guard had ridden ahead, spreading out in scout formation. Aisling rode back from Hilarion, whose mount was staying some two hundred yards behind the scouts.

At the very edge of danger she dismounted. Wind Dancer, still in his carrysack, was handed to one of the guards, and all three scouts retired out of range. Aisling and Hilarion conferred swiftly. Her hands flickered in shapes and gestures as she demonstrated her intentions. Then they both remounted, and Aisling started Teelar moving. He edged closer in a slow-walking spiral. The girl opened her mind, just enough to read the enticement that would reach for her shortly.

She felt it as they came in range of the slow-spreading pool of new evil. There was a mind-stench to the thing. And a drawing. She allowed it to sense her, not as she was but as a simple wondering girl, defenseless and ignorant. Its hunger quickened. The call changed: it sent dreams, visions of wonderful things. Only come to me and you shall have everything you want, it called. Come and find all you have ever desired.

Teelar moved in slowly, answering the careful nudge of her heel. His mind was blanked. The evil, eyeless and knowing only that a victim approached at the speed of one afoot, was less wary. Hilarion, his mind also blanked to it, but waiting, watching, sat his mount. He had no need to use mind-powers to read the time to strike. He watched Aisling. One hand was rising higher, out to shoulder level, the palm turned to hang edge down. There it stayed.

Aisling let her mind accept the offerings. They were wonderful. She'd be powerful, desired. She would be a leader, a ruler. Teelar moved a little faster under her signal. The evil roiled in its pool. A victim, young, innocent, and with the very faintest trace of untrained power. What a prize, a delectable tidbit to savor. It opened itself and called with all its strength, and Aisling's hand chopped down. Even as she signaled, her mind hardened to spear point and slashed in.

Behind her, less than a heartbeat later, Hilarion threw in his greater power. They carved through the mind of the evil like lightning through storm sky, the blue of their power against the smoky black of the Dark. It screamed once and was gone, small oily puffs of noxious miasma rising lazily from the land where it had anchored its being.

Hilarion closed in. He raised his hands, and began to chant softly. The land had only recently been used by Darkness. If he acted swiftly it would heal. His mount and Teelar added power. The scorched circle of land rippled. Aisling added her own gifts of healing, and the land shivered. A hint of green showed, then, in a rush, a tiny tide of grass swept over the circle, pouring from the edges to envelop what had been an ugly twenty-foot circle gouged deep into the earth.

The scouts moved in with cries of approval. One produced a pouch, tossing illbane seeds to spray across the new grass. Power urged growth, and with the grass, the tiny plants rose up to hold the land secure. Where illbane blooms no minor evil can live. Wind Dancer squirmed from his carrysack and pounced gaily across the circle. Aisling laughed.

"I think he's saying that we've done well." She watched as the big cat sniffed a flower and sneezed vigorously.

Hilarion nodded. "Yes, now we ride. Best we're away from here in case any come hunting whoever it was that killed their comrade."

They mounted again, and the renthans leaped into a steady rocking canter. They could hold that pace for hours and now they did. By dusk the small group was partway through the river pass. Hilarion watched his pupil as she rode. The false jewel would see that her brother could not steal her gifts to use against others. And the other ability implanted in the jewel might save her. He would have wished to tell her, but wisdom bade him to silence. Visions in his crystal warned that Aisling would fight better if she did not know that. In this way at least, she was being used. He glanced about him before signaling a halt.

They camped late, rose early, and rode again. As they traveled he taught her the passwords that would reveal whether those who came to meet her were truly his messengers. By sun high they reached the far side of the pass. Here Hilarion and the others would leave Aisling. She had supplies, all around her the land bloomed, and she had weapons with which to hunt at need. She would walk south with Wind Dancer.

With brief farewells, she did so. The weather was lovely. Not too hot as yet but warm enough at night to sleep under the sky if they wished.

She passed the large ruined keep which had once been the home of some family of the Old Race. It was half keep and half fortified manor. She did not go in; it was too sad.

She came to a small clearing. Wind Dancer, who'd been scouting ahead, appeared, his mind-picture sharp: Horses! Men who waited! Aisling halted. Then she circled cautiously, drawing power to cloak herself. Wind Dancer swept up to guard her back. She studied the waiting men. Two of them, nondescript, one who was perhaps in his forties, the other younger, maybe by ten or fifteen years. One, the larger of the pair, had medium brown hair; the other was fairer, almost blond. Both were moderately well dressed but without obvious jewelry, not even a ring. Purely Karsten from their looks, and that was strange. Why would men without traces of the Old Blood aid Hilarion?

She extended a trace of mind-touch, and both came alert. That was odder still. Those who had no gifts could not detect the touch when done so lightly. But here hands had dropped to swords as they looked about. She let her glamour fall and stepped into the clearing, where she could be seen. Then she spoke quietly.

"I seek those who wait at a gate?"

One bowed. "Lady, we wait for one who comes seeking."

"In summer the lawleaves feed many birds," Aisling said slowly.

He grinned happily. "And in winter, berries are few, and the lost die."

Aisling nodded. "Quite true, *but not the words I needed to hear*!"

She attacked, sword at the ready, swinging the keen blade in dazzling circles. It was a trick the valley had taught her, and it worked here as well. Moving into battle positions, both men involuntarily watched the sword. She trilled a battle shout, raised the sword as if to leap in, and struck savagely with her mind. Both men collapsed. Wide open, expecting a physical attack, they had forgotten to trigger any protections they might have been given against the power.

She stood with Wind Dancer, looking down at them. Her face was sad. In the valley where she had trained in the use of her power, she had learned to use her gift to attack if it was necessary. Now, she could not leave enemies at her back, yet she had never slain in cold blood. She did not believe she could do so now. Often enough she had seen her keep's butcher at his work, and while hunting she had killed deer and butchered them as any hunter must. Still, these were humans, not some bodiless evil nor beasts she had killed cleanly during a hunt.

Wind Dancer had left her and was trotting busily about the clearing. His ears went up, signaling interest, then he was gone. She caught a glimpse of him as he followed a trail, and her own curiosity was pricked. She hastily bound both men and followed her friend.

He led her to a half-cave in a rock outcrop. He padded inside and a young male voice spoke in astonishment.

"What are you? You're either the biggest of your kind I've ever seen or not what you appear. Are you . . . are you one of the power?"

Wind Dancer chirped a summons to his human. Aisling smiled and obeyed. If Wind Dancer called, then there was no danger for her here. She stepped into the half-cave and looked about. The man who'd spoken was bound in a positive cocoon of rope. He'd been gagged but he had managed to scrape that free. His face was a mask of blood and bruises, but he appeared little damaged apart from what had clearly been a nasty beating.

His face under the mess was vaguely familiar. She took out her leather water bottle, wiped away some of the blood from the man's face, and allowed him to drink. Then she stepped back.

"Who are you and what are you doing here?"

He looked up at her wryly. "I came with a friend to wait for one who came seeking those who waited at a gate." Aisling straightened. That was half of the password. Could it be this was the true messenger? She looked at him.

"In summer the lawleaves feed many birds," Aisling said slowly.

He nodded, grimacing as he moved. "And in winter berries are few, but bears may feast before."

It was the password, yet she must move carefully. She knelt at his side. "I have to be certain. How came you here, and who were the two other men I met first?"

"Two others? Are they secured?" She nodded. "Then I shall speak swiftly. We should be away from here as fast as we can. Where two found you, others may follow. Word came to me that my friend and I should bring a spare mount, meet a traveler here and guide her back to the duchy. We found four men waiting at a deserted garth. They challenged us and we fought. We escaped them, killing one and leaving another wounded, but still the others pursued.

"We came to a wood and circled it. There was in me a warning that to enter would not be worth the time we might save on the trail. Later we were ambushed by those we had escaped. It seems they did not fear the wood." He sighed. "A right choice still for us. They paid the wood with their wounded one for free passage. They boasted of it. One of them is skilled with a sling. I was struck on the head, and when I recovered they had my friend."

He looked up at Aisling, his eyes filling with tears. "I knew he was weak. I should never have allowed him to know what I did. The fault was mine. Mine the blame."

Aisling nodded. So this one's companion had talked, under torture or threat of it. "What happened to him afterward?"

"They cut his throat and laughed." His voice was savage. "But he had not quite betrayed you. He gave them almost the password twisting only the last portion. I can still see his eyes now, so hopeful on me. Begging me to understand and forgive him." He sobbed once. "I knew he feared pain. He was taken once when he was a child, because someone recalled his family had a trace of the Old Blood. When my family found him he'd been terribly treated. After that he always feared pain greatly. The men who took us hurt him badly . . . he could not withstand it. Lady, please. Do not condemn him."

Aisling remembered her grandmother's tale of how her family had died in the Horning. Despite his terror this one's friend had still lied, given her a warning and a chance to turn the tables. Aisling knelt and slashed the ropes. "Where does his body lie? We should bury him before we leave." The sudden light in his face was payment.

"Back by the edge of the wood. But what of these you left bound? Lady, it is too dangerous to leave them alive. They would not talk freely and I . . . I have little stomach for torture. But I would like very much to know who sent them and who they sought." As he spoke he was stretching, loosening muscles stiffened by a long time bound in one place.

Aisling smiled grimly. "Not torture, no. But they will talk." She offered him the water bottle again, and he drank. Better to remain wary, Aisling thought. She looked at him and felt again the sense that somewhere she had seen him before. He looked at her as he handed back the container, and she nodded. "What is your name?"

He looked worried. "Is it safe to share names, Lady? Yet I owe you a life. I shall give you mine and let you use another 'til such time as you are certain of my honor. I am Hadrann of Aranskeep."

Aisling bit back a gasp. So *that* was why she'd half-recognized his face. She'd seen his father at Teral Market. Her grandparents had been friends with the Lord of Aranskeep, and sometimes if they met at the market, they shared food in one of the larger private rooms. She searched her memory. Yes, this was the heir. They called him Rann for short, and he'd often been at Kars court. He'd also shipped on a Sulcar trader for a year.

She'd seen his father on a number of occasions but in her recollection, never Rann. Or maybe she had. There was a dim memory of a young boy with the Lord of Aranskeep once. Oblivious to her thoughts, Rann was continuing to stretch and work his muscles back into shape. The lady would give him a name to use when she was ready. Aisling finished thinking and nodded to him.

"My name is Jonrie of Jontor's garth at Aiskeep."

His brows went up. "So that is why you look familiar. I've seen Lord Trovagh more than once." He suddenly recalled she had claimed garth as home, not keep, and his face flamed. "Forgive me. I spoke without thinking."

Aisling had real trouble keeping her face straight. So he'd leaped to the conclusion she was her grandfather's bastard, had he? That was well enough. It explained a lot without giving too much away. She made her mouth droop a little.

"It is true the Lord and I are kin. I would not deny it. He and his have always treated me well. And from the line I received gifts." That last she emphasized a little and saw him understand. It was quite true, too, she reflected, just not exactly as he'd believe. "Now, let us seek out those I bound and require them to make accounting."

With Wind Dancer bringing up the rear she led Rann off along the trail. As she walked she wondered: just how had the heir to Aranskeep become mixed up in this affair. She'd like to hear, but at the moment there were other questions more pressing. She entered the small clearing and stood looking down grimly on the two bound and gagged forms that lay there still, glaring up at her defiantly. She needed answers and she would have them.

III

------◆◇◆------

*T*he two men had wriggled to a half-sitting position against each other, and as Aisling and Rann arrived, one had been attempting to chew the bonds. They flinched as Wind Dancer padded forward to smell them. He looked back at Aisling, his nose wrinkling in disgust. She chuckled.

"You might get free that way, but not for a month or so. Better you answer my questions. I might then let you go in a shorter time." She eyed them thoughtfully. "Kirion sent you." Her voice was flat. It had to be.

The older of the pair jerked in disbelief. "How——?"

"Did I know?" She wasn't going to mention that Wind Dancer had smelled Kirion's scent on the smaller, younger man and had sent her a picture. "Ah, but I know many things. And," her tone shifted to signal danger, "I shall know more. You will tell me. I already know who sent you hunting. You were sent to find me and take me prisoner. Kirion said you were not to lay hands on me on pain of death. I was to be brought to him untouched and undamaged, wasn't I?"

He stared up sullenly. "You know all, Lady. Why ask us then?"

"I know, but I'll hear it from you, all of it. To begin with, who are you two and why would you obey such an order?" Magic should not frighten Rann. He wouldn't be working with Hilarion if it did.

She gestured at the older man, her fingers leaving a faint trace of silver as they traced the painless spell. "Talk to me, *now!*"

His eyes glazed as the spell struck home, and he talked in a gush of words. She questioned him, Hadrann putting in a query now and again. When they were done Aisling stared at her captives feeling sick. What was it about her country that bred men like this? She felt fouled just being here close to them. From the corner of her eye she noticed that her companion was looking similarly sickened. Aranskeep at least did not indulge in such activities. Or did it? Could she be sure?

She shook her head slowly. There was no vice in Rann's face, only disgust at what he'd heard. From far back in her memory a small bell rang: something about Aranskeep. It would wait. She stared at the bound pair. To release them was to send word to Kirion that she'd arrived. They'd go back to him, tell him everything, endanger Rann as well. And how many other captives would they drag to Kirion's tower for him? They must die, for the sake of her mission. She'd talked to Hilarion about this kind of decision.

There are times when even the Light must make hard choices, he'd told her. Was this one of those times? But Rann, watching and listening, had seen the problem too. He moved away, circled casually. He drew his dagger and quietly, without the captives seeing him approach, moved behind them. The keen blade slashed twice.

Aisling vomited. She couldn't help it. Wind Dancer ran to her, pushing his head against her hands in comfort. Aisling had ridden with scouts and helped to battle the Dark, but that had been straightforward: her life or theirs, and her blood had run hot. This was butchery, and she loathed it. Hadrann knew that of me, she thought. He acted so that I did not have to. She turned, steadying her voice, smoothing her face. One hand was buried in Wind Dancer's warm thick fur.

"Thank you. And forgive me my weakness." She smiled wryly.

"As some faint or may have noses that bleed at a touch, so I have a stomach that heaves easily." She hid a smile as she remembered; it had saved her once. Ruart had not appreciated the event. She looked at Hadrann kindly. "I know it had to be done. It was kind of you to save me the doing."

He looked up from where he was checking the bodies. "Thank me not. It was necessary, yes, but I regret that it also pleased me a little. They tortured my friend before me. Broke him to betrayal. Then they murdered Brovar and laughed." He produced a pouch of coins and several items of jewelry. "Ah ha. Well, some of that they stole from us. The rest no doubt was payment for your swift return to this Kirion."

He broke off looking thoughtful. "Kirion? That wouldn't be the slimy little toad who encourages our lord duke in all his excesses, would it?"

"I'm afraid so."

"Kirion of Aiskeep, heir to Lord Trovagh."

"Well, of Aiskeep yes, but it's Keelan who's heir. That's part of the trouble. Lord Trovagh disinherited Kirion, and it wasn't a decision that pleased the . . . er . . . slimy little toad."

Rann grinned widely. "I'd bet it didn't. And I presume that being disinherited meant that Kirion wasn't getting an heir's allowance from Aiskeep either?"

Aisling nodded. Trovagh would not leave his ex-heir penniless, but he'd left him an amount that was only enough for a farmer's son in Kars. Kirion wouldn't have starved, but merely not starving wasn't what her brother had in mind. He wanted to live richly, in comfort and with influence. A man didn't do any of that on a few silvers a month. Kirion didn't need to. By pandering to the duke he'd been granted a keep, a tower in the palace, and a ducal allowance fit to keep Kirion in the luxury he believed his due.

She said so. "And if he had to do a few things for Shastro he wouldn't mind. He'd enjoy doing them and watching how the court feared him."

"I saw that the few times I was there," Rann said slowly. As they talked, he dragged the bodies toward a small deep hollow, bringing rocks to the edge of that to pile over the bodies. His gaze turned to her. "But these men were sent to trick you. They'd have captured you and taken you to Kirion's tower. Why? You're kin. Would he harm a kinswoman?"

Aisling snorted. "He'd harm his grandfather, his brother, or the gods themselves if it would buy him what he wanted. Shastro should beware. To Kirion he's just a useful tool. The day he stops being useful Kirion won't lift a finger to help him."

"But why you?" His expression was suddenly horrified. "He isn't, he doesn't . . ."

Aisling smiled bitterly. "No, he doesn't desire me. It's my abilities he has in mind. From what I already know—and his man confirmed—Kirion's found even better ways to leech power from any who have not the wards or power to prevent such a theft."

"But that's black sorcery. The duke, he can't know."

"He knows," Aisling said harshly. "Or what's more likely, he guesses and doesn't want to know. Then if he must turn on Kirion, he can always claim horrified ignorance." She had checked the dead men's packs. Lashed to one had been a small folding shovel, the kind often used in Karsten to dig a safe fire pit for a man on the road in wild country. Aisling looked about and considered her next move.

If she took earth from that patch of brush she could cover the raw soil with leaves. She pointed mutely to a hollow. Rann began to dig at the bottom of it, leaving Aisling to carry the earth away in an emptied pack belonging to one of the dead men. He curled the bodies down into the hollow. Over them he placed their bedding, tucking it in well. With the earth and rocks over them, it might keep scavengers from the bodies for a while. The longer the better, in case Kirion sent others in this direction.

With the earth and rocks replaced over the bodies, Aisling stood and straightened her aching back. She glanced at her companion as he brought dry leaves to scatter above the now level area. It was well done. To the passerby there were no obvious signs that here lay a grave. She picked up the money pouches and ran her fingers over them lightly, her mind open. No, there was no tracker placed on anything. Interesting. From what she knew of her brother he wasn't one to assume anything.

Wind Dancer had moved to stand on the grave and was continuing to sniff about curiously. Aisling received nothing from him until he turned to look up. There was something odd about them. Something she should investigate perhaps. She walked to stand by the grave. Her hands rose, then they lowered again as she nodded. Rann's eyebrows went up in question.

"Something?"

"Yes. One of them is wearing a 'here I am' spell. Very elementary, quite basic." So that was why Wind Dancer had smelled Kirion on them, she thought.

"Can you spoil it?"

"I could, but it's better to leave it alone. Kirion didn't know when I'd be arriving." She chuckled quietly. "All the spell tells him is that they're still here and that maybe they're still waiting for me. If he tries to scry where they are or what they do, with only that as a reference, what can he see?"

Rann stared at the leveled earth. "Would he see through their eyes with that connection?"

"Yes."

"And they see nothing." Rann was putting it together. "Only darkness where their bedding is laid over them. So that's all he would see. What happens when he tries harder?"

She shrugged. "Oh, if he tries hard enough he'll be able to tell they're dead. But it would take a lot of power to go beyond that. He could. But once he knows they've been killed he'll assume I did it in some way or another. He'll forget them and send out others to find me."

"They only just arrived here," Rann was thinking aloud. "He can't be sure when they'd trap you. It could be a day or a week. When he does wonder where they are, he'll scry. He'll see nothing. It could be another couple of days before he wastes more power and finds they're dead. He can't be certain that it was your doing, and where does he look for you then?" He answered himself. "At Aiskeep. We have their horses. And the two spare they brought on after my friend and I killed two of them. That's three horses each. Do you need to be home for any reason?"

Aisling had been following his reasoning. If she wanted to reach Aiskeep before Kirion was certain she was back, it could be done. She could stay a night, leave again, and lose herself in Karsten. No, not Karsten; Kars City, and in disguise. Let old Geavon know where she was and what she was doing. Her thoughts halted. Come to that, what was she going to do about Kirion?

Hilarion had said it was sister against brother. The geas must intend for her to stop Kirion in some way. But she couldn't simply march in and attack him openly. He had Shastro's support. She was a trained witch but not a full adept. Well, she'd daresay something, some method or idea would present itself. But if she wanted to see her grandparents she'd better keep moving. What had Rann asked? Oh, yes.

"I do need to spend at least a night at Aiskeep. And it would be best if Kirion does not know." Her voice was brisk. "I need to talk to Lord Trovagh and the Lady Ciara; they must know all of this."

He nodded. "I must bury my friend, Lady. Then we shall ride."

Aisling glanced at the sky. Wind Dancer would not like several days' fast riding; Rann was suffering from the beating he'd taken. She'd seen him wince now and again as he moved. The day was progressing, and the burial would take more time.

"Better if we bury your friend, then eat and sleep a night," she said gently. "It will rest the horses; theirs look to have been hard ridden. And I can craft a small healing spell for you. Nothing great, it will merely speed your natural healing while you sleep. But eat well and sleep you must."

As she'd expected he saw the sense in that. "Then follow me, Lady. My friend lies down the trail near the wood. On the trail that circles it is a good place to camp and shelter for the night." He too glanced at the sky. "I think it is likely to rain by the early hours."

Aisling had already noted the thickening clouds. She scooped up Wind Dancer, mounted, and followed Rann to where the body of a slight young man lay sprawled. He had some of the features of the Old Race. His hair was black and his open staring eyes were a light gray. But his face was round and the chin was weak. There was nothing evil or lecherous in that face, Aisling thought. But nothing of strength or courage either. Yet at the last he'd done his best.

Moved by that she stooped and closed the eyes and ran a fingertip in the sign of blessing over the wide young forehead.

"Go in peace." Her voice was soft. "I forgive anything I might have held against you." Rann straightened the undignified sprawl. He was casting about for a suitable place to dig. Aisling considered, as a trained witch, she had another method of disposing of a body.

"Rann?" He turned to look at her, and she spoke diffidently. "If you would prefer it, I can give your friend to the flames."

Rann nodded slowly. "We should be on our way, but will you ask for a judgment as well?" She nodded, and he stepped back in agreement. Wind Dancer caught her thought and moved away from the body. Aisling's hands swept out over Brovar. Her voice rose in the chant of one who calls.

"By cup and flame, I summon. This one died well. I speak for him at his going. Let fire judge." They were not the words of the standard calling of fire. This was a request for judgment. In her mind she drew the necessary runes. Then she spoke the word of invocation: *"Shalarin!"*

Pale silver the fire sprang up, flames racing the length of the body, sheathing it, hiding it from view. They reared up higher, died, and on the ground was nothing, not even ash. Rann bowed his head to hide the tears in his eyes. Jonrie had been generous in her words, and the goddess had judged. Brovar had not been denied.

Rann prayed briefly, then walked his mount back along the older trail. A mile farther on, he turned off to a jumble of rocks. There at the half-cave he began to strip gear from the patient horses. Wind Dancer trotted off into the trees. He'd provide his own dinner. It would be pleasant to hunt in the land of his birth again. He returned bearing a plump rabbit in time to find a fire lit and Aisling dropping a saddle blanket by the flames for him. He accepted the blanket at once with an approving purr.

Aisling laughed. "A warm fire, a soft place to lie, and a fat rabbit. What more does a cat ask?"

Rann laughed with her. "But is this one just a cat?"

"No cat is *just* a cat," Aisling warned him. "But with Wind Dancer we have all wondered at one time or another. His mother had never bred. She was four when she vanished into the hills and returned in kitten. Wind Dancer was the only one she birthed." She smiled remembering. "Since then many have asked her who she found in the hills. She refuses to tell."

She saw Rann was eyeing her doubtfully. "No, she is no more than a cat, but Wind Dancer, well, he's something extra. But he's also my good friend and traveling companion, and I owe him my life. Whoever Shosho found to father him doesn't matter."

Her companion nodded and half-changed the subject. "Do we

ride for Aiskeep in the morning? If we ride hard we could be there by the main road in a few days, but Wind Dancer couldn't keep up."

"He'll travel with me. I have a special carrysack so he can ride. He won't appreciate it, but he'll prefer it to being left behind." She reached out to stroke the big cat's head and sent him pictures of the plan. His ears flattened and he howled softly. Then he sagged back in agreement. It was better than being separated from his human. And it would be very good to see his dam and home once again.

While they shared food and drink they talked casually. Aisling was still being careful of her true identity but she could talk of Aiskeep, while Rann spoke of his own home and his father. She approved of his attitude toward her. He treated her as an equal, which, Aisling thought, was only fair. He might be a trained warrior, but she was a trained witch, with equal status, and she had reached her twenty-first birthday a moon before she left the valley.

Their talk drifted into a discussion of horses, then of sheep. All keeps had their own flock to provide wool for weaving into cloth. Aiskeep was proud of their colored sheep, which had come to the keep with Ciara, Aisling's grandmother.

"Black and . . . moorit, you say?" Rann was interested. "You have a true brown, not just a faded black?"

"Moorit, yes. Not just the pale kind that fades to dirty white after a couple of years, either. Some of our moorits are dark brown and keep that shade."

Rann looked wistful. "We've had good black fleeces, but a dark moorit is hard to find. I wonder if the Lord of Aiskeep would trade with us some time?"

"Perhaps," was all Aisling said, before the talk turned back to other topics.

They readied their gear before they slept. With daybreak they had eaten and were saddling the horses. After that they traveled steadily, at a slow canter much of the time, dropping to a trot or even a walk in the rougher going. Well-padded in his carrysack and cushioned by his human's back, Wind Dancer slept, his body yielding bonelessly to the movement. He woke when they halted in the early afternoon.

Rann was unsaddling their mounts and rubbing down the sweating beasts with care. Aisling laid out food while Rann changed saddles to a fresh pair of mounts.

"What do we do with their horses when we get farther into Karsten," he queried as he worked. "None of the four is much, but someone might recognize them."

Aisling grinned. "Oh, no they won't. I can do something about their looks. No, using the method I plan won't tire me," she added as she saw him about to object. "It isn't magic; just a couple of tricks. We'll push hard and get out of this area. Then we can head for my home by the old back-country trails. Once we're well on the way, there's a place to lie up a day and night. I can work on them then." Rann nodded. It made sense.

He finished what he was doing, ate, rested an hour, and then rose ready to move on. They used the enemy mounts steadily until they were in sight of the deserted garth. There Aisling halted her horse to sit staring sadly at the structure for several moments.

"What is it?"

"Three years ago when I was eighteen I came this way. I had trouble behind me and was traveling as fast as I could. Both Wind Dancer and I. Temon lived here. Kirion and a lord from Kars were hunting me and Temon had an Old Blood feud with the lord. He took me in, stood by me, and died for it." She turned impulsively to look at him. "I don't want you to die too. Go your own way from here. I'll be all right."

Rann made a small sound of outrage. "I'll do no such thing. Would you desert me if matters were in all ways reversed?" She hesitated, and he nodded sharply. "Exactly. At the very least, I'll see you to Aiskeep." His expression hardened. "I have debts of my own to pay, twice over. Brovar died at the hands of Kirion's men. You have some plan in mind to destroy him, kin or not. Will you thrust my help aside?"

Aisling bowed her head. "No, you speak truth. This quest is yours also. But it will not be easy, either or both of us may die in ways I do not wish to think of. Kirion will have no mercy on those who seek to bring him down."

"Nor will I have mercy," Rann said, memories edging his tone. "I saw too much in Kars. It is best for our land if Kirion is gone and Shastro is not in power longer than may be helped."

They rode on with Aisling considering the thought. She feared Shastro would not be easily deposed. He was weak, vicious, and pleasure loving. He had strengths though, and he would be no casual target. He feared enemies too much to take foolish risks. Kirion had catered to that and grown rich and powerful. But if he were gone, the duke would find another to give him what he demanded. There was always someone willing to step into a power vacuum. He might not be the sorcerer that Kirion was becoming, but he'd have power in some way.

The pendant warmed under Aisling's bodice. It flared, sending pleasant heat across her body before it died again. So, that idea was important. If they destroyed Kirion but left Shastro, it would be a job half done. She sighed. Was she supposed to destroy both sorcerer *and* duke? Heat from the pendant touched her again, and she bit back a stream of curses. It seemed she was. And just how, she wondered, was she supposed to do *that*!

A day later they swung onto a backcountry trail heading south toward Aiskeep. It had been a pleasant ride despite the speed. They had continued to exchange views, and at the noontime break, they had rubbed their mounts down companionably, comparing them to other horses they had known. They were now away from the roads and riding hard for a place where they could alter the horses' appearance, and so far they had seen no other riders.

Wind Dancer was tired of the carrysack. Almost at the end of the day's riding, Aisling allowed him out to scamper ahead, pouncing at grass heads and thistles to relieve the stiffness of his muscles. But allowing him his freedom took time, so that was the last break the big cat was permitted before they moved on again.

They reached a safe haven in the foothills a day and a half after that and still without seeing other travelers. Aisling dismounted stiffly. It had been a hard ride. Once she'd changed the horses' looks there'd be less haste. Nor did she have to arrive at her home by the front gates. From the cave they could travel deeper into the mountains at the rear of Aiskeep's valley, until they had threaded the rough land at the far end, where—for those who knew the path—there was a back way into Aiskeep's lands.

For the remainder of the day humans and horses rested and ate while Wind Dancer vanished to hunt. By morning Aisling was ready. In Escore there grew a small marsh plant with fleshy leaves. If the leaves were squeezed between flat stones they yielded a sap that, when heavily diluted, was an effective bleach. In Escore, where she had trained, it was used to clean wool. Aisling had brought plant seeds and a small container of the pure sap to show her grandmother.

Her grandmother would have to do without the demonstration. Aisling tethered the horses and studied them. Three bays and a rather shabby black. The black was easy: she'd give him a white stocking on one foreleg, a white sock on one hind. The main thing anyone would be remembering about the animal was that he had no white on him. After Aisling had worked for an hour, there was.

Then she turned to the three bay horses. *Hmmm.* Two had nothing that would distinguish them from thousands of others, but the third had a roman nose that flared like a war horn. She gave him a white star centered on his forehead and a lopsided blaze that slipped over one side of his muzzle. It lessened the effect of the roman nose considerably.

Rann was watching in amusement. "Anything else?"

"Yes. One of the other bays is young, and he's a good horse. I'd like to keep him."

"Him alone? So what about these other three?"

"They can be sold south once I'm home. But this one . . ."

"Yes?"

"I'll wash." Rann gaped at her. It hadn't been an easy trip. Had it been too much for her? Aisling saw the look and hid a chuckle. "Bring water if you will, please, lots of it." She added the bleach and washed the bay carefully. After that she soaked his mane and tail. She rinsed the placid animal and left him to dry in the sunlight. After the meal Rann glanced at the still-tethered animal. He blinked, looked away, and back again.

"I'll be the son of a sorcerer. He's gone chestnut colored." Aisling nodded, admiring her handiwork.

She'd known the bleach would work on horsehair. Once in Escore it had been done to give a soldier a familiar-appearing mount so he could ride openly in an area held by the Dark. She grinned at Rann and was pleased at his return smile.

They slept in peace that night, and even Wind Dancer was not reluctant to move on. He loathed hard riding—it left kinks in his spine—but the smells were growing more like those of home.

It took three more days, but then Aisling saw a familiar place, a small valley through which the trail led. Beyond that was a large cave that had been the haven of wolfshead outlaws before now. The trail bent, but she knew: around the next bend would be the cave itself and then the start of the trail into Aiskeep. Wind Dancer's head suddenly poked out of his carrysack. He paused only to send a brief picture, then he was over her shoulder and leaping up the trail. Aisling did not wait to explain. She dropped the lead reins, kicked her mount into a run, and tore after him.

Rann dithered. Was she chasing the cat or did she have some purpose in mind? From around the bend came a shriek. He kicked his mount into pursuit. Now was no time to sit and consider choices. He crashed through the bushes and found his companion being swung about by some male. The man tossed her over one shoulder laughing. It did not occur to Aranskeep's heir that if the plight were real his companion would have been using very effective methods to free herself.

But instead of using her dagger or the Power, she was beating the wretch about the shoulders and screaming to be released at once. Rann set about attaining that. He seized the man's arm, wrenched the girl loose, and flung her captor to the ground. His sword flashing free of the scabbard, Rann would have leapt on his opponent then but for Aisling, who stepped in quickly, her mouth curving in a small warm smile.

"Rann, I'd like you to meet my brother, Keelan." The good-looking young man grinned up from where he'd landed. Hadrann sheathed his sword hurriedly, then collapsed with a groan of exasperation and chagrin.

IV

—◇—

Keelan grinned "Good to meet you, aren't you Hadrann of Aranskeep? I met you last year at Kars."

Rann nodded, looking bewildered. "I am, but aren't you Aiskeep's heir?"

Aisling cut in. "We can talk about that on the way. Kee, why don't you ride ahead to warn everyone?" She leaned over to stretch out her arms to Wind Dancer. "We'll follow. *Ooof*!" The latter exclamation came as the cat landed in her arms, scrambling over her shoulder, and into his carrysack again. Keelan swung his horse alongside after he mounted. His hands went out to rub and scratch the cat around the chin, and Wind Dancer purred blissfully.

"It's great to have you back."

"Thank you," Aisling told him.

"I was talking to Wind Dancer." He prodded the cat. "Your mother is going to have to talk to you about overeating. If you get any bigger we'll be able to saddle you." Wind Dancer reached over to nip his wrist. "Ouch. I take it back."

Aisling laughed. "More likely he'd be able to saddle one of us." She patted a strap on the carrysack. "I'm already halfway there. Go on, Kee. Let everyone know. I need to speak to Rann before we arrive." Keelan looked at her. He nodded, reached over to give her one savage hug, and then he was gone, pushing his horse to a hard gallop as they cleared the upper trail. Behind him Aisling looked at the heir to Aranskeep as they started their mounts moving on at a fast walk after Keelan.

"I'm sorry I didn't tell you the truth. But when we met I'd just been attacked by two men supposedly sent to meet me. You said to use another name if I was uncertain of you, and I did." Her gaze met his. "Rann, it was a little too clear what I am. You know how many of the folk in Karsten feel about witches. Even a healer who is too good at her work may run a risk. There's always the chance it's because they have the Old Blood.

"If I had told you exactly who I was then, I could have endangered my family. I had to be sure of you. I *was* sure within a couple of days but I still felt it was safer to be silent in case we were split up, in case one of us was captured. Under truth spell you'd have been shown as ignorant of who I am. At least the duke could not have punished you greatly."

Her companion made an inelegant sound through his teeth. "Couldn't he! You forget it was Hilarion's message that sent me to meet you. How happy do you think our dear duke would be if *that* came out in his questioning of me? Yes," he said, in reply to a horrified look from Aisling. "I do have certain protections. How long would they last against Kirion? And even if they did, how long would I survive if he believed me to be involved in your escape whether or not I knew who you were?"

"I'm sorry. I still feel I was right," Aisling said miserably.

Rann grinned. "You were. I was just paying you back for not trusting me, I guess. And while I'm complaining about that I should live up to my own claim and trust you." He spread his arms and slowly turned his horse in a circle. "Look like a witch, do I?"

"No, why?"

"Because I'm not, but my brother was."

It came back to Aisling with a rush. Some talk, half heard, quarter remembered, when she was about eleven or so. She spoke slowly trying to recall what she knew.

"Your brother was older. He went to Kars and didn't come back. He was killed by bandits on the way home." She was watching Rann's face as she spoke and saw the terrible look in his eyes.

He spoke evenly. "Not quite. Jasrin was my elder by six years. I loved him. He was my half brother only. Father married his mother, and when she died two years after having Jasrin, father remarried. Mother loved Jas as her own, but she died too when I was five. I followed Jas everywhere after that, and he never said I was a pest or chased me away. I remember him teaching me to ride on his own pony. Father said I was too young to start sword lessons when I wanted, so Jas taught me until Father relented."

He looked up at her, his eyes blinded with memories. "He was a good, decent man. Then he went to Kars at eighteen. I was twelve and I missed him. He never came home again. During a party Jas said something rude about the way Shastro had come to the throne. He was drunk or he'd never have been so stupid. We heard about it from friends at court. Jas vanished. After the party he'd been seen drinking with one of the duke's men and was supposed to have gone on to another inn with the man. They found Jas dead in the outer ditch two days later. It was put down to robbers after his money pouch. The duke's man had disappeared, and no one knew anything."

Aisling dropped her gaze. The pain in his eyes was deep. Her mind worked quickly, putting together what she knew and what she could guess. Kirion would have had a hand in it. They had probably taken Jasrin, planning to forcibly change his mind about the duke. Once Jas was imprisoned, Kirion would have found that the boy had the gift of the Old Race in his blood, although he couldn't use it. However Kirion had learned how to drain those unusable gifts. Instead of turning Jas's mind as the duke had doubtless demanded, he'd drained the boy's powers, killing him. Kirion would have used scare tactics with Shastro. She could almost hear him.

"The boy was a witch. Did you want someone at court who could overhear your thoughts? Maybe make you do things against your will? Jasrin could have finished up by running Kars while you sat there agreeing with every word. It's a favor I've done you, my Lord Duke." She said all of this to Rann.

"That's how I put it together now. So did Father. I think he started quietly working against Shastro from the time he decided the duke had killed Jas. I was told when I turned fourteen. Father gave me the choice to help or simply to stay silent. I loved Jas. He was the best brother a boy could ever have had. I joined the conspiracy. I'm no friend to Estcarp, but they've always left us alone when we've left them alone. I want to see that's official policy in Kars."

"Is that all?"

His tone was hungry. "No, I want to see Kirion and Shastro pay. I want to see a decent ruler on the throne of Kars, I want all these stupid little wars amongst the nobles and clans of Karsten, to stop. We're bleeding the whole country dry. In a few more generations we won't have to worry about Estcarp. We'll have killed ourselves off without their aid." He swore. "It was that damned fool Pagar and his 'let's invade Estcarp.' So he did, and what did it get him but a really impressive grave."

Aisling shook her head. "It goes back further, to the Horning, and much of that was Kolder doing. You might as well say we should close our borders to everyone else. Let nothing and no one new in; they bring trouble always. But that's no solution either."

"No, it isn't. Isolate and when the world breaks in, and it will sooner or later, you're that much less able to deal with what it brings. A static society breaks more easily." Aisling was listening with some amusement. His face twisted into a sudden grin. "I think I've heard my father on the subject once too often. Let's change the subject. Who are you exactly?"

"Aisling. I'm Kirion and Keelan's sister. Kirion is nine years older than me, and Keelan's six. And before you ask, I loathe Kirion and his way of living as much as you do. I was only a child when he tried to kill me. He tormented Kee half of his life and almost destroyed him. Grandfather made Kee Aiskeep's heir, and Kirion hates us all for that.

"Grandmother Ciara says that Kirion's like his father Kirin. Both think that whatever they want, they have a divine right to take. The difference is that our father was also weak. Kirion isn't. He's convinced that the world owes him whatever he demands. But he's very fond of his skin. He doesn't take chances, and that's why he's sorcerer to Shastro. The duke is propped up in front as a target. Getting rid of him wouldn't make any difference to Karsten. Kirion would have another puppet standing up in a few months. Both of them have to go—permanently."

As she spoke they were descending the last slope into the cultivated lands of Aiskeep valley. Rann eyed her with amusement and interest. She saw things with clarity. The duke of Karsten and his black sorcerer must go. She knew they wouldn't walk away. So they'd have to be killed. He eyed her face, eager with the discussion, and felt a quiet warmth. She'd suffered at Kirion's hands too. She understood how Rann felt about losing his brother.

From the lower portion of their trail there came a clatter of hooves and the sound of voices. The two riders broke out of the narrow trail onto the broader valley and found half the inhabitants there waiting. Aisling hooked Wind Dancer's carrysack with its sleeping occupant over the saddle horn and was off her horse in seconds, running from one to another, hugging, chattering, being whirled by one elderly man as she laughed in delight. Rann caught snatches of talk and was quietly impressed.

This was how it should be with keeps and garths. It was this way in Aranskeep, but such affection and trust were all too rare in other places. The more so the farther north toward Kars one went. In many ways the situation in Karsten had always been unstable. Kars and the immediate lands surrounding the city were a duchy within which the duke was absolute ruler. Beyond the duchy were the keeps of Karsten, also ruled absolutely by their lords. Towns and villages, single garths—all were just as safe as their fortifications and fighters within.

He sighed as he watched Aisling welcomed home. There was so much to do and to change—if they ever could. He could foresee his grandchildren complaining about how far they had yet to go. But that was for the future. He shrugged and allowed himself to be pulled into the welcome. He was handed beer and cold meat on bread, as the horses were taken off to be fed and watered. After an hour of this he fought his way to Aisling's side.

"Shouldn't we be heading for the keep?"

She was flushed with the excitement and pleasure of homecoming but she nodded. "Yes, Keelan will have just about reached the keep by now. My grandparents will start riding to meet us but more slowly." She turned to ask the crowd about their horses.

The old man who'd whirled her first in greeting replied, "Your horses were weary. Let them rest. I have had others brought. They wait now." The crowd parted, and Rann gasped.

"Torgians? Surely that one is a pureblood?"

"Yes." Aisling hugged the stallion, checking that Wind Dancer's carrysack was hooked onto the saddle. The cat was gone but she knew he would return before she left the garths. The part-bred mare beside the stallion nudged for attention. Rann laughed and obligingly scratched her neck up under the mane. Torgians didn't look like much, but they were valued for their other qualities. A pureblood could outlast any other breed, could survive on far less, climb

like a cat in rough land or over mountains, and find a safe passage
through bog. They bonded to their rider and would fight for him
even before being trained.

The mare wasn't a pureblood but she was of the line. He admired her, scratching where she indicated and stroking her inquiring
nose. Aisling turned to smile at the pair of them.

"We should move on as you said. Oh, and that's Shira. She
knows her name." Wind Dancer had leaped for his carrysack again
and was making small impatient sounds. "If we don't go this awful
cat here will tear holes in me." Wind Dancer made a rude noise, and
everyone within earshot chuckled.

Rann swung up, took the cat-filled carrysack, and handed it
back once Aisling was ready. She settled the straps over her shoulders, cinched the waistband, and moved her mount off along the
road. Sudden eagerness overtook her. If it had not been for Wind
Dancer, she'd have had her mount racing up the valley to the keep.
Ciara and Trovagh would be on their way to meet her by now. How
she longed to see them both. It had been three years; even another
minute was too long.

She held her horse to a steady walk. On the smoother stretches
she allowed them to canter briefly. Soon her horse was infected with
her desire to run. He sidled when held back, passaging sideways with
hooves held high and hind legs flicking out in the occasional kick.
Aisling was firm until after an hour of increasing tension Hadrann
spoke.

"Why are we moving so slowly anyhow? I'm sure you have a reason, but you've been gone awhile. Are you sure the reason is that
good?"

Aisling stared vaguely at him. Why had she demanded this slow
pace? Well, because she'd gone away a child still and now she was returning as an adult. In Escore she'd sometimes ridden as a soldier.
She wanted her family to see she could control herself, a reason that

was starting to seem silly. It was natural to be excited, to want to run her mount. But what of Wind Dancer, who ended up shaken like a pea in a drum when she ran a horse full out?

From over her shoulder a nose was thrust against her neck and she received a message. Wind Dancer was as eager as she to arrive back. Stop all this foolish human indecision and move. He'd rather endure a brief shaking than this slow progress over the final few miles. Aisling smiled, then she flung back her head and laughed. She looked over to her companion.

"I'm a fool," she confessed. "Wind Dancer's just said so. Let's go!" She gave a whoop as she loosed rein, and her stallion exploded into full speed. Shira was right behind him as Rann in turn allowed the mare to follow. They tore down the road, a plume of dust indicating their whereabouts. Ahead sharp eyes pointed it out. A party had already left the keep, and now the pace of those coming from the keep also accelerated.

The two parties came together soon after. Aisling's stallion halted, plunging and rearing in excitement. From his carrysack Wind Dancer complained loudly. Aisling slipped from her mount and raced forward. Her grandparents, already on the ground, opened their arms. Aisling flung herself into them, holding, hugging, weeping in joy. She'd thought she'd never be home again, that she'd never again see the people she loved most in all the world. She could only hug them and weep, tears of happiness pouring down her cheeks as her brother and other friends crowded around to welcome her home, their straying lamb returned. Together they walked to the keep, where they celebrated in earnest with food, drink, singing, and dancing long after the sun went down.

It took a day for the celebration to wind down. When it did, the discussion of what to do about Kirion and Shastro started. Present were Aisling, her grandparents Lord Trovagh and Lady Ciara of Aiskeep, Keelan, and Hadrann. Aisling was indeed geas bound,

Ciara stated. She'd checked, using her witch powers. It was a clear and simple demand. Aisling must defeat Kirion and render him unable to practice sorcery. Trovagh looked sad at that.

"The only way I can see that happening is for the lad to die. He'll never give up power. If it is stripped from him, he'll spend his life trying to regain it, and he may succeed. He's bad enough as is it. If you strip his power and he regains it, he'll be like a rabid wolf. You can't take that chance."

Ciara agreed. "He's our kin, but that makes it worse in a way. If we allow him to continue his evil, then it besmirches our honor. And you're correct in what you say, Tro: Kirion is dangerous now. If he becomes completely paranoid, looking into every shadow for those coming to disempower him, then he'll be a hundred times as dangerous. What we do must be done quietly. He must have neither chance nor second chance to prevent us or take revenge."

Trovagh rose and quietly opened the door. He gave a low, clear, penetrating whistle, and Hannion appeared. The old master-at-arms for the keep had officially retired some years back, but he was canny. He'd ridden and fought in younger days beside Trovagh's father. Hannion was over eighty now but still upright, and his steps, if slower, were yet unfaltering. He had never been a fool, and his long years had brought added wisdom.

He gave a brief acknowledgment of the summons, half bow, half nod. Then he entered through the door as Trovagh held it open invitingly. Aisling rose to bring the old man a stool and place it invitingly beside hers. Hannion sat in obedience to Lord Trovagh's gesture and looked about at them, waiting. Ciara glanced at her husband, received a nod, and started. When her explanation ran down she sat quietly.

Hannion considered a little longer. "There is no question, Lady." His voice was firm as he spoke directly to Ciara. "Do you cherish a rotten apple until it renders the whole barrel worthless?

Does a farmer keep a rogue stud which may attack the farmer's family and which breeds other rogues? I am—I was a soldier. I give you a soldier's advice. A dead enemy lays no second ambush."

He nodded to her. "I know you have no love for the boy, yet you still consider him kin. Tell me, Lady. Do you remember the bandits who came sneaking into our lands by the back paths, when you were a girl? You and Trovagh fought and beat them with the aid of the garths-people. Why did you do that? Why not allow them free rein?"

Trovagh spoke slowly and sadly, his words a decision. "Because they gave us no choice. We had to beat them or watch garths burned, goods stolen, our people raped and murdered."

"But you took some of them prisoner, then you ordered them hanged. They were defeated; why did you do that?"

Ciara answered. "So they would not go free and harm others or return and harm us." She sighed. "You said it yourself. A dead enemy lays no second ambush."

"Then you have no decision to make here and now," Hannion told her. "Your choice was made long ago. Stick to it."

Trovagh reached out to take Ciara's hand in his. "He's right, my love. Kirion is this family's responsibility. We bred him, and he's gone rogue. Aiskeep deals with its own. Let Aisling do what she must. All we are here to do is work out how we may best help her obey the geas."

After that the talk circled endlessly. Toward midnight Aisling spoke quietly to her grandmother.

"I need to work a transformation. On myself and Wind Dancer."

Ciara smiled. "I wondered if he'd let you leave him behind again. I gather he won't. What shape would you give him?"

Aisling looked thoughtful. "I could make him appear to be a lap dog, but it could cause trouble. If he had to use his claws it would rather expose the trick. No, I think a smaller cat would be best."

Ciara agreed fervently as she imagined someone Wind Dancer

didn't like picking him up to coo over the sweet little dog and find-ing with disbelief that a lap dog had just scratched him to the bone with nonexistent claws. She smiled at Aisling. "I presume you know how to do that. It is a little outside my knowledge."

"I know," Aisling assured her. "It won't require more power than you have, just a different way of using it. Have a good night's sleep. In the morning I'll teach you." She pursed her lips. "Maybe I should tell you what other uses of the power I learned in Escore. We could work on anything else you think might be helpful to know. If we anger my brother and the duke with an attempt to lessen their power, and they realize who was responsible, there'll be storm-rack flying this way."

They slept well that night; Ciara had brewed a potion to make sure of it. With early morning the two women were up and already working on the first of their plans before they ate. On and off in the course of the next three days they worked together. Ciara already had the discipline and some power. She was experienced in using just as much as was needed, and wasting nothing.

At last she sagged into a chair. "My dear, I think I must rest. Many of the things you have shown me are too tiring for me to prac-tice now, but I do know them. I shall practice them one by one after you are gone, but I think that we should turn to considering your new details—what shape you will take, what name; how you know Had-rann; why you are in Kars—all the things that you must be able to say without hesitation if asked. And how you will move against Kirion."

Aisling mused silently, then said, "Much of that is easy. We've discussed it already. I shall look just like a girl I knew in Escore. She isn't ugly, but she's so nondescript you rarely notice her at all. I shall use part of her name as well. I'll be Murna Leshin, distant cousin to Hadrann, at Kars to learn court polish."

Hadrann, who had entered and was sitting nearby, sighed, as-suming a tired world-weary air. "And I shall be the dutiful cousin.

Bored to yawning with this dreep of a girl my father has landed me with but too polite to say so." He snickered. "I can bore a few of the court in turn with my complaints about it all."

Ciara smiled. "You are wicked children. Keelan, what's your part in this?"

"A little more complex. I shall appear to notice Murna when I discover she is a fine rider. Her only nonboring aspect," he added in an aside to them. "Gradually I shall appear to become mildly interested in her. Of course that will amuse Kirion. He'll watch, sneer, and count all three of us as negligible."

A gleam of hatred showed in Hadrann's eyes. "Kirion is used to being the hunter, and a man who is hunting often assumes that nothing is hunting him. He fails to guard his back."

"You will be . . ."

"Careful? Oh yes, Lady Ciara. We shall move as cautiously as redbirds when the hawk is about, nor will we assume nothing hunts behind us."

"And when will you leave for Kars City?"

"In two days. Keelan has hired a professional guard for us." Hadrann sighed. "I'd have used Aranskeep men, but they might be too open-mouthed on how they do not know my 'cousin.' "

Ciara considered that. "Then you had best be careful of Kirion. If he starts to wonder, it would be like him to send men inquiring at your home. The three of you decide why ordinary servants and men-at-arms might not know her, then write it down. I will send the letter to Aranskeep's lord by a trusted messenger." She looked at Rann. "Suggest one or two from the keep who can be trusted to allow some part of such a tale to leak to waiting ears. The sooner the better. I have found if that sort of tale is well-told the listener tends to accept it as truth and, moreover, usually believes he's really known about it far longer than he has."

Hadrann laughed. "By Cup and Flame, Lady Ciara. It is well

you are for us. It's a good trick, and my father will enjoy it. I know the very pair to spread the tale and what tale they shall spread."

"Then go and write. I'm for my bed."

Aisling hugged her good night, then she and Rann went to building wild tales of betrayal and true love. It was late in the night before they were satisfied with the letter and a fair copy was written and sealed. Harran, the keep's master-at-arms, took it to Aranskeep the next morning.

The three conspirators spent the rest of that day making final preparations. After a quiet, nervous evening spent waiting for Harran to return, they were almost ready to retire for the night, when Harran finally arrived, a reply clutched in one hand as he trotted up the stairs. Hadrann broke the seal and read quickly.

"My father is well pleased. He sends coin to help with our masquerade and says the tale we wrote is now circulating from one who believes he heard it some time ago. His memory was merely refreshed. Already it garners detail. He wishes us all good fortune." He smiled at Aisling and Keelan, omitting to mention that his father also bade them be very careful, since Lord Kirion was as quick to strike as an asp in long grass—and equally as venomous. All here had personal reasons to know the risk they ran. None would turn back. In the morning they would ride out to throw the dice, the table to be Kars, the stakes, lives. May luck and the gods be with them in this game.

V

·····◆◇◆·····

*T*heir arrival in Kars was uneventful. Keelan went to his own
suite in the main palace and Hadrann to the one held in readi-
ness for the lords and ladies of Aranskeep. Aisling went with him,
clutching Wind Dancer's carrysack, and admired the room allocated
her. Hadrann grinned.

"Of course it's the best one. I plan to make a point of complaining about that too. Now, you should really have a chaperone living
with us. But if we hire one she could be the sort of person who no-
tices things." Aisling raised her eyebrows questioningly. Hadrann
shrugged. "I say we don't risk it, but it's your reputation that might
be tarnished."

Aisling eyed her handsome companion then picked up a hand
mirror and surveyed her own appearance. "Dear cousin. Do you
really believe that anyone is going to look at you, look at me, and believe we're having a passionate affair? Just complain about me. Mention my looks, my boring personality, my inability to do needlework.
Note in tones of disgust that I can't darn socks. Don't complain so
much people wonder if your complaints are a sham, but make it
clear I've been foisted on you and you wish me in Hades."

Hadrann laughed. "That I can do." He looked at the nondescript face she showed him. "I have to say that is wonderful. Not
ugly, but I turn away and five minutes later even I can't remember

what you look like. I think it's because there's nothing outstanding. Hair that's just a sort of lightish brown. Eyes likewise. Skin neither warmly colored nor divinely fair. Ears: two. Nose: one. Mouth: well, you have one."

Aisling grinned. "And I dress the same way. Good quality in cloth and cut, but plain and in colors that never catch the attention. My manners are the same. Nothing outlandish but not country cousin, either. Women like me aren't seen. We can drift about the court in the evening, and you'd be surprised at what we hear. We simply aren't noticed, and if we are, those talking often assume we are too dull-witted to understand."

Hadrann's eyes sharpened. "You sound as if you know."

"I do. As I said, I took the appearance of a friend. Murna had been a spy in the Dales. Her appearance was carefully crafted over a long time. She was my friend in Escore. She talked to me often about her art and I listened. She was very good. I'm nothing against her, but I do know some of her tricks."

"Just be careful. Your brother isn't a fool, and he's always suspicious."

Aisling shivered. "I know. Now, tonight you'll introduce me to the duke. After that we'll have to see."

"At least he's unlikely to take a fancy to you," Hadrann said thoughtfully. "He likes beauty in male or female, and he doesn't ride that well. Since that's to be your only grace he'll be attracted to you still less. He doesn't approve of any who can do something better than he can." He stared about the untidy suite. Baggage was stacked everywhere. "Leave the servants to sort this out. We'll go for a ride before dinner is served."

They returned in time to bathe and dress in the elaborate court wear. Aisling had hired a maid on a part-time basis. The girl was to help her dress in the evenings, then go. She could return next day after their noon meal to put away clothing and care for anything that required washing, ironing, or mending. Hadrann had hired a valet on the same basis. If any asked, he planned to plead poverty and complain about his father's wasting of good coin on this cousin.

Wind Dancer, in his guise of ordinary-sized but attractively long-haired cat, spent part of his time curled comfortably on Aisling's bed. Among other things, he watched the servants when they were in the rooms and his human and her friend were not. The palace had an excellent stock of well-fed mice. Within days it was Wind Dancer who was well fed and the mice had all moved out—from Aranskeep suite anyhow. It made Wind Dancer popular with the staff, who were often blamed for damage committed by the rodent pests. As for maintaining his true identity, he had only to refuse to be picked up by anyone but his three friends, and he was safe.

Keelan had settled in comfortably. Keep lords each retained a family suite of rooms in the Kars palaces. Kirion had rejected them as soon as he was disinherited. He had seen that if he did not, then he'd find himself sharing with his detested younger brother and supplanter or, worse still, just possibly his grandfather. Not that he needed the Aranskeep rooms. He had his tower and, a day's hard riding away, his own estate and the well-guarded tower there.

True, the lands were neither rich nor wide. That suited Kirion; he had less work running an estate and fewer eyes to watch, noses to snoop into his business, and mouths to chatter about it. That stupid Ruart had gotten himself killed, but Kirion had benefited. He'd ridden straight back and quietly entered Ruart's keep.

As a friend of Ruart's he'd been able to convince the servants to allow him access, and Kirion had known where the man kept his wealth and how to open the main hiding place. He successfully distributed the best of that into places in his clothing before he departed, grumbling about friends who were always out.

He'd hidden an unpleasant smile as he did so. It was fortunate he was the only sorcerer in Karsten. It took time and an aptitude to be what he was, and Kirion kept an ear to the ground as well. If rumor suggested any other person was attempting to develop the same gift, then he or she died. Kirion saw to that.

After his single visit his spies had watched Ruart's keep. The servants had finally realized that their master might be gone for good. They'd appealed to Kirion as the only one they knew who might be able to discover Ruart's whereabouts, and he'd spoken to the duke.

It had taken time, months of it, but at last, when Shastro had been convinced Ruart must be dead, his keep had been given to a wealthy member of the court, for which transfer Shastro had wrung coin from the man. Kirion had suggested that. The man was an unnoticing idiot, and the coin would please Shastro: two birds with one stone from Kirion's sling.

Aisling was introduced to Shastro, duke of Kars, who condescended to speak briefly before turning away. She studied him thoughtfully while appearing to be listening to Hadrann. The duke was a man of medium height, slender, without real muscle showing in bulk or movement. He was fair-haired, blue-eyed, with a slightly gingery mustache.

He was overdressed, foppish, and as she watched he said something in a languid voice and tittered. Aisling smothered a snort of amused contempt. Hadrann half-turned to point out one of the tapestries—and to see what was amusing her. Shastro was recounting the tale of a recent hunt, making great play with his hands and expressions. Hadrann moved farther away, drawing his supposed cousin with him.

"Don't let him fool you. A lot of that is merely Shastro amusing himself. Under that fancy dress is a very good swordsman, not much stamina but excellent technique. He's clever and ruthless."

"And my brother leads him by the nose."

Her companion hastily glanced around. "Don't say that sort of thing without looking behind you; in this court almost anyone could be listening. And you are both right and wrong in what you say. Kirion leads by using Shastro's fears. But he's in somewhat the same position as a man with a tame bear: fine as long as he can keep the brute distracted, but should he just fail once, he risks teeth and claws turned against him. Shastro is weak in some ways certainly. But he can also be deadly."

He checked about them with a sweeping unobtrusive glance. "Circulate a little without me. Try to get a feel for the court. Chatter to some of the ladies. I'll be dropping hints about you elsewhere. Let me know when you wish to leave." They split casually and drifted away in opposite directions.

Keelan spent his first dinner at court listening. Later he circulated and dropped a quiet question here and there. All of the events were recounted little by little, and he went in search of his sister when the evening was nearing a close. He brushed past her, hissed a few words, and strolled on. Aisling went in search of Hadrann.

"Cousin, I grow weary. I'm for my bed. Will you escort me or see that one of your guards does so?"

Hadrann half-turned. "Oh, a guard. Yes." He snapped his fingers at one of his men. "See the Lady Murna to Aranskeep rooms. Stand outside the door on guard until I arrive." He nodded at her polite thanks and went back to his conversation. When she was out of earshot he sighed.

"These whims of old men. The girl's mother was my grandfather's leman in his old age. Somehow he managed to produce a daughter. Of course, her mother inherited little after my grandsire's death, but I suppose the girl *is* half of our blood, and the liaison was recorded. My esteemed sire feels guilty over how my grandfather treated the girl's mother; yet it is I who pay the price."

"How so?" A listener was mildly interested.

"Why, I must share Aranskeep rooms, put up with her foolish talk over a morning meal when I wish only to be silent, and obey endless minor demands." He sighed again. "But duty to one's father, you know. It isn't even as if she's pretty."

That last provoked a number of teasing remarks. Hadrann tolerated them, keeping his face set in an expression of mild irritation. Good, they believed every word. Now if he could only keep from overdoing this, Aisling would be all but invisible as she went her own way.

In her room Aisling had told the guard to wait outside as ordered, opened the small inner door within the suite, and allowed Keelan to slip in from where he'd been waiting. He talked at length, describing the events after Ruart's disappearance, Kirion's continuing influence, and the gossip on it all. Some was guesswork, but both knew Kirion, which helped them guess ways in which he might act.

"I haven't been to court since you left, so this is the first I've heard of most of it. No," he answered her questioning look. "I didn't go because I couldn't bear to see Kirion, and he was furious about losing Aiskeep too. I thought I'd give him time to simmer down, and time went by. There's always so much to do at home, and I'd rather be there than at Kars."

Aisling nodded. She agreed but inwardly she was marveling at the continuing change in her brother. She recalled what he'd been like when he first began to visit Aiskeep again. It had been years after their mother had taken Kirion and Keelan, abandoned her baby daughter, and gone to live in her family's keep near Kars. Aisling had grown up with her grandparents. Her brothers had been raised by their mother, with Kirion in particular, spoiled and indulged in almost every way. Aisha had never seen, or perhaps never wished to see, what her adored older son had become.

As for her other brother, it had not been until Keelan came first to visit then to live at Aiskeep that he had discovered a true home and that his small sister could be a real companion. They'd become friends, and when Aisling had to leave Karsten it had been Keelan who had gone part of the way to guard her.

She smiled at him, her eyes glinting in amusement. "That's one thing about Aiskeep: Kirion and Mother left us alone."

"And Mother isn't with us any longer." He'd not missed her in the several years at the keep. When Aisha had died a year earlier Keelan had felt only a dull sadness. He hadn't hated her but he hadn't loved her either.

It had been receiving a tiny half-dead kitten of his own at Aiskeep that had begun to turn his life around. He had worked to save her and had won. Shosho loved him unconditionally, trusted him, taught him to laugh and play, and finally to see that his young sister too could be a companion and friend. Aisling gradually had started to return his trust. Now they were friends, and in some ways this business delighted him. He liked Hadrann and being with them. The plotting, scheming, and pretending was an adventure.

Close to him as she was and with her abilities sharpened by Hilarion's patient training, Aisling read much of his feelings. They worried her a little. She would have to watch him for his own sake. Kirion bore no grudge against Hadrann or Hadrann's so-called cousin. He did hate Keelan, who was now the heir to Aiskeep and whom he saw as having cheated him out of his inheritance. If they were forced to draw Kirion out, then Keelan would be bait for their plan, but bait could be consumed.

She worried silently over that for some time as Keelan talked. Once he'd left her again she returned to her bedroom to think hard. She must watch out for her brother and convince Hadrann to do the same. Above all, she should watch any interaction between Kirion and Keelan that might threaten her younger brother. She would grieve all the days of her life if the demands of her own geas caused Keelan injury. She said as much to Hadrann when he returned late that night.

"Yes, but we will watch over him. I have friends at court; I'll make it my business to hear if Kirion ever speaks to Keelan. You're right, he is the most vulnerable of us all. Kirion has no conscience." He turned to look at her. "It has seemed odd to me ever since I met you and Keelan. How is it that two of you are worthy, honest people and Kirion is not?"

"Kirion was born a bully, I think. He has a desire for power, perhaps even a need for power, for the ability to direct events about him to his own advantage," Aisling said slowly. "The lords of Aiskeep are an old line as is your bloodline at Aranskeep, but we're of minor nobility as the world counts it. Kirion always wanted more power, wealth, and influence, and he's learned how to take those at the expense of anyone who crosses his path. He won't turn back now he believes he has everything he has ever desired."

Hadrann nodded. "So you think he's beyond redemption?"

Her expression was one of regret mixed with sadness. "Yes, Rann, I think he once might have been redeemed, perhaps while he was still a child, but now he's a man, and he's gone too far down the path he has chosen. He will never turn back."

He said no more on the subject. Instead, he too worried what could happen if any part of their growing plans went wrong. However for the next few weeks things went as intended.

Kirion was seldom at court but he liked to hear all the gossip. Varnar brought back all he could, eager to please his master. Kirion-intrigued was a master whose servant was not in pain. Varnar's memories—he believed—had grown a little clearer of late. He did his best to hide that, as he dreamed eagerly at night. He could see the face of his wife, the sweet blue eyes of his beloved tiny daughter. He could not quite recall how he'd come to be in Kirion's hands or what had happened to his family. Perhaps as the weeks went by he would remember. He waited impatiently, only partly consoled by his dreams.

*I*n court Aisling was developing a problem. Shastro, duke of Kars, had taken a liking to her. It had not been planned, and they'd been sure that he would be mildly averse to her if she was even noticed at all.

"It was your own fault," Keelan scolded when they convened a meeting in the Aiskeep suite. "You made that clever remark; he laughed and decided you were a wit, a possible ornament to his court."

"I didn't know he was there," his sister protested. "Maybe I can be rude to him?"

Hadrann scowled. "Shastro doesn't always jump the way you'd expect. He'd either toss you out of Kars or, being him, decide that he adored someone who wasn't afraid to be rude to him and spend more time with you. If you're out of Kars we lose a third of our force and possibly the most effective one. If he becomes really interested in you, he's likely to have Kirion look you over. And if that happens we could all have a problem."

"I can handle Kirion."

Hadrann looked at her seriously. "No. You can't. If he tries I'm sure you could block a mind-scan, but then Kirion would be suspicious at once. If he tries to drain you, then you can block that too, by which time Kirion will have reported to the duke that you're some sort of very dangerous witch, probably a spy for Estcarp. Shastro panics, has the three of us rounded up, questions everyone who knows us. And what happens to us if Kirion can drain or break you? Or just as bad for us and our plans, what if he can't?"

Aisling nodded. "He moves against both keeps for a start."

"He'd kill the three of us," Keelan said quietly.

"And everything we're working for is flushed down the Kars gutters," Hadrann finished for them. "We have to find some way of persuading him that my cousin isn't worthy of the duke of Kars."

It didn't look as if that was going to be any time soon. Shastro was charmed by a girl who made no attempt to catch his eye and who was not convulsed at his ducal wit and jests.

Two nights later he approached her again. "My dear, would you care to converse?"

Aisling smiled. "I'm always happy to talk, my Lord Duke."

Shastro's grin was suddenly less courtly and more honest amusement. "Only you, my dear Murna, could say it that way. You should say that you are always delighted to have the attention of your duke and make a play with your fan."

Aisling grinned back at him. "Why?"

"Why what?"

"Why the fan?"

Shastro's smiled widened. "Ah, my dear, you look at me over the top of it, flirt a little, let your eyes be alternately revealed and concealed. Make a mystery of yourself."

Aisling snorted inelegantly. "There's little mystery about me, and everyone's seen my eyes. They're brown."

"Ah yes, like forest pools, while your hair is a cascade of shining strands that could entangle my heart."

Aisling met his languishing gaze and began to giggle. Shastro dropped his affectations and laughed with her. "You have no taste for such compliments?"

"Not when they're not true." Her gaze met his frankly. "I'd accept honest compliments on something I do well, but not on my very ordinary hair and eyes."

"What do you do well then?"

"I ride well and I dance reasonably. Tell me about this new law, Lord Shastro."

"Which law?"

"The one you enacted last week. As I understand it, it limits the size of an estate within the borders of Kars."

"Oh, yes. That's so the city doesn't outgrow its walls too soon." He continued to talk on the new law, finding Aisling knowledgeable on that topic and on several others having to do with the problems of government. After that, he sought her out to talk on more than one occasion as the weeks passed. The truth was, that while she did not excite him, he did find her very good company. It wasn't something that had ever occurred to him before. He still had favorites and a current lover, but increasingly it was "Murna" to whom he talked seriously.

And as someone who was merely interesting to talk to, it did not bother the duke that she was by far the better rider. It would have infuriated him had she been desirable. Since she was not, he offered congratulations on her skill. He rode with her, danced and laughed with her, and the court gossiped with enthusiasm. If it continued, Hadrann, as her supposed kinsman, would soon have to take an official interest.

Aisling might have fallen into the trap of liking the duke. When he chose, Shastro could be witty, charming, and quite intelligent. She was beginning to wonder if he could not be reclaimed once Kirion was dead. That hope died one evening after she'd been at court for seven weeks and the duke came in search of her. He was laughing and flushed with anticipation.

"Come with me. There's something I'd like to show you." Shastro was tugging her hand. Aisling read his emotions swiftly and sensed nothing that signaled danger for her, but what she read she wasn't sure she liked. There was an undertone of anticipation to it that felt wrong.

"But my Lord, my cousin would not like me to be alone with you. Where are we going?"

"You'll see." Aisling was afraid she would. She did and afterward returned to the Aranskeep rooms just as Hadrann found she had vanished. He swung the door open, swept her inside, angrily slammed the door in the faces of those watching, and started to yell at her in a way that could be heard all down the palace corridor.

The door had not completely shut, so the fascinated audience outside was treated to a diatribe that convulsed many of them. Part of it was the speaker living up to their belief. Hadrann had built an impression of how he felt about Murna, and no decent lord would accept what looked like open immorality on the part of a kins-woman.

Aisling knew his anger for the sham it was and yet she knew too he'd been genuinely worried, fearful for her safety. It was too much. A tear trickled down her cheek, and she scrabbled in her sleeve for a handkerchief. Hadrann broke off what he was yelling and looked first stunned, then horrified. He shut the door, sending a glare at the listeners as it closed. Then he returned to Aisling.

"Cup and Flame." He dropped his voice to a half-whisper. "What did I say? It wasn't real, you know that." He looked closer and saw she was green.

In times of great distress other women fainted delicately, developed headaches, which they indicated with one slender hand to the forehead. Occasionally if the distress was real and not posing, a nose might bleed. Aisling had no pretensions; she went green and threw up—copiously.

He recalled how sick she'd been when he'd killed the pair who had murdered Brovar. She'd known he was right to do so and she hadn't blamed him. That she had made clear. But the death of the two men still had made her violently ill.

He dived for a basin, thrust it under her chin and seized a towel. Then he stood by as she was racked. Wind Dancer appeared and thrust his head against her arm, offering silent comfort. Keelan arrived just as his sister was finishing. Hadrann wiped her chin while Aisling sat back limply and in silence. Keelan was half-leaning against the end of the bed as he stared at them.

"Great comets! What happened to her? The last I saw she was with the duke." Keelan's eyes darkened in sudden worry. "He didn't—Aisling, Shastro didn't hurt you, did he?"

She swallowed. "Not me." Her voice was small. "But I don't think he likes me any more either."

Keelan fetched a cup of chilled wine. It was unwatered, and he held it to her lips. "All of it, dear." She gulped half, and he made her continue, watching as the color came back into her cheeks. The green hue receded slowly. Hadrann had brought water; now he wetted the towel and cleaned her face gently. Aisling sat up a little and looked at their concerned faces, knowing they needed to hear of the events that had distressed her so badly.

"Shastro said he wanted me to see something. I knew he wasn't interested in getting me alone or anything. He really was eager to show me something, so I went. It was along the west corridor and down a long flight of stairs that did a couple of half-turns. We ended up in dungeons." Hadrann, who knew Kars Palace better than either of them, made a slight sound. He could guess what was to come. He waved her to continue when she glanced at him.

"He left his guards at the top of the stairs. There was just me and the duke and a couple of horrible men, 'experts' he called them. They'd taken some poor old woman and said she was a witch." She looked up. "She wasn't. She had no power, none of the Old Blood. She was just a poor old woman whom one of her neighbors disliked. Shastro said he had to be sure of that though. He said witches were everywhere, conspiring against him and Karsten."

"You can leave out the rest," Hadrann said grimly. "I know what comes next and so does Keelan. But why doesn't the duke like you any more? Oh!" He started to smile.

Aisling mustered a small grin to match. "Yes, I was sick all over him. He said I was disgusting. He started to march me away. He was calling up the stairs for one of his guards there to take me back to my room. I was two stairs in front of the duke when I was sick on the stairs too." She produced a tiny giggle. "Shastro stepped in it and skidded. He didn't fall down the stairs, but he went to one knee and had to put his hand down for balance. He . . . um . . . he put his hand . . ."

Hadrann was already snickering. Her brother stared at her, envisioning the scene. "He put his hand . . ." he said blankly before comprehension dawned. He gave a shuddering indrawn snort then grabbed for a pillow. For a long agonizing time the three of them howled silently into muffling items. At length Keelan lifted his head. Tears of laughter had run down his face, and his hair was sticking up in tufts.

"Yes," he informed his sister. "I can see why the duke doesn't like you any more. I'm not sure that if it had been me, I'd like you either."

Hadrann surfaced to look at them. "And Shastro always so fussy about his dignity. Then he slips in sick and puts his hand in it, right in front of a couple of guards." That set them off again.

Wind Dancer, looking dignified, was sitting by Aisling. Humans did the oddest things, said his pose. Hadrann glanced at the cat, caught the eyes of his friends, and they too looked. Something about the cat's dignity reminded them of Shastro again, and they laughed until tears ran down their faces. Wind Dancer ignored it all firmly. You had to make allowances for humans.

Aisling sobered first. "Shastro doesn't have to worry about me. He knows no noblewoman would tell a story about herself like that. It's bad luck for the guards though. Unless they've cleared out pretty quickly he'll have them quietly removed. He'd know no guard would be able to keep a tale like that to himself for long."

Hadrann stood and reached for a purse on the small table. "I'll see if they've gone yet, maybe a few coins would give them a better chance to get clear." He smiled unpleasantly. "And it would be useful if they do get clear and can tell that tale all over the south of Karsten. It won't improve the duke's reputation with most keeps."

Keelan waved him to stop. "And what if they also spread the name of the girl across half of Karsten. Someone might start asking who this cousin is and why they don't know of her." Hadrann had halted and was listening.

"That isn't all, Rann. If the tale gets about and folk start laughing, the duke will think of some way to take it out on Aisling. I don't like it and I'm sorry for the guards, but they'll have to manage alone."

Hadrann turned back and very slowly and gently replaced the purse where it had been. His every controlled movement spoke of rage held under tight rein. "I don't like it either, but you're right." He went to the door and called an order before turning back to speak to his friends.

"We'll eat here tonight. I think it best Shastro doesn't see any of us about for a day or two. Let him get over it and believe Aisling has said nothing."

They stayed in the Aranskeep rooms the next day, all day. After that, they went hunting. They took food, water, a flask of wine, and had a wonderful time. No duke to placate, no courtiers to gossip, just the three of them and Wind Dancer, who'd been smuggled out in his carrysack. They came back after a second day of hunting with a deer, which Hadrann presented to the duke. It was a young buck and excellent eating for the ducal table. Shastro was graciously pleased. It appeared the girl had said nothing to anyone. He was pleased with that too.

As for the guards, he'd had them taken before they could flee. Oh, they had intended to run, to blacken his name all over Karsten, to make a laughingstock of their duke. There'd been no doubt of it; they'd been found packing, and one had already saddled his horse. It was well they'd been caught in time.

Probably they were witches themselves or in the pay of Estcarp. Kirion had warned him about all that. A good friend, Kirion. It was only his sorcerer who really looked after the duke of Karsten. Kirion was the only man Shastro could trust. So when his sorcerer had asked for the guards, he'd given them to him. He'd seen the bodies later, and Kirion had told him how right the duke had been and how clever to move so quickly. They *had* been spies from Estcarp.

Estcarp, he mused. One day he must clean out that witches' nest. If it wasn't spies it was assassins. He suspected that Lord Ruart's disappearance was due to some Estcarp plot. Kirion thought so too. Well, here were two spies who would not be reporting. They'd not be talking to anyone of the duke's loss of dignity. Estcarp would have to find something else to laugh about. Shastro's satisfied smile was a compound of smug approval and satisfaction—with an underlying hint of madness.

VI

----◦----

Shastro had decided not to have anything done to Aisling. Her cousin and that brother of Kirion's who always seemed to be near them had betrayed no knowledge of events. At first he stayed away from her completely, but after a seven-day he drifted back. He liked her. She was amusing and listened to him honestly, he could tell. Not, as many of his courtiers did, fawningly and with incomprehension.

No, little Murna understood the thoughts of her duke and she wasn't averse to pointing out where he was wrong, which was a novelty. She had done so just that evening, speaking of the poor people and how they looked to their leader, about how a good leader could guide rather than drive. Shastro had found it unexpectedly touching. It would be pleasant if his people looked upon him in that way, he said wistfully before everyone retired.

Afterward, in their suite, Hadrann looked at Aisling. "Be careful cousin. He's weak and he sees enemies in every shadow. That's how your brother controls him. If Shastro starts to lean toward hearing you, Kirion is going to start a rumor, probably that you're an Estcarp spy."

Keelan, who'd joined them by the small rear door, nodded. "And the first thing he'd do is to begin inquiries around Aranskeep. After that if he can't find any gossip he'll make some. Shastro is nervous enough to look under his bed and in his closets for assassins every night."

"You mean he really *does*?" Aisling looked astounded.

"That's the gossip in the servants' quarters. Our guard captain picked it up. I don't know if it is true, but I know that the servants believe it. Harran says they're scared of the duke and Kirion scares them into total terror, but, as I said, Shastro is a little crazy. He sees Estcarp witches behind it every time he trips over the mat. Kirion wouldn't have too much trouble convincing the duke that you're a witch, and since you are, if Kirion starts applying tests, too much is going to show up."

"Shastro likes me," Aisling objected. "He wouldn't want to hurt me. He didn't even do anything about that other stuff. Just didn't talk to us for a while."

Hadrann drank off the wine he had poured and sat down looking at her earnestly. "Aisling, you don't understand a man like Shastro. I've been at court on and off for several years. The fact that he likes you makes it more likely he'd move against you, not less." He waved a hand at her when she would have interrupted. "Keep it shut a moment cousin and listen."

"Shastro is weak, easily led, and Kirion has worked him up into a permanent belief that Estcarp has spies and assassins everywhere. I heard some nasty things about the duke's childhood. He fears to care about anyone. He believes that if he likes someone, then she or he has to be an enemy or will abandon him in some way. Kirion has built on that fear until he's the only person Shastro believes and trusts.

"That's because your brother has 'proved' to the duke time and time again that he *is* surrounded by enemies." He looked at her, and his voice softened. "I know that Shastro can be likable. What you have to keep in mind is that he is ruined now. Even if you married him he'd never be trustworthy. Kirion's taught him to enjoy certain things too much. He might listen to you for a while, but he'd go back to his old ways and then hate you if you tried to stop him."

Hadrann sighed quietly. "You do know that Shastro was a compromise? The lords of the city clans accepted him as duke since the last two had died with no heirs and they had to have a ruler. It was that or tear themselves apart fighting to as which of *them* would rule. Shastro comes from a previous line, one that lost everything they had several generations ago.

"He grew up in the low quarter, where they deal with those they hate quite simply. You would die. Oh, probably not an obvious murder, or if it was he'd have a scapegoat waiting, but you'd die. And then, just in case, he'd do his best to quietly wipe out everyone in Aiskeep so they wouldn't ask questions." Aisling had sagged back on her seat, her face sad. Hadrann took her hand.

"He isn't just weak, cousin. He's bad all through. He likes to play that he might change but he won't, and I don't believe he can or honestly wants to. You know your brother better than I do. Ask Keelan. Is Kirion likely to have chosen a figurehead who'd turn in his tracks to follow the Light? Is he?"

"No," Aisling said dully. "No. Kirion wouldn't make that mistake."

Keelan sat beside her and hugged her warmly. "So you be careful. No more encouraging Shastro to be a good decent ruler. He won't be, and it may alert Kirion too early." He gave her another hug, then stood to pour watered wine for himself. He returned to lean against the wall nearby. "But while we're on the subject of Kars's duke, has anyone noticed a possible ducal replacement?"

Hadrann nodded. "I did, but you can't look him over. I hear he hardly ever comes to court and when he does he's gone again as soon as is respectable. He's some sort of kin of yours, a man named Jarn.

His father died young in a hunting accident, and the boy inherited about thirty years gone, a big estate but almost worthless. Several square miles of poor mountain land and a half-ruined keep."

Aisling was thinking, her eyes half-shut as she concentrated. She sat up abruptly. "Yes. Jarn of Trevalyn." She looked across to where Keelan stood. "He's grandnephew to old Geavon. I think that makes him about our fifth cousin. Jarn's father settled land that had been abandoned after the last upheaval of the Turning. There'd been a keep, and since it was on the fringes of the mountains and massively built, it partly survived, but one wing collapsed, and the original family wasn't as lucky. They were inside at the time. Jarn's father improved the place, cleared that wing, got back some of the people, and brought in mountain sheep."

She grinned. "I remember Grandfather talking about it years ago. He said a lord could make a reasonable living there if he didn't mind living within a stone's throw of Estcarp in a great barn with a leaking roof, eating mutton stew and sleeping on beds harder than a merchant's charity. It was a carefree life: you had nothing to worry about but bandits, Estcarp, starvation in winter, lumbago from the damp, constant colds in the nose, and having your throat cut by disaffected peasants." Hadrann laughed. "Had he visited this keep?"

Keelan spoke dryly. "It certainly sounds as if he had. I'd think almost any other place would be a welcome change, but if this Jarn can keep an estate like that in order and survive it, then he should be able to handle Kars."

Aisling smiled too, then sobered. "I wouldn't leap to that conclusion, either of you. A man can love his home and not want to desert it no matter how awful it seems to outsiders; besides, we're talking casually of making him duke. Before we can even think of that we need to bell the cats. Kirion and Shastro aren't going to bow politely and usher Jarn onto the throne."

"No," her brother said slowly. "What we need to do is goad the duke into doing something really stupid that turns the people against him. They would be too scared to move yet, but if we get Kirion out of the way, then they'd act."

"Kee, we're going to get a lot of people hurt before all this is over, aren't we?"

"Yes. I don't like the thought any more than you, but the alternative is another war with Estcarp. If that happens Kars could be sacked and many of the keeps as well. Far more would die if that happened."

They retired to bed, each bothered by what lay ahead. Yet, as Keelan had said, if Shastro continued on the path down which Kirion was leading him, war was inevitable. The last major attack had cost Karsten an army of thousands. What could it cost this time? Turmoil in Kars, she thought ruefully, would certainly cost fewer lives than another war.

In the morning Hadrann went hunting alone. He took a small bow for waterfowl and followed the track to a small, reed-fringed lake some three hours ride from Kars. Aisling was to spend the day in her room. She planned to open her mind carefully and see if she could pick up from Kirion any sense of his plans. Wind Dancer would stay with her as company. Keelan had his own plans. Before Hadrann left, Kee spoke of them to him and Aisling.

"I'm going into the city. Is there anything either of you would like?" Aisling shook her head. Hadrann glanced up, considering the court finery his friend was wearing.

"I wouldn't go without a guard if I were you. That's an expensive neck chain."

The Aiskeep heir shrugged. "I'll take a guard, but I don't plan to go to the lower city, just the market. I need a new bridle."

"Well and good. Do be careful." They separated, Aisling scooping up Wind Dancer as she retired.

It was late afternoon before Hadrann returned from his successful hunting. Over one shoulder he carried a double brace of duck. He wore a satisfied expression and several pounds of lakeside mud.

Aisling held her nose when he tapped on her door, proudly displaying the results of his hunting.

"Phew! The ducks will be lovely, but I hope you're taking a bath before you sit down to dine with us."

Hadrann grinned happily. "I've already told my valet to start someone heating the water. I got another brace of duck, but they've gone to the duke." He glanced around. "Where's Kee?"

"Probably down at the stables."

"No." Her head came up at his tone. "I've just come from there. He left this morning, and the captain hasn't seen him since. He didn't take a guard either. You mean he hasn't been back here at all, not all day?"

Aisling's eyes widened. "No. I haven't seen him since he left either. I hope he's not in trouble. Wait, maybe I can scry for him."

His hand caught her wrist. "It's too dangerous. Just listening the way you were doing today is safe enough, but you go using magic to look and you're likely to alert Kirion. Let's go and talk to the captain."

But their guard captain was no comfort. "I'd say this was time to search, my Lord. It's still light enough to rake through these places without torches. We'll miss less if there's anything to find."

Aisling returned to her room determined to scry for Keelan. Hadrann followed.

"You can't risk it."

"I don't care, I have to find him."

He shook his head. "It isn't you. If you scry, you could alert Kirion. If he starts looking at us we're all in danger." He took a deep breath. "I have something to suggest that may work more effectively and be safer for all of us as well." As he talked, she listened. Then he watched as she left, half-running. Now, if only she could put Hadrann's plan into action without error, Keelan might be found.

She forced tears to her eyes as she rounded the corridor bend to find Shastro talking with a courtier. She waited, her eyes, brimming with tears, fixed on him. He glanced at her, smiled, and went to turn back to his conversation. Then his mind registered her distress. He swung back.

"Murna, my dear child. What has happened? Has someone been unkind? Only tell me and I shall have them punished."

Aisling looked up at him. "My Lord Duke, anarchy. A threat to your court." She watched as he stiffened. His gaze darted about them, and a small tic began at one side of his mouth.

"Anarchy? A threat? Speak, Murna, what is this?"

"My Lord, Keelan, the friend of my cousin is missing. He but went to the market to purchase a new bridle. That was many hours ago, and he is not to be found." She saw him relax, about to object that the disappearance of one minor member at court was hardly a threat. She bowed her head.

"My Lord, I fear for you."

"For me?" He tensed again.

"Isn't Keelan the brother of your lord sorcerer?" Aisling asked innocently. "If there should be a plot against him, perhaps a plan to use his brother as a lever. But worse still, what if they but seek to persuade him against *you*!" She saw the shot go home. Shastro went a greenish-white in terror. Sweat suddenly stood out on his forehead.

Absently he patted her arm. "Dear child. So sensible, so loyal to Kars and its duke. Yes, if it should be a plot against me. I must see Kirion at once." He looked down at her. "Go back to your cousin. Tell him I swear I shall do all possible to find his friend. If he has men searching he is to call them back. Better not to hamper what my own men can do. Go, quickly!" She went, running lightly back to the Aranskeep suite, where Hadrann waited anxiously.

"Did it work?"

Aisling was worried. "It worked. Right now he's on the way to demand Kirion find Kee at once. But, Hadrann, I fear Shastro is going to believe this an Estcarp plot again. I think he was starting to wonder as soon as I spoke."

"You can't worry about that. No, I think Kirion may claim this plot is homegrown. It would give him the chance to obtain a few more people for his experiments. He won't get those from Estcarp. It wasn't Shastro we were after anyhow. It was Kirion. He loathes Kee, but he'd hate to see anyone else hurting him; he prefers to do that himself. In a way Kee is *his*, and gods help the one who steals what belongs to Kirion."

Aisling sat as her knees began to feel weak. Wind Dancer jumped up and rose to pat her cheek gently with one large paw. She held him to her, the warm furry body and the rumbling purr a comfort. Hadrann poured wine, then looked at the cup, dumped it back in the decanter and poured them both fruit juice. He handed one mug to Aisling.

"Damn court habits. I always drink far more when I'm here. Tonight we want our wits about us if we ever did."

Outside they could hear an increasing hubbub. Aisling leaned out of the window to see. Below in the courtyard mounted soldiers milled. Shastro was nowhere in sight, but Kirion, haughty on a sleek black horse, was giving sharp orders. Aisling shrank back. Better that he did not look up and see her spying, as he'd think of it if he saw her.

She smiled wryly. Ten to one Kirion had no idea that she'd been behind Shastro's demand that his sorcerer find Keelan. The duke would never have admitted that the idea of a plot had been thought up by another. No, he'd have rushed to Kirion to alternately storm and complain, then to whine in fear. After that all the decisions would have been her brother's.

They waited through two hours that seemed to stretch to twenty. Then below there was a lesser commotion, and Aisling flew to the window. A filthy, battered figure was being helped from a trooper's horse. She bit back her scream of greeting. She must not betray them. Must not let any see how much she loved a man none knew to be more than a friend of her cousin's. But it *was* Kee, her brother, safe, and if not sound at least not too visibly damaged.

She flew to the door, snapping orders at their waiting guard. "Have someone bring hot water and our bath from the storeroom at once. Find a healer and tell him to attend the Aranskeep suite in half a candlemark. Send one of your men down to the stables to help the Lord Keelan back here. Lay out clean linen and outer clothing."

"At once, Lady." He was rapping out orders in turn as she shut the door again. Then she sagged into a chair to wait. Hadrann smiled at her. "If he could ride back he can't be too badly hurt."

"He's Aiskeep and proud."

"So?" The single word was provocative.

"So he'd stay on a horse if he were dying and be too proud to say so." Aisling snarled. She would have continued but for raising her eyes to see his grin. "Oh, I see. Start a fight and take my mind off worrying. But I am . . . is that them?" She would have flung the door open but for his grip.

"I'm the one who is so worried over my friend," she was warned in a low voice. "You are merely mildly concerned over my friend." Hadrann thrust her behind him and opened the door with cries of distress.

"My dear boy! What has befallen you? Are you injured? But you are so very dirty, one would think you had been rolling in the streets."

Keelan eyed him bitterly. "I have. No, I'm not much hurt, but I'd kill for a hot bath."

As he spoke a procession of palace maids bearing steaming copper cans approached. Behind them marched two men carrying a large bathtub stamped with the Aranskeep seal. Keelan gaped.

"Has someone added clairvoyance to his abilities?"

Hadrann glared at him. "Shut up with that!" he hissed. Louder he said, "No, dear boy. Merely common sense. I did . . . ah . . . see you from my window. You appeared greatly in need of quantities of hot water and soap."

"I am." Keelan assured him. "Very much so." He waved the bath procession through the door before him. "Get on with that and hurry." He took the hot drink handed to him by Aisling, allowing his gaze to meet hers briefly. Anxiety met reassurance, and he saw her relax slightly.

The bath was rapidly filled, and one by one the maids departed with watercans emptied. Aisling had laid out towels and soap meanwhile.

She vanished discreetly for five minutes as Hadrann helped his friend off with the filthy torn clothing. Alone she also opened her mind and listened for other minds. Ah. One came, slipping silently between the walls. Once her brother was safely ensconced in hot soapy water she returned. Her hands moved now and again in fluttering motions. They would look no more than the usual movements of a nervous woman were they overlooked, but Keelan could read hunter signals. He'd learned from her, and Hadrann had learned from both.

"All right. Now for the love of Karsten tell us what happened to you. My cousin was worried sick." Keelan ducked his head under the water, scrubbed vigorously at his hair, then surfaced to meet her glare. He grinned wearily.

"I made a mistake. All right? I should have taken one of Hadrann's guards with me. His captain even asked, but I was only going to the market. I intended to buy a new bridle, then come straight back." He lowered his voice to a slurred murmur. No one farther than a few feet from him would have been able to make out the words.

"I haven't been in the lower city for months. I had no idea how bad it's gotten. They're close to rebellion and they hate anyone from court. When the time comes we may be able to use that." His voice became louder again. ". . . and I bought a real beauty of a bridle too."

"What happened to it? You certainly didn't have it with you when you returned," Aisling digressed. Let them bore the listener. Keelan obliged with a long monologue on the best types of horse gear, the best place in Kars to buy it, and then a string of curses upon the heads of those who'd stolen it along with almost everything else he'd had at the time. Aisling allowed him to return to the subject of his attackers.

"So you wandered off into the lower city." She fluttered eyelashes. "How very foolish."

Keelan looked wry. "Quite so. But it was a pleasant day, I had my bridle, and I wasn't thinking."

"Obviously!" Hadrann snapped. "Will you stop discussing that witch-damned bridle and tell us what happened to you?"

Keelan's tale was interesting if only because it illustrated what he'd said about the lower city. He'd wandered along the streets, purchased food from a street vender, and when he failed to pay attention to his direction, managed to get himself turned around in the maze of alleys. He'd gone the way he thought to be right only to find it wasn't, not by some distance. Then he'd heard footsteps following. He'd dived around a couple of corners, which seemed to have been the intent. Now and again he glanced casually at Aisling, reading the words her hands wove. He nodded, following her lead as he continued.

He groaned. "I was an idiot, I admit it. They let me hear them following to make me hurry in the direction they wanted. When I came around a corner, someone dropped a roof on my head. I woke up in a cellar. I'd been stripped down to my underclothes, my head was killing me, and that place was *filthy*!

"That's how I got this way." A wave of his hand indicated the befouled clothing he'd dumped at one end of the room. "I'd been tied and I could hear them talking up the stairs. They were going to murder me, take my body out after dark, and dump it in the river. The tide would just be starting out, and I'd go with it."

Hadrann looked startled. "Whoever they were, someone wasn't a fool. They kept you alive just in case a major search was mounted. They could dump you out somewhere and stop the poking into everything any searchers would be doing."

"True. One of them checked me, and I played dead. He believed I was still unconscious. As soon as he was gone I wriggled all over that damned cellar, found a chip of stone and frayed the rope to where I could break it. After that I waited. They went off somewhere to check if I'd been missed and left the door at the top of the cellar stairs unlocked. I didn't waste time, I can tell you. I got out of there and made a run for it. Bumped into the duke's guards almost at once."

Aisling clasped her hands. "Thanks be that our duke cares for his people. And they brought you back. Did they find your prison or any of the wicked men who had attacked you?"

Keelan nodded, then yelped and held his head. "Ow. I must remember not to do that for a while. Yes, they found the cellar. No trace of the men though, but the duke will search. What an insult to him that a member of his court should be kidnapped in the duke's own city. And do you know, I really couldn't swear to it, but I thought one of those I heard had the merest trace of a mountain accent."

His voice became self-righteous. "I didn't mention it. After all, I'm not certain. It could have been one of those mush mouths from the very far South. But he didn't speak in quite the way of the city. Of that I am sure." He ducked down and continued to scrub. Aisling was listening. After a minute she grinned.

"He's gone. It's a nuisance that passage is there, but they can only listen to what's said in this room." She stared at her brother, ran her fingers through his hair to feel the lump. "Hold on and I'll do something for that. I can't fix it completely in case Shastro has the court healer check, but I can take most of the pain." She did so, and Keelan sighed in relief.

"Thanks be. That headache was killing me."

"Right. Now that you can think clearly, how much of that tale is the whole truth?" Hadrann queried.

"Most of it. I omitted that I think the whole house was a nest of spies. The leader was furious with whoever hauled me in. I gather I was a mistake on the part of some overzealous idiot who thought I was snooping. And," he paused teasingly, "they weren't Estcarp either. I recognized a voice. Remember Duke Pagar?"

"We're hardly likely to forget him." Aisling's tone was dry. "He got the whole Karsten army killed *and* our great-grandfather. Why? You aren't saying that it was Pagar's ghost returned?"

"No, I'm saying that Pagar married into a powerful clan who lost most of what they had when Pagar failed and would like to have it back. They weren't at all happy when the other lords chose to skip two previous ducal lines and accept Shastro as duke. That was the voice I heard: Lord Sarnor or one of his sons. They all sound alike."

Hadrann whistled softly. "Now *that* could send the hunter out. We must see Shastro gets the message. Set him against Sarnor's clan, and they'll keep each other occupied while we follow our own road." He lounged back against the wall. "This could be very very useful!"

VII

Keelan was summoned the next morning. But a long sleep and Aisling's minor healing had left him in shape to obey and be helpful to the agitated and inquiring Shastro.

"Now, Lord Keelan, please give me a full account. I want in particular to know any thing that could help us recognize your kidnappers."

So it had been the duke's man listening. Keelan nodded. "I shall do my best, my Lord Duke." He had nothing to hide so he was meticulous. He described every event in detail, every word he could remember, although here and there he shaded those a fraction. Once, when he mentioned the mountain accent, he added in his own ideas.

Shastro nodded thoughtfully. "Likely. Certainly not impossible. Those who've risen to power seldom like it when the wheel turns. I daresay they hoped to influence me to some action using a member of my court as leverage." He turned to address the heavy tapestry covering a corner at the back of his throne room.

"What do you think, Kirion?" His sorcerer emerged from behind the heavy embroidered cloth to glance at his duke and Keelan.

"I think my brother may have the right of it. It's unlikely he was taken to pressure you. More likely it was I they planned as a target."

"You?" Shastro looked disconcerted.

"Why not? Look at the facts. Keelan is a minor member of your

court, not a particular friend of yours, and of no strategic importance to Kars. On the other hand he is my brother. The kidnappers
may well have believed that they could force me to obey instructions
if they held him."

Keelan kept his mouth shut. He knew Kirion and was under no
illusions on that score. Kidnappers could have cut him into pieces at
high noon before the entire court, and Kirion wouldn't have lifted a
finger unless he saw an advantage for himself. But Keelan thought
there was an advantage his brother might not have noticed as yet. He
opened his mouth and spoke as if puzzled.

"It was a mountain accent. The more I think the more I am sure
of it. But what had Pagar's clan to gain? They're rich enough. They
have moderate lands, and they were almost destroyed by Estcarp.
Surely it isn't likely . . ." He let his voice trail off into silence as he
saw the two suggestions strike home.

Kirion's face had gone blank at the mention of lands and coin.
Shastro's look had darkened as he thought his way through possibilities. Then he erupted in fury.

"I—me. It was *me* they sought to betray when they took Keelan." He spun to stare at his sorcerer. "Look at the facts, Kirion. If
they could use your brother to force you to act against me, then I
would be helpless. Who in Kars has the power you have?"

"I would not have listened to them."

"No, no, of course not. But they wouldn't know how loyal you
are."

It wasn't loyalty, Keelan reflected. Kirion didn't know the meaning of the word. In reality Kirion hated the brother who'd inherited.
He would have made a great play of his anguish and higher loyalties,
then let the kidnappers murder Keelan and smiled happily in private.
Shastro was working himself into a fury of wounded pride and fear.

"Of course you wouldn't act against me, but they wouldn't
know that. They'd believe they could force you at the very least to

abandon me, to refuse me aid." He jerked upright, his eyes becoming almost crazed as thought followed thought. "How would they strike at me? Here, they must have an assassin here! Or spies to tell them when I'd be vulnerable."

Keelan bowed, drawing the duke's eyes. He had to get Shastro off that track before he started demanding Kirion question the court using some foul spell. "Servants tend to know everything that occurs in the court, my Lord Duke. And who would remark another of them walking in the lower city, whereas a courtier would be seen and remarked." After all, he reflected, that was nothing but the truth.

Shastro leapt at the idea. "Kirion." His voice was a command. "Have them close the palace gates. You will question all servants. See if any are from the mountains. Find out who is behind this plot against me. Find them, do you hear me? Find them, and I'll know what to do with them."

He had not been looking at his sorcerer when he made his demand. Keelan had been watching his brother out of the corner of an eye. He'd seen the sudden flicker of anger when the duke snapped that order. Shastro had spoken as if to another servant, and Kirion hadn't appreciated it. He'd say and do nothing, not yet. Keelan knew his brother. Kirion had in mind the acquisition of some of the land and wealth that might come his way if this clan was discredited.

He said as much later in private in the Aranskeep suite. "Kirion will do and say nothing to upset Shastro until he's had as much as he can persuade out of the duke. After that I wouldn't give two coppers for Shastro's continued existence. His paranoia is starting to show. At present it's useful to Kirion, but if it becomes too great it could be a danger to him. Shastro has only to begin doubting Kirion's loyalty and he could be in real danger."

Hadran listened. "Personally, do you think?"

"Maybe not personally or not unless Shastro really overreacts. Kirion could merely withdraw to his own lands, but Shastro could strip Kirion of much that he has and see that nothing more comes his way. If Kirion acted openly against his duke it would bring the clans in against him. He isn't that powerful a sorcerer as yet; if enough men were sent against him, they could drain his power to nothing, and he'd fall."

Aisling nodded to herself. Shastro and Kirion needed each other, not as master and servant but as allies. The duke was forgetting that. Kirion could use this business to remind him for a while.

But things could get messy if Shastro forgot again. They'd all heard the tramp of marching feet go past. The palace gates would all be shut by now, Aisling thought, the ones they could control anyhow. If she knew anything about servants, and she did, they'd have a half dozen other ways of getting clear of this place without using the gates. She said so to Keelan, who vanished hastily and unobtrusively to mention it to Shastro, who listened hard-eyed before snapping further orders.

Keelan excused himself. He left his brother and the duke discussing the actions the soldiers must take and hurried back to the Aranskeep rooms. Aisling opened the door, noticing several couriers who were within earshot. Her face stayed politely welcoming.

"Oh, Lord Keelan, have you come to tell us more of your adventures?" She simpered slightly, and her brother's eyebrows rose comprehendingly: there must be visitors as well. He nodded, stepping inside.

"I have come to speak to Hadrann, if you will tell him I am here." He spoke briskly, and she dropped one eyelid as she turned to call.

"Hadrann, cousin! Our friend Lord Keelan is here." She shut the door and turned. "Do come this way, Lord Keelan. What would you like to drink, and perhaps you would care for some bread and cold duck." She ushered him through the door, and Keelan stifled a groan. By the Flames, it would be old Lady Varra, the biggest gossip in the place, with her servants in attendance. He bit back a sudden grin. Ah. But he could encourage her to leave him alone with his sister and friend, and quickly. Her second cousin had married into Pagar's old clan.

He accepted food and drink, then approached. "Such a commotion. They're shutting all the palace gates to question the servants. They're looking for spies from, well," he lowered his voice, "from a certain clan." He whispered the name. "Our good duke has cause to doubt their loyalty. He'll question most rigorously those who are taken, I'm sure."

He watched as Lady Varra took that in. Within minutes she was heading for the door, a flurry of chatter bouncing about her vanishing form: a remembered engagement . . . so late and she must dress. She apologized for her unseemly haste, but it would not do to offend . . . Her explanations trailed off as she made her escape. Keelan and the other two looked after her with sudden lively interest. One would think there *was* a conspiracy, so keen was she to get out of here and away.

Hadrann walked over and opened the door to peer out. "She's gone." He looked at Keelan. "Now what cat have you set among the pigeons?" From the sofa Wind Dancer raised his head and uttered an indignant disclaimer. He disliked live pigeons; they had too many small feathers. Hadrann stroked a hand down the cat's spine. "Not you, my furred friend. Kee, was that true, Shastro has ordered the palace servants held here so they can be checked?" Keelan explained, following that with some speculation on the departed gossip and the speed of her going.

His sister nodded. "You were close to right. I listened a little as she went out. Just her emotions. She was scared to death. There is something going on, and she either knows about it or guesses enough to be afraid. But apart from her, if Kirion starts questioning servants he should find enough to keep him occupied for weeks. Shastro will insist on being present. They'll have a host of minor dishonesties to confess as well as a few major ones. Even if those have nothing to do with your kidnapping, Kee, Shastro will want to take action on everything he hears because he hates anyone except him to get away with anything."

"Kirion isn't going to like wasting his power pulling minor secrets from dozens of servants," Hadrann commented.

"No. And if the duke starts ordering him around as if he's just another lackey," Aisling added, "there could be trouble between them. It sounds from what Kee saw as if it's already been happening and Kirion is already annoyed over it. Let's wander out and see if we can stir things up. Just wait for me a moment." She darted to her room and returned tucking something into the back of her hair. She gave Wind Dancer a hug.

"If they come searching here you be careful." He squawked a reply. It sounded scornful, and she smiled. Hadrann took her arm, and they strolled the length of the corridor to the head of the staircase that led down to the more general rooms on the floor below, from where they could hear a growing noise. It appeared to be a large number of agitated people all talking at once. Keelan took the lead and began to descend the staircase.

A figure separated itself from the milling forms below and came hurrying up toward them: an older man who was dressed in the garb of a valet. His face twisted in fear, and sweat glistened on his face, shining in the candlelight as he neared them. He was terrified and desperate to escape, not to be taken alive. Aisling caught Hadrann's arm and Keelan's arms and drew them back to leave clear passage. She doubted the old man was one of those Shastro sought, but it was clear he had some major sin on his mind.

He barely glanced at them as he passed, but as his hand briefly brushed Aisling's bare arm she saw a tiny picture in her mind: this man and others together. She heard nothing, but there was the unmistakable air of plotters together. The man in her mind turned to look down at a figure lying motionless in filthy straw. She knew that face. She nudged Keelan and whispered hastily. He set off after the man at a slower, unobtrusive pace. Hadrann gazed down the stairs and whistled. Below them a palace guard peered up.

"Quickly." The soldier came running. "My friend saw a servant fleeing past us. He isn't at all certain, but he thinks it could have been one of the men who kidnapped him. They went that way. Look for Lord Keelan."

"Thank you, my Lord, my Lady." He followed Hadrann's indicating wave. A bare minute later there came the sounds of a struggle. Keelan's voice was raised. "Rann, help!"

Aisling and Hadrann raced up the stairs. In a half-open doorway Keelan was struggling with the servant. The palace guard was trying to rise, blood pouring from a head wound. The old servant was fighting like a madman and gradually overpowering the lighter Keelan. Hadrann leapt, his hand flashing out in a blow that sent the panicked man to the ground. The guard was on his feet looking unhappy.

"You haven't killed him, Lord?"

"No, he should wake again soon, and with so many to be questioned there may be no answers demanded of you. Many will be hauling in unconscious men." The guard heaved a deeply thankful sigh.

"I'll see they'll know if they must, Lord. My thanks for your aid. All of you. I would not be well regarded if this one had slipped through our hands."

He summoned help from comrades and hauled his prisoner away down the stairs. Aisling looked after them and shivered. She'd seen Shastro's dungeons and knew what would happen to the servant. She hated that she'd helped, but it was more important to bring down her brother and Shastro then to agonize over the fate of a man who was far from innocent. She took her companions' arms.

"Let us go back to the rooms. I want to make sure the searchers aren't wrecking the place and annoying Wind Dancer. We'll hear what was found out soon enough."

She was wrong in that last. Three days passed. Shastro seemed to be keeping the results to himself. He was seething over the discovery that an entire clan had been conspiring against him. Kirion had been unable to wring an admission from any of the servants of an intended ducal assassination. They insisted they'd been there only to watch and listen. Those who had taken Keelan had believed him to be following one of their number. Shastro didn't believe a word of it.

He was certain they'd been conspiring to kill him. Probably they were allied with Estcarp too. Shastro would die, and some puppet of the witches would be placed on the throne, there to talk treaties with Karsten's oldest and greatest enemy. He fumed, demanding the servants be questioned again and again. Kirion made soothing noises.

"They can tell no more." He shrugged. "They know nothing. It is likely they were never told to do more than watch and listen. It would have been one of that clan who'd have carried out their intent. Do you now plan to move against the clan?"

Shastro was storming about his room. He picked up a goblet and flung it hard against the wall. "And my proof? If I march every solider I have against their keeps I'd lose. The other clans would claim I was using this business to take the power of a clan. I could have them all banding together against me." He whirled on his sorcerer.

"Well, you're my advisor. Advise me!"

Kirion considered while pouring wine. He placed the dented goblet in the duke's hand. "Drink, my Lord Duke, and let us consider." Shastro sat, calming a little as he emptied the goblet and was poured another.

"You are right. We must move cautiously," Kirion mused. "But if plague strikes, or if enemies strike this clan in secret how can it be blamed on you? After all, you can point to witnessed testimony that creatures of theirs were stationed in the palace to spy upon you and your court. I suggest you hold an open ducal hearing. Let everyone speak who knows anything at all, or even those who just want to hear themselves talk."

"What good will that do me," his duke asked pettishly.

"Why, people assume that if there is talking going on, then nothing else is happening. We weary everyone with this discussion and in secret we act against the Coast Clan—nothing that cannot be explained as accident or ill-fortune."

"But they'll guess."

"Assuredly they will." Kirion's smile was dangerous. "They'll blame you, maybe even be stupid and reckless enough to attack you openly. You can then crush them the same way. You protest that if they did not have guilty consciences they would not be jumping to conclusions over a few accidents. I learned few things from my grandsire, but one trick I did learn. We kill two sorts of men from their clan. Those who are cool-headed and those who are clever. We kill the clever because they may see our intent and the cool-headed because . . ."

"Because if you kill the cool-headed the hotheads go to war." Shastro ended his sentence. "Yes. A good plan. I'll get the trial started. We'll try them on the kidnapping of Lord Keelan. I won't suggest anything more to begin. Let it come out from those who talk. I shall be shocked, horrified at the perfidy."

He smoothed his sleeve. "I can leave the rest up to you, my dear friend." His look was sly. "And do rest assured too, you shall have your share of any plunder these traitors provide." He strolled off leaving Kirion standing, his face blank as he fumed.

An hour later in his own apartments Kirion raged about the rooms, throwing small items at the wall and cursing his duke savagely, anger and wounded pride showing on his face. He hadn't worked for all these years, killed, tortured, and schemed, just to be told his master would toss him a few trinkets, like a bone to a good dog.

Shastro was getting above himself, forgetting who'd put him on the throne of Kars. There were a lot of Shastros out there, all mediocre, burning with ambition, and ready to do anything for the man who gained them their dearest wish. Perhaps it was getting toward the time when Kirion should think about that.

Shastro was the last of his line, yes, but the duke who'd sat on the throne in Kars before Shastro's great-grandsire had also left descendants. They'd jump at the chance to regain the rulership. Perhaps he should make a cautious approach there, just in case he needed a candidate quickly?

"Varnar!" Kirion tossed a small purse to Varnar when his servant appeared. "Take this, go, and drink at the Inn of the Merry Bear. Be careful, let no one realize what you do, but you are to make enquiries about the family of Jekkar the cobbler. I want to know all about them. Who is well, who may be ill, who is wed with children? Do you understand me? Be careful. I would not be pleased if you were too obvious in your questioning."

Kirion sniffed as Varnar scurried away. The man was useful occasionally, beyond the other, darker use Kirion would have for him if there was need. He continued with his latest experiment, wondering if he should also scry for his missing servants again. He'd done so a number of times in the past five moons, hoping they had found his witch-damned sister, Aisling. Not only could he obtain no sight through them but he also could not sense anything of the witch-cursed brat either. He'd try again when next he had a surplus in prisoners, although the way Shastro made demands, that wouldn't be anytime soon.

Varnar returned the next morning, smiling hopefully up at his master. "I found the cobbler, Lord, and I have all the news of his family." He talked while Kirion listened intently. Once Varnar fell silent, Kirion gave him a well-filled purse and other orders before sending the man away.

He did wonder how Shastro would react once the trials of the palace servants got underway. Kirion suspected a number of them were involved in wrongdoing, not always a threat to Shastro, but servants usually practiced some deceit that could be used against them at need. He'd bide his time and see how events fell out, and perhaps Kirion could give the events some assistance if that would help his plans.

The trial was unpleasant for many at court. Between the admissions of the servants, the careless talking of some courtiers, and the savage questioning conducted by Kirion, many clans were left with family in Kars under a cloud. The investigation had covered a lot of territory and uncovered some very illegal events besides Keelan's abduction. Six members of the Coast Clan were executed, and a number of servants simply disappeared once the trial was over.

But it had left the clans in exactly the position Kirion had planned. The Coast Clan was seething with rage, grief, and resentment. They'd leap at any reason to attack the duke. The other clans were frantic to prove their loyalty. If the Coast Clan made fools of themselves the others would see it as both a chance to impress Shastro and possibly also to garner a little profit.

So the incidents began. A lord of the clan, an old and wise soldier, was found dead, his neck broken. There were no signs of others. His family did not wish to accept that. It appeared that the old man had perhaps had a dizzy spell due to his age, fainted, and broken his neck when he fell from his horse. The clan trackers scoured the whole area and found no proof to the contrary despite their desire to prove otherwise.

Then a younger man died. Bandits, it was said. He'd been stripped naked and everything including his horse stolen. He'd been shot from a distance, the arrow left in the death wound. The family raged, but again the evidence fit the suggestion of bandits. Over the next few weeks eight clan members met their deaths. Shastro met with his sorcerer privately.

"Brilliant, my dear Kirion. Just brilliant. Enough of a hint in each case that they believe the deaths to have been at my instigation but never any solid proof, nothing they could bring to even a slightly biased court. And I shall arrange a court that is not. Oh, yes. Just as soon as you are done." He smiled patronizingly at Kirion. "And when will that be?"

Kirion noted the patronizing smile but allowed no resentment to show. He smiled in turn. "In a few days, my Lord Duke. We must kill their leader now. The lord of the clan is a sensible man. He sees that there's no proof and thus far he's holding the clan back. With him dead his younger brother will take over, and the man's a witless hothead. He'll attack you, and you'll have your excuse to crush the entire clan."

"Just let me know when you're ready, Kirion. I mustn't be caught unprepared."

The voice was preemptory, and Kirion bowed slightly. "Of course, my Lord Duke. At your command." Under the mild words was an ugly tone. It was definitely time Kirion found another figurehead, but for now he'd let the fool live; he needed him to direct events in Kars. After the Coast Clan was beaten and plundered, that would be the time to deal with Shastro.

"When do you intend to kill the man and where?" Shastro was demanding.

"In five more days. I have a servant within their main keep. He will poison their lord."

"Won't that be rather obvious?"

"A subtle poison, my Lord Duke, and a subtle man using it." Varnar, with his hopes of recovering his memory and his family.

Kirion had molded him well. "Their Lord will be dead with no signs to show what slew him. They will believe it poison, particularly when a new servant is found to have fled, but they will again have no proof."

Shastro chuckled. "The brother will mount a stupid and useless attack on me. I'll kill everyone with him, and the other clans will be more respectful in future." He smirked. "I'll teach them a lesson to remember. And once we're done with this, Kirion, you're to find some way of attacking Estcarp effectively. You haven't done that yet. Aren't your powers strong enough?" He laughed loudly before leaving Kirion to smolder alone.

Kirion sat swearing silently, then he smiled, a slow evil smile. Shastro would find out in time. Kirion had an agenda, and the duke was no more than an item on a long list. Kirion had men out searching for Aisling. So far the dammed girl had eluded him. There was nothing to show she'd even returned to Karsten although he thought she had. He scowled. That could be wishful thinking though. Then too, she had some of the Gift, and that could be hiding her from his own power.

But he'd find her, and when he did he would drain her power from her for himself to become the greatest black sorcerer Karsten had seen in its entire history. The witches should beware after that as well. Shastro wasn't entirely wrong; they were an enemy Karsten could do without. Their lands would provide wealth for Karsten—and maybe, if he was very clever, a throne for Kirion.

He had not considered that he might not be the only one with an agenda. Kars woke the next morning to find an army at the gates. The Coast Clan had a new and unexpected leader. He'd come to ask questions and to aid the memory of those questioned he'd brought a few friends. Shastro looked out on almost a thousand soldiers, a siege engine, an orderly camp that encircled the main gates of the city, and panicked.

VIII

⟨◇⟩

Aisling had again been looking out of the window. She'd woken early, and with sunrise lighting the sky, she had risen to enjoy the massed clouds as they changed from fire red to orange and then to a softening pink. The whole sky became light, and as objects sharpened she blinked.

"Hadrann? Hadrann, come and look at this."

"What is it?"

"I still can't see very well because most of it is almost around the window corner. But it looks as if there's an army out there camped along the city wall and across the main gate."

"*What?*" came the bellow from across the suite. Hadrann bolted in from his bedroom, hastily shrugging his robe about him. "Where?"

Aisling pointed in silence as he leaned far out of the window and gaped. He studied the single large siege machine and considered the orderly lines of tents and soldiers. His lips moved as he counted the horse lines. His eyes went to the pennants flying from a much larger tent to the rear. His mouth curved in a sardonic grin.

"Well, well, well. So Kirion's plans overreached. That's the Coast Clan pennant flying out there, and judging by the part of the army I can see, Lord Franzo must have over eight hundred men at least by the Kars gates. I can see a few independent keep pennants too."

"What will they do, Rann? Do you think Franzo plans to attack the city?" Her voice became thoughtful. "Hold on. Lord Franzo, that isn't the clan's leader, is it?"

"Nope. But it's Franzo all right. I recognize his personal pennant below the clan one. He's cousin to the main line but he's also a good, experienced, and canny fighter. He was a mercenary leading a small company in his younger days. Maybe the clan decided to give him war leader rights. Franzo isn't one to make a move before he knows what he's doing, and the next in line is or maybe was the sort of fool who would. If Franzo's in charge something must have happened to the next in line too. He's a hothead. He wouldn't give up his position for anything short of his life, not if he could prevent it."

In a palace tower some distance away, a hysterical duke was asking similar questions. Kirion tossed a spell at him that left Shastro sitting mutely in a chair, a dazed look on his face. Kirion went on with his scrying. Finally he stood up. He opened and shut his mouth, then in the end made no sound. Matters had gone farther and faster than a few oaths could relieve.

He thought of the duke. Bother the man. It looked as if Kirion would have to postpone any change of ruler for a while. He required Shastro to give the official orders and, he smiled sinisterly, to take the blame for any and all events if it came to that.

Apart from anything else, his own powers were only at any strength as long as he had those he could drain of their own gift. Shastro's soldiers found those victims for Kirion, and it would be better if the duke could also be blamed for those deaths if something ever went wrong. He flicked his fingers, and Shastro, unaware that he'd been briefly silenced, was off again. His sorcerer permitted him to babble until he ran down, then spoke slowly.

"It is unfortunate, but I am a sorcerer, not a god. I have questioned the powers that I can reach, and it appears that we have been temporarily outmaneuvered. That is Lord Franzo down there."

"I know that. But why is it him and . . ."

"And not the leader I intended to be rid of nor his stupid impetuous brother, whom we could have used," Kirion interrupted. "Because Franzo isn't the fool the brother would have been. He's been studying events too. My man hadn't yet acted when the clan leader was killed tripping and falling down his witch-cursed stairs. Franzo accused the brother of pushing him, had him locked up, and assembled the clan soldiers. Then he talked to the other lords of the clan. He only let the brother out, once Franzo had secured the backing of all the clan lords."

Shastro looked horrified. "But why here? They have no proof I've been involved with any of their misfortune." His voice developed a faint whine. "I was the victim, well, almost. They intended my assassination. So why is this Franzo here and what does he want of me?"

"Go and ask him," Kirion said tersely.

"But . . . but . . ."

"I doubt he'd harm you, not unless he wants the city to rise up and fall on him. He may have some nine hundred soldiers out there, but we have very good walls, defended gates, and a lot more people willing to fight for Kars." He refrained from saying that fighting for Kars wasn't quite the same as fighting for a duke, but Shastro was looking happier.

"Yes. My people wouldn't allow me to be murdered before them." Shastro drew himself up. "I shall invite this Franzo to appear before me."

"With safe passage?"

"Of course. I shall show him that the duke of Kars knows how to behave. I shall display my noble blood!" Kirion refrained from pointing out that, like Pagar before him, Shastro had risen from obscurity, noble blood or not, and in Shastro's case that had been four generations gone. Shastro was bleating on. "I shall show him he cannot think to intimidate the duke of Kars. As if he could!"

If that display of hysterical panic hadn't shown that Franzo had succeeded, Kirion thought, he didn't know what could. Aloud he agreed sincerely or, more precisely, with the excellent counterfeit of deep sincerity he could produce when required.

Shastro hurried off to have the throne room arranged, guards mustered to line the streets to the palace, and to first find a messenger and scribe. The duke could write but he felt that at the moment his writing might be a trifle shaky.

In the palace, Keelan and Hadrann were out and about, chatting, listening, peering out of windows, and generally putting together all the information they could uncover. Aisling sat quietly, motionless in a large chair in her room as she worked. Wind Dancer too had chosen to help. Aisling had covered him with a 'not to be noticed' spell and let him down from a window. Safely on the ground, the big cat had jumped from the basket and trotted off toward the besieging army.

Armies were rarely unpleasant to cats, and with Kirion engaged in coping with ducal panic, Aisling could safely link with her feline friend. Wind Dancer padded here and there, now pausing to listen to talk, now accepting a proffered tidbit from some cat-loving cook. After four hours he made his way back to the tower wall. Aisling let the basket swing down; Wind Dancer leaped in and sat comfortably as he was retrieved. Soon after that the men returned.

Hadrann spoke first. "Shastro is going to meet the clan war leader—Franzo, if that is him leading—tomorrow morning to, and I quote, 'Discuss the possible grievances the clan may have against the duke of Kars.'" His lips curved in a small smile. "Shastro is steaming. I think he'd forgotten that he may be duke and rule Kars, but out in the lands of Karsten beyond the city, the keep lords rule, and he has little effective authority over them. He hasn't enjoyed being reminded."

Keelan nodded. "The court is frightened. Gossip has it that if Shastro doesn't placate the Coast Clan the city could be taken. I don't know exactly how many men are out there, but it isn't likely." He considered briefly. "Although if that's Franzo, it might be possible." He glanced over to where Aisling sat with Wind Dancer sprawled across her.

"That is Franzo down there. He has nine hundred and sixty soldiers and the full backing of the Coast Clan," she informed them. "He also has the backing of a couple of allied lesser clans and several keeps that think Shastro wants taking down a notch or two. They aren't expecting it to come to an attack on Kars, but they will if there's no other choice."

"And if it does?"

"They'll strike straight through the city, not spreading out, not attacking any who don't attack them. When they reach the palace they'll depose Shastro. They aren't certain whom to put in his place. If this must be done they're intending to put Franzo in temporarily, and he's agreed to that until they find a suitable younger ruler."

Keelan looked surprised. "You mean Franzo would step down?"

Hadrann nodded. "He would. He's a good soldier and knows it. He isn't a man to enjoy sitting on a throne and dealing with a lot of paperwork and fawning courtiers." He grinned briefly. "I'd pity the court and the quill pushers if he did rule Kars, but he'd do that if it meant peace and time to find a man who can manage. The city has always needed a ruler who can balance Kars with Karsten." He looked wryly at his friends.

"Kars forgets as did Shastro that the city is large and densely populated but Karsten is a hundred times larger, and though the people may be scattered, they outnumber any Kars fighters ten times over. Moreover, of those out there perhaps half of all the men are fighters as well as whatever official trade we follow." He nodded to Aisling. "Many of the women of the garths also can use a bow. In Kars there is the watch and the guard; most people have never had to fight."

"No, they die for that when war comes to the city," Aisling said.

"True. But most still don't learn to fight. If Franzo decides he has to take the city make no mistake; he may well do so. I just don't know how many would die on both sides before he succeeded." He heard the clatter of hooves and leaned out to look. "The duke's messenger is back. Let's see if we can find out whether Franzo has agreed to the meeting." Word on that spread rapidly: Franzo had. Hadrann scouted quietly through the upper city after that and returned looking worried.

"I think Shastro may be about to make a very big mistake."

"Why?" Aisling queried.

"Because Franzo, being an experienced soldier and no fool, wouldn't take chances with this meeting. Before his army arrived he'd have sent a number of his less obvious soldiers into Kars, most probably dressed as ordinary tradesmen or farmers bringing in produce." His face was grim. "If the duke or that brother of yours tries to break truce and kill Franzo I suspect the soldiers would be there to either prevent it or strike back."

Keelan spoke slowly, thinking it through. "If everyone succeeds, if Franzo is killed and the duke and Kirion are killed in retaliation, then both sides will explode. Franzo's army will pour in to avenge him; Kars guard, with no one to give orders, will fight back. So will the ordinary people as best as they can, since they'll believe they won't survive otherwise. They—we—will lose in the end, but by that time Franzo's people will have gone crazy. They'll rip Kars apart. Loot, burn, and— Rann! We have to get Aisling out now or at least work out a way to escape once that starts."

Aisling made a small sound of disagreement. "No, listen, Kee. First we need to get word to Kirion about Franzo's men. He's smart. He'll see what can happen as well as we do and he'll put a leash on Shastro. Even if he doesn't or can't there still may not be a problem." Her smile flashed briefly. "Remember Shastro's spies. I did. I started doing some hunting and late last night I found a way to get into the secret passages."

She put Wind Dancer down gently then strolled toward the paneled wall. Her fingers pressed in one spot, thrust sideways in another. A small opening appeared silently, stayed open briefly, then closed again. It had been large enough for one stooped person to slide through. Both men walked across to join Aisling as she showed them the secret passage. It was uncomplicated but also unlikely to be done by accident.

"Aisling, have you explored along any of this?" Hadrann was curious.

"Of course. I went in the early hours when everyone was asleep and none of Shastro's spies were likely to be in here because of that. I can identify half a dozen other rooms where we can get into the system. One is right down by the great audience hall, where our beloved duke will meet Franzo. We go there to listen but we shall be ready. If things go bad we run for the passage. Get in, come back up here, and wait.

"If fighting reaches up toward this level we take Wind Dancer and vanish. I took the chance Shastro's spies would be busy somewhere else and explored again while you were away. Another branch of the passage goes straight down to the stables. If we have horses readied and order our guard to stand to in case, we might be able to get clear of Kars via the small north gate before matters become lethal. If not, I doubt they'll fire on the palace. We can hide in the wall's secret passages until things are quiet again."

"Makes sense to me," Keelan told her. "I'll go and tell our guards."

Hadrann was already moving toward the door. "And I'll see if I can drop a few hints to Kirion. I just hope he'll listen, because that fool Shastro won't, not to me, but he may to his tame sorcerer. Kirion can always claim to have come by the knowledge through his powers."

Kirion didn't particularly dislike Hadrann. As far as the sorcerer was concerned Hadrann was simply another young lord at court. It was a pity he was a friend of Keelan, but Kirion was shrewd enough to know Hadrann had been trained by the lord of Aranskeep, a good soldier. He knew the Aranskeep heir kept his eyes open: when Hadrann talked, Kirion listened and nodded. Then he went in search of his duke and laid down the law delicately.

He had to convince Shastro not to attack without frightening him so much that the duke would attack through fear that if he didn't, he'd be the vulnerable one. He succeeded for the moment but he was worried. Then he went off to make a few emergency preparations of his own. Shastro was becoming less and less stable. If Kirion lost his grip on the duke the whole city could blow up in their faces, a thought that did not inspire his confidence in the meeting's outcome.

Franzo came armed to the meeting. The duke eyed him nervously. If that soldier thought he'd start anything he was greatly mistaken. There were Kars archers unobtrusively stationed all around the walls of the main audience chamber. Franzo noted them and mentally crossed his fingers. He had his own men waiting as well. If that fool on the throne panicked, they'd have a bloodbath. He marched up to the throne, bowed, half-turned, and his voice boomed out.

"My Lord Duke of Kars, Lords and Ladies of Kars Court, people of Kars, I do not come as a soldier but as an envoy from the Coast Clan and its allies."

Shastro spoke, his voice thinner and reedier. "It is a strange envoy who comes with an army."

"The army was to ensure that I arrived. Strange things have been happening to those in power within the clan lately. Nor has Kars always shown itself a friend to the clan. It was felt that I should have an escort of friends to ensure my safety."

In the upper gallery Aisling muffled a giggle. "An escort of friends"—a lovely way to describe an army of almost a thousand. Franzo certainly wasn't short of friends. From the looks on the faces of those listening, his words were being taken with a grain of salt there too. Below on his throne Shastro had flushed in anger. He lifted his voice.

"It is a strange envoy I say again who comes with an army. What is it to me that men die in a clan far away. Am I now to be blamed if a farmer falls in the furrow and stubs his toe?"

Franzo eyed him. "It is not you, my Lord Duke, whom we suspect. But there is one close to you who has shown pleasure in, shall we say, acquiring such things as might have lost their owners to accidental death or execution."

From the gallery Hadrann and the two with him could see Kirion stiffen slightly. His face showed a hint of red across the cheekbones. Aisling shivered. Kirion would punish the man for that. Sooner or later in some way that could not be brought home to Kirion. The sorcerer stayed silent. Let Shastro do the talking. It could be useful to see if he defended the man who'd put him where he was.

Shastro had come to a similar conclusion. He planned to be rid of Kirion one day, but for now he needed him against Estcarp and his many enemies, enemies like this man and the clan from which he'd been sent. He looked down, trying hard to appear as if he were considering the man's words. Unobtrusively he cleared his throat.

"Lord Franzo. You accuse one whose name we both know. What proof do you bring against him? I gave him a gift. I gave it without his request but in gratitude for his aid to me at a time when I had need of it. Ask any in Kars if he walks hung with gold and jewels." He was safe with that; Kirion didn't care about them. "Ask any if he has vast holdings." Safe with that too. Kirion's tower keep was medium in size and quality. Kirion preferred it that way. He didn't have to spend too much time away from his studies, running a great estate.

The duke leaned forward earnestly. "Tell me, Lord Franzo. You come with an army. You say this is to protect you, that too many of the powerful in your clan die in strange ways. How strange are heart attacks and bandits? How unusual a fall from a horse that kills an old man growing weak? It is my understanding that the powerful in your clan themselves have decided that it was the brother of your leader who was responsible for his death. In what way do you hold me liable for that?"

With the feeling that he had the other man on the run he pressed on, his voice growing in strength. "You come with an army to protect you from the fate of those others. How does an army save you from a heart attack, from falling over your own feet?" The last sentence had been edged with sarcasm, and it was Franzo's turn to flush slightly. He opened his mouth to reply and was overridden.

"Lord Franzo. You accuse one who has been my aide and friend for years. You have no proof, only wild tales. It is I who have proof, not of his deeds but of yours, of an attempt by men of your own clan to assassinate their duke." He listened with satisfaction to the low rumble of anger from the crowd. "Yes. Your clan sent men to murder me secretly, and why? In what way have I harmed your clan?"

He had them now. All were intent on him alone. He stretched out his hands in distress. "Lord Franzo. If I had committed some evil against your clan, was it not their place to come here, stand openly, and speak out. We have laws in Kars and Karsten both. If I had broken these why did your clan not bring an accusation and proof against me." He sat back, his head bowed a little as if a weight of sorrow rested on him.

"But no one came. Not until you came riding to the gates with an army. You bring accusations but no proof. You terrify my people, you bear false witness, and you threaten me, your duke." His voice gathered strength. From where he stood Kirion subtly augmented his duke's voice with power, helping Shastro to produce deeper, more resonant tones. He bled a tinge of power into the words themselves as well, so that they impressed the listeners, even the clansmen and their leader. Franzo stood motionless as Shastro lifted his hands to him.

"Tell me, I charge you, in what way have they or I deserved this. If I have acted against your clan let you give proofs now. I will bow to them. I will stand before a tribunal of impartial judges and allow them to judge me and mine." His voice soared up. "Speak! I listen."

Franzo slumped. He had no proof and he knew it. He had never really hoped for any result in all this. He'd taken charge to prevent a lesser man who would have listened to no sense but attacked. He'd hoped that the duke might be made nervous enough to at least stop the deaths the clan were sure could be laid at Kirion's door. He'd hoped the duke would understand that the clan deaths must stop. If he'd done that, he'd done enough. But here and now Franzo spoke for the clan. He must get his men out of here with the best face he could.

He bowed low. "My Lord Duke of Kars. The clan has no proof of deeds. I can say only that they feel it." He paused to choose a word. "Unusual, when leader after clan leader dies. Coincidence may carry only so far. And within your court is one with the abilities to make such 'coincidence.' These beliefs I was asked to lay before you.

I have done so. I shall return to my clan." He bowed again and turned on his heel. His men closed in behind him as he walked down the length of the audience hall.

His back tingled. He wouldn't put it past the duke to signal an archer. Gods grant the man had more sense; it would trigger a massacre. His own men would strike back, and all were trained soldiers in a crowd of shopkeepers.

Shastro did have more sense but only because he was feeling smug. He'd stood up to the man, shown him that a duke of Kars could not be intimidated. Let the fool run back to his clan and bear them *that* message. He sneered at the retreating back.

Aisling stood and began to worm her way through the crowd, her brother and friend behind her. That had been instructive. She'd had her mind open in passive mode, her hand resting on her hidden pendant to help her shield in case Kirion scanned for such spying. She'd known when and where Kirion had helped the duke. She'd also read Shastro's emotions. He believed he'd done it all on his own. He was both pleased with himself and swollen with a feeling of power. He was also still jumpy from the discovery that there had been a plan to dispose of him. It wasn't a good combination.

Once back in his tower Kirion would have agreed with her. He was listening to the duke alternately rant of how he'd shown up that clan scum and demand that Kirion punish them further. Kirion was reluctant. Shastro had made a good point about coincidences, nor was he unaware of why Franzo had agreed to come to Kars. But if more of the clan died it would bring Franzo back or maybe another, less sensible leader, this time with orders to waste no time in talking.

It would not suit Kirion to be in a besieged city. He soothed his enraged master. As he muttered, his mind cast out frantically for an alternative. Something for Shastro to act against that might cause less harm to Kirion's plans. The keeps? Not enough to occupy the duke, and it would set every keep lord against them both. A common enemy? Estcarp? Perhaps. Not all-out war but a few small strikes along the borders in the Northwest.

Out past Verlaine maybe. That duchess was still alive. He could encourage Shastro to wonder if she and her crooked lord might not try to return, take possession of the keep in Estcarp's name. Come to that she was also still duchess of Kars in a tenuous legality. Kirion knew she'd as soon take the Kars throne as sit on an ant's nest, but Shastro loved power. To him it was inconceivable she wouldn't like to rule Verlaine or Kars if she could take either somehow.

He set out to hint the duke into the proper frame of mind. Shastro wasn't hard to convince. He'd feared the witches all his life, and over recent years Kirion had deliberately fed that fear. He mentioned Verlaine and the possibilities. Then he spoke of Kars, and the duke's gaze became horrified. Shastro bit on the thought.

"Yes, very likely. Think of the trouble it could cause. They'd be delighted to entangle us in our own laws."

"Then why not change the laws? Make it illegal to desert your holdings for so many years. As for Kars, she never reigned in the city. Hold a special sitting to formally and officially declare that she has no rights here in Kars."

"Yes, yes. I shall do that. I'll call a court tomorrow. Then, once that's settled I'll attack Estcarp. It's time they were taught a lesson."

Kirion bit back a groan. Then he settled to explaining why that would not be advisable just now. Shastro was obstinate, so Kirion was forced to wheedle, then to talk in alternate obscurities and sorcerous hints. Handling the duke was like dealing with a high-strung horse. He must not be reined in too hard nor allowed to run wild. Kirion was beginning to feel he'd like to shoot this nag and buy himself another.

IX

———✦◇✦———

Shastro held his court not the next day but the next week. Kirion had worked hard delaying, suggesting additional points of discussion and soothing the fears of his duke and the courtiers. Keelan, Aisling, and Hadrann had assisted unobtrusively. The three of them agreed with Shastro's plan to sort the inheritance of Verlaine and Kars once and for all. Aisling said so to the duke when they talked two days after Franzo had departed with his army.

"Then you agree. You think it right that the succession be clarified?"

Aisling nodded. "I do, my Lord Duke. As to Verlaine, the girl held title through her mother, but she fled the responsibilities. Verlaine is a border keep. Karsten cannot risk having it held by one not committed to our country's welfare." Shastro was listening eagerly. Murna was so sensible, so intelligent. She was saying everything he believed and in words he could use when he spoke before his court.

"And what of Kars?" he asked eagerly.

"Now that is far different. The duke ruled; she was merely his duchess, and from all the evidence, the marriage was never consummated. That means that she was not legally his wife. Had she born a child to him that child would have ruled and she would have been its regent. However, with the duke dead, her marriage not ratified, and another holding the throne, then she could not have taken power—

unless a convocation of the Kars council agreed that there was no other suited and that it was necessary for her to do so to reduce civil disorder."

Shastro was all admiration, particularly as Murna was saying what he wanted to hear. "You are right. That's so clear, so well said." He drew himself up. "And so I intend to say to the council myself." He drew her arm through his and walked slowly along the balcony. "With all that cleared up I can consider what to do next. I'm certain that Estcarp was behind the Coast Clan's attempt to attack me."

Aisling sighed. "That may be so, my Lord Duke, but it seems to me that our people can think up their own follies without assistance." She allowed herself to frown a little. "And people agreed with the clan. All those coincidences. It was so very strange. Almost as if the witches were working against the clan. Could it be that they wished to divide you. To lose you the support of one of your strongest allies?"

Shastro gaped, then took the idea to his heart, momentarily forgetting that it had been he who had caused the Coast Clan most of its troubles. "Aye, indeed. That would be a witch trick." He remembered then, but it would do very well to placate the clan who might well believe it. "By Cup and Flame! Yes. I shall send envoys to the clan at once. They must stand with me against the witches and their evil." He patted her arm. "Thank you, my dear, your insight is always valuable. But I must go; a duke has many calls on his time."

He was gone, sweeping hastily across the room and out of the door in search of Kirion. Aisling looked after him and hid a grin then a startled look as the latter portion of his words sank in. Yesterday Hadrann had said he wondered about Shastro, if the duke was becoming enmeshed in his own lies. To Aisling's ear that last speech had held a ring of truth, as if the duke really had believed that the witches could have been responsible for the clan problems.

But Aisling knew that the clan deaths had been Kirion's doing and surely at the Duke's command. Hadn't Shastro honestly known or was he rehearsing his speech to the council? Or could Hadrann have been right? Was Shastro becoming confused amongst all his lies and plots? She went in search of Keelan and her friend to discuss it.

Shastro had swept through the long corridors to Kirion's tower. Once there he ignored the guards who dared not halt their duke and burst unceremoniously through the door. Kirion had been at work and was not pleased with the abrupt entrance of his duke, but he had to keep the fool happy. He listened, and once he'd heard it all, it was Kirion who wasn't happy. Gods, the man was indeed losing his mind. He set out to delicately remind the duke that far from the witches being involved in the clan's troubles it had been the duke who caused them or, rather, Kirion, at his duke's command.

Shastro looked blank briefly then rallied. "Oh, yes, I know that but I mean that I shall give this as a possible explanation to the council." He nodded to himself several times. "It makes good sense, does it not. They and the clan will believe it." He beamed at his sorcerer. "Then I can attack Estcarp. They'll all be behind me against the witches."

Kirion stifled a moan. Dear gods, the man was obsessed. He bowed. "Let us first convince the council, my Lord Duke. Then with Verlaine and Kars rulerships cleared, we can make approaches to the clan. It may take a little while. Not all have your insight and understanding." He watched as Shastro preened.

Not that it was a bad idea, Kirion thought. The Coast Clan was likely to accept it, at least enough of them to make peace between the clan and the throne almost a certainty. But Shastro could not be allowed to attack Estcarp with the full army of Karsten. Such an attack would have meant disaster. Apart from that, Kirion had no wish to find himself playing lone Karsten hero against the might of the massed witches of Estcarp. It had been the three times Horning that had started Karsten's woes. It had lost the country most of its healers, the effective ones anyhow. It had caused riots, started feuds and hatreds that in some places still continued. It had led to that stupid assault on Estcarp and its incredible defense, which had lost Karsten an army. Many of those in it would not have been missed, but it had weakened the country and divided it for too many years. Estcarp was bad luck. A prudent man left the witches alone, except that Shastro wasn't prudent. He intended to thrust a stick into an ant's nest and stir vigorously. Being Shastro he'd then be surprised and furious when the ants rushed out to bite.

Kirion considered. Let them get this council done, then the clan's ruffled feathers smoothed down. He could see that both events were slowed. Give Shastro time to lose the edge of his fears; time for him to work on the duke and suggest caution in this matter. Maybe, too, Kirion could plant evidence suggesting it had been witches still in hiding here who were causing strife. He might use that to obtain a few more of the part-bloods for his own purposes.

His "bandits'" quiet little raids along the northern border had already netted him a sample or two from Estcarp, none with true power but all of the Old Blood. He'd gained something from each person taken. After the council and the clan matter he'd find a way of keeping the duke quiet awhile. If he did that the fool might let this attack idea rest. If not then they could make a few minor forays against Estcarp's outermost defenses. Kirion could make them sound far more than they were.

Shastro was tugging at his arm. "Well, Kirion. Don't you think we should show them we weren't fooled?"

"Of course, my Lord Duke." How the man loved that title, Kirion mused. You could see his chest expand every time it was used. "But first the council. You must not allow enemies to distract you; that might be their fell purpose. To prevent you from clarifying the succession of keep and Kars or from making peace with the clan."

"Of course, of course. They shall not succeed. I'll have the council convened as soon as possible, all the most learned judges. I myself shall address them on the subject. While I have them assembled, there are a few other matters I shall discuss. I must have a list written down so that I remember every point I wish to make."

Resisting the desire to tell him to run away and play with his quills then, Kirion agreed. He only hoped Shastro's speech would be effective.

To his mild surprise it was. The duke used Aisling's arguments with force, and the council saw the sense in them that Shastro had seen earlier. He received a standing ovation; the laws passed in record time and with no dissent. Envoys went almost immediately to discuss some of the implications with the Coast Clan.

But shortly before they left a man arrived at the court to speak to the Aranskeep heir. Hadrann listened, dismissed the man, and sent his valet for Aisling and Keelan.

"Let's take a ride. It's a lovely day."

Keelan stared out to where the late fall rain hammered sullenly on streaming roofs. He looked at Hadrann wondering if he were drunk, then caught the warning in his friend's glare.

"I wouldn't go as far as to say that." Keelan grinned. "But I'd like to get out into fresh air. We could take my carriage. We could even visit old Geavon for a couple of days."

Aisling nodded. "That would be pleasant. It won't take more than an hour to pack. Geavon has most items we would need. Wind Dancer can come if he likes."

Two hours later they clattered downstairs, laughing, talking about the need for fresh air, and generally letting those about them know what they planned. Wind Dancer was curled along Aisling's shoulders. With the horses harnessed, Keelan's man driving, Hadrann's six hired guards and their captain riding after the carriage, and the city left behind, the three were free to talk in safety.

Strangely Hadrann had chosen to circle and drive to the north-east once they were clear of the main Kars gate. Aisling and Keelan trusted him and said nothing even when they headed in that direction. Wind Dancer did not care anyway; he was comfortable in Aisling's lap and content to nap. It seemed Geavon's keep was not their objective. Keelan and Aisling would have to wait to see what was. If they stayed on this road they would eventually reach the turnoff to Jarn's Trevalyn keep, a good place to talk privately.

Here, where the Turning had wrung out mountains, magic was altered. Used from farther away to probe toward them, it would be blurred. Kirion would know that. Aisling looked out of the window. Her hands moved in slow passes as she laid wards about the carriage. Kirion could scry all he wished. He'd see and hear little but three people chatting about the weather, the council, and the hope of clan peace. And if that seeing and hearing was blurred or vanished at times, well, Kirion knew that all this area was something of a blind spot for scrying. She turned to look at the two waiting.

"We're safe. Now, Rann, what did you have to tell us?"

"A message came from Hilarion. Escore has made a large advance in driving evil from the land. One of the Estcarp witches died, but in doing so she has empowered the Light. The Darkness falls back. There is increasing traffic between the two lands. Estcarp is also strengthened, and increasingly they resent Karsten's attacks on them. Hilarion has read runes and omens. With many settlers from Estcarp in Escore there comes great danger. If Karsten is foolish enough to attack Estcarp openly with a strong force the runes say that both lands may combine."

Aisling stared down at the plank floor of their carriage considering that. Then she raised her head to meet Hadrann's gaze. "I fear he could be right. Many of the new settlers in Escore come from Estcarp. Many of those were families of the Old Blood driven from Karsten and never to find a true home again. If Karsten attacks across Estcarp's border, such people not only would wish to assist

Estcarp but also in the back of their minds hope to return. If Karsten were very badly beaten they might be safe to return and take up their ancestral holdings once more."

Keelan gave a grunt of disapproval. "That would be folly; the wounds are still there. Many of their neighbors took what they left. They wouldn't give it back after so many years, and others innocent of wrongdoing or bloodshed bought the abandoned keeps and garths. Are they to be flung out penniless? Two wrongs will not make a right."

"That I know," Hadrann told him. "I have no solution, only Hilarion's message. Escore and Estcarp grow stronger and closer linked. If Shastro attacks, then Shastro will lose—and all our land with him. However, if we stay within our borders, then they have no reason to do aught but leave us be. They'd prefer that."

Keelan snorted. "Of course they would. They are two to our one. If they have time to grow strong they can turn to rend us at their leisure."

Aisling stared. "Keelan, my brother. You forget we are of their blood. When have we ever attacked merely to steal land. I lived three years in Escore. I spoke often to those from Estcarp. They do not wish to drown us again in blood."

"Maybe not. But I'm sure they wouldn't mind a little blood if they could recover all they lost. They're people too, Aisling. Not saints just because they have the power and the Old Blood." He turned to the silent Hadrann. "What do you say?"

"I say that if you, who should know better, think this way, then many who know less will already be fearing it. But tell me, Keelan. Think back to all the history between the lands that you have ever heard. How many times have we attacked Estcarp, and how many times have they attacked us. Who always began the wars?"

Keelan sighed. "I know. It was Karsten that was the aggressor, but maybe Estcarp grows tired of that. And if they do and this other land aids them, then we could be crushed. I know we have the Old Blood, but this is my land and I love it. I would rather stay here and die than desert it to die without me."

"And we all work to see no land must die," Aisling snapped. She turned to Hadrann. "Was that all the message?"

"No. There have been a couple of minor raids on Estcarp's border where it meets the sea toward their south keep. Farms have been burned and all those there murdered save for a couple of their people each time. Those seem to have been taken away to Karsten. No scrying can find them, so they are believed dead."

"Kirion?"

"Likely enough, but worse still. It seems that from the second farm a witch was taken, a sixteen-year-old girl on her first visit to kinfolk since her departure to be trained. Hilarion knows little more save that she is now missing, taken, they believe. The raid was only a few days gone, and she may still be alive. It is asked that if we meet her we aid her if we can. They know it's not likely, but she's almost a child still, only just trained, and they grieve for what may be happening to her."

All three shuddered. "We can guess," Aisling said in a low voice. "If Kirion has her, the girl's death will be neither easy nor slow. Could the messenger tell us anything of how much time has elapsed? When was she taken?"

"A week ago," Hadrann said, "but they had soldiers in the area who rode to cover the border at once." He looked at them. "If those who took her were Kirion's creatures, then they must bring her back alive and undamaged. For that they must move slowly and carefully. I believe they may have circled southeast toward this area. I spent an hour wringing out all the messenger knew, then I studied maps. I think it likely they'll try to come back past Trevalyn keep. Jarn might like to hear about this, don't you think?"

Keelan grinned. "Jarn doesn't like Shastro and he loathes Kirion.

I think he'd be happy to help us foil any of their plans, if that was why we drove this way. I'd wondered."

"He's your cousin."

"Sort of. Old Geavon is grandfather's third or fourth cousin I think. Jarn is his grandnephew. Aisling has never met him but I have. I liked the man. He's sensible, a hard worker, and he isn't against the Old Blood. His great love is his estate, his own lands, and his family and their name. He's the sort who would rather work his land and live in peace, not that he always gets that. This area has become dangerous with bandits again."

Hadrann looked thoughtful. "So if we all arrive at his keep even unexpectedly, we'd be welcomed?"

"With the best he has, which may not be saying much."

"Still, we'd be welcome." Hadrann thrust his head through the window and gave orders. The carriage lurched on its springs as it turned into the narrower rougher road leading upward. Wind Dancer opened one eye to complain of the bumps before going back to sleep. The horses settled into their traces to pull harder against the steepening slope.

"We should be at Trevalyn before nightfall. Once we're there we shall go hunting. We'll split up into three groups. We'll hunt and shoot all over the whole area. Bring back deer, duck, anything edible for the table. It's a good excuse, and as long as we do bring back something most days, no one will question it," Hadrann continued.

"What about me," Aisling queried. "Am I myself or cousin Murna? I'll have to stay as Murna, I know. Our guards would ask too many questions otherwise. But do we tell Jarn?"

Keelan considered. "I say we keep quiet. Tell him if anything goes wrong and we must, but apart from that we say nothing. The fewer people who know a secret the fewer there are who can betray it, even by accident."

"That's sensible. Very well."

The carriage lurched upward. Within the jerking vehicle Aisling felt a sudden warmth against her breast. The hidden pendant was warning her but of what? She opened her mouth to speak. Behind the carriage the hired guard were riding slowly on the rutted track. One halted his horse and gaped down, then he dismounted hastily. His companion saw and then he too was off his horse, scooping up the small coins. Why, there must be a week's pay here in lesser silvers and coppers dropped by some careless fool. The guard captain turned to find all of his six men groveling in the dust.

"What . . . ?" An arrow took him in the chest, but the captain was an old soldier and knew his duty. With his dying breath he screamed a warning. His men too were experienced. Three fell to arrows, but the other three took cover. Ahead, Keelan's driver recognized the danger. He swung the carriage horses up and behind an outcrop of stone. They halted obediently as the driver fell hurriedly from his exposed perch. He thrust his head through the window and explained to his master in a frantic gabble.

Keelan listened. "I see. How many of the guard are dead?"

"Three at least, Lord Keelan, and the captain. Others of them may be wounded."

"Did you see any of our attackers?" The man denied it. He did not explain he hadn't looked—he'd been too busy—but Keelan understood. "Good man. You did the right thing. I want you to keep a lookout. Watch where the guards went to cover and keep a sharp eye out for any of our attackers. I must talk with my friends."

Aisling was waiting outside the carriage with Hadrann as Keelan returned. "If I sit on the floor of the carriage where I can't be seen, I may be able to read them. I should be able to tell you their numbers. Maybe something of their plans."

"Do it," Hadrann ordered.

Aisling slipped cautiously back into the vehicle. Wind Dancer greeted her with a thrust of his head against her cheek. She smiled, hugged him gently, then sat down on the carriage floor. She slid into a comfortable pose, shut her eyes, raised her hand to cup the hidden pendant, and easily found the trance Hilarion had taught her.

The pendant's mists welcomed her back. She moved through them as they swirled, then she opened her mind a crack. Thunder roared, deafening her, but within the sounds had been emotion, maybe words. She crafted a light shield and opened her mind once more. Yes, emotions, terror, disgust, horror, nausea.

She touched them very lightly. A warning. They faded to be replaced with a query. *Who?*

Half-friend, maybe. Who?

One taken by evil men for an evil purpose. They seek now your carriage to bear me more quickly to that end. Aid in the Light's name.

Automatically Aisling gave the reply to that. *Aid in the name of the Light shall be given.* Then she knew. She must talk with the others swiftly.

She reached again. *I have friends here, but also some who would recognize you and be a danger. Give me time to speak to them all.*

There is a little time, but hurry.

Aisling half-fell from the carriage, grabbing Keelan. "Kee, that's Kirion's men out there. They want our carriage so they can get their prisoner to Kirion."

"Pris—They have the witch?"

"Yes. Kee, she's only a girl and she's terrified. We have to save her. You know what Kirion will do to her."

Both men scowled. They knew. There was one easy way to disarm a witch of her powers. Kirion would find great pleasure in it. Both he and Shastro had done so before. And as it happened it would break her wards, allowing Kirion to leech her power. As a trained witch with her witch jewel she could bring him power enough to make him almost invincible in Kars. Aisling felt sick. She could not allow it to happen. They had to rescue the girl, but how? She left her brother and Rann discussing it and retreated to the carriage again.

I am here. Is there any way you can aid us?

None. I am bound and gagged. Oh, please . . .

Aisling wavered. Should she tell the girl. *Do you know where you've been taken and why?*

To the death of all I am, better I die clean. Sister, I beg you.

If she did not know all of it she knew enough. *Is there any way I can slay you mind to mind?*

She felt fear, then a firming of the girl's resolve. *Those older and better trained can stop their own heart.* Her voice in Aisling's mind was bitter. *It is something our kind have had to learn, but I am not yet trained in that. If I were free I could slay myself.*

If you were free you could slay them, Aisling sent.

Yes. Maybe if I open my mind completely you could stop my heart for me?

Not yet. There is hope of freedom. I will speak to my friends. She paused to reach out and count. Nine men with the girl, and Aisling had her two companions, the driver, and three guards left—bad odds. But then the bandits would not expect nobles to fight when they had guards and servants to die for them. They believed the odds to be far better. She returned to Hadrann just as a gurgling screech rang out. Rann grinned cheerfully.

"One gone."

"What, how? Kee . . . where's Keelan?"

"Evening our odds a little. Kirion's bandits aren't that good. Maybe they sneak about, kidnap girls, and burn garths very well, but they aren't trained the way Keelan was trained."

Aisling reached out with her gift, then jerked her mind away. A man had died, a second was gone even as she touched. There was panic among the others of the enemy remaining. She felt Keelan.

His concentration shut her out, but she could feel the competence. He'd learned well from old Hannion and Harran in the past six years. Since then he'd been an excellent stalker and hunter. Now he used his knowledge on other more dangerous game. Hadrann had strung his bow. He slid around the edge of the rock and waited.

Aisling took up her own lighter weapon reluctantly. An arrow was nocked and held ready as she watched from another rock edge. If the bandits had discounted her companions in the carriage, they'd have doubly ignored her. She'd give them reason to recall her if there was no other choice. One of the enemy was made careless by the sounds of his comrades. His companions were dying although they were hidden from those in the carriage.

Other enemies must be behind them. Perhaps Estcarp's borderers had found them. He knew of those ones. They had a reputation in Kars as being utterly deadly. In attempting to see the new and unknown enemies he was seen by Aisling. She held her shot until she felt she must let the arrow fly for the sake of those with her, then she loosed it, closing her mind tightly as she did so. There had been nine against seven. Now there were six. They had hope.

X

················◄◇►················

isling watched the surrounding land keenly. Out there in the jumble of rock and scrub Keelan was hunting. It was for her to back him where she could. She could not link with him—they'd never had that, brother and sister though they were—but she could tell where he was. She allowed that direction to settle into her, then she let her eyes drift out of focus. She would notice the slightest movement as she scanned across the area.

There! Another flicker. Her gaze sharpened on it but before she could let fly, another arrow had flown. Hadrann too had watched. Keelan came slipping back.

"Five to go, but they have the girl in a hollow back there." He spat dust. "Filth. She's been tied so tightly she could be crippled even if we do free her."

Aisling looked at him. "Her choice, her choosing, Kee. But if I were the one bound I'd rather be freed. Her friends may be able to help her once she's back among them. If we can't get her away she's asked me for a clean death."

"Can you?"

"We have an idea that may work, but better we get her out. Rann, what do you think?"

"I think we stop talking and do something."

"True, my friend," Keelan agreed. "So we leave Aisling out here to watch and we both go back into cover and see how many more we can pick off. I wonder what our brave guards are doing. There were three of them alive." He turned to his sister. "Aisling?"

She concentrated. "Fear, anger, pain. Two of them are hurt, one badly. The one less injured tends him. The one unhurt is circling toward us. He wishes to find out if we are unharmed and to aid us either way. He comes from that direction."

Her hand lifted to point as she forced down nausea again. She was fighting for all their lives, and the life of a young girl who had done no more evil than to be born with the Gift. But she hated the killing.

Hadrann nodded. "We'll wait for the one who's circling." He blinked down as a furred weight thrust past his knee. "Ah ha. Wind Dancer. And what are you doing out of the carriage?"

The big cat ignored him. He went to Aisling, raised his front paws to place them against her, and uttered a low imperative cry. She dropped to one knee. He lifted his face and laid it against hers, rubbing his head along her jaw as he purred. Pictures came to her as they touched. Small, sometimes fuzzy, but clear enough. She hugged the cat sending pictures in return. His reply carried undertones of impatience. Aisling grinned.

"All right. As you wish, Wind Dancer. It's your turn to be a hero."

"Aisling?" Keelan was watching them. "What are the two of you planning?"

His sister smiled. "Wind Dancer wants to help the witch."

"No," both men protested.

"I rode as a warrior in Escore. If the distance to be traveled was not too great, Wind Dancer rode with me more than once. We work well together."

She looked out across the rough land before them in which a girl was being held for a terrible death. "Wind Dancer's coat blends with this land. We will go, each knowing where the other is and both knowing where those who hold the girl are hidden."

"And what do we do?" her brother asked sarcastically. "Wait to be called for dinner?"

"No, Keelan," Hadrann interrupted quietly. "You collect that guard and go back and help the two injured. Then you start making a noise over in that direction. Leave all three guards hidden together as a diversion. You and I will split and cover them. That gives us all a better chance no matter what Kirion's men decide to do. Tell the guard Aisling is in the rocks above the carriage with her bow, guarding it in case the bandits try to steal it while you're gone."

Keelan grunted. "Sound good enough?"

Hadrann eyed Aisling. "You just be careful. Kirion would be quite happy to exchange you for the witch, I'm sure. But we wouldn't!"

She managed a small smile at him. "I know. Now go and find that guard before he blunders into Kirion's men. He's turned around, and I don't think he knows where we are."

The two men slid off silently in the direction Aisling indicated. Left alone with Wind Dancer she looked down at him. A long affectionate look passed between them. Then they too slipped noiselessly into the scrub. Wind Dancer took the lead. If any heard them coming they would look at human height for the makers of the sounds to appear. Wind Dancer would have seconds to warn Aisling and to be missed by any hastily loosed arrow. He and his human had indeed played this game before.

They moved silently through the scrub and harsh upthrust rock. Aisling had her mind cautiously open. Just enough with her shields in place to know the direction of the enemy and no more. She came through a patch of high bushes, Wind Dancer well ahead. She halted as he came trotting back. His picture of the scene below, sent as he reared up to touch his head to her hand, was clear this time.

A hollow large enough to take almost a dozen horses and a bound motionless figure. Over it stood two men. Three others were placed around the hollow's rim. All smelled of fear, anger, and spite. As Wind Dancer watched, one of the men had kicked their captive casually and cursed her. Another spat on her and added his curses. Aisling bit back sudden rage. That witch down there was only a child, but it was folly to let fury sway her. That sort of emotion led people to do dangerous and foolish things. She would be cold, calm, and, her mind added, when she had the chance she'd finish those sons of diseased hogs.

She circled, with Wind Dancer helping to pinpoint each of Kirion's men. Then she moved back a little and waited patiently. Some minutes later there came a growing commotion from the south. The three men up on the hollow's rim came running to join the two below. Aisling remained in wait. Below her there was a hurried conference, then two of the men were left with their captive. The other three vanished in the direction of the sounds.

Aisling tracked them with her mind. They were heading directly for the noise, and she grimaced. "Like shooting bound leapers, eh, Wind Dancer? I don't know what Kirion's paying them, but I think it's too much."

Wind Dancer gave a small chirrup of agreement, then padded back toward the hollow. Aisling slipped after him until they reached the rim and could look down while lying in the surrounding scrub. The witch lay as she had before. The two remaining men were standing together trying to watch in all directions at once. They had been some fifteen strong at the start of the raid. Estcarp had accounted for six of them. Now this group they'd expected to slaughter like lambs had turned out to be wolves. Kirion's men were staying alert.

Aisling cursed to herself. Then she grinned thoughtfully. From here she could take out one cleanly before he knew. But the other could drop into cover before she could shoot again, and that cover

could block her sight of him. Both men had bows of their own as
well as swords and daggers. The survivor might shoot the witch out
of spite before Aisling could reach him. She dropped a hand to
Wind Dancer, what suggestions had a great hunter to offer?

The big cat placed a paw on her knee. Slowly he flexed his claws
in and out, keeping her attention upon that wicked display. His
mother had been a normal-sized cat. Wind Dancer was the one kitten she'd ever produced, and that when she was four. Who or what
Shosho had found in the hills behind Aiskeep to sire her only kit
none knew, but the end result, some thirty-five pounds of muscle
clad in short thick fur, armed with claws that would not have shamed
a young snow leopard, now offered a battle plan.

His was an intelligence that was all cat in many ways, and in
others, Aisling felt, perhaps something else. Not that she ever in-
quired. He was Wind Dancer, her friend, her battle companion, and
each owed their life to the other several times over. She watched the
pictures he made in her mind and agreed. It might be dangerous for
him, but she would be swift. They inched back to the rim of the hollow. The two guards remained on edge and close to one another.

Aisling stayed where she was, waiting as Wind Dancer circled.
When he was in position, she shot. Even as the first man went down
and the other dropped into cover Wind Dancer was moving. He was
behind the guard still living and he sped down the slope in a silent
savage rush. The guard heard the faint sound, turned, and screamed
once before the big cat was upon him. Aisling wasted no time.

As soon as Wind Dancer struck she too was in motion, leaping
down the slope in flying strides. She watched her feet. It would not
do to trip in case her cat had need of her. He did not. Taken unawares by a nightmare the man had flung himself backward, tripping over a dead branch as he did so. Wind Dancer followed him
down, claws and teeth striking home before the terrified man could
do more than scream and then try vainly to protect his throat.

Putting aside his mail scarf would be the last battle error he ever made. By the time Aisling reached them it was finished.

"Well done, furred warrior." Aisling knelt to hug him, stroking along the still bushed neck and shoulders. "Now, let us see what we can do for this one." She drew her dagger and strode across to the captive. Kirion's men had taken no chances. The girl was not only bound and gagged heavily but also blindfolded. Aisling would have spat. Wind Dancer had been right. The bonds were brutal and she only prayed that they had not been on so long the girl would be crippled.

She cut loose the girl's feet and hands then lifted away the blindfold and removed the tightly drawn gag. She smiled. "Peace, sister. The Light has sent aid. Are we in time?"

The girl worked her mouth painfully, then gave up the attempt to speak through a mouth too long dry from lack of water. She nodded, then lifted her hands to study the deep red and blue weals. Aisling was digging through saddlebags. She found a canteen, poured a few drops of the contents on her palm and sniffed, then tasted cautiously. Water laced with Karsten brandy. She brought it back.

"Drink a little of this, slowly. Hold each mouthful a while before you swallow." She was obeyed. Wind Dancer had disappeared to prowl about above the hollow. He returned to signal that no one was returning as yet. The witch eyed him with interest and some nervousness. The big cat walked across to her, sat, and purred. Then slowly he pushed his face toward her sniffing, continuing to purr loudly. The girl suddenly smiled. Her faltering hands went up to cup Wind Dancer's face.

"For your aid in time of trouble, my thanks, great warrior. The Light knows its own. It seems that even amongst our enemies Estcarp may find help and friends unlooked for." Her gaze met that of Aisling. "And you, sister? What do you here in this barbarian land."

Aisling felt anger flare in her. "This barbarian land is my home.

I was born here, and my mother and mother's mother before me. Is it your custom to insult one who has risked all to save you?" She saw with some satisfaction that the shaft had gone home. The witch flushed.

"Your pardon, sister. Yet . . ." She studied the woman before her. "Surely you are of our blood and you have power. I could not be mistaken. I feel it. There is more also. I feel a power about you that is yours and not-yours. Old . . . old . . ." her voice trailed away, then rallied. "I feel another thing too: a spell, a power that is a trap. What is it that you bear?"

Aisling had been chafing the wealed wrists, pausing to inspect the damage every few minutes. She ignored the comments. "How long were you bound so tightly?"

"Only since we halted. They planned to steal your carriage, kill the guards and nobles; you, they wished to take alive. They were forbidden to use me, but for you they had no orders."

Aisling snorted. "They'd have regretted that. I'm no court maiden to squeal and faint if I'm seized. And the man who sent them would have killed them all very very slowly if he found out I'd been violated."

"Why?"

"Because he's my oldest brother. A fool who thinks his path to power is black sorcery," Aisling told her briefly. "He'd like to have me in his hands even more than he'd be pleased to have you."

The witch looked apprehensive. She was cold, exhausted, hungry, and her wrists were a flaring agony. She began to shake. "Your brother? And the men with you, what will they say of me?"

"Don't worry. I loathe him a lot more than you ever will. He's tried to kill me or have me kidnapped more than once. The men with me are a friend and my other brother." She surveyed the shaking form. "Now, we have a problem. We had seven guards with us. Three survived the attack. They're hirelings from Kars. They'll take one look at you, recognize you for what you are, and either try to kill you or denounce us the minute they return."

Aisling rose to look over the patiently waiting mounts. On one saddle she found a long cloak, on another a mail jerkin with attached coif. The owner had not been a large man. With extra padding it would fit the witch but, she looked back at the girl, not now. The freed captive was clearly in no condition to be hauled around the countryside in forty pounds of mail and on a weary horse,

They needed to stay here and rest but for the problem of the guards. She took up the cloak. "Wear this, wrap it well about you, and pull down the hood. Wind Dancer, you lie beside her and listen. Witch, hide in that patch of scrub. I must get my brother and friend aside and make plans. We have to rid ourselves of the guards we have with us else we are all betrayed. I shall return as soon as I can." She produced a bag found with the cloak.

"Meanwhile, eat. There's oatcakes here and cold meat. You have the canteen. I'll be as swift as I can. You should be safe here for a while, and there's no more I can do for you just now." She ended her instructions with a questioning tone, inviting comment. There was none, so she turned to climb the slope.

Once at the top she heard small sounds as of someone approaching. There was no attempt to be more than reasonably quiet. Aisling drifted behind a tree and waited to see, as she'd expected, that it was Keelan who came seeking her. She stepped out to meet him, smiling.

"All's well, brother. The two of Kirion's men who remained are dead. The witch is freed. I left her eating and drinking, cloaked and hidden with Wind Dancer. What of the three who came your way?"

"Dead also. Of our guards, the one badly injured should be returned to Kars in the carriage. How many horses are with your witch?"

"Eleven. They are no fine bloods but they're good hill-country beasts. They're leg weary but not in ill condition. But my witch as you name her . . . Kee, if the guards see her, we're all in great danger."

"I know. Rann and I made a plan. We knew you'd free her then come seeking us. Listen, Aisling. Rann is telling the guards to take their friend and return to seek a healer in Kars. They're willing to listen since their captain is dead and the badly wounded man is cousin to the other two. We said we would take the bandit horses and ride on to Jarn's keep. It is no more than a few hours from here. They are to return with a full guard and the carriage in a ten-day."

"And us?"

He grinned cheerfully. "We sneak back into Estcarp with our witch, turn her and the spare horses over to the first small patrol we find to help repay what those scum of Kirion's did there, and pray that the patrol doesn't decide to kill us as a better repayment."

His sister eyed him. "And just what did Rann say to this?"

"I won't repeat it. He cast some reflection on our parentage and soundness of mind."

"I bet he did!"

"Well, can you think of a better idea?"

Aisling sighed. "No."

"Nor could Hadrann, so that's what we're doing. He would like to send you to Jarn at Trevalyn keep. I told him if we all went we'd never get away from them in less than a week, and what did we do with the witch? Not much sense in rescuing her then letting her die out here. And if he tried to send you alone you'd just double back and join us again past the border. So he cursed some more and agreed to the plan."

Aisling chuckled. She could imagine the exasperated conversation that had prefaced Keelan's return to find her. Poor Hadrann. But he'd succumbed to Kee's argument finally. That was good. She didn't have to waste time doing her own arguing. As they talked they'd been trotting back toward where Hadrann waited with the surviving guards. Once there Aisling looked over the injuries. Many keep ladies were skilled in herb lore and wound care.

The injuries were minor in one case—a sprained shoulder easily treated with a sling—and the same man had a shallow messy cut along his side. She cleaned it carefully, dressed and bandaged the injury, then turned to the other victim. That was far more serious, as they'd feared. The cut was deep into the leg, a sword slash that had also broken the bone. The man would be unable to ride, and the wound should be stitched. She could do that as a temporary measure.

Once the man was back in Kars the healers could cut the stitches and redo her work more skillfully if such was needed. Wound fever was likely, and they could treat that better in Kars as well. Both guards were watching her, concern on their faces. She spoke quietly, telling them her beliefs. One hesitated.

"Lady Murna, we hired on to guard you."

"And well you did so," she agreed. "But the keep of our friend's cousin is only three hours' ride away. The bandits left good riding beasts saddled, bridled, and able to get us to the keep in that time. Better you take our carriage and make for the city. Your kinsman will find skilled help there for the wounds he incurred in aiding us. I will write a letter to go with you. My cousin and his friend will also sign it so none query you and your return without us."

He nodded wearily. "My thanks, Lady Murna. We shall obey."

Hadrann and the unwounded guard lifted the injured man. He was carried gently to where the carriage and its patient horses still stood. Once there he was placed carefully within and padded about with spare clothing to ensure he was not easily jolted from his reclining position. The horses belonging to the dead guards and those who had survived were hitched in a line. The lightly injured man would drive the carriage. His unwounded cousin would lead the mounts. They took up their places, then waited for the promised letter.

Aisling removed her bag, took out a scrap of paper, trimmed her quill and unsealed the tiny bottle of ink. She wrote swiftly before passing the paper on to her brother and friend to be signed. Then she waved it in the air. The ink dried and the paper was folded, sealed with Hadrann's seal ring, and the guards farewelled.

"Return for us in ten days." The man addressed acknowledged the order with a slight bow.

"That I will do, my Lord, and a full six-guard with me. On my life I swear it."

Aisling read his sincerity and smiled. "I know that only if you yourself were slain would you fail to keep your word. Care for your kinsman and bring word back with you. I would know how he does."

The guard's bow this time was as deep as a man on horseback could manage. "I will bring word, my Lady. The thanks of my house for your healing." He nudged his mount into a steady walk, the carriage swung in behind, and the small procession vanished down the trail. As soon as it did so Aisling was also in motion. Trotting quickly back toward the hollow where the witch waited in hiding. Keelan and Hadrann made further plans as they followed.

"I think we should stay out here, don't you, Aisling?" Keelan's voice carried, and his sister slowed.

"Yes. We can hardly appear in Trevalyn complete with a whole bunch of horses and a witch and without any of our baggage and hope the servants won't gossip for years after about it."

Hadrann coughed. "I'd bet they would. No. I suggest we camp out for several nights while the witch recovers but *not* in the hollow. We showed such a place isn't safe from attack. We'll go farther west and a little north, swing past Verlaine, and cut around the hill cliffs over the Estcarp border. That's probably the way Kirion's men brought the girl. We may even find her people hunting that way for her."

"That'd be nice," Aisling commented. "We could then be shot as the ones who stole her away after burning a garth and murdering its people. Going that way is good, but before we go too far I want to talk to the witch. She may know how we can be safe while bringing her home." The witch, when questioned, had her own ideas.

"The borderers will be out in strength searching for the trail and myself at the end of it. The council has forbidden a breaking of the border, but there are always those who are deaf to such a command. Let us find a safe place nearby and sleep. Tomorrow we ride as you say, west and a little north, for another day. Then I shall see if I am able to contact friends to report."

Aisling looked at her. "Report then so that those who come do not start shooting first and ask if you had need of a rescue later."

The witch smiled shyly. "That I would do, Lady. I swear I will permit no harm to come to any of you at the hands of my friends." Her eyes lowered and she glanced sideways at Aisling, her cheeks showing a slight flush. "I am sorry I miscalled your land. I spoke from the pain of my body and the fear of what was to happen, but still I say it: you have the power. How are you safe here, where the power is feared and hated?"

"It would be a long story," Aisling said. "But quickly then. My grandmother was but a young girl when the duke of Kars ran mad. He ordered the three times Horning, and of her family only she survived. She was found by a keep lord who owed her mother a debt for healing. He took the girl in. Later she wed his son, her true love. There was the Old Blood in the lord's family also, thinner and further back, but he remembered." Aisling smiled as she too remembered.

"My grandparents yet live. They love still and are happy. The old lord died in the Turning. I am one of three children born of my grandmother's son. My brother Kirion is nine years my elder. He seeks power, and having none he turned to black sorcery. He has found a way to leech it from those of the Old Blood. Keelan, my other brother, who rides with us, hates Kirion, as do I, both for many offenses and because he would bring down Karsten in war again. Shastro, duke of Kars, is Kirion's puppet. Thus it pleases us to set you outside Kirion's grasp."

"And the cat? When first I saw him I thought him perhaps one of the Old Ones." She cast a look at Wind Dancer where he rode in his carrysack on Aisling's shoulders. The cat looked back and yawned, and the witch laughed. "Truly it is said a cat is his own master."

Aisling grinned back. "Very true. We don't know who his sire was although my teacher in Escore had his suspicions. Wind Dancer says nothing, if he knows aught to tell. But he aided you by his own choice, and it was at his claws and teeth that one of your guards died and I was able to free you."

The witch leaned over to smooth the cat's fur. "My Lord Cat, I do give thanks for your valor. Your name shall be known with praise among the council." Wind Dancer opened an eye, looked at her, yawned again, and apparently slept. But the aura surrounding him was one of smugness.

XI

------◄◇►------

*T*hey rode only another hour before Hadrann, scouting ahead, found a place he deemed suitable and safe. There they made camp. Wind Dancer vanished at once, to return, dragging a large mountain hare just as they lit their fire. The beast was a young buck, plump and already in winter white. Wind Dancer thrust the hare upon Aisling, then trotted off again. She smiled after him. Her brother took the beast from her and began the skinning and cleaning.

"Roast hare will do very well. Those filth of Kirion's don't seem to have had many supplies left."

It was the witch who answered that. "They did not and kicked me the harder for it. I think in the way of that kind they had swilled and gorged all the way from Kars. By the time they took me they had eaten all the best they'd had. They stole somewhat again from my kin's farm, but that too they wasted in riotous evenings. All that they had remaining was oatcakes and journey bread."

"Your kin's farm? Lady, I grieve for you. Bitter is it to lose those you love." Hadrann was sincere and the girl knew.

She shook her head. "I too grieve for honest folk murdered. They were not close kin. My parents died while I was training. Once I would never have been permitted to return. But now the council allows a witch to return to visit friends and family once her training is completed. These kin were cousins I barely knew, but with them my parents had left their personal property that I might have it when I was free to come for such things."

"What happened to it. Were the things burned?" Aisling was curious.

"Not so. A man of the guard who had ridden with me borrowed a packhorse from my cousin's farm and took it with him well-laden with my parent's legacy. It has gone to a friend. She is recently wed, and it pleased me to be able to give her these gifts." She winced at the memory. "Now that horse may be most of what remains of a good farm. Those men burned every building. They lost six of their own to the good shooting of my kin, and they were angered. Everything is likely lost."

Aisling, who knew the garths of Aiskeep, was the one who spoke. "I think not. No doubt there were sheep out in the pastures, if only a few. Unless you saw him die, likely the sheepdog fled to them. And your attackers may have fired all buildings, but in my experience not all burn to the ground."

"It is true they had sheep that were pastured afar, nor did I see their dog slain, but I saw much smoke. It was a great plume against the sky as we rode for the mountains."

"Yes, that was likely the hay barn, but houses burn less easily from no more than one flung torch." She grinned at the witch. "I seem to recall rain only days before this. Was that not so in Estcarp also?"

The witch smiled back. "Why, yes. It was so. I remember riding in the rain to the farm and wishing my cloak let in less water. Then you think much of my kin's home may have survived?" Her face fell again. "Oh, but they themselves are dead. I did not know them well, but I liked them and they were good, kind people."

Hadrann gave a resigned grunt. "It is that sort that Kirion and his type most despise. But what Aisling said before is true. It's possible the house did not burn. You may also find some of your kin live yet as well. Not everyone who falls with blood on his face is killed. Such wounds about the head or face bleed hugely but may be no more than a knockout blow."

The witch's face lit with hope. "It may be so. I shall pray it is. The men hustled me away quickly once I was taken. I saw only that Osland lay across his doorway without movement, blood still trickling down his face. I saw nothing of his wife or daughter."

Keelan nodded slowly. "Then, Lady, it is not impossible more of your friends live than you know. Dead men do not bleed, and if Kirion's filth had laid hands on the women you would have seen and heard . . ." He paused. "Too much." He half-turned from his patient cooking of the hare on its improvised spit. "I would say, do not hope too greatly, but some hope is warranted. But what of you. Was there time for you to cry the alarm to your fellow witches?"

The witch hesitated, then answered. "There was. It was for that I believe that Osland fought. I could say little. Only that we were beset. Then he was struck down, and I was seized. After that they saw to it that I could work no magic nor call for further help."

Even as she spoke Wind Dancer came plodding in, so that the discussion broke off. With him he bore another hare, large, winter white, and delectably plump. He sat smugly by Aisling as praise was showered upon him. The first hare was done. Keelan removed it carefully, divided it, then as they ate, he quickly skinned and cleaned the latest catch. That he spitted in turn.

He looked up, his face shining greasily in the firelight. "If Dancer keeps this up we'll have enough furs for a new cloak." He wiped his mouth and looked at the grease. "Not to mention getting fat. But with a second hare we have no need to hunt tomorrow. We shall have oatcakes for breakfast and our noon meal. Then cold roast hare and journey bread before we sleep."

Aisling glanced across the ebbing fire. "And watch for berry bushes. If the hares up here are already in white, then the berries should be ripe for eating also." She smacked her lips loudly, and everyone smiled.

The fire became coals, Keelan banked it for the night, and they lay down to sleep, Wind Dancer tucking himself into the curve of Aisling's stomach. The night was quiet. The air was cool but not yet the true chill of winter. Hadrann took first watch and roused his friend short of midnight. Keelan watched until the early hours, then woke his sister. She sat after that, watching the stars fade and first light brighten the sky. Once it was light enough to see she stirred the fire.

Then she went to the small stream, filled the water pot, and hung it over the flames. In one of the saddlebags she had found a small packet of trennen leaves. It was not a large amount, but it would give them a hot pleasant drink for several mornings. The trennen tree grew mostly to the very far south of Karsten. Its leaves had a sweet lemony taste when dried then steeped in boiling water. She waited until the water boiled, added the leaves, and laid out the oatcakes. Then she roused the camp.

They ate and drank peacefully. Once they were done Aisling would have moved to ready their mounts, but Hadrann stopped her. He turned to the witch.

"Lady, are we close enough for you to call your friends? I would not have us walk into ambush, and if they are following your trail they may well be close."

The girl nodded. "I will see if I can reach them." Turning her back, she walked apart. With what she did safely hidden, her witch jewel could fall free from where it had lain hidden in her bodice. She took it up and concentrated. There was nothing. She hid the focus again and returned to shake her head silently. Hadrann looked at her.

"How far can your seeking travel?"

"If they were within a day's ride I would know."

"Then we halt at noon," Hadrann said. "You can seek then and again when we camp."

Aisling and Keelan had the saddled horses waiting. The line of the other unridden beasts was hitched to Keelan's mount, and they moved off. At midday the witch could find nothing. They halted only briefly and moved off again riding steadily deeper into the coastal foothills. Keelan had handed over the line of spare mounts to his friend and ridden ahead. He came trotting back along the narrow trail.

"There's a good place half an hour ahead. Grass for the beasts and an old fire pit. It doesn't look to have been used this year."

The news was cheering as was the small fire Aisling lit before setting the trennen leaves to bubbling in the water pot. The lemony scent relaxed them as they ate and drank the hot sweet liquid. With the meal done, Aisling turned to the witch.

"Try again, but if you fail maybe I can aid your search. Power can be linked. Two together can do far more than two apart." She saw the hesitation and spoke reassuringly. "I would force nothing on you, sister. It was a suggestion only."

The witch considered. "You speak aright. I will try alone. If I fail, then let us attempt to search together." Her gaze met Aisling's look. "I trust you, and I do not wish harm to come to any of you. It is unsafe for you to continue across into my own lands if friends do not await us."

Hadrann spoke wryly. "So it would be if it were you who came with us. But your land may be the safer. If you were openly seen with us in Karsten, no matter who our friends or what our oaths, all of us would probably die. If not sooner then later, maybe after torture as Estcarp spies. Like the lady here," he indicated Aisling. "I love my land, but I know its faults. Go now and see if you can keep us safe."

The witch drew apart and sat, cupping her jewel secretly in her hands. She shut her eyes, reached, and then a slight satisfied smile curved her lips. Several minutes later it had curdled. She returned to the fire.

"There are those who search for me, but they have no other witch with them. I cannot speak to their leader. I have not the strength alone."

Aisling stood quietly. "Then I shall lend you that strength. Come and let us try."

She hid her own thoughts as they moved away from the camp. Hilarion had taught her well, although from what she had heard in Escore, the training was somewhat different from that the witches received. But she suspected they were equal in strength, she and the witch. And if the girl had her witch jewel, then Aisling had the pendant. She took her companion's hand as they sat facing each other. The witch cupped her hand about the jewel within the cloth of her robe. Aisling spoke very gently.

"I know that you use a focus. It is safe to use it openly before me. The cloth that covers it will otherwise act to lessen the power. Look, I too use a focus." She drew the pendant free from its secret pocket as she spoke. The witch bent to stare at it and gasped.

"Old, so old. It is what I felt when first your mind touched me. From where did it come, Lady? From what land?"

"It is a treasure of my house," Aisling said evasively, "but let us not waste time."

The witch nodded. Together they slid into the mists of power. Aisling reached out and found the witch. She fashioned a broad beam like a light in her mind, then held it out before her, sweeping it in slow arcs. There! It was the witch who cried out in recognition. The light narrowed, focused, and touched. In a camp many miles away a woman jerked awake. She choked off her instinctive desire to wake her company, then deliberately she lay back, opening her mind to their call but cautiously. There was a change in the familiar feel to the mind-touch.

Lady, Lady Witch, is it you?

It is, good Selarra. I am unharmed and I ride with friends who saved me. One is a woman of power who aids me in speaking with you.

What should I do?

A strange voice came into her head. A woman's tones with the accent of Karsten. *Lady, the witch does not say, but I must. We who have aided her and now travel with her to bring her to safety are of Karsten. I and my brother and his friend. We slew those who had taken her, and with us we have their mounts. It was in our mind the beasts might go some way to rebuild the damage done by their owners. Look for four riders and many led mounts. We travel west and a little north. I think we may meet toward noon tomorrow.*

Lady Witch?

She speaks the truth, Selarra. She and her companions are of our blood, not wholly but in part. You will greet them in all good seeming. I owe them my life and more.

The emotion touching Aisling's mind was doubt, but the soldier was obedient. *At your command, Lady Witch. We shall ride east and a little south.* Again the strange woman's voice struck in.

Not so. Stay in your camp, Selarra. You have not traveled deep into Karsten as yet. Better you do not. Let us come to you. That way if aught happens you may ride swiftly to the safety of your own lands and be within them before you can be taken.

The witch's tones were wistful but resigned. *She speaks for me also, Selarra. I did not think. We will come to you near evening. Do listen for our arrival.*

I shall. Ride carefully.

Contact thinned and was gone. In a far camp a woman lay thinking deeply. It could be that those cursed filth had somehow broken the witch to their hand. Selarra would ride very carefully indeed. Aisling opened her eyes and released the witch's hand. At the camp she spoke quickly before laying down her blankets. Wind Dancer appeared and snuggled in. She hugged him.

"Well for you that whenever you accompany me I always take your carrysack. You'd not be so pleased with this journey if you had to run afoot." He chirruped to her, thrust his head hard against her shoulder, and settled in to sleep. As she drifted into slumber a small picture came to her of a cat draped comfortably across a saddle while a human, recognizable as Aisling, walked and trotted beside. Aisling slept, her mouth still curved in a smile at the picture.

They rose and ate at first light. Soon after, they rode on. The day and the riders were quiet. There was no light speech nor laughter. All were apprehensive save the witch, and she felt her heart silenced by yearning. Only in Estcarp would she feel safe again. Only there, where she had a place, respect, and honor.

The others were silent because they listened. They watched for birds to fly up or the quick sideways jump of a disturbed leaper. The wind blew toward them from the northwest. None of the three doubted that Selarra would be laying an ambush just in case. It was common sense, but none of them wished to die because a soldier shot too quickly. At last, toward mid afternoon Wind Dancer leaned forward from his carrysack. His paw patted urgently at Aisling's neck.

She halted her horse to stroke him. "What is it?" She caught a blurred picture of soldiers in hiding ahead. Aisling drew out her pendant, sinking lightly into the silver mist. With Wind Dancer still in link she caught a glimpse of those ahead. They crouched in a thicket of old brush, by a rock above the trail. It was shaped like the head of a bear, and she noted it. The sight lifted her above the land. Her eyes swept back along the trail to where she sensed her own group moved.

Wind Dancer patted her again, and for a brief instant as his paw rested on her bared skin she had the scent of strange humans in her nose: the smell of horses, harness, and meat cooking on a fire. Aisling held up a finger to the breeze, looked down to where the trail curved along the side of the mountain, and smiled grimly. She sent her mount forward to swing it around before the line.

"They're ahead. No more than half an hour's ride. They wait above the trail for us to pass so that they may take us from behind."

The witch stared. "Do you say that Selarra plans your murder?"

"No, but she fears, I think, that you may have been broken to our purposes. Ride on ahead of us. We shall wait ten minutes then follow more slowly. She must see that you are unharmed and free." She looked the girl full in the eyes. "We have no wish to start some foolish fight with those who seek you, but if we are attacked we will not stay our hands. Ride on and see your friend understands."

Wordlessly the witch drew ahead as Hadrann, Aisling, and Keelan kept their mounts from following. Keelan eyed his sister.

"She'll be with her friends very soon. Is there need for us to wait once she is safe?"

His sister looked down as she thought. "I do not think there is a need, but we should be sure she is safe. Let us ride after her a ways. Until we see them come to meet her. Then we can ride away . . . slowly."

Hadrann laughed. "So that if they really wish to thank us they have only to ride after us more swiftly."

"And with their hands empty of weapons," Keelan added.

"Exactly!" Aisling said dryly. "I find that while I am of the Old Blood even as they may be, I am also Karsten's daughter and I do not quite trust those of Estcarp."

Hadrann reached out to take her hand. "And is it not sad that this is so, that they feel the same way. They must; why else do they seek to see us first? We are all kin, the woman of Estcarp and we three. Yet we watch each other as if we were mortal enemies. I think this is why the geas was laid."

"Yes," Aisling answered him softly. "Yes. It is so. When Shastro and Kirion are dead another must be duke in Kars who has no dread of the witches. Let us first put our house in order, then may we open the door to kinfolk."

She had remained in a light rapport with the pendant since the witch had ridden ahead. From that direction Aisling felt a sudden surge of emotion. She turned to look at Hadrann and her brother.

"She had met her friends. Let us ride on until we can all be seen. Do not talk. I wish to probe ahead."

This time her linking was stronger. Her body swayed on the horse, but her mind hovered high above the narrow winding trail. She looked down with eagle's eyes to where a tiny figure was talking, gesturing, to a group dressed as the border patrol of Estcarp. She counted ten, a common number for a patrol. She scanned the area but could see no others. Then below her the witch and the group's leader broke away and rode back. It was enough. Aisling fell back into her body and looked out at her companions.

"The witch is returning with another: Selarra, their leader, I believe. Let us ride to meet them."

She felt Wind Dancer scrambling from his carrysack and halted again to let him jump free. He landed neatly and trotted past them along the trail. Ahead she heard a cry of surprise and felt a sudden fear. What if they thought him to be attacking or some creature of the dark. Her mount was thrust into a wild gallop even as the thought hit home. She rounded the bend ready to cry out for his life only to find the two women dismounted and making a great fuss over the delighted cat. Aisling laughed, slowed her horse, and advanced, her hands held out empty but for the reins.

"I see one friend knows another." She glared down at the purring cat. "Foolish beast. I feared they might think you attacking and loose an arrow at you." Wind Dancer looked up and chirruped a remark that was clearly sarcastic: "And a thousand fleas to you also."

She looked higher, into laughing eyes. "I think you must be Selarra?"

"I am indeed." The smile vanished into a serious and formal salute. "Estcarp owes a debt to you, Lady. To the House of . . . ?"

From behind his sister Keelan spoke, not loudly, but his voice seemed to ring against the mountains. "That is my sister, the Lady Aisling. I am Keelan, heir to Aiskeep. My friend who stands with us is Hadrann, heir to Aranskeep." He saw the stiffening, the halted move of hand to dagger.

"What you ask yourself is true. My sister and I are sibs to Kirion, the sorcerer of Kars. But, Lady Selarra, far more than any injury to you has he injured both of us. So much so that my sister lies under a geas of the Power. We must destroy both our brother and his puppet duke or die in that attempt."

The woman addressed turned to the witch. "Does he speak truth?"

"The Power says he does."

"Then I may thank him with all my heart." She beamed up at Aisling. "Join our camp, Lady. Eat and drink in friendship before we must ride hard for the border." Keelan led up the string of spare mounts. Selarra ran a knowledgeable eye over them. "Good beasts. We will take them with still greater thanks. Now, let us not stand here in the road. You have ridden all day and would enjoy a rest I daresay."

Hadrann assented so heartily everyone laughed. He made a comic face, stood in his stirrups, and rubbed his backside, provoking still more amusement.

"I would not do for a borderer I fear," he sighed. "You must have softer saddles or tougher skin. Mine is almost worn through. If you have food and drink for us why are we standing about here?"

Selarra led the way back, still chuckling. At the camp her patrol was drawn up in a line. The woman swung down and nodded to them. "We are all friends here. Bring the best we have to share." She sat indicating that her people would care for the horses. Wind Dancer marched up and sat beside her purring. There were exclamations of wonder, and he looked smug. Dancer loved to be admired.

Leather bottles of plum brandy appeared and went around the circle, then again. They were watered down with water from the good stream near the camp and there was ample for all. No one was drunk, not even the guards taking turns watching the trail below. But they smiled more swiftly, laughed more readily, and for that evening forgot that blood might be in common but country was not.

When they slept at last they slept without fear. They rose to eat and laugh again. Selarra took Aisling aside to consult. To a woman of Estcarp, a woman of the Power must be senior in any group.

"Lady, will you ride with us to our border or shall we part here?"

Aisling drew in a breath. "Best we part here. Your border is a day's ride, but with spare mounts you can ride more swiftly. Before nightfall you can be across it and safer. We need to be back in the mountain keep of a kinsman before our guards come seeking us again."

"Then I will thank you with all my heart. I know the witch will not have spoken of something between us. It is against their teaching." She paused. Aisling smiled.

"But you and she are kin. There is much likeness, and she was so sure, so positive one would come searching, even across the border if need be. She said the council forbade that, but the one she knew would not care for such. You are sisters? Is power yours also?"

Selarra gave a soft snort. "Barely. But they'd have taken me for the training anyway although it's little use I'd have been; my heart was set on being a border rider and wedding the man I loved." Her grin was wicked. "So the night before I would have had to go with them I climbed from my window, and in the morning I was no fit witch." Aisling giggled. "Oh, yes, there was a commotion, but they had no choice but to leave me. They took my little sister, and she is content. Her desire was always for knowledge and the witch powers. We have both our wishes, and I am content as is she."

Aisling nodded. "What of your husband?"

"He was slain by your raiders some time ago." She reached out taking Aisling by the shoulders and looking into her eyes. "For too many years I have hated all of Karsten. Now that Karsten has given me back my sister alive and unharmed, I will hate no longer. I saw how it rent you also. That you are kin to us and enemy too. Yet you saved her even from your own." She drew Aisling slowly to her and kissed her cheek.

"I am Selarra Briarthorns Kin. If ever you come to my land ask for me. All that I have is yours, even to shelter against my own."

In a rush of happiness Aisling hugged Selarra hard. "I'll remember." She reached deep into her memory. "And if you find any in your land who recall one, Lanlia, a healer whose grandmother was of Trasmor's line, say to them that the Old Blood lives on in Karsten yet."

"That I will do. But I see that the others wait for us to be done talking. Ride well, Aisling. May the light above you be strong, the way smooth, and evil always far from you on all the roads you take."

She vaulted onto her horse and trotted off down the trail after her patrol. At the first bend, she and her witch sister looked back and waved. Then there was only the sound of hooves receding along the trail.

XII

⟨◦⟩

Aisling sat her mount thinking. Then she glanced down at Wind Dancer as he sat placidly waiting for them to move. He was thinking of roast mountain hare. So was Aisling but for other reasons. She turned her horse to stare about her. Excellent country for hares. They'd come back to those areas twisted by the Turning. Pockets of grass and clumps of brush had grown up quickly. The hares lived well.

They would be the perfect excuse for the wanderings of Aisling and her companions. Wind Dancer had already provided several winter-white hares. If they could find more they would show them off at Trevalyn Keep. She looked down at the big cat and projected the feel of hare, the delight in the hunt, and the taste of prey. Wind Dancer licked his lips and moved off. Aisling nudged her mount to follow, leaving the reins loose as she removed and strung her bow.

"What are you up to?" Keelan queried.

"The guards who return for us will find out we did not go straight to the keep. They'll wonder, and where they wonder they'll talk. But what if we had a good excuse, one that any guard would think only reasonable for the nobility."

Hadrann smiled. "Such as?"

"Winter-white furs. For a cloak. Down in the lowlands or South the hares won't turn white for another couple of months. Up here they are already. What if we hunt all day and again tomorrow. If we come back with a heap of furs, won't they believe that?"

The men nodded. "They'll think it quite sensible," her brother said slowly. "A whole cloak for you and trimming for us if we get enough."

Hadrann agreed. "We save the skinned and cleaned hares too. It's chill up here. There's already small patches of snow in the shadows. We can be at the keep in three days. The hares will be fine, and the whole place can eat roast hare. That will ensure us a most hearty welcome."

"It'll ensure they believe us too," Aisling said. From hoof level Wind Dancer chirruped impatiently. If they were hunting let them get on with it. She broke off to laugh and signaled him. "Go then, move ahead of us. Catch what you can and beware of arrows."

He trotted off, moving silently in long sweeping zigzags across their front. The three humans spread out in a line, each with bow at the ready. The first hare was young and nervous. He panicked, ran, and died abruptly. Keelan dismounted to pick up the body. He dropped back to skin and clean the beast before tucking body and pelt in a saddlebag, then he trotted his mount to rejoin the line.

Wind Dancer caught the next two hares, both older wilier beasts that chose to sit tight from the riders, missing the feline who led them. Wind Dancer did not miss. As they hunted they were also working their way back along the trail but parallel to it. By nightfall they had killed five more hares and made a comfortable camp. Keelan had broken off the hunt to ride ahead and light the fire, start food, and prepare hot drinks.

He'd also found a willow from which he could cut springy switches. These were curved in a circle and tied. The hare skins were stretched over them and scraped as the friends sat talking. Aisling plaited fine grass rope. They'd tie the stretched skins in flat stacks to the backs of their saddles. The horses wouldn't approve, but that was too bad.

The next morning Wind Dancer was tucked into his carrysack, and they rode hard, pushing their tough little horses into early afternoon, when they made camp. Wind Dancer emerged from his carrysack and stretched luxuriantly. Aisling received a picture of hares followed by other pictures. She giggled.

"Wind Dancer says we're ruining him one way or another. Either he'll have all his fur worn off in the carrysack or his pads worn off hunting hares." The big cat marched off down the slope looking back to see they followed.

Keelan had halted them here because he'd seen signs of hares. He'd been right. Hares seemed to explode from the grass almost every time Wind Dancer swept out to look. They shot until there was no more room in the sacks to carry the skins and carcasses. When they returned to the camp, Hadrann looked over their spoils.

"Wonderful." His expression turned serious. "You know, we could do worse than to return here to this spot with a packhorse once our guards reach us again. The court wouldn't come into land this rough."

"Or this close to the border," Keelan noted.

"True. But they won't be averse to a few gifts of this fur: enough to make Shastro a cloak for instance and fur trim for Aisling to give to a few of the ladies. Maybe a share in the meat to a friend or two? Hare meat will keep well in this weather, and a hare should be hung for some days anyhow."

"And I can pick up the latest gossip at the same time as I offer meat and skins," Aisling added. "Yes. If we sent the carriage back without us, hunted here, then rode direct for Kars early in the morning we'd be there well before the meat went bad. We could keep a couple of guards with us to do the skinning and cleaning and stake out the skins. If we hunt for a couple of days then ride hard for Kars we could easily be back in one day."

She paused, then spoke thoughtfully. "It would also keep our guards away from the Trevalyn servants. That way they'd not start to wondering or gossiping about us. It would be safer for us all."

Hadrann hauled out one of the skins he'd taken. He studied it closely, parting the fur and looking at it in various angles. "They're good furs, and Shastro hates to spend money if he can get something free. He'd love enough of these for a cloak. But I'd better present it. We still don't want him to pay too much attention to Aisling in case Kirion starts noticing her too."

"So maybe I should give him the furs," Keelan said thoughtfully. "Kirion could put that down to my trying to get into the duke's favor. He already knows all about me. He'll just sneer about it to Shastro and forget it."

Aisling nodded. "That makes sense. Rann, if you'll share out some of the meat, I'll gift a few of the spare furs." She stared around the darkening landscape. "The hares are breeding too well anyhow. I've seen dangerously many gnawed tree trunks. A good many of the animals will die when the real winter comes. So if we hunt them hard now we'll only be getting what wouldn't survive winter anyway. A couple of packhorses would be suitable. If we sent the carriage back slowly with only one pair we could use the other pair for that."

Once the fire had died to coals they slept peacefully. Hadrann took first watch. The morning was bright and clear, chill but it would warm a little later. Keelan slapped his hands together briskly while preparing breakfast. They ate quickly and were saddled and away soon after. They reached the area of their fight with Kirion's men by early afternoon, before the sun was too low in the sky. Aisling checked the hollow. Foxes and wolves had found the bodies, which were mostly eaten down now to bones and tattered rags of clothing.

She choked down her feelings as she looked on what was left of the men she'd had a share in slaying. She had a job to do here: anything that would identify the bodies must be gathered and taken away. Apart from that, it would be folly to leave anything of value that could be used. The remains were revolting to her, but it was something that had to be done.

Aisling began, saying nothing as her brother and her friend moved to help her, accepting her right to do at least a portion of the task herself. They moved from body to body, swiftly gathering coins, silver buckles, and anything else that was of value or that might identify the dead. The girl locked herself into the task. It must be done, and she would do her share.

Once they were finished, they moved away from the bodies, and the gleanings were piled into Aisling's hands. She tucked them all into a saddlebag, pausing to look down thoughtfully at some of the items.

"Rann, some of this we'll have to hide. We can't keep it in case anyone finds us with it. Kirion would love to know we'd killed his men and freed a witch. I've kept apart the bits that could identify his men. What do we do with them?"

"I'm older than you." It was Keelan's voice, and Aisling blinked at him in puzzlement.

"By six years. So?"

"So, I've visited Jarn before. The old keep owners mined in a couple of places to the west of the keep. They struck water and gave up, but the mine shafts are still there. Jarn fenced them off to stop stock falling in, that's all."

Aisling's face lit with understanding. "If we drop these bits and pieces down the shafts they aren't likely to be found. Which way, Kee?"

"Give them to me, and I'll do it. You two keep checking, but we did check for anything like that from the others toward the road. I think this precious pair must have been the ones Kirion trusted, as much as he'd ever trust anyone out of his sight."

He received the small handful of belongings from Aisling and trotted away. Hadrann and Aisling moved off slowly. They found the sites of the fight and again the bodies were no more than scattered bones. Aisling collected coins, buckles, cheap weapons, and one good dagger. She looked over the weapons with Hadrann.

"We can sell everything but that knife. None of the swords or other daggers are more than the basic stuff sold in the market. That dagger has no identifying marks, but if anyone's seen it before they'd recognize it."

"I should think they would," Aisling said dryly. "It has Kirion's crest on the hilt. He must have given it to the leader as a token, maybe as proof to someone else that the man came from my dear brother. We have to be rid of it, but before we do that I'll have to check it over. Knowing Kirion there's a good chance it's sealed to him in some way. I just wish we'd found the damned thing earlier."

Hadrann spoke comfortingly. "I doubt he's even started to wonder about them yet. He wouldn't expect to take a suitable captive at once, so he'd have given them time. I'll go up the trail a little way and stand guard. Wind Dancer can go down trail. You get that thing checked and cleared. Then Kee can ride back and dump it. He won't like having to make the trip again but better safe than ambushed."

Aisling sat on the chill ground. Her mount cropped grass peacefully nearby as she took the dagger into her hands. She sensed nothing, but then Kirion wasn't a novice. She probed deeper. Ah! There! She considered the spell, sealed in the owner's blood, and wrinkled her nose in disgust. Typical of Kirion.

She wove a masking spell in her mind, spoke the words, and allowed the result to settle like a smothering curtain over the knife. That should do it. Kirion would have felt nothing since the spell was still intact, but if he scried for the owner, he'd see nothing. If the weapon was disposed of where it could not be easily retrieved, Kirion should never know what had happened to the owner or the men with him.

She stood looking over the now innocuous weapon. A pity to throw away a good knife, but it was too easily identified. She whistled, a long clear note and soon heard hoofbeats as Hadrann returned. Wind Dancer crawled in and sat purring. She held the dagger down for him to sniff, and his purr was confirmation. The knife was fully cloaked. She laid down the carrysack, Wind Dancer crawled in, and Aisling mounted her horse, settling the carrysack across her shoulders.

They rode slowly up the trail until Keelan joined them with a clatter. He groaned when told the dagger must also be disposed of in the same place but rode off with it. He rejoined them just short of the keep. After that all went as they'd hoped. Jarn greeted them with genuine pleasure. The hare carcasses went to the great kitchen and appeared as roast hare, minced and spiced hare, and hare pie over the next few evenings. The guards arrived a few days later, complete with additional members and the carriage.

They reported that the badly injured man was recovering, and the city healer who had attended him had been loud in Aisling's praise. His kinsmen were gruff but honest in their thanks to the "Lady Murna." Aisling accepted their gratitude gently. She casually mentioned their hare hunting and also saw to it that they saw the furs and heard of the feasts the keep had enjoyed.

"My cousin and I and our friend are also considering a second such hunt. We would like to do even better this time . . . if you will assist us by taking the carriage back?"

"Lady, I chose good men. They will take your carriage back safely. My brother and I will remain with you if it be your will. Both of us can skin and clean and stretch furs. They'll not be spoiled in our hands. And we can take it in turns to stand guard. We owe a debt for our cousin, Lady. It would please us to pay it."

Aisling smiled and agreed. She'd done no more than she would have done for any man of Aiskeep, but such attentions to one's people were rarer in the city. If the man felt he owed a debt, then it would be wrong to deny it.

The hunting was good. Wisely Hadrann chose a system that kept the two guards in camp working on the game brought back to them in turn by Hadrann, Aisling, or Keelan. That first day they hunted hares. Between their successes and those of the cat they had a heap of furs and meat by day's end.

Aisling took up five of the plump bodies and walked away. Hadrann turned to the interested guards. "It will be moonlight, and I see well. We'll stake these out and see if the foxes that come for them have changed coats as yet. If so, then we may have more work for you."

The foxes had. The first Aisling shot was winter white with only a black tail tip. Keelan was acting as runner with the dead beasts and at the same time making sure the guards did not leave. Out in the night around a mountain shoulder Aisling was using witch light. It did not alarm the foxes who came to the bait, but both she and Hadrann could see their prey clearly. They shot only those they could identify as not quite full grown and hence probably still unmated. There were a number of them, so that Keelan and the guards were kept busy.

When they were done they had returned fifteen foxes to the camp. Keelan had brought back the discarded carcasses as the foxes were skinned, and the constant supply of those ensured more foxes continually arrived to feast. But after fifteen Aisling spoke softly.

"Enough, I think. There's sufficient to make the guard think we had very good hunting. More and they'll wonder."

Hadrann shrugged. "That's true. Better to take no chances. Thus far it looks as if we've got away with everything we've done out here. We will share out the furs slowly. By the time anyone realizes how many we took, the mountains will be snowed in."

"What of the hare meat?"

Keelan, who'd just returned to them, spoke up. "We send one of the guards back to Trevalyn with some of it. He can catch up with us. We send a message to Jarn that the meat we're sending him is a midwinter gift from us since we won't be there. We send a couple of the fox furs to him too and four of the hare furs. Does that seem good?" It did, and when they reached camp again the guard was dispatched.

They left mid-morning after sleeping well. The ride back to Kars was uneventful. The second guard caught up with them that afternoon, and by nightfall they were entering the main gate of Kars city. They went straight to their rooms, Aisling immediately calling for hot baths, hot food and drinks, and a warmed bed. Wind Dancer, who'd slept in his carrysack all the way, vanished to hunt mice. They'd be a pleasant change from hares.

Hadrann took the great heap of furs to a tanner. They'd been rough dried on the stretchers and were of fine quality. The tanner was very impressed. Yes, he could begin working on them at once. Certainly he would treat them as the valuables they were. Hadrann settled to haggle over the tanning price. With that done he went back to the stable to split hares.

One third to their own tables. One third each to Aisling and her brother, who would quietly share them out to friends and acquaintances. By late evening a number of diners were extolling the generosity of Aiskeep and Aranskeep. That included Shastro's cook, a middle-aged woman who was tyrannical in her domain. Her cooking and the smooth way in which she ran the duke's household affairs allowed her license in his eyes. Where she was pleased, he was pleased to listen.

The next night the three friends dined with him. Shastro was merry, inquiring after their hunting, Jarn of Trevalyn keep, and if there had been any trouble on their journey. Hadrann laughed at the latter.

"Oh, indeed, my Lord Duke. Some scruffy collection of bandits, but we killed most of them, and I suspect the others simply ran. We took the horses we found to go hunting. It was all most amusing."

"There was nothing to say they were from Estcarp?"

Hadrann looked horrified. "Cup and Flames preserve us all. No, my Lord Duke. They rode a scrubby lot of ponies of our own mountain breed. We did look over a few of the bodies briefly. They had Karsten weapons—cheap rubbish too—Karsten clothing, and no looks in common with any of Estcarp I've ever seen. No, I think them no more than a band of wolfsheads such as even Karsten can breed, a vicious-looking bunch."

He laughed. "No, my Lord Duke. They were not so formidable. I myself shot a couple. Even my cousin here with her lady's bow was able to strike one down. My young friend also slew his share. We counted half a dozen dead but did not bother to search far for any others." He laughed again. "If any lived I would think them running still. It was fair sport. If only you had been with us, sire, no doubt the score would have been higher against them."

Shastro flushed in flattered pleasure before asking more questions. Hadrann answered casually. It would be Kirion's hand behind this. The guards had talked, and Kirion suspected that the bandits had been his men trying to reach Kars in a hurry but he only suspected. There was no proof, and if Hadrann and his friends kept their heads . . . Well, they'd keep their heads. Shastro was asking to see the looted weapons.

"Of course, my Lord Duke. I dumped them in a bundle in my outer room. Cousin Murna will be pleased to fetch them for you."

Shastro disclaimed any wish to disturb the lady. A servant

should go. Hadrann gracefully agreed. Let the servant do that. There was nothing else to find, and he would add an item or two Shastro would find interesting. Several years back Hadrann had chanced across a body and a couple of items it bore. A small voice was saying that now was the time to use the trinkets.

When the servant returned, Hadrann took the bundle from him, allowing it to unroll across the floor. Plain, poor-quality swords, knives, and a shabby bow jumbled across the sheared sheepskin carpets. Shastro gave a sharp exclamation and pounced.

"This trinket, it was found on one of them?" He held up a jewel. It was a pale flawed amethyst held in a circle of plaited silver. It was of small value, but someone had spent time carving the gem into the likeness of a cup with flames surrounding it. The work was well done, and the trinket pleasant to look upon. Hadrann stared at it in apparent surprise.

"Why, yes, my Lord Duke. It came from one I thought to be their second-in-command." He laughed. "If such a wrangle-tangle group could be said to have a command." He stooped, thrusting the cheap weaponry aside. "The man had this on him also." He picked up another small item and proffered it to Shastro, who almost drew back. At Hadrann's blink of surprise the duke collected himself and took it in slender fingers.

"Yes, yes. Very interesting. I wonder where the wretch obtained them?" There was something in his voice that said he was indeed wondering. Aisling craned to see. Another trinket. Probably from the same hand. This time a small tawny cat's eye carved into the shape of a sitting cat. It was attractive without being valuable, and Aisling cried out in delight. Shastro turned and forced a smile.

"My dear Lady. You find it pleases you, then it is yours." He pressed it into her hand. "Say nothing. Count it as some small recompense for a fine meal and the destruction of a dangerous band." But his voice was tense, and in one white-knuckled hand he clenched the amethyst trinket. After that he angled to bring the meal and the evening to a swift close. There was a half-worried half-considering look in his eyes. Aisling knew it had something to do with the trinkets. She reined in her impatience until they were able to bid the duke an elaborate farewell. Once back in their suite she pounced on Hadrann.

"I did the searching of some of those we killed," she said precisely. "And of the others, I saw all you gleaned from their persons. None of them had those pretties on them. From where did they come and why did the sight of them so distress Shastro? What game are you playing and why were we not let into it?" From his comfortable sprawl on the couch Keelan seconded her words.

Hadrann looked bleak. "The first and last questions are easily answered. I added the trinkets to the bundle as I unrolled it. I did not mention them to you since I had no idea of using them until Shastro gave me the opportunity, and once I thought of it I had no chance to speak to you apart." His tones grew harsher. "As for whence they came and what the game was, that is a long tale, but I can tell it in brief." He poured them glasses of wine, drank deeply of his own, and refilled it.

"You know Shastro came from the city's low quarter and there he had two cousins whom he loved deeply. The man was his best friend, and it was whispered that the girl was his lover. They vanished while traveling with a carriage and driver. Shastro searched. Indeed he all but had the city and land about it torn apart by his men in the year of the warhorse. Then he stopped, and it was as if they had never been. There was a rumor they had been found. Do you not recall, Keelan?"

"Vaguely. I was not at court that year. Kirion was though. It was after that he consolidated his power over Shastro."

"Exactly." He looked at them. "I was hunting the year after the cousins vanished, being sick of the court and fawning men. It was nigh a year and a half since the two were missed. I found a place where a carriage had been ambushed. Out of interest I tracked what had occurred. I found a body, bones by then, clearly found before me since foxes do not carry away weapons and coins, and there were signs another body had been removed. I was caught up in my hunt by then, so I tracked on. There were women's clothes, shreds of them, in the wrecked and hidden carriage. What clothing was left after the weather and small creatures."

"And you found her?" Aisling leaned forward. "It was she who had my trinket and the other one you used?"

"It was. I found her bones huddled deep into a small crack in the rock. It was early winter when they went missing. I fear she died of exposure, afraid to leave her shelter until she was too weak to struggle forth. She may also have suffered some injury, enough to weaken her before even the cold struck home. Those who searched had found the carriage, the driver, and a passenger. The passenger they had taken, for honorable burial I presume. The poor lady they had never found.

"I scraped a hole by the crack, wrapped her bones in my second-best cloak, and laid them inside. Then I filled the grave with rocks and covered it with earth. I took from her the two charms she wore. I knew who she was by them. Her brother, Shastro's cousin, was a skilled carver of such semiprecious stones. It was how he earned a living for them until Shastro rose in the world. The duke bragged to a group of us once and showed a charm he had that his cousin had carved."

Aisling's voice was soft and slow. "They were in a carriage and attacked, murdered by bandits. We were in a carriage and attacked by bandits. Shastro believes that her trinkets were found in the bandit's possession, but I am sure it was Kirion who dispatched him on to ask questions of us. What questions will Shastro now ask of Kirion?"

Hadrann looked at her. "That passed through my mind when I saw he would demand to see what we had scavenged from them. For some time I have carried those trinkets in a secret pocket. One day I hoped to use them and now I have. The cousins were a strong influence for good on the duke, and I swear that he did love them deeply and honestly. By now he will know how little Kirion likes to have his own influence diluted. Shastro becomes more unstable and suspicious of those about him by the month. He will wonder about the deaths of his kin. He will think about it while the question eats at him.

"Did Kirion have our duke's much-beloved cousins murdered? Was it done by the same men Shastro was asked to use for a raid into Estcarp? He won't ask those questions of Kirion directly. He'll seek out others to question. I think he will return to the site where they found the bodies but secretly. Among other questions, he will wonder most whether or not Kirion took the girl for his own purposes.

"Was she tortured, raped, slain quickly, or flung into some cesspit to die drowning in filth after being mind-emptied by Kirion? That question would haunt any man who loved. It will haunt Shastro, who knows his man's ruthlessness. And, I saw Shastro grieve. If he has never loved or cared for any others, he loved his cousins with all his heart."

Hadrann's eyes were pitiless. "I am certain Kirion murdered my brother. Let him answer for these other deaths to his duke. I think sooner or later Shastro will ask questions, then let Kirion beware."

XIII

---◦---

Aisling murmured agreement, then looked at the two men. "Something else occurs to me. We know Kirion was, shall we say, persuading those girls that Shastro wanted to love him, to get them to cooperate. But I've seen no signs of that since we arrived. How willing will Shastro be to give up having the women he wants?"

Hadrann grunted thoughtfully. "Well, the last was young Jedena of Carmorskeep. Shastro wanted her. Jedena preferred a young man of the court, then seemed to change her mind and fall madly in love with our dear ruler. Everyone guessed that had to be Kirion's influence. The girl lasted quite well, but Shastro tired of her a couple of weeks after you and Keelan got to court. You wouldn't have noticed the girl much."

"I haven't noticed him with anyone."

"Which, knowing Shastro, means that this time it's someone willing. Likely some merchant's daughter who thinks it an honor. He likes to flaunt the noble or unwilling ones far more."

Keelan shrugged. "But his loves rarely last more than a few months. He'll be looking for another very soon. What did happen to Jedena?"

"I don't know. I'll make inquiries."

Aisling glanced up. "Leave that to me. I'm lunching with the Lady Varra. She's the biggest gossip in Kars as we all know. I have only to get her onto the right subject to hear everything she has heard or suspects." She grinned. "And if she doesn't know about Jedena, then no one will. I'll take her a fox fur and a pair of the hare furs. After that she'll talk all day if I am prepared to sit and listen."

She disappeared to change her garb and reappeared an hour later carrying the furs. She blew a kiss to both men and hurried out of the door. Her return was unnoticed some three hours later. Her companions were engaged in a hard-fought game of fox and geese. Aisling hung over them watching until the game resolved. Hadrann had beaten his friend, and they became lost in further discussion on strategy. Aisling waited, but when it showed no sign of abating, she coughed. They looked up.

"I think assassins are about to be hunting our dear duke again." That brought swift concentrated attention from Hadrann and her brother.

"By whom?"

"Jedena's father."

Hadrann stared, then looked grim. "I can guess the rest. The girl's killed herself. Where and how?"

"Varra only heard yesterday. From some relative who lives near Carmorskeep and knows the lord and his lady there. I think Varra writes to every relative she has. It's no wonder she has a bevy of servants; she needs them to take all her letters," Aisling added.

"Never mind Varra's servants. What about Jedena?"

"Well, according to Varra the girl left court and went home once Shastro tired of her. Apparently they had a fight before she went, and the duke said that he never wanted to see her again; that she was a bore, and he was tired of her. The girl went back to her keep, poured out everything to her mother, then went up to her room, apparently to sleep for the night, and hanged herself instead.

"Her father isn't sure exactly what went on, but he believes one of three things. That Jedena refused the duke, who had Kirion twist the girl's mind into compliance. With her mind twisted, even when Shastro fell out of love, Jedena couldn't, so she hanged herself for her lost love or she killed herself in despair at what she'd been made to do. Or the duke seduced Jedena, then threw her over so brutally the girl felt she had nothing more to live for. Whichever way it was, the old man blames Shastro. According to Varra, he's breathing fire and threats."

"Ineffectual ones," Keelan commented. "I seem to remember Carmorskeep is poor. It's a week's travel away by coach at this time of year too, and the roads will soon be impassable by that method. The old man will probably rant and rave awhile, then it will all blow over. But how stupid of Kirion not to have taken the love spell off the girl. He could have done that and blurred her mind or something. Made Jedena believe she'd been in love but had fallen out of it like Shastro."

Hadrann was looking serious. "There's more to it than that, Kee. Jedena was keep heir. She was the only child. Carmorskeep looks to the Coast Clan. Worse still, its lady is close kin to Franzo, and the keep is actually hers, not her husband's, which is why Jedena would have inherited. Under clan law and with the heir dead, keep lord and lady must choose an heir from amongst the clan. There's very little doubt who they'll choose."

"Who?" Aisling was interested. "And why will that affect things?"

"The who is a boy named Lorel. The why is because he is Franzo's youngest son. Franzo and Carmorskeep's lady are half brother and sister. They've always been close. He'll be deeply distressed over young Jedena's suicide and just as upset to see his sister's grief. Knowing Franzo, if or once his son is formally named as heir, he'll feel he should avenge Jedena's death. He's been at the gates of Kars with an army once already. I think he could be back here in spring with another."

"In spring?"

"Franzo was a professional soldier. He won't be silly enough to start anything at the beginning of winter."

Aisling stood, stretching. Wind Dancer chirruped from his seat beside her, and she stooped to stroke him. Her mind received a clear picture as her fingers touched. It was overlaid with a hopeful wistfulness. She straightened, her face lighting suddenly.

"Wind Dancer's just asked why we have to spend winter here? Let's go home, back to Aiskeep. Hadrann, you'd be welcome to come with us. Oh, Kee, let's go home. I miss Aiskeep so much. I want to see Grandmother and Grandfather again. I want to see our friends. I want to laugh and not feel that someone is always watching in the walls in case I say something treasonous. I want to be me again." She drew the word out in a soft humming hunger. "Hoooommme. Let's go hoooomme!"

Keelan groaned. "Aisling. Yes. I miss Shosho and everything else you said too. If we left in the morning we could be back in a few days." He turned to his friend. "You could come with us. Go on and stay with your father awhile then return, whatever you wanted. But I know we'd be very happy if you spent time at Aiskeep."

Hadrann was considering. "I could spend a couple of days, but my father's old. He'd like to see more of me than he does. I'll ride with you, stay three days, then go on to Aranskeep for the winter. Maybe I can come back in spring before you leave, and we can ride back to Kars together."

Aisling had walked to the door to call the guard. "Find my maid please, tell her she is required. Start getting ready in the stables. We plan to leave for our keeps in the morning." She shut the door and looked at them. "One other thing. Who tells Shastro he's losing us for the winter?"

Hadrann grinned. "You can. Give him that speech about how much you miss your home. He's sentimental."

Aisling's answering smile was rueful. "Just as long as he isn't sentimental about us staying in Kars." She went to change into a more formal robe. That was something else she'd enjoy about being home: it would no longer be necessary to change her clothes for almost everything she did. Court etiquette required clothing that ranged from casual to very formal and the appropriate level of garb for each occasion. Aisling was bored with it all.

In Aiskeep she could spend the day in riding clothes if she wished. There was no need to dress for breakfast, change to ride, change for lunch, change to spend time with an acquaintance, change for the evening meal, and change yet again for a later court revel—and that was a minimum, she thought. If you did more, you had to change more. She could recall days when she'd had to change her clothing as often as every second hour of the entire day. She bit back a groan as she flung off her robe and reached for a formal gown. Cup and Flames but she wanted to be home again.

Her maid pattered hastily in, and Aisling was caught up further in trying to dress, do her hair, and give orders all at the same time. The maid's face fell as soon as she understood she'd be unemployed over winter. Aisling understood the look. She made a quick estimate as she brushed out her hair. She flicked a glance about their suite and asked a question.

"You also help Lady Hirrisyn. Does she remain in Kars over the winter months?" The girl nodded. "Then you will spend the winter with less to do." She saw the girl's lips thin in annoyance. What good was more time if you had no money to enjoy the time? In winter the palace would be chill. With no money to buy fuel, the maid would be cold and damp. Aisling continued, and as the maid listened her face lit with pleasure.

"I know what it will be like here in winter," Aisling was saying. "I want you to do us a favor. We will be leaving many of our possessions here in the Aranskeep suite, as will the Lord Keelan, my cousin's friend. If you will stay here, keep the suite warmed and cared for, we will leave money with the fuel merchant. We will pay you one third of your usual wages for the time we are away. I will give you half of that before I leave; the other half I will leave with the Lady Varra to be given to you the day before midwinter."

She watched the maid's happiness. "Is that satisfactory?" The girl was nodding before the question was completed. She'd be warm and comfortable in a noble's suite all winter. She'd have less coin, but she wouldn't have to pay for fuel either and she could let her rented room go for the time. She would be doing half her usual work and in the end she'd have as much coin as if she were caring for both ladies. Moreover if she made a good bargain with the fuel merchant they could both slip a few coins extra from the lady's purse. Aisling understood all that.

Aisling had grown up in a keep. She knew the economies of a maid's life. The girl would have a wonderful winter. Aisling would have to remember to give Varra the money for the maid. She would also leave the girl a small midwinter gift to be given with the coin. She finished her hair with the maid's help. Then she sat and scribbled briefly before reaching for sealing wax and her ring. She turned, offering the sealed note.

"Here. This says what I have asked you to do. It says you have the right to be here caring for our rooms while we are gone. If anyone disputes that show them this letter. To make sure you are safe I will leave a copy with the Lady Varra. Go to her if you need and, in any case, for your payment before midwinter." The elderly Varra would enjoy helping. She adored having a finger in any pie.

Aisling swept out, leaving her maid beaming and clutching her letter. Shastro was not so happy. He whined and complained. He would be lonely without her. The palace was always dull over the winter. His companions bored him. Aisling snorted.

"You'll be surrounded with sycophants all competing for your attention; you'll hardly notice my absence." Shastro grinned, the truth for once amusing him.

"I'll notice. There won't be anyone among them who says the things you do or who dares beat me soundly at fox and geese, but go." He looked oddly sad for a moment. "I understand your wish to spend time at your home. Once I would have wished to go home. Now there is no home for me and nothing any longer to wish for and no one else I may trust for the truth." He forced a smile. "Be safe. I will send some of my guards with you to Aranskeep if you like?"

"To Aiskeep only if it please you, my Lord." Aisling spoke quickly. The last thing she wanted was to be forced to ride on past her home. "Keelan has asked my cousin and me to stay a few days there before we continue. His grandfather will send keep guards with us after that."

"Very well. To Aiskeep then." He kissed her hand gently. "Go safely and return in spring." He sighed theatrically. "Long will the winter be without you, my Lady."

Aisling snorted in disbelief. "You'll have dances and revels all winter, and there's the midwinter celebrations: masques, ice-skating, and dancing. By spring you'll have a new love most probably. I'll arrive back, and you'll say, 'Oh, were you away? I hadn't noticed.'"

Shastro laughed. "Away with you, you insulting woman. I do not forget my friends so easily. Any light love of mine will still never do as you do." Again she saw that flicker of sadness as his hand closed. "You speak the truth to me; you treat me as a friend, not as your duke. I value it. Come back safely, and I swear I'll notice you've returned."

Aisling smiled gently. "And I swear I shall come back. Take care of yourself, my Lord. Tell your guards we leave mid-morning." She bowed and hurried off to speak privately to her companions.

She had noticed something very interesting that they should

hear. She found them at the stables with their hired guard. With Shastro's arrangements explained and the hired guards paid off but engaged again for spring, Aisling was free to link arms and walk the men to the Aranskeep suite, where they found Wind Dancer asleep on a seat in the main room.

Once the door was shut Aisling checked quickly. The pendant's mists swirled about her, as she listened with her mind for any who might be about, but the passages within the walls were empty. Her hand went out to stroke Wind Dancer's soft fur.

"Listen for any spy in the secret passages. Let me know if you hear anything suspicious."

Then she removed from its shelf the small carved cat charm Shastro had given her and held it, looking down on the object thoughtfully before looking up to catch their gazes in return.

"You remember Shastro kept the other of these trinkets. Well, all the time I was talking to him he was playing with it. And he was . . . strange, twice. He spoke of not being able to go home again and that if he did there was nothing there to wish for any longer. He said he'd miss me, that I was the only one left to tell him the truth." She looked up from the trinket. "I think he was remembering his cousins."

"That's more than likely." Hadrann said. "I've seen him play with that amethyst several times of late. I saw Kirion noticing it once. I don't think he liked it. There's been gossip too that Kirion doesn't spend as much time at court as he used to before this season. I've noticed that since we gave Shastro the trinkets and something to consider, Kirion's hardly been seen. I'll be glad to be out of this place for the winter. I have a feeling this may be blowing up to a storm."

Aisling shivered. "I have the same feeling, but not in Kars, surely. There hasn't been real war in the city since the Sulcar sailed in and burned half the docks and warehouses there. Even Franzo backed off from an attack before."

Keelan's expression was hard. "That doesn't mean it can't happen. Our guards were talking to some of the others from along the coast. They say Jedena's father and mother are taking the girl's death very badly. They've announced Franzo's son as the Carmorskeep heir. They seem to be pushing for the formal ceremony to be completed as fast as possible. And I wonder," he paused. "I wonder if they don't want the lad in place as heir before they do something else, and there's only so many other things that something else could be."

"Franzo?"

Hadrann shook his head. "We don't know, Aisling. But Shastro should have remembered that other people besides him love their kin. Franzo isn't a hothead. He isn't likely to attack over the Jedena business, but if anything more occurs, then I wouldn't depend on him staying out of it. His clan will want him to lead them in any attack, and he'll obey. If he's given a more personal motive he might insist on acting anyhow. He isn't a hothead but he isn't stone either."

He left it at that and was soon caught up in packing and choosing what he would take. Keelan had vanished to his own suite and was sorting rapidly. Most of his clothing could be moved to the Aranskeep rooms to be kept aired and dry there. It had been a good idea of Aisling's to use the maid. Everyone worked briskly for the afternoon. They spent a last evening at court. Aisling danced once with the duke and a number of times with other acquaintances.

The morning was good, not hot nor too chill but calm and clear. By the tenth candlemark they were away. Aisling had firmly rejected the coach. The horses could not drag it swiftly. The roads were becoming muddy, and in places holes were forming under the growing drifts of snow. They would travel quicker and more easily riding horses and with their gear on sturdy pack ponies. Shastro's guards agreed. They would have to ride back in worsening weather. The faster they reached Aiskeep the faster the guards could return.

The party clattered out and down the road at a brisk canter. Wind Dancer slept curled in his carrysack against Aisling's shoulders, much to the amusement of the guards. Shastro had provided six guards, all arrayed in the screaming purple and gold uniforms that shouted their status. No bandit would be stupid enough to attack anything or anyone marked so clearly as the duke's. Shastro had a reputation for resenting hands laid on his friends or property. Anyone who did lay hands on such was likely to draw back bloody stumps.

Aisling was thinking of that as she rode the last miles to Aiskeep mid-morning six days later. The duke knew his reputation, knew that few would be that bold or that stupid, and he'd cared for his cousins. They were traveling with only a driver but still, knowing Shastro, they'd have been marked as his in some way. Probably the carriage doors bore his crest. The driver would likely have been in the duke's colors, and Shastro would wonder, would always have wondered, who would attack what was his.

Her hand went to her waist-pouch and she felt the shape of the little cat. What had the duke's cousins been like? Fair, dark? The guards rode spread out. Two ahead and behind. Another one each scouting far ahead and trailing the party far to the rear. None could hear her. She nudged her mount to range alongside Hadrann's horse and asked her question.

"You saw Shastro's cousins. What did they look like?"

"I never saw them alive but I heard."

"Well?"

"The boy was slender, not tall but wiry, blond but that tawny shade with a faint hint of red, and he had blue eyes. The girl was slender, with long blonde hair, quite a pale color, an oval face, and dark blue eyes. Not beautiful but pretty and with plenty of character in her face. She wore pale soft colors a lot; so did the boy. Is that what you wanted?"

"Yes." She allowed her mount to move away. The trinkets had been a vanity in one way. The amethyst would have shown well against a blonde. The small cat, she suspected, would have been a contrast to the boy's hair. She wondered why both trinkets had been with the girl. Perhaps it was she who carried them for safety when they traveled or for luck. Or perhaps she was wrong, and the girl had always owned both small trinkets.

But Hadrann had confirmed something she'd observed before. Men often sought out loves similar to their first. The men Shastro most often befriended were wiry in build and blue eyed. The women he chose as lovers were always blonde, slender, and young and most had eyes of dark blue. If he had loved his cousins enough to seek out only lovers or friends who reminded him of his lost kin, then he'd loved them indeed.

For a moment she felt tears sting her eyes. Shastro had sounded almost forlorn as he bade her good-bye. And he was fond of her, that she knew. He did not desire her but he enjoyed her companionship and the time they spent talking together. Surely he might yet be reclaimed for the Light? Then she remembered the old woman he'd had tortured. He'd believed she'd be interested to see the ghastly spectacle, but perhaps she could teach him differently? She didn't want him as a lover, but if she wed him perhaps it would help Karsten. And perhaps not, a harder part of her mind said. Where would she be if she failed?

She wondered now if . . . speculation disappeared in a sudden blaze of joy. Keelan was yelling as they rounded the bend to the last stretch of road. Ahead she could see the walls of Aiskeep. She bit down on the desire to scream and shout with her brother. The duke's guards must not be surprised at how pleased she was to see a keep supposedly foreign to her. It would be so good to be home and free of that kind of caution.

She could hear Keelan's shouts echoing back. "Open, in the name of the heir. Open the gates."

And old Harran's welcome acid tones. "All right lad, all right. I'm old but I'm not deaf yet." She pulled up in front of the gates as they swung back slowly. From the corner of her eye she saw the amused looks the guards were casting about. Keelan was shouting back upward.

"You sure you aren't deaf? These gates need oiling; you don't seem to have heard that?"

"I heard, I heard. What about you doing something around here. I'm an old man. I can't do everything."

"Why not, you've always said you did it all before," Keelan retorted at full volume. His target spluttered. Keelan started to laugh, Aisling giggled helplessly, and Hadrann and the guards joined in. Old Harran spat in disgust.

"Humph! You get in here before bandits come looking to see who's making all that noise. We can't afford no ransom not even what they'd ask once they got a good look at yer." Still grinning Keelan rode through the now fully opened gates. The guard captain turned to Hadrann.

"Lord, there's half a day yet and an inn within reach by nightfall if we ride hard. It would save us a day on the journey back to Kars. Give us leave to go."

Hadrann reached for his pouch and pressed coins into the captain's hand. "You'd be welcome to stay the night here I know, but if you wish to go we won't delay you. Thank you for your care." The man accepted the coin and bowed slightly.

"Thank you, my Lord. We decided earlier. We will ride back now and be in Kars the quicker." He reined his mount back to join the others who waited. He spoke briefly, and seconds later they were riding northward.

Hadrann rode through the massive gates to join Aisling and

Keelan where they had dismounted. Wind Dancer had jumped from his carrysack and was prancing eagerly about. The horses were taken away, and it was Aisling who ran toward the door first. It opened, and within stood two familiar figures. She embraced them both, hugging and almost weeping her joy.

Ciara was practical. "I can't greet you properly, dearling. Let us rid you of that shape first." They linked, and "cousin Murna" melted away to be replaced by Aisling's laughing face.

"That's better." Wind Dancer trilled, and she smiled. "Him too, he says." They dispelled the big cat's disguise, and he bounced merrily. Aisling stooped to hug him and straightened.

She looked at the beloved faces of her grandparents and allowed brief tears to fall. This was what Shastro had lost and now sought in every light love. This she had missed every day at the court, where all was false and smiles hid hatred or fear. This was her place no matter how far she went or how long she was gone. Home. She was home again.

XIV

⸻◈⸻

They swept into the keep in a joyous laughing noisy group, Wind Dancer butting knees, bouncing, and bawling with the best of them. He was swept up and hugged as often as anyone else. After a short while he left his humans and went to find his dam. Shosho didn't like noise and excitement. Being a normal-sized cat she sometimes got stepped on during such celebrations.

Aisling had spared him a thought as he padded off. The picture she received was Shosho rubbing happily against her giant son. She grinned and turned back to the welcome. Ciara had sat finally on her large comfortable chair before the fire, before speaking to her grandchildren.

"Dearlings, I'm so happy to see you home again. You are home again, I hope. For the winter at least?"

Aisling knelt to hug her. "Of course we are. Hadrann can only stay a few days though. He must ride on to Aranskeep. I said we'd send guards with him for safety?"

"Of course. Harran can go with six men." Ciara waved down polite objections from Hadrann. "No, lad. There're bandits about at this time of year. It's on the edge of winter, and like bears, they too seek to lay up fat for winter." She turned to Aisling again. "We have new neighbors in my family's old garth. I forgot to tell you when you were home last."

"What happened to the others?" Aisling remembered them as a pleasant rather stupid family from one of the smaller garths on the keep's lands, garth born and bred, doing their work by rote because it had been good enough for their grandparents. Nothing new, never any innovations. They'd saved up all their lives to buy a garth. Everyone down to the small children contributing coppers where they could. Ciara had sold them the land and ancient sturdy house on a sliding series of payments. Now her grandmother looked sad.

"I should never have weakened. They wanted a garth so much and they'd worked so long and so hard for it. But you remember what they were like. They were one of our families, hard-working but not really very bright and too trusting. They could never remember a time when they'd been anything but protected by the keep. That garth is outside our lands at Aiskeep and isn't protected, so it's the perfect target."

Aisling looked at her. "Bandits?"

"Bandits," her grandmother confirmed with a sigh. "Just at this time last winter from the signs. We rode that way in spring to find them all dead. The door was unbroken. I think one of the bandits simply knocked, said he was stranded and could they offer shelter, and they let him in. The whole family down to the little children perished. Some of the walls had holes hacked in them, but all the hiding places were empty."

Lord Trovagh made an angry sound. "The family gave us every copper they had. There was nothing to find, but the bandits had tortured one of the women to be sure. They left sometime in early spring. Anyway they were gone by the time we arrived."

Ciara completed the tale. "We mended the holes in the walls, scrubbed blood from the floors. Then we sold the garth to Jontar's second son. The lad's smart, and so's his wife. First thing they did was hang heavier doors and shutters. We paid for the wood." She sighed. "We saw to it this time the door was on iron hinges inside, iron barred, and of real strength. There's been too much blood spilled in Elmsgarth."

For a moment her eyes were bleak as she remembered her own family, murdered in the Horning so many years ago. Ciara had been nine. She'd survived because her mother had got her into hiding and because the Lord of Aiskeep owned a debt. She recalled further and smiled. She'd repaid him by wedding his sickly son although that had been her wish and no sour bargain. Tro was her life and her love. She'd kept him alive through every winter ailment since, cared for Aiskeep as the old lord would have wished. And if that had meant she could never leave the keep or wander as she'd once dreamed, well, there had been other dreams worth the price she'd paid willingly.

Without thinking she began to hum her song. Aisling chuckled softly and joined in, singing the words in a small clear voice. It was an old song, come over-mountain with the Old Race when they first trickled across the bordering range to settle the wild empty Karsten lands. A peasant song, it had a gentle wandering tune in a minor key and words that were in one sense banal, in another, full of the meaning of life itself. But it changed key and strength in the last lines, soaring in power and passion.

It had been Ciara's favorite ever since Lanlia, her mother, had sung her to sleep with it often when Ciara was barely a toddler forcing herself to remain awake until the last lines. She in turn had sung it to the baby Aisling. Ciara sang the words softly. Oh, yes. Her dreams had changed. Now she hoped that Aisling would be safe and happy, that Kirion would be defeated and his puppet duke unstrung, that Keelan would come home in time to rule Aiskeep wisely but not yet.

She smiled at them all and sang louder. Keelan had picked up a pipe and was accompanying them. Old Hannion had trotted away and reappeared with his bagpipes. Hadrann had picked up two spoons and was providing a rhythmic accompaniment. The welcome home became noisier, more musical.

One by one servants trickled in to join the music making and dancing. Enthroned in his chair Trovagh laughed as he watched Aisling swung in the circle dance by Harran.

His gaze met Ciara's, long love and alliance shared in that glance. He stood. "Can't let the youngsters think we're too old to celebrate." He bowed low over her hand. "Do me the honor of dancing, my Lady." He spoke a few quiet words to Harran, and the tune changed. The impromptu band slowed then swung with the pipes into the soft "Lament for the Fallen Hills," written by a great musician after the Turning.

Trovagh danced, Ciara with him. It was a slow dance but beautiful and very graceful in its simplicity. They finished and sat again as the pipes broke into a wild swinging skirl of sound. Aisling was on her feet with Hadrann. Keelan joined them, holding Jonrie from Jontar's garth by the hand. Their feet hammered the floor as they leapt to battle and music and the equally old tune of "Beware, the Clans Are Riding!"

They danced it twice through before Ciara signaled a halt. Then Aisling came with her companions. They held food and drink and formed a small circle around Ciara and her lord. Ciara looked at them.

"And are the clans riding? I do not like the latest news Geavon sends from Kars. How close are you to fulfilling the geas, Aisling?"

The girl looked worried. "To the first question, I think the clans are too close. To the second, I'm not so close to fulfilling the geas." She looked at her brother, and he took over.

"Kirion's been stupid. I think Shastro wanted to weaken the Coast Clan. So he persuaded Kirion to use sorcery to make accidents happen to their leaders. However they had a few too many accidents. No one could prove anything, but the clan became suspicious and angry . . ."

"I heard about Franzo's army," Ciara said seriously. "Whatever possessed the pair of them to think the Coast Clan would not suspect more than 'accidents?' It's only fortunate it was Franzo in charge."

Hadrann spoke grimly. "That good fortune may be about to be lost." He quickly told the tale of Jedena and her death. Ciara whitened.

"Then the clan may ride to war. If Franzo rides there isn't a man who'd hang back. What would make him act?"

Hadrann considered. "He loves his half sister. She's half-mad with grief over her daughter. Franzo's youngest is heir now that Jedena's dead. Franzo is an old friend too of his sister's lord. It's all a big tangle, Lady, but I think that if anything else happens to his sister or her man, Franzo will forget his cool head and call out the clan. He loves others also; if aught happens to them it could be sufficient."

"What could happen?"

"Anything. Even if it looks like an accident it could be enough. The clan have seen too many accidents or coincidences. They no longer believe them to be either."

Ciara's eyes lit with anger. "That stupid pair. Karsten doesn't need another war, least of all one among ourselves. I swear there are times I wonder who cursed us. Ever since that half-wit of a duke and his Kolder friends." She looked at them eyes still furious. "And what about Kirion and the duke?"

It was Aisling who replied to that tart query. "It's difficult. I'm supposed to keep both of them from starting a war with Estcarp. That's how Hilarion read the geas. It means I probably have to see both destroyed because they won't stop otherwise, but that isn't simple. I can't attack Kirion openly; if I attack him and fail he'd use it to set the duke against me."

She bit her lip. "Kirion would probably start by claiming that Kee was involved in any attempted assassination of his brother. At the very least Shastro would have Kee murdered for that. He'd almost certainly have Hadrann killed too, since everyone knows he and Kee are good friends. One of the Escore leaders once said that assassination is easy and impossible to prevent if the assassin is willing to die and doesn't care what may happen to his kin afterward. But I do care, and I don't want to die either. Not when my death could refuel Kirion's sorcery for him. If I fail and survive he'd have that chance."

Ciara nodded. "I see the risk. What of the duke then? If he were gone Kirion would have to seek out another puppet?"

Hadrann smiled ruefully. "He would indeed and he'd make sure whoever had wrecked his plans paid for it, if he could find us. But he'd inflame the people against Estcarp for a start. He'd claim Shastro's death was a plot to weaken Karsten, and many would believe him. He'd step up raids across the border using that excuse to gather in others he can leech of power. I fear our disposal of the duke, even if we succeeded in that, would help rather than hinder Kirion."

Ciara glared, her own look exasperated. "So what do you intend to do?"

"We play a waiting game, Grandmother." Aisling's voice was soft. "If we are patient, then a time will come when we can reach Shastro without Kirion being able to claim it was Estcarp's doing. Or Kirion will relax his guard, and we can strike before he knows. Perhaps they will turn one against the other. I rode to war overmountain. I learned one thing from that: patience is seldom amiss; impatience is almost always an error. We wait."

Her grandmother nodded unwillingly. "If the geas will allow it who am I to argue?"

"Thus far I have not been urged to act more swiftly." Her face became thoughtful. "This business with Franzo may be a chance. If he moves against the duke again and then we struck, all would think it to have been the Coast Clan's doing. Kirion could scream against Estcarp all he liked. Few would listen to him."

"No, they'd be busy escalating a civil war against the clan," Hadrann groaned. "I swear, there are times when I feel like a kitten tangled in a ball of wool. There's trouble whichever way we turn."

Ciara laughed and stood. "To bed with you all, my children. Winter comes. Rest, play, relax, and make plans. Spring will be time enough to worry about what must be done." She walked across to where Trovagh sat watching the dancers. "Come, my dear Lord. Us for our bed." He gave her his arm, and they left quietly. Behind them the celebration continued until dawn. But like her grandmother, Aisling had sought her bed earlier.

She slipped between sheets warmed with a warming pan and was almost asleep when a heavy weight joined her. A purr made the identity plain, and she slid a hand down to fondle soft fur. Then she slept and dreamed. Under a soft spring sky an army lay at the Kars gate. Above the main tent floated the pennants of the Coast Clan and Franzo, followed by those of many septs and keeps. Down the main avenue of the city sped a group of men, soldiers by their gear.

They were followed by a hail of arrows. Now and again a man was struck and fell from his mount. At such times he was killed by the crowd who lined the way. They gave a path to the thundering soldiers but closed about the wounded, their faces twisted in a madness of rage and fear. The soldiers gained the gate and fought there. It opened at at last, and three men spurred free toward the safety of the war host outside. One reeled in his saddle, and another rode alongside to support him. As he did so he looked back and she knew the face. Franzo!

Her eyes scanned swiftly. The clan leader had come previously to talk in Kars, but it had not been in spring nor had his men died about him by treachery as he left. This could be a true-dreaming. Her gaze flashed about trying to see and remember all she could. It was late spring. How late she was uncertain, but it must be close to the summer's beginning. The trees were all in leaf, blossoms showed on some bushes that did not bloom until winter's chill was well gone.

In the camp outside Kars gate war horns were blowing. From behind trees horses dragged a siege engine, then another. She shivered. Franzo was not wasting any more time. Now he would beat down the walls first and talk after. Many were going to die in this harvest time of death. Into her dreaming mind came a small quiet voice.

"Your time, geas bearer, and three are stronger than one. Three and three: three to accomplish, three to aid." At the last words the voice faded, as did the dream. Aisling awoke in the darkness of her room. She lay, carefully committing to memory all she had seen and heard. Her heart raced, and she felt sweat gather on her forehead. She was afraid, yet if any action of hers would save the city and her land, then she would act. There was nothing she could do as yet.

She would talk of the dream and its meaning to Ciara but she'd say nothing of it as yet to her brother and Hadrann. She lay awake another hour, trying to tease plans from her tired mind, but at length she fell asleep again, to wake late but refreshed and hopeful.

Ciara, found sewing a new wall hanging, only listened and nodded. "You are right. Let it be forgotten until you must return to Kars. Such dreams sometimes do not happen because there are others involved whose actions may change the course of events. It may be that no army will be at Kars gate in late spring. It may also be that it is not the spring to come that was the one you saw. A city does not change swiftly, and Franzo is likely to look the same for years yet."

She picked at her feltwork as it lay across her lap. "It may also be that the dream is symbolic. If that is so it could mean powerful enemies are moving against the duke. That a rash act of his will bring destruction and death. Wait, say nothing. You will know when the time is right to tell your brother and Hadrann."

She watched her granddaughter run laughing across the courtyard later that day. Snowballs hurtled through the air. Ciara smiled, remembering another snowball the child had thrown. Kirion hadn't appreciated that. He hated the child then. If he discovered that Aisling masqueraded as Hadrann's cousin in the Kars court he'd see to it she never returned to Aiskeep alive—for more reasons than his precious sorcery.

On the other side of the courtyard Hadrann flung a snowball at Keelan. He followed it with another before launching himself at his friend. They rolled over and over in the snow, Keelan yelling for his sister to help him. Aisling joined the battle. Snow flew. Wildly excited, Wind Dancer jumped and pounced indiscriminately on any person who temporarily emerged. Nearby the Lord of Aiskeep leaned against a wall laughing so hard he was all but bent double.

Ciara grinned before strolling back inside to arrange hot drinks. They'd need them once they slowed down and the cold made itself felt. It was good to have them home. She liked Hadrann too. Her grin widened. And if she was not mistaken the boy liked Aisling. The Old Blood was often slow to mature. Slower to age. Slow also to look for a mate. It was not that the blood ran colder. But most males were in their thirties before they found women of more than mild interest.

Part bloods like Aisling and Keelan would seek out mates earlier but still later than those who were of Karsten incomer blood alone. Keelan was closing on thirty; thus far he'd shown little interest in women. Aisling was twenty-two now; she'd begin to look about her soon. Ciara considered what she knew of Hadrann. There was a little of the blood in the old lord, his father. It wasn't wise to play sex games with one's own people. Tarnoor, her lord's father, had never approved, and she thought that Hadrann's father too would be of similar mind. The lad had probably done no more than the usual brief adventuring about court or while on the Sulcar ship.

But he was getting ready to move on. That light in his eye was unmistakable to a woman who'd lived long and seen much. The daughter of Aiskeep, sister to the heir, would be a good match for

Hadrann. And Aranskeep was only a three-day wagon ride away, two by horseback and a good inn between. Aisling could come home often. She sighed. That was, if they all survived this spring; if Kirion and his duke lost their lives, and her three did not.

She stopped her gloom and poured boiling water into mugs. The hot lemony scent of the dried trennon leaves was wonderful. She inhaled with pleasure, chuckled, and thrust aside her worries. Hadrann would be here only another day. She'd not cloud his pleasure nor that of her grandchildren. Let Aisling live in the joyous present this winter. Spring would come soon enough.

In that she was wrong; winter lingered. Hadrann left for Aranskeep. Harran and his men fought a snowstorm to return. The storms dumped huge quantities of snow across the south of Karsten all that month and the next. Great fluffy drifts piled up and collapsed the roofs of less-well-built garths. The cold froze the deep mud of roads and the shallow water of streams. It even froze solid the river that ran from the Turned Mountains through northern Karsten between Kars City and the southern lands.

Karsten had not known such a winter in living memory. Whole families of peasants died, frozen to death in their hovels. While in outlying garths, even well-founded ones, the struggle to survive the cold was great. Many garth-folk did so only to find they had lost all their beasts. None from Aiskeep were suffering so, but then Aiskeep had a long and strong tradition. Their people were housed in weather-tight garths and their beasts in good solid barns. They had cut great stacks of hay, and two huge stacked banks of surplus firewood were placed, one by the keep and the other at the far end of the valley. Aiskeep people might suffer in the worst winters but never because their lord and lady did not care.

In a lull between storms Aisling was sitting hunched over a game of fox and geese with her brother. Ciara was sewing by the fire, Trovagh dozing on the other side. They had all risen early, woken by a short but ferocious windstorm. Once up, they had eaten well and settled by the old long fireplace. Sometimes in midwinter the snow abated for a few days or as much as a week, but it would come again. From outside the room came a growing commotion, and all raised their heads to listen.

Hannion's voice could be heard, then his footsteps before his head poked around the door. "Lady Ciara, there's trouble at Elmsgarth. Young Jarria has ridden to cry aid of us."

Ciara rose, Aisling came to join her as the garth-girl staggered in, old Hannion steadying her steps. The girl stood, shivering on her feet, half snow-blind, white patches of frostbite showing on her cheeks and nose. She lifted her mittened hands imploringly.

"Lady, the House of Jontar has always looked to Aiskeep. Help us now or we die, all of us." She slid to her knees as Aisling ran forward. Jarria's eyes rolled up, and she collapsed into the waiting arms. Lord Trovagh moved in his chair.

"Harran." His voice was quiet, but it cut through the babble of voices. "Call out the guard: yourself and eight chosen men. Prepare two wagons. Outspan spare horses. Heaviest beasts only to be used. Warmest clothing to be worn. All suitable arms to be carried. Hold the wagonloading until we can find out the problem that brought the child through such weather. Go quickly!"

Harran stayed not on the order of his going. They could hear his running feet as they hammered down the stairs and the stentorian voice of Aiskeep's master-at-arms as he bellowed orders. Both Ciara and Aisling were examining the motionless girl. Ciara looked up at her husband.

"Exhaustion mainly. Some exposure. We can heal the frostbite. Aisling can give her sufficient strength to speak briefly. But after that the child will have to stay here and be abed for a few days."

"Do it!" Aisling complied, reaching within to summon her healing power. He watched as the white patches faded to a healthy pink.

The eyelids fluttered, and at once he was on his knees, holding Jarria's hand. "Speak, lass. What is the danger to your kin? What aid can we give?"

"Bandits came, Lord. Mebbe a dozen of them. They could not force the house. They said they were desperate." The garth-girl spoke in short panting gasps. "They said they would destroy all our firewood if'n we didn't let them in. M'father said they'd destroy us for sure if'n we did. Better to keep them out an' mebbe live. They burned the winter wood we had stacked outside, all 'a it. When we still wouldn't open the door they rode away. After that we used the wood careful. Not enough left. House got awful cold, an' the little ones was crying."

She looked up, her face desperate. "'Twas night, but there was moonlight enough. I rid all night usin' our plow horses. I pray I ain't ruined them, but m' dad said I should ride. If I didn't make it 't would be a quick painless death. If'n I got here at least I'd live to claim the garth and mebbe you'd help us." Her hands clutched at his. "Lord Trovagh, please, they's dying?"

He looked down at her, his eyes gentle. "I have already given the word. Men and wagons assemble. My grandson and granddaughter will ride to the aid of Elmsgarth." Tears began to drip down her face, and he brushed them aside with a forefinger. "Child, child. You spoke the truth. Jontar's House has ever looked to Aiskeep, as Aiskeep has looked to your kin. When Ciara and I were less than your age Jontar fought beside us against bandits. We won then; we shall win now. Go with the Lady Ciara and sleep, knowing all you could do you did."

Keelan scooped her up as she slumped. Ciara led the way while Aisling went running to bring word of Elmsgarth's danger to Harran. He grunted.

"Firewood. Yes, but that weighs. A wagon of it shall go first, not too heavily laden and with food also. After that my men will ride each with two axes. In this cold ax heads can shatter if used too long or carelessly. Elmsgarth has dead trees still unused as firewood along its stream. We can cut those onsite and haul the wood." He studied her.

"Who else rides with us?"

Aisling grinned. "Who else? Keelan and I, of course. My grandmother will be tucking Jarria into bed right now, but she'll be sorting medicines as soon as she's done that."

Harran chuckled. "And complaining about not being able to go too, I daresay."

Aisling grinned in agreement. "I'll leave it to you. Kee and I'll be down soon and ready to ride."

She was gone in a rush as Harran looked after her. She was a good lass, and he thought that after a poor start her brother too was shaping up as a lord to follow. He bawled orders for Keelan's and Aisling's horses to be saddled. At home both rode Torgian mounts, which would deal well with the snow. He saw the horses led out and seized their reins from the stable boy, just as two figures came running toward him. At the door behind them stood Ciara. He could hear her indignant muttering from where he waited, holding the reins of the stamping mounts. He grinned. As he'd thought, his lady wasn't pleased others were having adventures without her.

His men piled into the wagons. The first team threw their weight against their collars, and the wood-laden wagon rolled. Old Hannion ran up panting to hand Aisling a small parcel. The gates opened, Keelan and Aisling cantered up to head the line, and the rescue party moved out, through the gates, along the winding road.

The snow had mostly halted for several days, but now the sky was leaden again. It had always been difficult to reach Elmsgarth in winter. This winter it could be impossible; yet they had to try. The lives of nine people depended on it. Aiskeep had never yet let its people down. This should not be the first time. The wagons rolled on down the rutted icy road as the first flurries of snow began to fall again from a slowly darkening sky.

XV

————◈————

On horses it was normally only a few hours ride to Elmsgarth, but with the drifted snow, the freezing temperature, and two wagons, it would take every minute until darkness and maybe longer. Aisling and her brother left the ordering of the mission to Harran. They ranged out along the road ahead. Their mounts helped to break a trail, and they watched for problems that might slow the procession.

Harran knew winter. For any garth it was one of the great enemies. The bitter cold taxed the endurance of the strongest as cold sapped their strength. The snowdrifts swiftly exhausted those who fought them. And here they fought not only snow and the cold but also time. But he had a trick or two up his sleeve. He'd taken double teams for each wagon. Then there were the two riders and the axmen with all the keep's spare shovels in the second wagon. Oh, yes. His lord was relying on him, and the lives of a family depended on his skills. Harran did not intend to fail either keep or garth.

For the first hour they plodded on. The men who rode the wagon were beginning to shiver. Then Aisling came riding back, her face serious.

"Drift across the road, not high but long."

Harran grinned happily as he turned to his men. "All right, lads. Here's where you earn your pay. Let's look at this drift." A mile farther on they found it. Keelan, who had climbed it on foot to investigate the extent of the piled snow, was just returning to his waiting mount.

"It isn't a bad one. Too deep for the wagons as it is, but we can either cut or tramp a path quite easily. Which do you think, Harran?"

Harran dropped from the wagon and studied the drift in turn. "Tramp it, I reckon." He waved, and the men climbed down to join him. Aisling had climbed the first wagon and was ready to drive. With her far lighter weight she'd be of most use doing that. Keelan took the second wagon seat after hitching both their saddle horses to the rear of his wagon. Harran's men linked arms in rows of three. They marched forward tramping the snow into a path.

Step by step they advanced again until they reached the clearer section of road, then they returned. Their breath stood like smoke plumes in the air. They warmed as they worked. It took no great length of time before Aisling could set her wagon in motion. She allowed the beasts to take their own time. They'd be careful. All she had to do was keep them in motion and on the tramped-down path. This she did until a call signaled Keelan that it was safe to follow.

It took several minutes after that for the men to climb back into the wagon. Harran took the opportunity to change the teams, the led teams coming up to replace the original ones. Aisling had taken her mount and disappeared around a bend ahead. Keelan followed to find her several miles later. He halted in dismay.

"Gunnora, preserve us. How in Hades did Jarria get over that?"

"She didn't. I'd say that she went off the road here and cut across country, which we can't do with the wagons." Aisling surveyed the drift. It was as high as her own head, and while she suspected it did not extend far it would be a massive weight of snow to move. Keelan looked at her.

"Could you do anything? The wagons are a fair way behind us. Harran was changing the teams when I followed you."

Aisling's eyes narrowed thoughtfully. "Maybe. I daren't exhaust myself. From what Jarria said I may be needed as a healer, but I learned a few things in Escore. There was one . . ." She spoke to her mount, who planted his hooves and stood stolidly waiting. Aisling's hands rose. Her fingers wove as she spoke words too softly for Keelan to hear although he could feel a kind of prickling in the air.

He reined his mount back to the bend, from where he could see if the wagons came in sight. Aisling was chanting softly now. He saw lights begin to dance over the drift, then with a rush they were gone, though not far. He heard the sound of brush creaking, then the snapping sounds of branches. He looked back in time to see the first wagon plodding into sight. The road ahead was clear as far as he could see.

Keelan kicked his mount forward cautiously. "What did you do?"

"I just shifted the drift a few yards. To that patch of brush." She pointed. "The snow on the brush swapped places. With some kind of balance like that, it's a much easier thing to do."

"Why the snow from there?"

Aisling chuckled. "Because, dear brother, it would also look a bit suspicious for Harran to find a completely cleared path, no snow at all, and us standing here looking pleased with ourselves. With that exchange there's some snow, enough to make everything look normal, and the shorter the distance I moved that weight, the less power I wasted. He knows both Ciara and I have some of the Gift, but he thinks it is only for healing. I would rather not burden him with the knowledge that my power is more than healcraft. Now, let's ride on. See what other problems we're going to face."

Keelan followed, mentally estimating how much extra time that drift must have cost the garth-girl. Jarria would have had to circle far out. Right around the large patch of brush, which covered many acres. The road bent away after that, and she'd have had to ride over more rough country to find it again. Chilled to the bone as the child had been it was a marvel she'd made it. Old Hannion had said the two plow horses had been exhausted but would recover with a rest, hot mash, a warmed stable, and good hay.

Keelan nudged his mount to overtake his sister's horse. He rounded the bend and halted with a groan. "Flames take the luck. That won't be so easy to deal with." Aisling muttered a searing agreement as she cast her gaze over the fallen tree. The look sharpened in both pairs of eyes simultaneously. Keelan dropped from his mount and walked up to touch the wood. He peered, rubbed the bark in his fingers.

"It's dry. I think the whole thing was rotten ready, just waiting for the next high wind."

"So it's much lighter than green wood," Aisling said slowly. Her head came up. "Kee, ride back to Harran. Tell him to keep the wagons moving slowly, but two men are to bring the loose teams up as quickly as is safe. We'll try swinging this to one side, just enough to let us through. Once we get to Elmsgarth a wagon can return with ax men. We slay two birds with the same shot."

Keelan obeyed. His mount had all the cat-footed sureness of the Torgian breed and cantered back along the slippery footing of the path with a comforting steadiness. Once back at the wagons Keelan spoke quickly to Harran. When the heir was done Harran called orders, and the loose teams trotted heavily off ahead. The wagon horses were reined in. They would keep moving but at a slow walk. They'd stay warmer than if they had to stand waiting for the tree to be swung aside.

Up at the tree Aisling and the men were fastening the chains to the roots. It would have been easier to pull at the other end. Branches were lighter, but they were also more likely to catch on rough places in the road or against other branches below the snow. To get a firm anchor it would have been necessary to affix the chains well down toward the trunk, which would also afford less leverage. The tree was large, but with two six-horse teams, they should be able to move it.

Aisling finished, checked her fastenings, and stepped back. A man moved to the head of each offside leader. They called, and the teams responded, huge hooves digging into the icy surface. The tree moved with reluctance. The beasts strained, snow and small gobbets of ice flying as their hooves gained traction. The tree creaked, scraped, and slid, branches grating against the roadway. Little by little it moved until just as the wagons reached them it was far enough to one side to permit them passage.

Aisling looked up. "Harran? Should we rest here?"

He looked up at the leaden sky. "Better not, lass. I think it will snow again soon. We should make time while we can. If we have to stop, then we can use that as a break, but until then we should keep moving."

The road wound on. Jarria would have cut across some of the bends, Aisling knew. When they came to another of the longer low drifts, Harran had the men out to tramp a path at once. They were losing a little time but not a great amount thus far. Brother and sister continued on. They'd been traveling well, covering almost half of the distance already. Keelan rounded the bend ahead of her, and she heard his groan, loud in the clear still air.

"What . . . ? *Ooh*, damn!" They faced a drift. It was huge. It towered above them as they sat their horses. Here the road fell away on either side as it followed a slight ridge. For that reason it rarely flooded, but it made it dangerous to leave the track. They couldn't go around. The country was rougher and even if they pulled back up the road and tried from there it would be impossible to take the wagons safely. Much of the lower land would be water-logged, ice over deep mud. The drift was aslant the roadway, and they could see it extended some distance. Keelan looked at his sister.

"What if you could exchange just part of it. It'd make a difference between digging that out all day and having to spend the night outside or having a chance." He looked at the immense barrier. "Can you do that?"

Aisling sat her mount, closed her eyes, extended her hands and reached out. Her mind mapped the shape and weight of snow. Tentatively she prodded the problem. It wasn't impossible. She could halve the drift, take away the portion closest. That would mean that Hannion had only to carve a path through one end. It would take an hour, maybe a little more with all of them digging.

But such use of power would leave her depleted. What if healing was needed for those at Elmsgarth when she arrived? Keelan was watching her closely.

"If we can't get to them they will die," he said quietly. "If we can but you cannot heal we may still save most. Use as little of your gift as possible, but use it." He grinned suddenly. "The wagons won't be up with us yet, and I have a plan."

Aisling slipped back into her silver mists. Along the side of the road where it dropped—that would be a good place to dump the snow. She wouldn't even have to lift the weight, just slide it over. Little snow clung to the steep slope, but the exchange would be helpful. She chanted softly, finally sitting back on her patient horse as the power flared. Snow cascaded down the slope while a dusting of snow appeared in its place.

She sagged in her saddle. After this Harran would have to do things the old-fashioned way. She watched wearily as Kirion took the short-handled wide-mouthed shovels from both horses. He scraped at the snow, then with hard twists of his wrists cascaded more snow from the drift face. He nodded at his handiwork. There, that looked as if two people had dug hard and vigorously for the hour they had been ahead.

He packed the shovels again. Reached over to take the reins of his sister's mount and drew it to one side. The wagons creaked around the bend and halted by the drift.

Keelan looked up. "Looks as if this is the break you had in mind. We dug away some of it, but Aisling should rest. She worked too hard in this cold." He allowed the eyelid away from the other men to drop slightly.

Harran had served the family all his life, and he'd known Ciara and Aisling had the Gift. He hadn't known until now just how much power Aisling had, but Keelan guessed Harran would still not be greatly surprised. It wasn't discussed, and both women were always careful to make no display even of their healcraft, but Harran could no doubt guess why Lady Aisling was exhausted. The master-at-arms said nothing of that, merely nodding to Keelan as the men climbed down to dig.

Keelan took the small lit brazier from the second wagon. He scooped snow into it and set that to melt. Beside it he placed a box filled with hay into which a lidded pot was tucked. It was still hot to the touch. Aisling had tied her horse to the back of the wagon and climbed in to join him. He waited until the water was bubbling, then added a handful of dried trennen leaves and several huge spoonfuls of honey from supplies. He filled a mug with the result and passed it to his sister. She drank eagerly and sighed.

"That's so good. I'll get down and help dig in a minute."

"No, you will not!" Keelan said firmly. "Once you've eaten you'll wrap yourself in a couple of blankets, dig into this straw, and go to sleep for the rest of the trip. I'll see you're wakened if we have to have your help. Otherwise you'll rest until we arrive at Elmsgarth." She would have objected, but he fixed her with a glare. "Don't argue, sister. This way you'll have some of your strength back to heal if you're needed. The men think you've spent the last hour or more digging."

"Harran won't."

"Harran isn't a fool, and he's served Aiskeep all his life. He'll know but he won't say anything. I wouldn't be surprised if half of them guess, but they'll say nothing either and they won't mind you sleeping awhile." He leaned over the wagon edge to call. Men arrived in pairs while their comrades continued to dig. They drank from the proffered mugs and accepted the plates of steaming mutton stew as Keelan spooned it from the pot in the hay box. Then they returned to digging. Aisling nestled into the straw, and her brother tucked her down into it. He pulled the blankets tighter and patted her arm.

"Sleep. I swear I'll wake you if you're needed."

Her eyes slid shut, and he watched protectively as her breathing slowed. Good. They'd have that drift cleared soon. Nine men digging hard make a path quite quickly. Although, he thought when he looked up to estimate the daylight left, it would be close. If there were no more delays they would make it before dusk. If not, they'd be arriving after dark. Not a good time to be out in winter. The temperature would really start to fall then, and the gods know it was cold enough now.

A candlemark later the road was sufficiently clear for the wagons to move ahead. Keelan swung onto his horse's back and rode ahead. In the second wagon Aisling lay curled asleep. Harran had threatened to call down curses on the head of any fool who woke her. Very soon after that the wagons met two smaller drifts. One could be tramped, but for the other Harran ordered logs tied to the chains and used the spare teams and logs as horse-drawn rollers to flatten and compress the longer drift.

With care they persuaded the nervous wagon beasts to surmount the flattened drift and continue on along the road. Keelan ranged up beside the first wagon and looked at the driver.

"Harran, if I rode ahead with a couple of the spare horses loaded with wood I could be at the garth in an hour."

The master-at-arms nodded. "So you could, lad, if the road was clear, which the main trail may well be until it ends. However, it's been some time since you visited Elmsgarth, and it was in summer. Remember how far it lies from the main road."

Now Harran asked that, Keelan did recall it. He bit back a string of oaths although his face was eloquent enough. His grandmother's old home lay at the end of a valley. Jarria would have left over two days ago. All that time the wind had blown, sometimes softly, but rising now and then to a howling blizzard. Within the narrow valley entrance the snow could have piled higher and higher, confined as it was.

Nor was it possible to circle and come at the garth from behind. The land rose past the valley entrance. The valley stayed lower, but on either side and behind it the cliffs became higher and steeper, the land outside the valley rougher. Nothing save a bird or one of the small mountain deer could have circled past the entrance along the tops and then found a way down the cliffs. And even the deer would most probably have failed. Keelan allowed his mount to pace slowly beside the wagon while he thought.

"What then if I ride to the valley entrance? I can return with word. If the gate is shut, then some could ride the spare team and come back ahead of the wagons. They could start the work. I could try my mount over the drifts then with them there in case I need aid." His face twisted. "I could take a light load of wood. Harran, there are small children there. Jarria said it was for them that her father let her try. Am I less?"

The man bowed his head. "No, Lord's heir. Go and do what you can for your people." He watched as Keelan turned his horse. Hoofbeats faded along the icy road. Harran looked back along the wagons and then up at the sky again. The promise of snow was closer. His lips moved silently as he prayed.

"Lady of the Light, Lady who watches over those who love, have a family in your care tonight. Gunnora, keep them alive until we come to them." He flicked the reins, and the heavy horses leaned harder into their collars. They were Aiskeep born and bred. Like the people, they would die trying if that was the need. It seemed a very long time before hoofbeats sounded again. Keelan was looking bleak.

"The whole mouth is choked. I don't know how far back it extends, but at the valley entrance it must be two men high, maybe nearer three. Give me the team and men. I'll start them digging."

From behind in the second wagon a long clear whistle rose up. Keelan grinned. "I think we have company again." He halted his mount until the wagon came level, then he smiled at the face that grinned back from the heap of blankets. "I see you're awake."

"I woke up awhile ago. I've been listening to what you said to Harran. Kee, it's easier to move things that have less weight on the one spot. Harran has snowshoes in this wagon. Two pairs. We could make a light sledge and pile that with wood. We'd have to walk and drag it the length of the valley, but we'd have a better chance."

He looked at her a moment. This was why Kirion had hated his small sister. She'd grown up at Aiskeep. She knew far more than Kirion ever would about the land, the animals, and people. She understood how to work with the land rather than to fight insurmountable odds and fail. Kirion had hated her for it; Keelan loved her. And her knowledge could save a family right now. He nodded.

"We'll be at the entrance soon. Get out the snowshoes and start the men making a sledge. Find a couple of ropes to drag it. It's the best idea I've heard all day." Her face flashed into pleasure as she moved to excavate the snowshoes, then seek out lead ropes brought for their mounts. Several of the men dropped from the wagon's tailboard to hunt out suitable pieces of wood while Harran contributed lengths of rawhide as ties to bind the sledge together.

They arrived at the snow-choked valley entrance still working feverishly. Most of the men moved in with shovels. Aisling fought her way up the shallow cliff. She was light, climbed like a cat, and could unobtrusively use her gift to help her. She could not travel along the cliff top but she could see what faced them. Once at the top she dropped a rope, and Keelan joined her. They stared along the narrow way. From below Harran hailed them and was in turn helped up. He studied the aspect carefully, then grunted.

"It could be worse. If we dig along one side and use a wagon to take the snow away we may be in before morning. The men will work until they drop. They know in some other winter it could be their family trapped." He glanced downward. "They have the sledge done. Take time to eat and drink first. Then go with the blessing of Cup and Flame." He started to scramble back down the rugged cliff face. Keelan followed. Aisling unfastened the rope, dropped it to them, and climbed down like a squirrel.

At the bottom she found the men looking over the sledge. It was crude but solidly made. It would do well enough, and wood was piling up onto it. With the load agreed, a couple of blankets were lashed over the chunks of wood to keep them from falling off if the sledge overturned. Aisling sat on the rear of the wagon as she ate and drank. Keelan sat beside her. Once their impromptu meal was concluded both stood. With no more than a hug for Harran from Aisling and a smile to their men from both, they marched forward, their snowshoes digging into the slope of drifted snow.

It was hard work, but within minutes they stood panting atop the drift. They bent to haul, and inch by inch the sledge came upward. Once it was there Keelan looked out along the snow-filled valley. He took up one sledge rope, laid it across his shoulder, and began to walk. Silently Aisling took up the other rope and fell in beside him. They moved with care. The minor snow flurries were thickening as they marched. Aisling cast a look upward. Harran and the men had better dig hard. There was a blizzard on the way.

Harran was anxiously aware of that. He spelled his men in twos, allowing each pair in turn to rest and warm his hands at the small brazier. Hot trennen was always simmering, and Harran, carrying his whetstone, kept the shovel edges sharp. Even snow or the granules of ice would blunt good steel in time. He watched the sky and his men alternately, praying for all of them and in particular the two who forged ahead of the rest.

Aisling was keeping up with her brother. On top of the heavy drift the going was almost easy. The wind had flattened the top, scouring away loose snow. She could see her footing plainly, and her lighter weight made the walking easier. Keelan was stronger but he sank deeper and had to use more energy to walk. The sledge glided along behind them.

Keelan glanced over toward the valley wall. The drift height was dropping slowly. Through the Elmsgarth valley the wind often blew almost in a direct line from garth to entrance. It was this which had piled the snow up high, but at this end the drift was quite a lot lower. They reached the end of the main drift and looked downward. Climbing down would not be difficult; the snow looked to have slipped right to the ground. But Aisling measured with her eyes.

"The snow down there must be still deep. Look at that tree. I remember the way the branches grow. From that it looks as if the snow is at least waist-deep along the track to the garth."

Keelan didn't recall the tree but he wondered. "Are you sure that's all? That isn't very deep even for us. There must be some other problem, or Jonro would have been out chopping wood. Even if the bandits took his ax he could still gather broken boughs." He thought back. "Harran said there's dry wood along the stream. Why wouldn't Jonro have broken those up? He could have made a temporary ax of some kind."

"Let's go down. We take it carefully, use probe sticks to check ahead. You're right. There must be something else."

They moved down the drift until they and the sledge halted at the bottom. Aisling moved to the trees and stripped a long branch from one. With that probing ahead she stepped out slowly, Keelan behind her hauling the sledge. In this way they progressed until halfway down the valley, well past the trees that should have been firewood for the garth if they were desperate. Then Aisling stopped, her face puzzled as she probed. She squatted, shoveling snow away.

"What is it?"

Aisling leaped back, her eyes wide with horror. Her hands flew as she chanted, the words gabbling out as fast as she could mouth them. She finished with a word of command that made the snow shimmer silver momentarily. Then she stared at Keelan, answering the anxious question in his face.

"Rasti!" she said.

"What? They're from Estcarp and the border there. I thought they never came so far south."

Aisling was back checking the burrow mouth. "They have them in Escore too," she said. "Huge ones, far larger than the ones from Estcarp. These are the Estcarp ones, but there must be forty of them. It takes three or even four to equal Shosho's size but they're crazy in winter. Sometimes they form a pack and then they fear nothing. They must be recent; Jarria said nothing."

"So what do we do. It certainly explains why Jonro isn't out cutting wood. I suppose these things have burrows all down the valley from here?"

Aisling looked down. "Probably not, but Jonro would bring a pony down to haul back the wood. After that he'd not risk it again." She pointed. "See that white branch sticking up out of the snow over there? I think that's a bone for a horse or pony. Dying peacefully of the cold's a lot better than being eaten alive. But Jonro must be dead or injured; otherwise he'd be out cutting wood regardless." She toed the burrow edge.

"I can deal with them, Kee. But I made a mistake just now. I panicked when I found that burrow. I used too much power making sure they didn't move against us and I could feel them beginning to stir. I can put them into a deeper sleep. The smaller the animal the more often it needs to eat. In a coma they'll burn up all their fat and die in a few days. I can spell that to happen, but then I'll collapse. Leave me here and get the wood to the garth. Get a fire built up, then come back for me. It's the only way." She made her look stern and held her gaze on his until he nodded.

Aisling dug out the protective herbs she always carried. Some of Hilarion's teaching could be used as well. Around her throat was the pendant. Rasti were of the Dark, the pendant of the Light.

Keelan stood watching her prepare. So he was to leave her in the snow, was he? Leave her to freeze and die if her warming and protective spells failed? No, that he'd not do. As a trained witch she was in charge while she was conscious and where the problem could be solved best by her gift. She could give him orders, but once she fell over, it was up to him what he obeyed. He hid a rueful smile. She'd be furious, but better she was alive and angry than dead while he explained to his grandparents how he'd let it happen. He waited for his time to come.

XVI

---◆---

Aisling set her feet firmly. Before her was gathered a sheet of bark with the herbs crumbled in a tiny heap. Dry twigs lay in a circle around the herbs. In a separate pile lay nine leaves. Three from each of the two main types of trees that grew in Elmsgarth. The last three contained one each of the other bushes. The shrubs that clumped toward the garth-house. Her hand went up to close about her pendant and she freed it. With the chain shortened the pendant lay against the pulse as it beat in her throat. She could feel the power rising with each thump. Keelan stood behind her his sword drawn.

He stood firm even when silver mist rose to enclose his sister. From within it Aisling was chanting again, very softly. Fire came to her call, blooming a soft gold wavering back to silver and then to gold again. With a final word she sent it to the herbs, adding the dry twigs as the herbs burned. Sweet smoke rose. The fire blossomed, but beneath it, a barrier to the snow, the bark remained whole. The fire flared, a candle reaching upward in a warm gold pillar of light.

Aisling bowed her head in salute as she took up the first three leaves. "Elm, guardian and namesake, come now to my call. You for whom the home was named. Who sheltered my grandmother in time of death. Who stand tall about the garth protecting it from the winds that blow. Come elm, share your strength again that those who have cherished you might live."

She felt the spirit of the elms stir. "Come elm, how often have you shared your sap with those here. It has salved their wounds. Brews from your bark they have drunk and been healed. They know you, as you know them. Always have they given you honor. Come elm!"

The spirit woke. A faint sense of inquiry came to her. She opened her mind showing the rasti, showing how Elmsgarth's people could die without aid, reminding the elms how the people here had ever given honor and how if the rasti struck or even remained in waiting, the honor would be gone. The power flowed into her then, freely given.

She added the leaves to the small fire and took up those of the willow. "Come willow! You who have lined the streams a hundred hundred years. Whose bark has soothed fevers, relieved pain, and aided winter sickness. Come willow! Whose spirit has been honored by those who share the land." She felt it stir and smiled, her voice becoming coaxing. Old Willow disliked to wake but it would. "Come willow, aid those who have cared for you, those who are part of you as you are part of them." The power roared, given at her asking.

She flung it into the fire, which soared up, a slender pillar of light. Then she took up the last three leaves. Her voice was gentle. "Come winterbloom. Come lawleaf. Come cheel! Healers, friends, and sharers of the land. Share healing now, share strength and friendship." These spirits were weaker, more fragile but they came at once. She felt the power slip into her softly, and she bowed her head. All living things had spirits; if honored they thrived.

Here in Elmsgarth there had long been a tradition. Once each year in spring there was an honoring of the trees. A ceremony that thanked each species for returning to life after winter. Water and a small portion of some sort of nourishment was given to the smallest sapling of each type. Across much of Karsten this custom had lapsed. Aisling smiled; in Kars they would laugh heartily at the very idea. A peasant folly. Not in Elmsgarth. Here the ceremony had never died. Trees died or lost their leaves outside these lands. It was different here.

In Elmsgarth trees lived longer, grew larger, and were slower to lose their leaves, swifter to regrow them in early spring. Ciara had learned from her mother, Lanlia, who had learned from her husband's mother. Even when Ciara had left her home, left her dead behind, she had still insisted on returning each year for the ceremony. She had taught it to those who held the land after her.

Aisling wondered now, even as she chanted, combining the power given her, aiming it carefully, if perhaps someone from the previous family would have survived if they too had honored the tradition? They'd promised, making it clear that they were only humoring a superstitious fool when they spoke of it to Ciara. It had been too late to refuse them the garth they'd paid for. It was almost certain they'd never carried out their promise. The girl shrugged. The trees hadn't saved Ciara's family, only the child herself, and that had been as much by her own strength and sense and that of her mother. But then, they had not called on the spirits that day.

Aisling slowly moved her hands apart. The power within the flames split, each half bending away. No time to worry about ideas. Now she must keep control. That was hard. Raising the spirits had been easier. She stretched the flames, teasing them out into long slender ropes of fire. They burned, a woven rope that shimmered gold, silver, and a sparkling blue-green.

She pointed with each hand, signaling with an index finger that each rope was to circle the rasti burrows, then to meet again. They must blend in a perfect circle without weakness. They obeyed, swirling out and melding to form the chain that would bind. Aisling began to chant again, crafting the power.

> *Those within the line of fire,*
> *enemies are to all that is*
> *within this garth that honors well*
> *spirits of land that here do dwell.*

She switched to the older tongue that would bring the power flooding.

> *Long have they lived*
> *and shared your lands.*
> *Given you honor from their own hands.*
> *All is one over earth, under sky.*
> *Let enemies sleep, never wake—and die!*

She waited tensely as the power circled, then, with a lowering of her hands she emptied it out around the circle. Within herself she reached to the rasti: no pain, no fear, just a slow sleeping into death. She regretted the need, but they would die anyhow. It was just over halfway through the winter. If this rasti pack was so desperate already, then they would not survive the rest of the cold time.

The power sank into the earth. Through her pendant, clutched in one hand, she felt it touch the small sleeping bodies. They slept, deeper and deeper. Coma. She laid that upon them. Then she laid on the bonds that would keep it so. Behind her Keelan was alert. He saw her eyes open and caught her as she slumped.

"Is it . . . ?"

Her whisper was fading. "It's done. They will never wake." Her eyes closed. Keelan scooped up the slender body and laid it on the sledge. It would be a hard bed but only for a brief time. Another quarter candlemark on foot. Maybe a little longer with the sledge. He turned to look down the valley and bit back a cry of dismay. The garth was gone from his sight, so too the trees that towered along one side of the valley and encircled the rear of the home. Nothing but whiteness. He knew the snow had returned.

By now Harran and the others must be almost through. Harran knew Elmsgarth; he'd see to it that they kept to the track along the left-side valley wall. It would give them all shelter right up to the garth-house even if the way was slightly longer. But Keelan was out in the valley center. No wall to guide him and his sister helpless, depending on him to save her. He cupped his hands about his mouth and took several slow deep breaths.

Then he removed his scarf and wound it about his face. He had to breathe slowly. Gulping air this cold could freeze his lungs. He took up the sledge ropes, tied them, and stepped into the loop. It lay across the back of his neck under his jacket collar, then passed under each arm. That way he had his hands free. He must not try to move too swiftly. A fall could break an ankle or leg. If he did that they would both die. Even a sprain would be dangerous.

For long moments he was almost paralyzed with fear. If he moved he might kill them both. Then common sense reasserted itself. If he didn't move they'd both freeze anyhow. He muttered a quick prayer, then leaned into his harness. The sledge moved slowly behind him as he plodded forward. The snow was falling more heavily, blinding him, sliding coldly down his collar. He adjusted the scarf as he walked.

Keelan considered as he advanced toward the unseen house. He'd been facing directly up the valley when the snow came. The wind in winter almost always blew down the valley in one direction but not in a completely straight line. It veered slightly to the southwest. So if he traveled directly into it, hopefully he wouldn't walk in circles. And old Hannion had told him that a man moving in a snowstorm tended to veer to his right. Keelan paused a moment to study his hands as he held them up. If so then the two angles should cancel each other out.

Right. He leaned into the harness again remembering the lay of the valley. From here he should meet nothing until the garth-house. He would still have to walk with care though. The stream ran swift in the thaw and it had carved out a deep bed. If he strayed too far to the right he could stumble over the edge. A step at a time he marched forward. The wind and snow on his face, icing his lashes, blinding him to more than one step ahead.

The sledge was becoming heavier. It dragged him back as he leaned harder into the rope, or maybe it was the blowing wind. Each breath was icy, biting into his lungs with every inhalation. He paused and turned his back to it for a brief respite. Aisling lay wrapped in the second blanket they'd used to hold down the wood. He touched her face and smiled. She was warm. He took up her hands in their heavy knitted mittens and chafed them briskly. Hands could become frostbitten even if the body was warm.

He could do nothing for her feet. His own should be well enough. He swung his arms, beating his hands against his sides. Then he took up his march again. A step, another, his prints in the snow behind him filling in almost as fast as he made them. He glanced back to see that they left a line, the most recent footprints still deep. The next shallower, until some five steps back the print was a slight dimple in the snow. The sixth was gone, filled in.

He shivered and moved faster. He was counting as he walked. A man walked a steady four miles per candlemark over country that wasn't too rough. He'd had less than a mile to go when the snow started to come down. Maybe only half a mile. So count that the sledge halved his speed. He shouldn't take more than that one mile's speed. He'd gone perhaps half of that before he began counting.

His brain felt fuzzy. What was he trying to work out? Oh, yes. If he'd come halfway, how many more paces would it take to reach the garth-house. But he'd lost count. He'd have to start again. One, two, three. Was Aisling all right? He should check. Twenty-six, twenty-seven . . . His own feet were feeling numb. Not frostbite, please not frostbite. Fifty-two, fifty-three— Oops, he'd lost the wind again. He had to walk straight into it. Not easy. It hurt against his face and eyes.

Eighty-six, eighty-seven— He was sitting down. How had that happened? He didn't remember falling. Maybe he'd stopped for a rest. Can't rest here. Must get to the garth. See Aisling is warm. Build a fire with the wood. The wood, where was it? Was he to cut down trees? He remembered loading axes into a wagon. The axes would be following. That was it. Someone was bring axes—and wood. Oh, and he must keep counting. Thirty-one, thirty-two, thirty-three . . .

He was sitting in the snow again. How foolish. Aisling said sitting on cold ground gave you— What did it give you? He couldn't remember but he mustn't sit down, Aisling said. Aisling, his sister. Yes! He had to get Aisling somewhere and keep the wind on his face. It stung. He didn't want to do that but for some reason he had to. He had to count too. He giggled breathlessly as he tripped and almost fell. Two left feet. Yes. Two, three, four, . . .

Why was he bothering to count? For that matter why was he bothering to walk when it was so hard? If he lay down very soon it would be lovely. He could sleep and be warm. It was warm now, really. He'd could lie down for a while in the warm and rest. Aisling wouldn't mind. She was a good sister to him. She'd understand. Keelan took another step while he considered where to lie.

Something huge and solid loomed up, and he ran into it. The impact half-jerked him from his stupor. "Ouch!" He ran his mittened hand down the heavy planking. It was either the house or one of the barns. He turned to follow the wall and remembered Aisling as the sledge dragged at him. Lords of Light, he'd been dying on his feet. He could dimly recall the decision to lie down and sleep in the lovely warm snow once he'd walked just a bit farther.

Well that the wall had been there to wake him. He groped down its length until he reached a door. He looked above that. The garth-house. Long ago someone had carved a spray of elm over the door to the main house. The carvings over the barn doors were different. He groped for the latch. The door swung open slowly to reveal a room full of still bedding-wrapped bodies. The fire was out. Ash, a soft gray-white on the hearth. No time to check the garth-folk. He must see to the fire. He hauled the sledge inside, slammed the door, and turned back to the hearth.

He tore off his mitten, thrust a hand into the ash. Warmth—it might not yet be dead. He leapt for the sledge, dug hurriedly beneath Aisling, and produced the bundle of kindling. He dived back and stirred the ash with a stick. Coals! One still showing the faintest hint of red. He laid a handful of twigs on it, blew with all his strength, and prayed. Gunnora, Lady, these here are in your hands. Let there still be an ember. He blew again and watched with incredulous joy as the tiny flame crept up.

Gently he fed it another twig and a second as it grew. At last he had a fire, a healthy vigorous infant fast growing in size and strength. He sat back on his heels, hands to the warmth. Of all the blessings given to man, surely fire was the greatest. He reveled in the growing heat. Then he remembered Aisling. He untied her carefully, lifted her, and laid her by the fire, wrapping the blankets about her. Then he took her wrist and felt for a pulse. It was there. She'd trusted him with her life, and he'd not failed her.

But had Aiskeep come too late for these others? He stood, half-reluctant to find out in case he had. Slowly he walked to turn back the blankets on face after face. His fingers groped for the throb of life in slender children's wrists, in wrists sun tanned, work thickened.

In wrist after wrist he found life. Only in one could he find nothing. He piled more wood on the fire, then went into the freezing air briefly to gather snow, a pot of which he placed by the fire. Then he sought out the larder, assembling the ingredients for a mighty stew. That pot went onto the swingle over the fire.

He dug around and found soup bones, added some of the snow water, and other odds and ends. That would cook faster. Then he sat down to feed the fire and luxuriate in the warmth. It was as if he'd never known the heat of fire before. Now he loved it. He took it to him and held it tight. It was life, a talisman against winter and death. A sun men made to bring back summer in the midst of the snow. From the bundle beside the fire Aisling lifted her head and smiled at him.

"You made it."

Keelan smiled back. "Guess we did." His smile widened until he was grinning like a fool, unable to stop as he found tears leaking down his face. He grasped her hand. "We made it in time. They're alive. I haven't done more than check, but they are, Aisling. They live, all but one I'm not sure of." His voice broke, and he sat in silence holding her hand.

Aisling lay gathering her strength. Her mind scanned her body slowly. No damage: the spell-sleep had protected her long enough. The strength of her gift was still a lot lower than she would wish but it might yet be sufficient. She touched Keelan with her mind, evaluating. He was weaker, exhausted still from his walk to reach a haven and save her. She quietly augmented his strength. There was nothing else necessary apart from a possible slight frostbite in several toes, but that was minor.

She'd heal it later if she had the power left. For now she had to know about Jonro's family. She could feel the life sparks about her. Keelan's glowed strongly; the others all were much weaker. They would live but they would wake disorientated, starving for food.

They could wait though. She touched them lightly. They'd all live. But there! One dimming to nothingness. She staggered to her feet, leaning on her brother. He guided her across to the limp form, guessing which patient she needed to see first. Aisling laid back the bedding to study the wan face.

Keelan moved the covers lower, and his breath hissed out. Aisling looked. The rasti. Jonro must have gone to chop wood by the stream. The vibration of his ax had roused the rasti, and they'd streamed forth to battle. She'd sensed no injured in their burrow, but then they were cannibals. Any injured would have died quickly. Jonro had escaped. His family had bound his wounds and laid him nearest the fire. Keelan was peeling the bedding lower and lower.

Aisling shuddered. From toes to lower thighs the man's legs had flesh bitten from them. There were bites up his left arm. Several more were scattered where his clothing must have pulled back to bare his flesh as he fought the horror. Keelan was staring down.

"Can you heal all that?"

"I could but I won't." Her flat gaze met his own stunned gape. "Kee, listen. If I make this as if it's never been, someone will talk. If I healed every wound I still couldn't make them forget that the injuries had existed, but Jonro won't die. The wounds are already starting to fester. Rasti are filthy little beasts. It's that which often kills humans bitten by them. I can heal the infection that is beginning. I'll burn it from him so it does not return."

Keelan was turning Jonro's arm. "One of them has severed a tendon in his arm."

"I know. I can fix that too." Her grin was wry. "I'll collapse again once I've done what I have to. You're going to be the only one on your feet until Harran gets here." She studied the injuries on the unconscious body before her. "When I'm done there'll be no more infection. He won't develop wound fever, and any real damage like that tendon will have been healed as well. But the bites will still be raw and open. He'll have huge scars." She took in a breath.

"Get clean cloths, salve them, and bind them on only as firmly as it takes to keep them in place. Tell Harran when he arrives that the deeper bites should be stitched. That's if I'm not awake again by then." She turned back to her patient. "Now." Her hands closed around Jonro's throat. Her thumbs lay softly feeling the pulse through questing fingertips. She drew strength from herself. Her power was dangerously low, her gift straining to obey her demands.

She first burned out the infection. Then she treated the wound fever also starting to race through his blood. Her mind sought out the injuries that could disable: the severed tendon in the arm, the fraying ligaments behind one knee where another bite had savaged flesh and sinew. She sought out any more that could leave a farmer unable to work his land. There was nothing, only the weakness of body that was dragging him down. The endless cold followed by the shock that was draining him.

She took up the last of the Gift she had to give, thrust it home, felt his heartbeat strengthen, and sagged to her knees. Dimly she felt her brother lift her back to the warmed blankets beside the fire. Keelan stroked the hair back from her forehead.

"An interesting life we lead," he mused. "You keep falling down. I keep picking you up. Just make sure if you continue falling over, that you do it when I'm around." He tucked her blankets around her more securely and moved to stir the stew. The soup would be ready shortly. Keelan stretched, sighed, and moved to open the door. Outside the blizzard was picking up power. Gunnora aid Harran and the Aiskeep men out in this.

He poured soup into a bowl, found a spoon and settled to spooning a bowl of soup into every patient in turn. With that done he refilled the soup pot and set it to heat again. It had just begun to bubble when sounds from outside caught his attention. That sounded like Harran's voice. Thanks be! But just in case . . . The door opened, and the first man entered to find Keelan lining an arrow.

"All's well, lad. It's us."

Keelan lowered the bow. "How do you know that makes it well?"

Harran gave him a hurt look. "Now, now. And after all we did to get here." His nose twitched. "Is that soup I smell?"

Keelan laughed. "It is and it's ready to drink. Everyone here is alive. Jonro's family have all had a round of soup, and there's mutton stew cooking too." He took the bowls handed him and began to fill them with the steaming savory concoction. "Sit down and get outside this."

Harran checked off the Aiskeep men, saw to it they had a bowl each, then sat. He was weary to his bones, but they'd made it. Aiskeep had not failed its people.

Ten days later, during another lull in the storms, the Aiskeep men rode home. Jonro was recovering well. He'd have terrible scars but no physical impairment. Everyone else had been up and about for days. Aisling had slipped out twice to monitor the rasti. The first time their life sparks had flickered low: they slept, dreamed of blood, and the hunt, and the joys of mating. The second time no sparks remained: the rasti were gone. Only the small corpses remained, deep in the cradling snowdrifts.

As soon as the ground began to thaw Jonro's family would dig them out, taking the pelts with care. Unmarked pelts were valuable in the market. Then they would fill in the burrows with stones. Elmsgarth would leave nothing that offered an easy refuge to the rasti should others come this way.

The rest of the winter was quiet. Aisling was happy about that. The spring looked likely to bring enough excitement. They still had to find a way to dispose of Kirion and the duke. Neither would be exactly an easy target.

*I*n Kars Shastro was bored most of the winter. He enlivened that by taking a new love, a slender blonde woman, the wife of one of his courtiers. It amused him to flaunt her in the man's face, but it was the courtier's own fault. Marry a lovely innocent woman and talk constantly about her before your duke. What did the fool expect? Besides, she hadn't been that innocent, or Shastro was no judge. He was annoyed to find them both gone near spring. Fled Kars and away. He shrugged petulantly. There were always other lovers.

Kirion had spent a busy season in his tower. Varnar was coming along nicely. He dreamed often now. Sweet dreams of his loving beautiful wife and his adorable little daughter. Kirion could see that even when awake the man was remembering. It would be so amusing later, once he was ready to let his toy know the truth. He was interrupted by the need to bespell a courtier's wife. Then again, later, to scry for the fluttering idiot and her gawk of a husband.

He wasn't pleased at having to lay aside his experiments. Shastro was less pleased to hear that his prey had gone to the Coast Clan. He hadn't known the dratted woman was kin to one of their bloodlines. Spring came, quietly surrounding the city with greenery. A season when life began, at least usually. This year the opposite might apply.

XVII

———◇———

Keelan, Hadrann, and Hadrann's "cousin Murna" arrived back
in Kars as soon as the roads were open. With them came the
attractively marked domestic cat who had made friends with the servants the previous year. The servants were pleased to see the animal
again. It was pretty, a ferocious hunter, and somehow things seemed
to go better when the beast was around. Mice had reinfested the old
palace, and the cat caught them by the score. He caught rats too. He
often took the trophies down to the cook in the lower palace.

Wind Dancer, being intelligent and fond of his stomach, had
made certain the cook favored him from the start. Now, as soon as
they were settled in, he caught a plump incautious rat and stalked
down to lay it at the head cook's feet. She beamed.

"So, great hunter. You have returned to help me." She surveyed
the rat with disgusted approval. "That was well done. One less of the
filth to steal my food. Here, a gift in return." Wind Dancer received
a thick slice of venison carved from the evening roast. He accepted
with pleasure and departed to eat it out from underfoot. Wind
Dancer liked the palace. The prey was abundant and often unwary.
As something of a rarity he received attention, admiration, and a regular trickle of delicacies.

Out in the south of Karsten cats were becoming less rare
amongst the keeps and larger single garths. But the original line

brought in by Ciara's trader friends were not prolific breeders. They tended to produce only once every two years, usually twins or sometimes a trio of kits. Unwary kits had accidents, and adult cats had their own problems, so across Karsten the population growth rate was insufficient to fill the demand. Kits were cherished. Cats were admired and often loved.

Keep lords and their ladies were seldom stupid. It had been observed over a couple of generations that a keep with cats had fewer diseases and more food safe in storage. So from Ciara's feline friends the ripple of keep cats had moved out slowly. But the lords of the North and toward Kars were often unfriendly to those of the South. Cats were slow to come to that area and slower to appear in Kars City. Although after many of the court had seen the disguised Wind Dancer, there had been a number of attempts to obtain kits.

Wind Dancer approved of that, just as long as the courtiers understood that they were the cat's humans, not the humans' cats. People were there to serve and protect. Aisling, who knew his feelings, had grinned and stroked his ears.

"Don't worry, brother in fur. If they ill-treat a kit it will leave them, and a dozen will stand ready to take it in. They want your kind to kill mice and rats. Much good that will do them if they must shut the cat away to keep it with them. And Shastro likes cats." Wind Dancer who knew that very well sent her a picture of the duke forgetting his dignity to trail a string and feather.

Aisling giggled. "I know. I'll talk to him about a cat law, that they may not be ill-treated nor confined." Her thoughts were wistful. In some ways she liked the duke. He was interesting to talk to when he forgot to be pompous. He was weak; that was the trouble. Yet there was an underlying dark side to the man. She'd never forget their brief visit to his dungeons. She knew too how he used his lovers. She'd already picked up the gossip from several court ladies. They'd talked about the girl and her young husband who had fled.

Aisling had imagined herself bespelled as Shastro's prey and felt sick. How must it be to know that your emotions, the love and desire you felt were produced by a spell? And if that spell wore off unexpectedly, as by all accounts had happened here, how would you feel to know you'd lain with a man you despised? Wounded your adored husband, flaunted your lust before the court, and through it all, been only something used by your ruler, who should have been the first after your husband to protect you?

Aisling shivered. Thanks be that she was immune to that sort of spell. They wouldn't work against one with the amount of witch blood she bore. But it was for that reason she was Hadrann's "cousin" and very plain. Shastro would not wish to be on bad terms with a large, powerful, and independent keep. Rann's father was friends with other keep lords in his area. Nor did Shastro desire plain women.

And yet, she sighed slowly. She could have liked the duke. He wasn't the fool many believed him to be. Aisling sighed again, reminding herself of other things about Shastro. He was self-indulgent and determined to have his way at all costs—to anyone else, that is. He was overly conscious of his rank and too ready to listen to flatterers. Under all that, though, there was a child who'd been starving poor once and who'd loved his cousins. A man who, years after their deaths, still grieved over their loss.

But both Kee and Hadrann believed him beyond saving. Even if Kirion was dead, Shastro would still lean toward finding another powerful advisor who'd get Shastro anything he set his heart upon.

She heard footsteps and turned toward the door. Hadrann entered, his gaze worried in a glowering face.

"How much did you hear about Shastro's last woman and her man?" His tone was abrupt.

Aisling sat up. "She was married to young Damon. He's third son to Lord Darrar. She's the daughter of a minor lord from somewhere along the South Coast." She thought back over some of old Lady Varra's gossip. "I was told the girl's illegitimate. No one seems to know who the mother was, but the girl was pretty. I thought her to be only around sixteen or so. I never had much to do with her, but I never heard anything bad. The gossips say Shastro had Kirion love-spell her. My dear brother did a damn good job because Shastro flaunted her all over the court, and the girl had no shame at anything they did even in public."

"What about her husband?"

"Nice boy, about eighteen, seemed to be really in love. From what I saw last season, so was she. I'd have said she adored him. That's why I think Kirion must have laid one of the more powerful spells on her." Aisling looked disgusted. "Poor girl. But they did get away. I heard they bribed a gate warden to let them out after dark toward the end of winter. Once Kirion discovered who it had been, Shastro had him flogged to death as a warning to the others. I don't know any more than that." She eyed Hadrann. "Why, what's going on?"

"More than either that idiot Shastro knows or Kirion considered." He sat, thumping into the seat with a furious expression. "I've just had a long letter from Geavon."

"Geavon, why's he writing to you?"

"Because he usually has his own man bring his letters directly to you. This time he was in a hurry, and it came by the Kars messenger, which means others saw it. If he writes to Keelan someone might be interested. And if he writes to you they'd ask why to my obscure cousin instead of to me. But it was meant for all of us. Keelan will be here in a minute." He stood again to wander restlessly to the table where wine stood waiting. "A drink?" Aisling nodded, and he poured glasses of the gentle southern vintage, adding water. Keelan arrived, took one of them, and drained it, holding it out for more.

They sat to listen as Hadrann unfolded the letter. "I won't read it all. Geavon has gone into a whole lot of genealogy and things about old family feuds, but the gist of it is bad for Kirion and Shastro. It could be even worse for Kars." He turned to a page and read. "Lord Darrar is one of the old school. He's never let an insult go unanswered. As for the girl, maybe none at court knew her mother, but it's been no secret to some of us. Her father is Lord Ershmon. As a lad he took a woman as mistress who was believed to be his half sister."

Keelan grunted. "So his father wouldn't allow him to marry the girl?"

"Exactly. But it seems he did love her. He later wed a woman who proved to be barren. His mistress had two children, and he kept her decently. Never cast her off and continued to see her discreetly. Once his wife was dead Ershmon had the children declared his heirs."

"So what's this Ershmon like?"

"One of those lords who live only a step or two above their peasants. Poor land although quite a lot of it. Sea coast. A bit of wrecking now and again maybe. They get by. His line has held the keep there since the incomers first arrived. But if he has little he does have his pride. What Shastro did has touched that." Hadrann looked up at them. "Would that what Shastro did were all."

He returned to the letter. "I'll summarize. We should get out of Kars without wasting time, Geavon warns. It's a long tangle of history, but briefly Ershmon's girl is related to the Coast Clan through her grandmother, who is still alive and powerful as the daughter of Franzo's great-uncle. Darrar is also related to the clan through a different connection. The two children got away, straight into a bad storm."

"They died?" Aisling's voice was distressed.

"Worse in one way; they survived. But the girl had been pregnant to her husband. They only were sure a few days before Shastro had Kirion bespell her. I won't go into all that seems to have happened about that, but she lost the baby and almost died. She may have been left barren. Her husband got her back to their keep and to safety. But to do it he took chances with the storm. He lost a mitten, pushed on to get her under cover and developed frostbite in that hand."

"He lost it then," Keelan said in knowledgeable tones.

"Yes. So Geavon says. If the two of them had died, their families might never have known much of what had been going on. Or if they learned, it would have been months later, when some of their grieving would have been done and they'd have been less likely to be rash."

Aisling sat straighter. "Do we take it from that, they *are* going to be rash?"

Hadrann nodded. "According to Geavon the two are in Lord Darrar's keep. Since they got there Coast Clan people have been coming and going, and listening hard. It isn't a very nice story. A duke who wanted a girl and didn't care she was wed, didn't care she was with child. Didn't care for her name, family, reputation. Didn't care for her life even. Didn't care about her husband or the lad's name and kin. As a result the girl may be barren, and the boy is left one-handed. The names of both keeps have been smeared with stinking mud."

Keelan whistled softly. "And instead of two dead to mourn, they have two live embittered people reminding everyone daily of the insult simply by being alive and present."

"Yes. Geavon says that there's no doubt this time. The whole of South Coast and its clan is seething. Allied keeps are sending men. They see it as not only an insult to the clan but also a clear indication of just how the keeps and their lords are disregarded. Franzo is already assembling an army. If we don't get out of Kars now, we'll be under siege."

"But if we do, what guarantee is there that it will work out our way?" Aisling questioned. "We need to see Kirion stripped of his sorcery and dead. Shastro deposed at the least. I daresay Franzo would like to ensure Shastro's death, but what does he do about Kirion?"

"What? Kill him too, I'd think."

Aisling shook her head. "Kee?"

"No. Kirion will say he merely obeyed his duke as is his oath. He will spread his hands and look innocent. He'll be horrified at the things Shastro forced him to do. He'll wriggle, use his power to cloud minds and issues. He'll hole up in his tower and make sure he's forgotten. When a new duke is in place and things calm down he'll drift out again. Once he finds what the new ruler wants most, what his weaknesses are, he'll move in on them. In a year or two it will be 'my Lord Duke,' and 'my dear advisor' all over again."

Hadrann looked from one to the other. "And you both think that will happen?" They nodded. "So we need to stay." His voice was heavy. "But not here in the palace; there are too many eyes. Better we take a small estate in Palace Lane." He studied the last page of Geavon's missive. "According to this, Franzo could arrive in another week if he's moved almost impossibly fast. But Geavon thinks three weeks is more like it. Aisling, you and I will go out to consider houses this minute. Kee, I want you to ride to Geavon."

"For supplies?"

"Clever man. Yes. Take a couple of packhorses. Hire them if you have to. Buy food made to last. Nothing fancy, siege food: journey bread, spiced sausage, dried meat, hard cheese. Get what you can from Geavon and buy the rest carefully. Not too much of anything from the one market stall. We'll try to find a storage place in whatever house we move to, a hidden cellar or secret room perhaps, one that can be secured and spell-hidden."

"What of servants?" Aisling asked. "The three guards we had at Jarn's perhaps. The brothers and their cousin. They aren't clever men, but they're solid. If they take our money they'll not betray us."

Hadrann nodded. "Good idea. I'll start looking at estates, you find the three guards and see if you can hire them." He turned to Keelan and grinned briefly. "Hire a woman too if Geavon can recommend one who doesn't mind getting her hands dirty and would be loyal. Bring her back with you."

"Anything else you'd like me to haul to Kars? A few guard dogs maybe, or would you prefer geese?"

"Geese are a good idea," Aisling said seriously. "They're excellent watchdogs, they won't cost to keep, and they taste a lot better than dog meat if we get desperate."

Her brother groaned. "Why didn't I keep my big mouth shut? I have to bring back half a pack train of siege supplies, a woman who'll probably boss us about, and a herd of geese to keep us awake half the night."

"A flock," Aisling said absently. "Geese come in flocks. You could bring a half dozen hens too."

Keelan stared at her in horror. "I'm going, in fact I'm gone, before you think up any more awful ideas." He vanished through the door with the air of a hunted man. The two left behind laughed.

"Hens!" Hadrann said, grinning. "Do you have any idea of what house we should hire?"

Aisling grinned. "I do. Come and look at it first. If you don't think it's right we can split up. You keep looking, and I'll find the guards we want. But I remember Merrian, Varra's granddaughter's best friend, talking about it one afternoon when I was chatting with Lady Varra. Merrian's family keeps the house because they have to. Something about her great-grandfather's will. He was a merchant, and I think she's a little ashamed of that."

"Merrian's at court now?"

"Yes, her whole family is in the palace. I'll talk to her at once." She departed, to return three hours later, brandishing a ring of keys.

"Perfect timing. Merrian and her lot are leaving on a tour of family outside of Kars. They leave in three days and they don't expect to be back for a month."

"By which time if Franzo's army has arrived, they won't be getting into Kars to rejoin us."

"No. Merrian says to look over the house. If we like it we can rent it by the quarter year. I didn't tell her we were planning to live in it ourselves. She'd have wondered why we'd want to leave our suites in the palace. I said we were expecting family and needed a place to put the servants and lesser family members."

"Good work. Let's go and look over the place."

They did so, enjoying the chance to leave the court awhile. They peered into every corner of the old house, walked about the grounds, and forced open long unused doors to various sheds. The place was a good size as to grounds. Perhaps five acres enclosed by an immensely thick stone wall built from huge stone blocks. Aisling looked at that. The original builder must have been paranoid, she thought. Or else he'd had some very dangerous enemies.

Around the house the land was landscaped with a formal garden and beds of brightly flowered shrubs, many of them with medicinal uses. But there was ample land left unused. Someone had planted that with lassin grass. The grass grew rapidly to some three inches before stopping until it was grazed down again. Then it swiftly grew back. Geese and hens would do well left here to live as free-range birds, Aisling thought.

She looked back at the house. It was two storied. Hadrann had counted seven bedrooms in the main family section, all double-sized with their own hearths. The servants quarters had another two and a small dormitory. The house was massively built, like its surrounding wall, and old. It would have secrets. And with Merrian's attitude, perhaps secrets no longer remembered. She returned to the building, found an empty room, and locked the door. She took out her pendant, called the mists, and chanted softly, allowing her power and her will to fuse with her question.

"Let what is hidden be revealed. Let that which is shut be laid open to me." She sank into the silver mist, opened her inner eyes, and saw. Here and there in the rooms, gold light flickered. She noted all the places it indicated, then turned her inner eye to the grounds about the house. Under an edge of the house, extending well out across a corner of lawn she could see the light outline a shape. She followed that with the inner eye. It carried on under the house and out again.

Aisling studied the area, memorized the outlines and dimensions carefully before relaxing. The silver mist slipped away as she tucked her pendant back in concealment. She wondered if Merrian had even known that her despised house had what seemed likely to be large cellars. Hadrann could be heard walking down the corridor toward the room. Aisling unlocked the door and seized his arm.

"This may be better than we knew. I spelled to seek out hidden places here. I expected hides within the walls. Any merchant would have those. But I think there are cellars as well." She recalled the thin line of gold that had arrowed away to the surrounding wall. "There may even be an escape tunnel. Oh, let's go and look quickly. I can pay Merrian this evening before her family leaves, if I'm right."

Hadrann laughed, catching her hand in his. They ran along the passage and down to where the large ancient kitchen stood in all its stone-slab paved glory. Hadrann looked down. That was interesting. He could vaguely remember something he'd seen once as a young boy. His father had taken him to visit friends in a keep far south. They had a keep kitchen that was paved with large flat stone slabs. The keep's heir and Hadrann had run and played, and his friend had shown him a secret.

Watching him think, Aisling remained silent. Hadrann turned

around, letting his eyes glide over everything to be seen. He halted at the huge old hearth. There were two. One on each side of the kitchen. That was not uncommon. You could use whichever was not affected by the prevailing wind at the time. But in the southern keep, he remembered, they'd had another use. His eyes fastened on the massive iron spit and the wheel to which a handle could be affixed.

You could roast a small ox on that or—his memory broke open and poured out—you could run a cord through the wheel, move the brick in the hearth corner then, and reveal an iron bolt set in the bottom of the hearth stone. He was doing so even as he remembered. The bolt was there. A cord? He stared about and saw a light iron chain hanging on the hearth wall. He looped it around the wheel, finding that it had a small hook at each end. One around the bolt, one back to fasten the chain. Then he heaved on the spit handle.

The stone hearth lifted slowly. Aisling gaped. That was clever. Using the spit and wheel, one strong person could raise the stone. To make it impossible all that was required was to remove the spit handle. Of course another could be found. But if she was right and an escape route led from cellars beneath the house, then those fleeing could be long gone before the cellars were again open. The slab came up and tilted back to lean against the rear hearth wall.

Hadrann looked for Aisling to find her examining the other hearth. "Rann? I'd say this one works the same way. Both entrances probably connect somewhere below. That way you can escape through whichever one isn't being used to cook at the time." She rose to look at him thoughtfully. "And we could keep a stack of light kindling, paper, and heavier wood by the side of the hearth not in use."

Hadrann understood at once. "So the last one down lights a fire, maybe someone else can use a lever to hold the slab a couple of fingerwidths open." He watched Aisling as she experimented with a couple of abandoned lengths of firewood on the hearth. "Pull the paper and kindling over the slab. Prop heavier wood up to fall in when the kindling burns in a few minutes. Then drop the slab slowly."

Aisling giggled. "And Eloiha! No one came this way." Hadrann laughed at the expression she had used, it was one much favored by street conjurers when making a leaper disappear.

"I think we can go this way though; there's steps, with the first a wide one. Room for two to stand there. Let's go."

They climbed down quietly after Aisling had returned from locking the wall door and both outer house doors. Aisling paused to look at the stone slab. The underside had two iron brackets set in the stone. Even better. Intruders might be certain the slabs lifted, but with a bar through these they'd find raising the slabs impossible. She pattered after Hadrann. For some time they explored underground. The cellars must have originally been dug and paved above to hold all the merchant's considerable goods. Aisling discovered two more hides in the cellars walls and finally the escape exit.

Dust lay thick on all surfaces. One of the hides held a solid scattering of the small gold coins of Estcarp mixed with some from the Dales. Aisling picked them up carefully. Estcarp coins could not be used as they were, but there was nothing to prevent her hammering them unrecognizably flat. They could then be given to Keelan. If he came back quickly they'd already decided that he should make another run for siege supplies.

She looked at the heavy weight of coins wrapped in her scarf and the layers of ancient dust. "Merrian never knew about any of this."

"From the depths of this mess," Hadrann said, poking his toe into the dust, "no one's been down here since her great-grandfather the merchant died. If they'd known of the cellars, they would surely have known there were hides. They'd have come looking for that gold." He glanced at the scarf. "How much is there anyhow?"

Aisling hefted the parcel in one hand. "A lot. Enough for Kee to

load several more packhorses. Geavon will exchange this lot for
Karsten coin. With the amount of room down here we could empty
a whole pack train of supplies without completely filling all of the
rooms. I wonder if the merchant had this lot dug. And if he did
would anyone remember?"

Hadrann looked closely at the walls. They were stone blocks,
massive in most places. He shook his head slowly. "I doubt it. I think
this may date back a lot further. Maybe to when Kars was unwalled.
It was more likely to have been built by some lord. This wasn't just
storage. We still have an escape route to find."

They found it after a long time and another pause to use Aisling's gift and her pendant. Even knowing where the entrance had to
be, it took more time to discover the secret of its unlocking. The
tunnel was narrow, only a fat man wide and the height of a short
one. It came out in two places. A shorter branch of the tunnel exited
in a clump of ancient trees against the wall but within the grounds
still.

The second and longer branch exited into where a small deep al-
cove slanted deep into the street side of the surrounding wall. It held
a statue of Gunnora, and someone standing within the tunnel end
there would be able to look through the artfully pierced carving
around the inner shrine and see if anyone was present. No one however would be easily able to peer back. There was a small plate of
iron that covered the hole when not in use.

With the inner latch unlocked, the whole statue swung outward
on its plinth. That left a gap just wide enough for a person to slip
through and appear to have been innocently praying within the
niche. They returned the way they had come, ending up in the
kitchen once again. Aisling nodded to herself. She'd find Merrian at
once and pay her a three-moons rent.

Keelan returned two days later. With him came three laden
packhorses and a strapping six-foot woman with brawny arms and a

love of cooking and cleanliness. Her family had been in the employ of Geavon's line for generations, Geavon sent word. Amara could be trusted with their lives. She had brought a half dozen loudly furious geese and two sacks of ruffled hens. Keelan had hoped for a short rest and was not pleased to be handed a scarf full of hammered coins and told that he was leaving again at once.

But he went. He had heard enough from old Hannion. Aiskeep's retired master-at-arms had lived through sieges of Aiskeep twice and remembered them. He'd shared his wisdom on the subject with Keelan, plus other older tales of longer and more desperate siege times. So too had Ciara, who remembered both of the sieges of Aiskeep and recalled too the stories her father-in-law had recounted. Lord Tarnoor had ridden as a soldier in his younger days and had seen much.

Merrian was paid and departed with her family. Hadrann moved his entourage, complete with poultry, into the Palace Lane estate, where Keelan joined him in the kitchen on his return.

"Any sign of trouble out there yet?"

"Not yet," Keelan grinned wryly, passing Keelan a mug of mulled wine. "But I had a nasty feeling between my shoulder blades as I rode through the gate. I think someone was watching Kars. Maybe several someones. If Franzo is coming he'd be a fool not to have scouts watching Kars and spies within the gates. When do our three guards move in?"

"Two more days. They'll sleep in the servants' quarters. I said they have room and stabling but no board since I'm paying them five silvers a week. They're happy with that, and I'd wager Amara will slip them the occasional meal. I just don't want them demanding food as of right. There may come a time when we cannot share."

They looked seriously at each other. Wind Dancer, who adored the new lodgings, pranced in with his fifth rat, and released the undamaged beast to scurry hysterically about the kitchen. The solemnity broke up in disorder.

The guards arrived, settled in, and Aisling was left counting the days. Geavon had believed it would take Franzo three weeks at most to assemble his army and surround Kars in a siege. It had been eighteen days since then.

Franzo was right on time. His scouts appeared openly the next day. There was a prompt exodus of people who recognized the danger, and an immediate influx of others with similar motive, who believed city walls afforded sufficient protection. All were permitted their decisions without hindrance. But two days later Franzo marched in three thousand men with their gear and surrounded Kars. The siege had begun.

XVIII

⟡

t first the siege created few problems. Those who'd fled outnumbered those who'd entered. The first great pack trains of spring supplies had arrived earlier, and there was ample food in the city. Kars water came from a number of deep wells. Estates like the one Aisling and her companions had rented had not only well water but also great rainwater tanks. Aisling had entered these through an opening in their roof and swept them clean. Then she had reconnected the pipes that would carry the water from any rain showers down from the roof area to fill the tanks. In one of the cellars she found a pair of hand pumps.

"Rann, where do you suppose these fit?"

He walked over. "Down outside by that lowest corner. I think I saw two outlets there." They carried their prizes outside and discovered he was right. Keelan looked at the angles.

"Whoever built this was smart. He sloped the tank so that even a few light showers will let you pump water from here. And when the tank is full the weight of the water will make pumping much easier. But I wonder . . ." He thrust bushes aside and gave a yelp of triumph. "Look, Aisling. There's a trough. It would have been meant to lie under the spout of the second pump."

The stone trough was filled with rubbish, and bushes had grown up around it. Hadrann called their guards and gave orders. By the next day they had the wide trough cleaned and hauled into position. It would serve to water the horses. Amara had found two large shallow pans in a dust-laden storeroom. One was complete with a pierced metal lid. This was cleaned and placed by the trough. The geese and hens could drink through the holes without the geese climbing in to foul their drinking water. The other deeper lidless pan was filled for them to swim there instead.

With the siege a reality all three were able to buy openly. Other prudent families would be doing likewise. Aisling visited merchants with her necklace of hammered coins. Supplies flowed into the estate. Hadrann received a large allowance from his father. Keelan and Aisling had gold of their own. They poured out all they had. Soon traders would realize that gold had no value against the necessities now barred from entrance to the Kars marketplace.

The three bought more food, firewood, bales of hay for the horses, and grain for both them and the poultry. The hens had settled and were laying busily. Amara was delighted with that and produced a stream of delicacies based on a number of eggs. Aisling had looked over the amount of grassed land and purchased ten yearling sheep as well. These grazed on the wilder parts of the estate, keeping a nervous eye on human comings and goings.

On his second trip to Geavon's keep Keelan had taken their carriage team and left them in the keep stables. In the livery stables the three now had only a riding beast each, and the guards had a pair of plain mounts of their own. Aisling would bring the horses back to the estate and feed them there no sooner than she must. Geavon had exchanged their found coins for other coin of Karsten. He'd then refused to keep the found coin. Keelan expressed their gratitude before using the exchanged coins to buy supplies from those leaving the city. Those fleeing had no time to waste. Gold was gold.

The siege wore on for weeks, then a month. In the city tempers grew short, as people gradually understood that the siege would not go away. Food prices climbed slowly, then more swiftly. After two months Keelan retrieved his horse from the public stables. The animal was added to those that grazed the pasture about the estate. Rain had fallen earlier, the short but heavy showers of early spring. Most came in the early hours and lasted half a candlemark but with violence. The great stone water tanks had begun to fill.

Amara's kitchen storerooms were filled to bursting with bags of flour, sugar, salt, and other necessities. Even through the first month there'd been those willing to sell for gold. They would regret their decision soon enough. The three took every opportunity to eat at the palace. Shastro kept his usual table, ignoring the growing shortage of food. He would have what he wanted, or why else was he duke of Kars. Wind Dancer came with them and hunted happily. He made certain to bring his prey to the cook each time.

She praised him eagerly. She'd lived through sieges herself. The rats this clever beast offered might one day be all that stood between her and starvation. By late spring the estate's tanks were brimming. But in the city other items were in short supply. Shastro was being unpleasant about servants who ate his leftovers. He claimed they stole the food and sold it. Three horses now grazed about the house. The guards had sold their two mounts. By mid summer Aisling considered the sheep and poultry thoughtfully.

"I think we may have to kill a sheep."

Keelan stared out at the tiny grazing flock. "Why now. The grass looks good still?" Hadrann who was present, answered that.

"It is. At the moment the grass growth keeps pace with the number of mouths to eat it. But with the heat the growth will slow soon. If we have too many grazers then there will be no grass left by fall. We have to kill some of the sheep."

Aisling joined them in studying the flock. "Two, I think. We could offer one to Shastro for the high table. Have you noticed? I think he and Kirion have been arguing. Kirion never appears at the evening meal any more."

"I noticed. And Shastro scowls if you mention our dear brother. I think there may have indeed been some unpleasantness."

Aisling grinned cheerfully. "Well, you know the saying 'When thieves fall out, honest citizens come into their own.' I guess Shastro wanted his own way. He'd have told Kirion that he didn't care how it was done, he should just get rid of Franzo and his army."

"And Kirion would play Hades trying to explain no one has *that* amount of power. He can't just spell three thousand men and a whole siege camp's worth of gear to vanish."

"Shastro would ask what use was power if it couldn't be used when you needed something done . . ."

"Kirion would say the duke had done well enough from Kirion's power thus far—"

"Shastro would lose his temper and demand something be done right now, or else he'd find someone who could—"

"And our brother would call him a fool, tell him to see if he could do that, and stomp off."

"The duke would . . ." Aisling started, then reconsidered. "No, he wouldn't dare have Kirion arrested in case Kirion wouldn't lie down for it. Anyhow, he needs Kirion's powers. They'll be using them to spy on Franzo and cause mischief. There's a lot you can do to an army even using minute amounts of power. Kirion would know tricks to make those out there very unhappy."

Hadrann had been listening with amusement. "You both know your brother and the duke well. So what will Kirion have been doing?"

Aisling snorted. "Oh, that. Well, seeing that tether ropes fray or come loose on the most restive mounts. Making yeast for bread making work too fast so all the loaves spoil. Seeing that a cook adding a handful of salt to a cauldron of stew slips and adds the boxful. Encouraging rain to move in right over the army and stay as long as possible."

She laughed suddenly. "When I was over-mountain one of our witches caused a plague of fleas. It drove the other side totally crazy. The brutes got into everything from bedding to armor. Everyone was scratching. There's a host of things like that one can do. It doesn't take a lot of power and it drives the other side wild."

"And if they do that, then it confirms the Coast Clan's belief that Kirion and the duke are behind every bad thing that has ever happened to them," Hadrann said soberly. "If they get into the city after a year of those sorts of tricks, there'll be no mercy. They sack the place, kill a lot of innocent people whose only fault lies in living here."

Aisling nodded. "But if we had something they wanted," she said slowly. "If before they crack the walls we could offer reparations? You said Franzo isn't a cruel man? If Kars showed it had risen against those who'd caused all this . . ." Her voice trailed off as they thought.

"We don't want to go up against Kirion directly," Hadrann said at last, "but if Shastro did, one or the other of them would lose. We might be able to deal with the other then. Franzo would accept that the two who'd caused his grief and all the clan deaths had been punished."

"Which brings us right back to where we were when we decided to stay," Aisling said in exasperation. "I must see both are dead and beyond creating further evil. The only things we've achieved in all this time are that we're trusted by Shastro and haven't yet been unmasked by Kirion." She departed slamming the door in a way that showed the siege was shortening her temper as well.

Keelan looked after her in surprise. "That isn't like Aisling."

Hadrann shook his head. "Kee, what happens to cities when a siege works? When the besiegers break in? Maybe if their leader has declared the cityfolk as wolfsheads?"

Keelan recalled tales. "They burn buildings, steal everything portable, murder the people, even children."

"And what happens to the rich, more especially to the noble-women?"

Keelan went slowly white remembering his grandmother's tale of her own family. "Dear lady. Why did we let her stay?" His eyes turned to the wall as his face slackened in relief. "The cellars. She'd be safe down there with Wind Dancer. This place won't burn. There's water, food, bedding. She could be safe down there for months until Franzo gets his men under control again. We can say that. She'll feel better then, won't she?" Hadrann said nothing. "What is it?"

"Kee, that land where she was, she rode as a soldier a few times, didn't she?" Keelan nodded mutely. "She's always known what she risked. She isn't stupid. She knows about the cellars; she was the one who found them. But she's made friends, Kee. And she knows what will happen to them if Franzo's men break in. But she knows too that we can't risk bringing half the court here to hide."

Keelan wrinkled his brow. "We could hide a lot of women and children."

"For how long? The army could be occupying the city for months if they broke in. You can't hide and feed dozens of people. We don't have that many supplies, and people will be people, Kee. Some woman would decide she wanted her husband. She'd sneak out and if she was caught she'd talk fast enough with what they'd do. Or some child would make a game of getting out and be seen." He sighed heavily.

"Aisling's thought about all of that. We talked about it while you were at Geavon's keep. Our removal of your brother and the duke is more important. With them in power the whole of Karsten will be at war with Estcarp again in less than a handful of years. Set that against a few hundred dying here in Kars, and there's no contest. She knows that." He looked at his friend. "You and I know it too. But we don't think about it. Aisling does. She sees what will happen to those she likes in the court. She feels helpless, and it makes her angry."

"I see. I hadn't thought about any of that. Listen, Rann. She needs to feel she's doing something. Let's ask her if we can spy on Shastro without Kirion knowing. Even if we can just eavesdrop it will make Aisling feel she's making a move toward our goal."

Hadrann brightened. "Not bad. Let's find her."

They discovered her sitting in the palace suite window seat with Wind Dancer sprawled half across her lap. She was looking out of the window at the land as it sloped to where the army lay encamped. She glanced up as they entered and spoke directly to Hadrann.

"You said Franzo isn't a cruel man. What would he do if women and children fled the city now. Before his men become too angry and too hard to hold back?"

Hadrann stood in silence. At last he answered. "I think he'd let them go unharmed. He'd question them, find out all he could about the city's condition. Get some idea of how long they may hold out. But he's not cruel, and he's smart as far as a siege and soldiers are concerned. Men with those they love to protect will fight like madmen. Men with those they love safely away are more likely to listen to an offer, and a man who shows himself honorable will be heard if he offers terms."

"Then we could get some of the court women and children away."

"If they'll go. Talk to old Lady Varra. Her knowledge isn't restricted to gossip; she also knows people. If it were me I'd talk her into leading the escape if she'd agree." He grinned briefly. "Even Franzo would listen to her. She's a wicked-tongued old battle-ax, but she has a good heart and a lot of sense. The women would follow her, where as they'd hesitate to go with anyone else."

From his sprawl on the seat Wind Dancer uttered a low chirrup. Aisling caressed his ears. "And what have you in mind, my furred one?"

The picture came clearly. Wind Dancer was being let down in his basket. The window on the far corner of the suite was set into the outer city wall, the palace occupying one corner of that wall. Aisling recognized the scene. It was the time of the previous brief siege, when Wind Dancer had been their spy. She watched his sending as he scouted the camp, was fed and indulged by Franzo's cooks, and amused the men with his games as he listened to their plans and talk.

Then his picture changed. Again Wind Dancer was being let down the wall, but this time it was summer in the city. He jumped lightly from the basket with a sealed note tied to his collar. Wind Dancer's pictures stopped abruptly. He'd made his contribution; now he wanted his ears stroked some more. Aisling obliged as her face lit. She began to speak quickly, and across the room two other faces became animated with hope.

The arrangements took time, but days not weeks. The old battle-ax, as Hadrann had named her, saw the sense and the advantages of their plan. She counseled them to say nothing to the duke. She'd see to it that the others kept their mouths shut. Shastro might use the idea to attack Franzo. Let him do that later, not at a time that would endanger women and children. They could admit what they'd done once their refugees were safely away.

Two days later a cat basket was lowered slowly from a window high up over the city's outer wall, a section of which was formed by a portion of Shastro's sprawling palace. It was in that section the Aranskeep suite lay. As far as anyone but the servants knew, Hadrann, Keelan, and "cousin Murna" were still spending much of their time in the suite. It was a convenient ruse, allowing them to use a single window that looked down from the city wall.

Wind Dancer's basket settled with a soft thump, and the big cat leaped lightly out. His collar bore a letter, sealed carefully, addressed in large writing to "The Most Noble, the Honorable Franzo, Lord Commander of the Army of the Coastal Clans." Inside it was a frank plea from Hadrann. He reminded Franzo that he was known to him, mentioned briefly that the duke might well hold out until the last, in which case the city would be ravaged by soldiers driven mad by the waiting and the deaths of comrades.

He said that fearing such, Hadrann had persuaded women and children of the court to flee the city, to take refuge with friends and family who had keeps close enough to be reached. Food was growing short in the city, and soon riots would begin in the low quarter. He begged Franzo to treat these innocents with kindness, to allow them safe passage and an escort if Franzo could spare the soldiers. This he asked in the name of a brief but honest friendship.

Several hours later Wind Dancer returned. His collar still bore a sealed letter, this time addressed to Hadrann. Franzo had responded with generosity and sense. He offered an escort, a wagon to carry the weary, the old, and the very young. Safe passage to neutral keeps for all women and children trusted to his honor. He ended the note with his name and titles in full.

Hadrann read them out slowly, his lips stretching into the first genuine smile in days. "He's sworn to carry out his offer. With that full signing he's staking his own and his family's name that all will be carried out as he's said. Any soldier who lays a hand on a woman or child does it as to Franzo himself. And he wouldn't take at all kindly to it." He looked up. "Aisling. Go and ask Lady Varra to attend us. I want her to read this for herself."

The lady came, read, and pronounced herself satisfied. "I know that boy. Not terribly bright but honest. If he swears to something, he'd rather die than fail. And he's decent. He'd hold his men back from sacking Kars as far as possible, but he knows that may not be far if the fool who names himself duke holds on beyond what is sense."

Her mouth set grimly. "And he will. Him and that Gunnora-cursed sorcerer. They'll ruin us all and never understand how it happened."

She rose, winced, and swore. "Thrice damned joint ills. It's sad to be old. Never live past your children. Not that any of mine had the sense the gods gave hens, and their offspring aren't much brighter. But I'll get them and their children away." She grimaced. "Not that I fancy being lowered down any walls, but if I'm the first down the others won't be so afraid to join me." She looked at them, a sudden bitter humor gleaming in her eyes.

"Don't think you've pulled any blindfolds over my sight, the three of you. I know there's something else going on. But I have the feeling I'd approve if I knew what, so I'll let it be. I'll have everyone here and ready to leave once the revels become rowdy tomorrow night. I'll order the children to bed after an early meal so they'll have slept well by the time we must wake them to go."

She stumped to the door and turned to look at them. "Watch out for Shastro once he finds we're gone. He's always been one to act before he thinks. My advice is to go and tell him the next morning what you've done. Say you did it to help him and make him believe it. Mention how much less food he'll be using now. Tell him it was all my idea if you wish. He'd find that likely." She gave them an evil grin and departed.

The hours slipped by. All spent the day at their rented estate, asleep in various beds. Wind Dancer cuddled beside Aisling. He could feel the emotions that roiled within her and he knew the feel of his fur against her skin was comfort. The three humans rose and attended the duke's usual lavish evening meal. The waste of food angered Aisling, and she was dull company when Shastro sought her out. Aisling took the opportunity after that to slip away, as the after-meal dancing became boisterous. She was joined in the Aranskeep suite by a steady trickle of nervous women and excited children. Hadrann and Aisling's brother arrived after midnight.

"Kee? Did anyone notice you leaving?"

Her brother snorted. "Notice. Most of them wouldn't notice if I walked in naked. Shastro's blind drunk in a corner with his latest leman. She's throwing him walnuts, and he's trying to catch them in his teeth. Kirion left before we did. The rest of them are cross-eyed with drink or so stuffed with food they've gone to sleep in their seats. Let's get this started." He dug into a corner chest to produce knotted ropes. Aisling took one rope, fastening it securely. The other ropes the two men were busily tying to the corners of a leather sling.

Lady Varra plodded forward. "Right. Gently now. My old bones don't like bumps." She turned to look at the apprehensive group behind her. "You lot come after me. Don't waste time. Any silly fool who decides to stay after all, I daresay these good people won't throw them out after us. But if the siege breaks the city, she'd be better off being thrown through a window. Soldiers play longer games." She indicated three children to the fore. "You three come as soon as I'm on the ground."

She arrived swiftly below, lurched from the sling, and raised an arm. At once three children, great-grandsons and a granddaughter, were climbing nimbly down the knotted rope to join her. She laid her arms over their shoulders and peered about. A man approached and bowed. She spoke so quietly that none about could make out the words until he looked up and moonlight lit his face. The old woman nodded to him and signaled with the wide arm sweep that meant all was well and the others should join her.

Above them, Hadrann allowed a small smile to linger. That was Franzo. The commander himself had come to make sure his honor was not besmirched.

By ones and twos they lowered those waiting. Some whimpered in fear, but none changed their minds. When at last they were done almost two hours had passed and over fifty women and children were crowded below. Hadrann looked down. Then in a clear emphatic movement he cast off the ropes to land in a tangle below. He knew Franzo would understand. Any others who came down would not be doing so with Hadrann's blessing. It was also a warning that others might.

Hadrann watched as below the women and children were formed into an orderly group. He leaned out of the window, allowing the moonlight in turn to reveal his face. Franzo looked up. His arm rose in a slow salute, then he turned to take the old lady's arm. Slowly, with respect and care, the commander of the Coast Clan Army conducted the refugees to safety.

He'd ridden as a soldier or a mercenary for half his life. Now he rode as war commander for his clan. He'd seen war, seen the awful aftermath of sieges, and knew both the horrors and the long-festering hatreds that could stem from them. Kars would fall or surrender those the clan wanted. They would give the ultimatum soon. He would do what he must and as the clan commanded, but here and now he could save some innocents from the city's death if that went as he expected. For a soldier, it was much better than nothing.

XIX

———◇———

*I*n a small room off the ducal suite Shastro faced his sorcerer. His face was twisted in fear and rage, his eyes determined. Kirion had scried. The results had not been good, even less so when he drained the last power from a captive and used the results to push for a reading on the besieger's terms. The duke had heard them with terror, and fear in Shastro always became rage. The greater the fear the hotter the fury burned. Now he faced Kirion and shouted.

"Do it again. You must have got it wrong."

Kirion was cold. His wagon was hitched to a fading star, and he was wondering how he could disengage. "I am unable to do so. It required great power and the power supply is . . . gone." He looked down and prodded the body with a casual foot.

"I'll get you more then. I'll order my men out into the low quarter. You can direct the sweep, take as many of the Old Blood as you like and can find, but get rid of that clan."

"I'm not a miracle worker," Kirion snapped. "I can't just wave my hands and make an army evaporate. It takes work and power to do anything at all. I'm learning all the time; I can do things I could not manage months ago. The power is getting harder to find though. And without huge amounts I can't do more than harass that bunch across our gates. If your useless lot had found me real power, someone of the almost pure blood. Or got over-mountain into Estcarp and brought me back a witch."

His tones became exasperated. "It's like pulling a wagon, Shastro. You yourself can't haul one even loaded lightly. It takes a horse. More load, more horses. I need power to haul the load you demand." He eyed his red-faced sweating Lord. A slight sneer colored his voice. "And it's no use shouting at me either just because you're scared. This is a realm where being a duke gains you nothing."

He knew as the last words left his mouth that he'd gone too far. He was exhausted from the morning's work or he wouldn't have made that slip. Shastro was fanatical about receiving the respect due his rank. Kirion had always been careful to provide it, though in appearance only. He had no genuine respect for either the rank or the man. But it kept the relationship on a smooth basis. Of all the times to lose his temper, he thought as he watched the duke react.

He hastily smoothed his voice, dredging up the last scraps of his power to inflect his tones. "I speak only as others would, my Lord Duke. You yourself in your wisdom once commended me that I spoke always the truth to you." Shastro hadn't, but if he believed it was wisdom to have done so, he'd remember it. Shastro was good at changing his memories to suit his self-image. Kirion's voice became sweetened cream pouring from a jug.

"We must work together, my Lord Duke. You with your rank and power, the many men who look to you for orders. And I who serve you in my own humble way. Get me power sources, and I shall strain every nerve to strike down your enemies. At the least, be the power sufficient, I may be able to spirit you away." He couldn't do that, but he could always blame his inability on Shastro's men by claiming the power needed was greater. It was their fault if they hadn't found enough sources of the power Kirion required. In truth such a spell was beyond him at present.

He wondered if Shastro could find any of the purer blood.

Kirion was starting to suspect the duke had his own schemes. Kirion's man amongst the pseudobandits had reported they had a girl from Estcarp they believed a witch. Then silence. Nothing, no word until that Aranskeep pup had reported an attack by bandits. Then he'd produced, to Kirion's bewilderment, trinkets Shastro had recognized. Since then the duke had eyed his sorcerer oddly. Kirion would have given a lot to be sure in what direction the duke's thoughts went. And more still to know about the trinkets.

It was true his false-bandit leader had been involved with the death and disappearance of the duke's kin, but Kirion could not believe the man had been stupid enough to have retained items from the girl. And where had she gone in any case? Could his man have played him false and let her escape? But Kirion would have known. He could swear the fool had been as baffled as he at her vanishment.

Shastro was calming. He moved away, fingering some of the items Kirion had been using. His eyes, if the sorcerer had seen them, would have shown a thoughtful look. The duke had never been quite the fool Kirion assumed. He was weak, pleasure loving, and his darker delights ruled him strongly. Nor was he clever. But he'd survived by cunning over the years until Kirion had aided him to a throne. He glanced at his sorcerer from the corner of one eye. It was almost time he rid himself of this arrogant witch.

Yes, let the army at the gates be driven away, and Kirion could be felled by a silent knife. Choose a time when his powers were exhausted, send in several men with orders to fail at peril of their family's lives, and Kirion would die. It might even be necessary to do it before the departure of the clans out there. He could claim all the evil deeds done in Kars had been committed by the sorcerer without Shastro's knowledge. That once the duke realized how he'd been used, he had struck back to preserve his innocent people's honor.

A singularly nasty smile lit his hidden face for a moment. Franzo was an honorable man. He'd swallow every word. Now, Shastro would leave this dreamer of power and see some further source was found. He turned, a penitent look pasted across his features.

"My dear Kirion, I understand. We are all on edge with this damnable siege. Do you prepare while I order up soldiers for your sweep of the low quarter. Do your best, and I shall accept it gratefully." He swept out leaving Kirion to eye his departure with speculation.

Shastro never forgot hasty words or an injury. Kirion was being used and he disliked the idea. Maybe it was time the duke stepped down. His lord had been very slightly different toward him ever since that business of the trinkets. Family—they were usually a nuisance in one way or another. Shastro's hangers-on had been no better: the boy always wanting his cousin to be kinder to his subjects, protesting the usage of those Kirion took to drain.

And the girl was a danger. She'd had too much influence over her cousin. As long as she was about Shastro would take no other woman to wife, and Kirion had it in mind to breed a dynasty. With heirs to Kars's dukedom Shastro would not be required further. Kirion would continue as lord advisor, consolidate his influence over the heirs until he ruled in all but name. It was better that way. Let his figureheads be targets. He looked after Shastro. He'd failed there. Perhaps it was time to reconsider and select a new duke. The old one could be tossed to the Coast Clan as a sacrifice to deflect their demands for both master and man.

Outside Shastro strode along the passage. He was met by Hadrann, who bowed low. "My dear Lord. I have a confession I must make to you."

"Come then, sit and drink with me, and I'll hear it. I'm no priestess but I dare swear my penance would be more welcome." In better humor Shastro led the way to his rooms. He liked young Hadrann, and the lad's father had large lands and much power amongst other keep lords. He listened to the tale and nodded indulgently. It fitted well with his new decision. Franzo should see that the duke of Kars had been gravely deceived by his advisor. Undeceived, the duke would put all right.

He leaned forward. "You once knew the commander, you say? He was in some small way a friend of yours? Would you then bear him a message from me?"

Hadrann hid his surprise. "I would, my Lord Duke."

Shastro finished his glass, poured another, and drank it as he thought. It confused an enemy if you did as he wanted before he asked. Kirion's scrying had revealed that the clan was preparing an ultimatum. They'd demand the bodies, living or otherwise, of the duke and his advisor to be delivered up to them. They would wreak what they'd consider justice on the two. Then they would aid the city in choosing a new ruler before disbanding.

But if Shastro made the first advance, offering to deliver up the evil sorcerer who'd spelled him into much of what had been done, then Franzo might just accept the claim as truth and be content with Kirion. But Shastro must stall once initial contact had been made. His advisor had genuine power and was a dangerous man. It would take time to prepare an ambush that would not backfire on the duke.

He smiled. "I thank you for your confession, Lord Hadrann. Your penance shall be to bear a message as I have said." He allowed his mouth to droop in distress. "I fear I may have been gravely deceived by one I trusted. But you I can trust to help me put things right. Be at my private room tonight. I shall have a letter for you and a safe-conduct from the city." He rose, tossing back the last of his wine. Hadrann stood obediently, understanding that the audience was over.

"At what hour shall I wait on you, my Lord Duke?"

"Midnight." Shastro's eyes gleamed in a flickering wicked mirth. "A very suitable time. Until then, go, and speak of this to none."

"At your command, Lord."

Hadrann got himself out of the room in haste. He could hardly wait to reach Aisling and Keelan. Something was up, and he'd gotten the impression that it concerned Kirion as well as whatever plot Shastro was hatching. He swept his friends up from a game of fox and geese. His manner was casual, but both felt his urgency and came without discussion. With all safe in the Aranskeep rooms Hadrann checked the corridor. No one in sight. He shut the door and dropped the bar across it.

The other two kept silence, but their attention sharpened. "Sit," Hadrann ordered softly. "Aisling, have Wind Dancer listen for any spy within the walls, we want no listeners for this."

He saw her gaze turn to Wind Dancer. The cat's head came up, and his attention focused on the wall behind which the secret passage ran.

Aisling nodded. "All's clear so far. He will alert me if he hears anyone approaching."

"Good. Now, as you know I was to attend Shastro as soon as possible to tell him of the escape of those we aided. He had something else on his mind. He took my confession as if I'd mentioned that I like grapes. Then all of a sudden it was as if I'd brought him a gift. Listen, this is what he said."

He recounted the conversation, carefully watching their faces. Keelan was frowning as he considered the words. Aisling was serene, but Hadrann knew under that serenity her mind would be checking, adding, measuring intent, and making leaps of intuition based on her understanding of her brother and the duke. She was so sensible, so wise, so . . . Hadrann's mind made its own leap. So sweet, and he loved her. He'd always loved her, he suddenly realized. From the day they met.

He'd have her to wife or die unwed. He forced the realization from his mind. Now was not the time to speak of it or even to think on it too much. They had deadly plans to carry out. They might not survive them, nor would Aisling be pleased to be distracted. He crushed the ache in his heart as he looked at her. She must not fail, nor must she die. His body between her and death, his love a shield. He forced back his thoughts and concentrated on the raging discussion again.

"For Gunnora's sake, Aisling. We can't know, I agree. But it sounds to me as if Shastro might be going to surrender."

Aisling snorted vigorously. "*Shastro?* His idea of surrender is to offer someone else—" She broke off, and they stared at one another. Aisling spoke in a small voice. "Someone else, yes. Like his sorcerer. His dear advisor, who could be blamed for everything."

Hadrann picked that up. "I told him how kindly Franzo had received those who fled. He started wondering perhaps if Franzo would believe that Shastro had been fooled. But why now?"

"Because," Aisling said slowly, "I could feel the Dark power being used last night. Maybe Kirion was scrying the army's plans. What if those plans included a demand to be made very soon? Wouldn't it be good to preempt that. To make first another offer?" She looked at them. "But we don't have to sit about wondering. If we have everything prepared, if Hadrann moves fast, we can read the letter before it leaves with him for the camp."

"A risk," Keelan commented.

"No, I can shield the power use, and the power needed to read a short letter without unsealing the envelope isn't great. However it's a delicate spell, and not something I can use more than once or twice without either exhausting myself or risking Kirion's picking up the emanations."

The men looked at each other then back at Aisling. "Get everything ready," Hadrann said at last. "I'll bring the letter back as soon as I have it but to the Aiskeep rooms, not here. If Shastro has that reported and questions me I'll say I asked to borrow Keelan's mount for a ride in the city. Mine is lame."

"Is it?"

"I regret the necessity, but he will be after Aisling has paid him a visit. She'll mention it to me over dinner."

Aisling nodded. "I can plait a hinder cord. I'll leave it on while I fuss with my own beast. Then have your beast led out into the street to be trotted up and down. All shall see he's lame. I'll give orders for him to be treated, remove the cord, and he will be well again by tomorrow. But if any of Shastro's spies come asking, there'll have been a lot of witnesses."

"And I shall go down to see for myself after the meal. I'll hear some of them, agree I can't use the horse, and seek Keelan."

"Who won't be found until after you have Shastro's letter," Keelan added cheerfully.

The plan, as plans occasionally do, worked out. A quarter candlemark after midnight Hadrann was watching Aisling as she held the letter in slender hands. Her eyes were blanked as she concentrated. The scent of herbs caressed the room. Power tingled gently. Then she began to speak. It was a brief letter, the words of a man feeling his way cautiously, but the intent, the approach was clear.

Shastro was gravely distressed. After the last aborted siege he had been bothered by a feeling that the clan might have honest grievances. He had begun inquiries. He'd been forced to move secretly since the man he suspected was his friend, his trusted advisor, and had power of his own. But at last it seemed that he was finding out unwelcome truths. He had been deceived, tricked, and used. Evil deeds of which he'd known nothing had been done in his name.

Did Franzo wonder, the letter continued, that the clan had been denied justice? A duke relied on those about him. If Shastro had erred, if death and sorrow had been brought down upon the clan it had not been his doing but the scheming of another who would take power once the duke was deposed. It had all been a monstrous plot against them both. They were to destroy each other, and the plotter would take power in the ruins.

The letter was couched in obscurities. It never spoke clearly or named the one suspected. It did not have to. Those listening understood every word as would the man to whom it was addressed. He might even believe it. The three knew better, and did not. Aisling let the letter fall from her hands. She lay back against Keelan's arm. Hadrann stopped to pick up the still-sealed note.

"I'll likely be two or three candlemarks. Sleep a little if you can. I'll come here when I return."

Keelan was assisting his sister to stand. "No, better we go to the house. Meet us there once you've returned and attended the duke."

"Very well." He took Aisling's hand in his own and held it briefly. Her gaze rose to his. "Take care, cousin," he said. His voice harsh from the emotion he was suppressing. "I would not wish to see you in danger."

Aisling looked into his eyes. Without intent her mind reached out to sense the emotions he was so clearly feeling. Not fear for himself, not anger at Shastro's lies. No, his mind held only warmth, love, desire, and a terrible fear for her. That they should die and never have time to touch.

She spoke then, not from the surface of her mind, which was wrenched with surprise that he should feel as she did, but from the deeper instincts that rose to her need.

"By Cup and Flame go you forth. By Cup and Flame come you back. Fire's heat hold you safe. Wine give you strength to return. And until you lay hand in mine once more I hold Cup and Flame in my heart."

It was the ancient oath, given to a warrior as he rode on a quest. It meant love and remembrance no matter how long he should be gone. In a few of the older keeps there were shrines to a warrior who had ridden away and never returned. Given by a woman unwed and free, it was an oath of another kind. Love and remembrance, yes, but also a promise that if the warrior returned he would be a welcomed suitor.

Hadrann heard it with incredulous joy. His hand closed with crushing force on Aisling's fingers enveloped in his. He said nothing, but his eyes held hers, half in fear, half in wild hope. She gave him a small comradely grin and nodded. He said nothing, released her, took up his cloak, and left. But the grin he now wore threatened the stability of his ears. Behind him Aisling massaged her ill-treated fingers. Keelan laid an arm about her shoulder.

"I would like another brother, and you've chosen me the best I could ever have, dear sister. But 'cousin Murna' will have to walk wary."

Her returned grin was half rueful. "I know. Too many know Hadrann's honor. He'd never take a kinswoman as a lover, nor would his father countenance his marriage to a woman who is close kin and penniless. Until this matter is resolved we shall have to be content with words and the touch of hands. Yet I could not let him go without so much as I could give."

Her eyes were wide. "He loves me, Kee. I knew it when he took my hand. He feared for me if this siege goes awry."

Keelan snorted. "For Gunnora's sake, girl. I've known he cared for you for months, even if he didn't. And if the siege breaks Kars, I'll take care of you. I'll have you safe into our cellars if I must drag you there. Now, stop fluttering and get ready. We want to be away to our house quickly just in case Shastro turns up asking why Rann called on and why you're here alone with one who isn't kin and no woman to company you."

They rode quietly along dark streets. Their three guards flanked them looking menacingly into not always empty shadows. Kars alleys after dark had oft been dangerous. With the siege and the growing shortness of food and money to buy it, the nightlife had become lethal to many. Few would risk three guards and a noble who rode with a sword at the ready, but soon they would. Desperation was a stink in the air that all who rode in this small group could recognize.

Hadrann rejoined his friends at the third hour after midnight. He had nothing to report save that Franzo had received him with friendship then gone aside with his captains to read the letter. Some time later Franzo had returned with a letter for Hadrann to take to the duke. It had seemed wiser to return directly to Shastro with it. The mood of Franzo and his men had seemed to be one of cautious optimism.

In other words, as Keelan summed it up, "Franzo's nibbling the bait, but our duke will have to offer something more than a scent on a hook to get a bite."

"Shastro is playing his cards against both sides," Hadrann said soberly. "I was delayed on my return. Soldiers are sweeping the low quarter, and I'm sure I caught a glimpse of Kirion with them."

Aisling shuddered. "Gunnora preserve those they take. When Kirion starts his next power-working I'll scry to see what he and Shastro are planning."

"And for now, let us to our beds," her brother added. "Has anyone seen Wind Dancer?"

Aisling smiled. "He's hunting. There are fat field mice in the grass, and he says he must do his share to save our supplies. The truth is he likes field mice." She looked worried. "But he says that a servant tried to catch him in the palace yesterday. Shastro has forbidden the cook to give scraps or leftovers to them. He says that he must pay for what he eats, and they shall do likewise. He's ignoring that they haven't the coin to eat more than once a day now that prices are so high."

Hadrann nodded. "So they'll catch and eat anything they can. Cat is acceptable now. Soon it will be rats, and finally their own dead. By the time that happens the city may rise against Shastro, more quickly if they hear what the clan may be offering. I caught a few words. Aisling was right. They'd originally intended to halt the siege if they were given the duke and his advisor. Let that news be known about the city and Shastro may be sitting in a frying pan on a fire. Stay where he is and fry slow. Leap and burn faster. And the people of Kars will be adding fuel."

In that he was correct. Franzo and his captains had considered the letter. Their reply had suggested that Kirion be sent as an envoy to prove the duke's good faith. The army would be responsible for taking and holding the sorcerer once he arrived.

Kirion had rejected any idea of being an envoy when the subject was broached. The duke wrote back to report failure. Franzo thought the problem understandable and offered another idea. Open the gates and allow the army to enter, solely to capture their quarry.

This time it was Shastro who rejected the plan. He wasn't opening any gates to allow any armies to stream in, for whatever purpose they had in mind initially. Purposes changed. They weren't going to change in his direction. Within Kars food was scarce now at merchant level. The poorest folk were desperate. Hadrann moved between their rented house and the Aranskeep suite at the palace, but Aisling and Keelan had chosen two days earlier to move permanently to the estate. They still returned regularly to dine with Shastro and to be seen at court in the evenings, but now they always slept behind their own walls.

No one bar a few servants realized that as yet; all three of them had left clothing and some personal possessions in the suite. But both men felt it would be safer for her if Aisling was out the palace, and where she went, Wind Dancer went too.

In the dungeons Kirion held scores of those with the merest trace of the Old Blood. He was working, or so he believed, a spell that would bring Shastro wholly under his sway. With the duke obeying his every word, Kirion would have him confess to crimes, absolve his advisor, and then commit suicide in expiation before the people. The Coast Clan Army would accept that and leave quietly.

Then Kirion could choose another suitable man and begin the long careful work of raising him to be the new duke of Kars. It was all a nuisance, but these things happened. He soothed his anger at events by continuing to send sweet dreams to Varnar. His servant was so amusing. The fool really believed his dreams of a small happy family waiting for him somewhere. What pleasure it would be to reveal the truth when the time came.

Hadrann rode back and forth between their rented estate, the duke's palace, and Franzo's army. Summer had been and gone, and the fall was almost over. Soon it would be the full chill of winter, and if times had been hard for the poor before, they would be thrice as hard once the cold closed in.

Originally the anger of the people had been directed against the army that besieged them. Gradually that had changed. Now it was the duke's men they hated with their gaze as the soldiers clattered by. Kirion had demanded and been given a second sweep of the low quarter. He'd returned with few and with several dead soldiers. The human rats of the low quarter, backs to the wall, had fought. Shastro refused to order a third sweep.

On their rented estate Aisling encouraged the geese to sleep along the bottom of the wall furthest from the house. There too she had placed wards with care. They were shielded from Kirion's observation, which took more power. Yet it was essential he not be able to find traces of her gift. The working had been done very slowly, built up layer by layer as she recovered her strength each morning.

Her work was not done with the brute powers Kirion used to smash home like flung stones but with delicate interweaving that was added little by little. The wards would warn, waking any of the three if intruders tried to enter. They proved their worth the night of the first food riot, when true winter came to the low quarter.

XX

———◄◦►———

*I*t began when a merchant ran out of grain. At least, that was what he said, but a servant talked of how his master had decided to sell no more of what was still held within his storehouses.

The merchant had come to an understanding that gold could not be eaten. He'd keep the remaining grain for himself and his family. But he was the only one whose storehouse had stood on the edge of the low quarter. Kars guard drove back any from that area if they tried to reach farther warehouses.

To this one place then they had come with their pitiful coins. They had purchased by handfuls rather than by the basket or bushel, but it had been enough. Now that chance was gone. The grain was there but not for them. A woman hammered on the door. Her man had been taken in one of Kirion's sweeps. He'd never returned. She'd sold herself over and over to the Kars guard to obtain a few coppers. Her children wept with hunger. And a woman from the low quarter does not love her children the less.

When the merchant would not open the door she broke a window. Then another. A crowd had gathered, and she turned to them.

"The pig within this building piles food high to eat. My children starve. He will sell us nothing. When has he ever dealt honestly with us?" The gathering crowd responded with a sullen muttering of agreement. The merchant was well known for weighing down the scales with his finger when he measured grain for purchase. The woman picked up another stone and smashed at the storehouse lock.

"Let him be the one who hunts rats. Let it be his daughters who must sell themselves to eat . . . if they can find any takers." The sneer in that curse would have etched glass. The merchant's daughters were arrogant and unlovely. Their servants hated them and with cause. None of that was any secret to the dwellers in the low quarter. She smashed again and again at the lock.

Inside the merchant made his error. Had he been content to stay inside and do nothing it is possible the woman would have found the door immovable and given up. But the merchant, facing the loss of his food, acted. He called out his guards and flung them against the crowd. The woman fell, run through and dying. She screamed her dying hate as she fell, and the crowd became a mob surging forward.

The guards killed again and again. Trapped in the narrow street the crowd could not escape and then it no longer wished to. The mob roared, swirled, coalesced, and struck back. The guards were pulled down one by one until all five were dead. Then the mob moved in on storehouse and home. They smashed in the doors, looting the food and all else portable.

The merchant, in the end a brave man, tried to protect his family. The crowd reached for him, and he died quickly. His wife and daughters did not, although they were dead by the time the mob scattered and were gone with their loot. When the Kars guard arrived there was only an empty warehouse, a looted home, and a number of dead bodies, stripped and left where they had fallen.

The guard reported, and Shastro, white with rage at this challenge to his authority, went in search of his sorcerer. "You wanted more specimens for your studies?"

"You said it cost too dear in guard's lives last time." Kirion hid his amusement. He'd already heard about the riot and could guess the rest.

"I've changed my mind. Outside I have twenty guards waiting. Another dozen will join them once they reach the low quarter. Go with them if you wish. You can smell out those with traces of the power; they can't. Take whomever you find. Do what you will, just find a way to rid Kars of that honor-lost Franzo and his damned army!"

Kirion went out to guide more than thirty guards in a ruthless sweep, but the mob had come to understand it had power of its own. The people fought, taking to the sun-baked roofs, dropping stones, throwing rotting offal. And when a small number of the guards were cut off, the ambushers descended to fight them with a trapped-rat-like courage. The guards retreated with prisoners enough to content Kirion for a while, but the mob was left with a greater sense of its own strength.

That night they emerged from their warrens and rioted again. Guards quietly drifted in the opposite direction. They usually patrolled in threes. Three men could not stop fifty, and they were too smart to attempt it. When none appeared to halt the trouble, the mob knew they were the masters now. One of them reminded his friends of past grievances. They closed in on the home of a justice. That prudent man had an escape route and reached it together with his family. But his home was burned to the ground before he returned with help.

The mob split, gathered to itself others, blossomed into hundreds and split again. It flowed through the quarter where more affluent tradesmen and minor merchants dwelled, lighting fires, smashing doors, committing atrocities, and moving on. Guard horns blew as Shastro was informed and gave orders, his face red with fury. Guards formed up in ranks, pikes and heavy horses— mob smashers.

In his throne room the duke snarled. "There's always more rats. I don't care how many you kill. Let them taste blood. You'll march in and kill until I give the order to withdraw. I'll teach them who is master in Kars." He pointed a finger at his guard-sergeant. "I and my advisor are coming with you. Detail your six best men to cover us. And empty the barracks. I'm going to smash the filth who defy me."

"Yes, sire. At your command." The sergeant had dead men of his own to avenge. "If it be acceptable I shall use the guards in three companies. We'll circle the quarter, strike simultaneously from three directions, and have them encircled. We can then drive in, killing as we go until we have them well reminded who rules, sire." The sergeant had been disgusted at the rioting and horrified at the failure of his men to prevent it. He'd redeem his own honor as well.

Shastro eyed him with approval. "Excellent. Give the orders. I will be with you shortly." He waited until the man was gone then turned to Kirion. "You'll come with me."

"I am a sorcerer, not some bloody-handed guard," Kirion said coldly. "Am I to waste gathered power dueling filth in the alleys?"

"You're to guard your duke," Shastro said savagely. "Half of this trouble came because of your advice and your constant demands for more sources of power." He became angrier as he felt the truth of his words. "Get out into the gutters for once, Sorcerer, and do some of your own work. See what trouble your advice causes."

He shut his mouth abruptly, but Kirion had caught the undertone. None of his advice had been responsible for this. It had been Shastro who'd wished to punish the Coast Clan, Shastro who'd demanded Kirion use his sorcery to bring them grief and deaths. But was that what the duke would say to others? Or was he trying to load all the blame, all the actions onto his advisor? Kirion's mind jumped forward. And if the duke *was* blaming his sorcerer, to whom was he saying that? Kirion could guess.

If only he was placed behind the duke. But Shastro made certain his sorcerer was before him as they rode off surrounded by armed men. The engagement was savage. It lasted three candlemarks, and in the low quarter whole streets lost some from every home. When it ended the people were cowed. They crawled into their hovels, hating sullenly but too afraid of their duke to emerge from the quarter again or not for some while.

But if Kirion thought that would be the end of it he swiftly learned he was wrong. On a quiet estate in the nobles' quarter, letters had been written. Aisling had scried the first riot. Keelan thought of the plan.

"Look, Rann. You're going back and forth with letters. What would happen if you dropped one and it was read?"

"The duke would have me strung up," Hadrann said promptly.

"No, listen. I don't mean the real letters. We could write new ones. The city would love to hear that its troubles would be over if they just handed out Shastro and Kirion."

Aisling looked thoughtful. "That's very true. And what if they also read letters that were offers. One, say, suggesting that Kirion hand over Shastro only as the real cause of the troubles?"

"And another the opposite?" Keelan queried. "Yes. It'd raise some eyebrows."

Aisling grinned. "And four of them would belong to Shastro and Kirion if the letters fell into their hands. I could set the merest trace of a spell to help that along. Just so they'd see the right letter for each. I'd wager each has in mind selling out the other anyhow, even if they haven't offered it yet. Rann, you can disguise your writing. Let's see what we can do."

"How do we get the letters somewhere believable?" Hadrann was cautious.

"Write first. The opportunity may arrive."

The letters were written, masterpieces of innuendo and suggestion, at least the missives supposedly from duke and sorcerer. The one apparently signed by the army's commander was quite straightforward, and it also turned out to be straightforward as to how they were discarded for discovery. With Shastro's punishment of the low quarter he'd been seen by hundreds, as had his advisor.

Keelan and his friend had donned the garb of bullies, hired swords, and skulked away once Aisling had scried the duke's intent. They'd left through the shrine's secret door, with a spell from Aisling laid over them that rendered them nondescript and almost unnoticeable. They'd slipped about the fringes of the fight, dropped the letters as the guard retreated with their dead and prisoners, then vanished to reappear through the shrine's hidden door.

Once the people ventured forth the letters were found. Few could read, but one by one in the different streets someone was found. The letters were read to savage groups who snarled, their eyes showing a red madness. After that rumors began. One came to Kirion's ears. He drained every scrap of power, hid himself in night, and came at last to where he could lay hands on the letter of which he'd heard. Hadrann had written well. He'd even initialed the bottom of the page with the mark of one of the duke's scribes.

Kirion read, burned the letter, and withdrew, his face thoughtful. It seemed as if it really was time to dispose of a duke who'd become dangerous to his creator. That night he worked long and hard, draining a half dozen prisoners to search yet again for his sister. With her in his hands he could work the miracles Shastro demanded. Then he could move against the duke. He found no trace of Aisling and cursed, kicking the bodies that littered the tower floor.

He tried again to find the men who had waited at the ruined garth. They too were nowhere to be found but, straining all his abilities, he was for the first time able to learn one thing: they were dead. They had been dead all this time. That had to have been his sister's doing, he thought. He would wait, lay hands on some others of the Old Blood and try yet again. He would have her, and with her, the power to do as he wished.

Another rumor had reached Shastro's ears. He marched with thirty guards, seized one letter and another. He looked at them. Maybe Franzo had tried to reach him with a messenger who'd been killed. That would account for the first missive. The second he read, and for long minutes he raged about his room. Flinging items that smashed against walls and floor. He paused to read it again.

So it was he who had ordered his sorcerer to attack the clan. It was he who had ordered the murders of . . . He looked down at the page. By the gods, the wretched man had named him as instigator of the deaths of his own cousins. Shastro froze, suddenly silent. The letter said that in proof if a spy was sent secretly, he would find the body of the woman buried in such and such a place. Kirion claimed to have spied on the duke and seen the murders and the woman's burial. There was even a small neatly drawn map.

Shastro slumped back into his seat. "Sharna!" he said softly. "I loved you and your brother. You were light in my darkness. Warmth for the chill of my heart." He bowed his head remembering. They'd come out of the low quarter together. He and Sharna, his love, and her brother Paran, his friend. Anything they had they'd shared. When he rose to be duke he'd shared that with delight in having something to give. He'd planned to wed Sharna in all honor and have Paran declared his chief advisor.

He clenched his hands, tears standing in his burning eyes. He knew his darker side, the things he took pleasure in. While Sharna and Paran had been with him he'd been able to resist temptation. Without them he had fallen, listened to Kirion's prompting, accepted the pleasure offered. He'd been told that as duke, to him no delights were forbidden, and they hadn't been. Kirion had been quick to offer spells. Any lover his duke desired should be his; they dared not reject their lord.

Shastro had taken as and where he willed. His fingers were rolling something over and over. He looked down: the trinket Paran had made. Paran, who had delighted in his skill and loved to make small baubles to please the eye and caress the fingers. He looked down on the carved amethyst, at the insignia of Cup and Flame. Sharna had been devout. He'd paid Paran to make it for her name day.

He picked up the letter again, studied the map. Kirion had said that his duke's cousins had been attacked by bandits. They had found the bodies of Paran and his man but no trace of Sharna, though Shastro had ordered a search that lasted for days. Kirion had led it. The duke's eyes became lethal with hatred as he remembered.

But whoever had written this letter knew where Sharna lay. If it told the truth—and it seemed that it was Kirion who had written—Shastro must discover if the letter lied. And if it did not, there would be a reckoning. His lips drew back from his teeth. Oh, yes. There would be. Then his anger collapsed, and there was only a richly dressed man who leaned against the back of his chair and wept slow burning tears for his love, who might have saved his soul but had died too soon.

A siege is not to prevent the escape of one person here and there but to hold a city within its walls until such time as it is ready to surrender and open its gates. Shastro sent out two men from different points over the walls. One returned. It had taken him long weeks first to find the grave, then to elude the tighter army lines and reach Kars again. With him he brought an item his ruler knew and a description.

"A woman for sure, sire. Small, delicate bones. Long blonde hair. She was well wrapped in a heavy cloak. No, sire. It was plain. Black wool with braided ties. Under it she still had the rags of a gown in lilac. I searched according to your orders. She had this on a braided leather string about her neck still."

He stepped forward to place an item on the polished wooden table. Shastro waved his permission for the man to depart, casually tossing him a purse as he did so. But his eyes were on the deadly lovely knife that lay before him.

He knew this object. It had been a jest between the three of them the midwinter he'd become duke. Paran had carved tiny cats from semiprecious gems, gifting one each to his sister and cousin. Sharna had embroidered handkerchiefs using her own hair for the initials. Thus, she'd said, they could each have something of her. And Shastro had ordered his court silversmith to make the knives, tiny delicate razor-sharp blades fitted into silver-chased sea-ivory hilts.

They were grace knives to be worn about the throat and used as last resort. He'd jested that now he was duke and they of the nobility, they had honor to defend. He turned the hilt in shaking fingers seeing the initials twined in the chasing. Sharna, Shayril's-daughter. He lowered his head to lay it on the knife, praying for some fading echo of her to reach him.

"How did you die, love?" he whispered to it. "My spies found no wounds they could swear to. Did you die calling my name, trusting me to help, and I failed you? But I trusted too. I trusted a man who came offering me a throne, saying I was the strong one Kars and Karsten needed. A man who swore that no one found your poor body. Did he even look? Or did he already know!"

The duke raised his head, and his eyes were frenzied. "How did you die, love? To give him power? I say he *knew*!" His hand crushed the letter he had been rereading when his spy returned. "He drew the map." His voice dropped to a hissing whisper. "He'll pay, love. I swear. For the years without you both. For the years he tempted me and I fell." He kissed the knife gently. "With this, on this, I swear. He'll murder no more, love, once I am done with him."

Shastro stood. He reached up to take a pendant from about his neck and replace it on the chain with the knife, dropping it into his

tunic with an air of finality. He smoothed his face. No sign must
there be of what he knew. Kirion saw too much if a man was careless. Shastro did not intend to be careless. He would lead his sorcerer
on, use him, drain all the power the man could summon up, then
strike.

He found Kirion working a spell and interrupted without ceremony. "I want something done." Kirion bowed silently, but a newly
alert duke saw the quick flare of anger. Yes, his advisor did not like
taking orders. Had that been contempt mixed with the rage? Shastro
drew himself up. "You are to scry Franzo's army. I want him
watched whenever he is in conference with his captains."

"That will take power."

"What else is power for?" He softened his tone. "Besides. I may
have a gift for my most useful sorcerer. A spy has bought me word
that there is a whole family with the Old Blood hidden somewhere
in the city. He is closing in on them. Six, maybe more, but six at the
least. All half bloods. He says the parents are both that, and hence all
four of their children. The city is closed; they cannot escape. What
could you do with all of that power at your command!"

Kirion turned to hide his face. What could he not do? Rid himself of this arrogant fool for a start. Raise a duke who'd hang on
Kirion's every word. And win a war with Estcarp to give him an endless supply of victims to drain until his power could open gates, tear
down the sky, and— He turned back avidly.

"At your command, my Lord. No word from Franzo shall escape me. But let it be soon that this family is found. It will take all
the power I can leech from those we have now to overhear Franzo for
any great length of time."

"You shall have them as soon as possible, my dear advisor." He
swept out smiling to himself. Once the dungeons were empty he'd
claim that the family had been taken, on the way. He'd arrange as-

sassins then. That would drain any power Kirion was withholding. With his sorcerer powerless, Shastro would take great pleasure in cutting his heart out with Sharna's own small knife.

*B*ehind him Kirion had a blank look as he thought furiously. Shastro was up to something, but what? This family. If he had them in his hands he'd have all the power he needed. He'd do as the duke demanded until then. After that Shastro could beware.

Varnar entered and Kirion smiled at him. His hands rose to weave hypnotically. He'd see what Franzo and his army planned, but for now he'd ready this tool. It would amuse him afterward. He spoke in a quiet, compelling rhythm. Varnar sat, his eyes becoming blank as he saw his family: his adored wife, his beloved daughter. How he missed them. He'd be with them in his master's home outside Kars if it were not for this siege. Kirion laughed soundlessly at the entranced dreaming figure.

He'd taken the fool from the low quarter. A man so ugly, so scarred that no woman had ever looked at him beyond a commercial transaction. Kirion had first drugged the man in wine offered a good servant, then started to insert the dreams.

Now Varnar believed in the lie his master had created. Kirion had made him straight, strong, and handsome. Only the strength was true. Out of Varnar's dreams Kirion had created a family. They were an idealized portrait that had never existed: the adoring wife, the lovely gentle loving little daughter. Neither had ever existed.

The dreams had become the man's reality, and soon Kirion would end the dreams. He'd show Varnar the truth and drink in the man's utter despair. Varnar would die of grief for phantoms. Kirion would drain the pain and use it. He'd slash away the picture the man had of himself and allow Varnar to see his real shape, that of a man

ugly beyond redemption. He smiled. It would be so much fun. But
for now he must do as Shastro wished. He drew on his stored stolen
power and scried. How interesting. Franzo was talking to that pup
of the duke's. The one with the plain, stupid cousin. He drew more
power and settled to listen.

isling was talking with Shastro when she felt the tingle of
magic. She had spelled bracelets, given one each to her
brother and friend. The signal was different. It would warn if Kirion
listened alone or if the duke was with him. Hadrann felt the prick of
warning and switched smoothly to another tack. He'd been speaking
of the city. Now he spoke of the duke, praising him.

"My Lord Duke feels he was grievously misled. He listened to
one who was unwise, perhaps even deliberately so. Perhaps if your
terms could be adjusted there might be agreement. After all, you
would have no wish to punish the innocent?"

Franzo was slightly puzzled but agreed. Hadrann continued in
this vein until the sharp tingling faded from his arm. Then he resumed the original discussion.

n Kars a furious Kirion sagged back. Damn. He'd lost focus. He
called for Varnar and gave orders.

As the days slipped by the last of the scourings from the low
quarter filed in one by one to be used up. Kirion chanted, drew
power, and had the lifeless remains removed.

He focused again on Franzo's camp. Now that was interesting.
The man was sending out soldiers. Kirion split his attention trying
both to hear the orders given and follow the first troop as they left. It
drained his power slowly over several weeks so that by the time he
found that one troop was merely on a run to collect supplies and that

Franzo's orders for the other were to ride about the walls on watch to ensure no spies slipped out, he was drained.

$\mathcal{M}$idwinter came and went, and spring would sweep over Karsten in another few weeks. The city was desperate. Of those outside the palace, only Aisling and her comrades and servants had enough to eat. Twice the guards had been forced to beat off thieves who had succeeded in scaling the wall after food. The yearling lambs were eaten. The hens too long since, and only one pair of geese remained. Grain and hay were rationed; the horses grew thin. If the siege held much longer they would be food for the guards and Amara. Only Wind Dancer did well. The rats and mice were bolder and more careless.

Shastro had his own spies. He knew the dungeons had emptied. He must see to it that Kirion needed more power. He spoke quietly to men, one by one. They departed. In his tower Kirion summoned Varnar. It was time to use this fool. He must know what was being planned behind his back by his duke and the commander of the besieging army. He could draw on no more prisoners; it must be Varnar's pain and grief that fueled a final scrying. He could afford to spend the man. Soon Shastro would find the hidden Old Blood family and bring him power to spare.

On the rented estate Aisling jerked from her seat as the geas bit at her. "Keelan, we have to go to the palace."

"What about Rann?"

"He took another letter to Franzo. He'll go back to give a reply to the duke first. Wait for him near the duke's rooms then come to our suite."

They left, riding swiftly. In Aisling's carrysack Wind Dancer rode with them. He'd flatly refused to be left behind. With cat senses he knew that he too was a part of this. He'd be needed. In time, Hadrann was able to leave a preoccupied duke and join them. Aisling laid out her scrying tools, slipped into her pendant's silver mists and waited patiently.

Over-mountain Hilarion felt a shift in the lines of power. A geas moved to conclusion. For success or failure he did not yet know, but he would know soon enough. In the Valley of the Green Silences those who'd known a girl, prayed for her. Prayed too that war from their cousins in another land might be averted. The lines of power firmed. It was time.

XXI

———◆◇◆———

Kirion had ordered his servant to sit in a corner. He'd be wanted shortly. Kirion did not wish to waste time calling for him when the time came. Varnar sat obediently. He allowed his memories to surface and smiled as he sat. If he must wait, the gods and his master knew how long he'd pass the time in remembering. He frowned a little. It had been some time since he'd seen his wife and daughter, hadn't it? His brow wrinkled. It was strange, he couldn't quite recall.

Kirion had called in another man and a boy. They had been held in a place unknown to the duke. His master drained the poor wights, and the guards removed the bodies. Kirion smiled slowly. Varnar in his corner shivered. When his master smiled in that way it boded ill for someone. The sorcerer waited. He'd had that pair in reserve for many months. The man himself hadn't known he bore the Old Blood, a full quarter and much power. Or why it was his master had hired him and allowed him to have his son live with him. Well, he knew now, if he could know anything at all wherever his soul had fled.

Shastro had called men and given quiet orders. Six assassins bowed and left to deal with the man their lord had come to distrust and hate. They died as they attacked. It drained almost half of their target's recently stolen power, but he had a little left and in the corner his fool sat dreaming and smiling. The sorcerer cursed. Trust

Shastro to pick the wrong time. But then Shastro probably considered the time right, before the family he'd promised could be brought. Kirion prepared the word that, when said, would dispel Varnar's illusion, releasing all the man's emotion in a great wave of pain and grief. Then he waited for his duke.

Shastro came quietly, and, unknown to any but those who followed, behind him came one under a geas and those who aided her. Wrapped in her mists Aisling laid the unseen over them: over herself and Wind Dancer, who padded at her heels, over her brother, and Hadrann, her love. It was time to cast the dice, letting all ride upon the outcome. Life, death, and love. She walked to a destiny not knowing what it would be, only that what she did was necessary for the sake of her beloved land. That they all knew. If they died, then they'd accept death to buy Karsten life.

In front of them Shastro reached the door to his sorcerer's tower. The guards stepped back. Their master had forbidden entry to any, but it would take far more reckless men than they to deny their duke passage. Shastro wasn't known for a placid acceptance of insolence. He swept by, one hand rising unconsciously to clutch at the shape of a small knife within his tunic. He entered the large room, his gaze flicking quickly from side to side.

Kirion eyed him with amusement. The fool really thought he had power here. Kirion would show him power. It would be the last thing this creature he'd raised to rank would ever see. He leaned forward in his chair and drawled a greeting. Shastro turned.

"What have you seen from your scrying, sorcerer. What plans has Franzo?"

Kirion smiled. "Plans that change, my Lord Duke. Once he demanded the lives of two men. Now it seems he would settle for one." He was referring to the letter he'd seen, which had offered only Kirion. But the duke had seen a different missive. His face reddened. This man, this thing who dared to taunt him, was bold enough to refer to his own treachery against his ruler. His voice developed an edge.

"Yes, indeed. Franzo would accept one instead of two. So I also heard." He took a pace forward. "An interesting thought, but perhaps not so welcome for the one being sold."

Kirion nodded. In a room off this, lay six assassins, bodies cooling. He hadn't found the idea of being sold to Franzo welcome, no. And this duke he'd raised from the low quarter to rule, dared to taunt him with it. At least Kirion had drawn off some of their power as they died, enough to replace a little of what he'd used to stop them. In his corner Varnar dreamed, oblivious to the sound of voices. Kirion glanced at him. Not yet. Not quite yet.

"My dear Shastro, why not sit and drink a little wine with me. You are weary."

His dear Shastro straightened. "I drink no wine with you, sorcerer. There are too many things in your cup." His voice dropped to a tone half regret, half memory. "And I have drunk too often of the cup you have offered." His eyes fixed on Kirion's face as his voice became accusatory. "What cup did you offer Sharna and Paran, sorcerer? No, do not lie to me. I have proof. It was your men who killed them and not bandits as you said. What have you to say to that now?" Kirion shrugged as Shastro raged on.

"My cousins, my friends. You murdered them and for what? So yours would be the only voice I heard. Well, I have stopped listening." His face hardened. "As you will stop speaking. I'm done with you."

His hand dipped to draw the grace knife even as Kirion rose. Shastro flung himself forward. Kirion lifted a hand, and the duke halted, unable to move. Kirion concentrated. Fire came to his fingers and he flung it in an arching spear of white flame. Shastro cried out as the shaft of fire sliced through him. He dropped, writhing, and lay, his fingers clutching the knife hilt. Kirion walked over to look down at the man he had raised to a throne.

"You were quite right about that, my Lord Duke. You are indeed done with listening, but not because you wished that. It is I who am tired of talking to you." He laughed scornfully. "What, did you think to best me. I *made* you. If I had those pitiful idiots you called cousins murdered, it was my right. You've had years of luxury, any lover you desired. Power, rank, wealth—all have been poured into your lap, by *me!*"

His voice came as a hiss. "And you'd have betrayed me to Franzo. Sold me to him with your lies. I did as you demanded, my Lord Duke." The sarcasm in the last words slashed out. "You demanded the Coast Clan be punished for its refusal to bow to you. I merely obeyed your command." Kirion was coldly angry. He'd done only what had been asked of him, and see how he was repaid? Nor had the last fiasco been his fault.

"You demanded those who wished nothing of you turn to you with desire instead. I saw to it. You commanded I spell that brainless woman with her young idiot of a husband. I spoke and she was besotted with you, allowing you any liberty, even before the whole court. Then your own gatekeepers were bribed to allow them to go free. And once again it was I who had to seek out the guilty one for you. Wasting my power on minor needs over and over. So very well you ran the city I gave into your hands. But you weren't mentioning any of this to Franzo. Oh, no. It was all my doing."

He kicked the duke viciously. "Listen when I speak, my Lord Duke. Yes, I had your stupid cousins ambushed. You must have suspected all these years, but you took what I offered anyway." His tone mocked savagely. "What does that make you, my Lord Duke?"

Shastro felt only the fire. It was consuming him. But underneath it he heard the words. If he'd had the strength, he'd have denied that change. He'd never known, never even suspected. He'd have taken nothing at Kirion's hands, not even his life, if he'd had any idea. A single tear of blood gathered in the corner of one eye.

Paran, his friend, the brother of his heart, and Sharna, whom he'd loved as he'd loved nothing else since she had gone. He'd looked for her in all his light loves and found nothing but brief pleasure and a momentary distraction.

In the flames he saw Sharna. She was smiling, holding out her hands. Paran stood at her shoulder, love and welcome clear to read in his face. They did not condemn him. Kirion kicked again but his victim made no sound, did not move. It was unsatisfying. The sorcerer muttered another word, and the white fire drew back a fraction.

In the passage outside the corner tower Aisling had halted. She touched her pendant and drew power. The witch jewel gleamed openly on her breast, but the pendant lay hidden still as her teacher had warned. She touched the jewel, keying it with the word of command. She could feel the power rise in it; the trap was set.

Her hands lifted, wove slowly, and a glittering web of light sprang from them. She cast it forward. It settled over the guards, and they stiffened into immobility. Unaware of the intruders, they would see and hear nothing. She walked past them to open the door. The others followed. Aisling spoke under her breath and the guards returned to duty unknowing.

The four who had entered slid quietly behind the drapes that cloaked the entrance. They'd arrived just after Shastro was struck down, in time to hear Kirion's ranting. Now Aisling drifted past the drapes sparing a glance for Shastro. He would not survive. The fire her brother had called was eating him alive. Her eyes as they met his showed pity. His lips curved into a tiny rueful grin of acceptance and regret. In his eyes was a faint hint of surprise at seeing "Murna" here. Aisling moved on and appeared, undiscovered, to one side of her angry brother. She said his name in soft command.

"Kirion!"

He turned and laughed, Hadrann's brainless cousin. "What are you doing here, cousin?" He sneered. "It's the wrong time to come calling on a sorcerer. Do you want a potion to make you pretty, to make men love you, is that it? Well, once I'm done here I might even give it to you. But you'll have to wait."

"No," Aisling said quietly. "I'm done with waiting."

He turned sharply. "You'll do what you're told, you brainless clod."

"You could not order me as a child. You will not order me now," was her reply. Kirion stared. Something teased the corners of his eyes. By Cup and Flames, the girl was beglamoured. His hands wove a swift spell and cast it outward. It passed over her, and she changed before him. Kirion gave a strangled yelp of recognition, then smiled, a slow evil smile of anticipation.

"Sister. My dear little sister. Come out of your kennel at Aiskeep to see your brother. What a prize for me. What a morsel of power. I'll drain you and that jewel dry, and feast."

"No."

"Oh?" She was too confident. Allies! That was it: there were others. He cast his power out again and winced. Two humans and—he blinked in amusement—a cat. Kirion flung back his head. A high whinnying laugh rang out from him. "Dear little sister, you bring help against me but what help? Two without training and a cat. If that is all you can conjure against me, then I have nothing to fear. Let me deal first with them."

He hurled power so that it flowed about the three who stood behind her. Kirion poured out more of his darkness until he knew them held fast. Then he turned back to his sister as she waited. He studied her a moment, and his smile was hungry.

"That jewel, it tells me where you were, but it is a gateway into you, sister. I have the power to draw from it all you are." He raised his hand slowly, speaking soft words that seemed to smoke across the room. The chain that held the jewel fell into glittering dust, the jewel flew to Kirion, seeming to nestle into his hand. He smiled.

"Now, sister, I shall have it all."

"Ishari!" She spoke aloud the word that would free the jewel's power, even as his mind probed into it.

She was still near the door, her allies behind her, and Kirion was almost in the center of a large room. The jewel exploded, but Aisling was able to shelter herself and those with her. Kirion too was more fortunate than Aisling would have wished. He had always feared some trap of the power might strike at him, so about himself he had layered protections.

The jewel's force beat at those like a whirlwind. Kirion reinforced his words from within, spending recklessly almost everything he had left. The trap tore at his protections, tearing them down almost as fast as he could reinforce them. For long moments they contended, but Kirion had sucked just sufficient power from his two victims. When the storm was over, he was unharmed, yet there were only the dregs of his power remaining to him. Now, it seemed, was the time to use Varnar.

Kirion spoke his word softly. In the corner Varnar shuddered. His eyes snapped shut in a reflex of agonizing pain. His wife, his adored child. In that instant both died, and he knew the bitter truth: he'd been tricked, betrayed, cheated of all he'd ever wanted and come to believe in. They had been lovely illusions, his life with them crafted perfectly to cause him the greatest agony a man could bear. He was Varnar the ugly, Varnar the scarred. Varnar who walked alone and always had, always would. He groaned, a slight breathy sound redolent of the agony that filled his mind and heart. His master drank in the torment and felt dark power swell within him.

Unseen by the sorcerer Wind Dancer padded forward. Hadrann and Keelan were bound by Kirion's spell, but the big cat was untouched. He moved with the slow flowing gait of the hunter.

Aisling had learned from Hilarion, but her gift was mostly for the land, for healing and growing. Her spells were more defensive than those that brought death or destruction. Kirion was chanting. His power slashed out, striving to reach her again, to drain from her all she had or was. She shielded as step by step she closed with him. For a moment she felt despair. He was too strong, too skilled. He'd had longer to learn, and his sorcery was overcoming her mists.

But Kirion too was growing fearful. The girl was still advancing. Involuntarily he stepped back a pace, then another, half-turning as he retreated. Wind Dancer had circled. His paws were silent as he padded around behind the fringe of wall drape. He moved until he was just inside his enemy's edge of vision, paused to be sure Kirion caught the movement, then leaped.

As he did so, he howled, the wild tearing cry of a cat about to give lethal battle. Kirion flung up an arm and screamed a word. Fire surrounded the leaping cat. It dispelled the glamour Wind Dancer still wore and more. To Kirion's amazement the attacking beast swelled in size. It was now twice, three times the size of a normal cat, but other than that, Kirion's power had left it unharmed. He cursed and drew savagely on Varnar's pain.

It flooded in, transformed into the rawness of dark power. But Wind Dancer had reached the sorcerer. His claws and teeth fastened to a leg, and Kirion howled as they dug in. He seized the beast by the scruff, dragging him loose and casting him aside with all his strength. Wind Dancer hit the wall with stunning impact. As he landed, Kirion struck at him again with a hammer blow of force. No spell, no finesse, merely brute power. Wind Dancer wavered up onto his paws. His ribs were flaring pain where he had met the edge of the wall.

Across Wind Dancer's shoulders he felt a touch. The pain was gone. It was Kirion alone who saw a dim upright shape standing behind the big cat. It turned slanted, emerald cat-eyes on him, and scowled even as one hand touched away Wind Dancer's injuries. Distracted, the sorcerer stepped back once more.

From his corner Varnar came crawling weakly. He'd lost every-thing. His wife and child had been illusion, all their happy years to-gether illusion's bitter ash. Everything he'd remembered, dreamed, rejoiced in—all had been dreams to sow a harvest of power in pain for the man who used him.

He crawled forward, not knowing why, only that he wanted to hurt the one who'd torn out his heart and feasted on his pain. If these people wished to harm his enemy, then he'd aid them with his last breath. Wind Dancer had paused. He felt a hand stroke lightly over his ears. There was a scent in the air about him. No human would have smelled it, but the nose of a cat is far keener. It reminded him of herbs his human used. He took in the room with one swift cat-eyed glare.

There two of his human friends were held unable to move. There, a man who stank of pain, crawled. There too another lay shuddering. One who'd been kind to Wind Dancer, now struck down by an enemy. His human was closing with that enemy. She should not fight alone while Wind Dancer, hunter, warrior, son of Shosho remained alive. He felt approval flow from the presence that stood by him. It warmed him, although he had no need of approval. He was a cat; he would do what he willed, and he willed to attack. He screamed again as he leaped.

Beset on two sides Kirion lost his temper. He cast a curtain of fire about Wind Dancer and Aisling. The cat ignored it and appeared on the other side before the surprised Kirion. Aisling had diverted the fire cast at her. To one side the wall hangings were smoldering. Her fingers wove frantically as she tried to contain the dark power her brother had stolen. Varnar reached his master. The strength Kirion leeched from him was slowly stopping his heart, but he had strength enough to reach up.

He ignored the duke, crawling past him as Shastro sprawled, deep in his own pain. The white fire was consuming the man who'd ruled, but Shastro didn't care, not since he'd seen his cousin's faces. He'd seen Aisling's transformation and dimly understood she was the sister Kirion had spoken of before. The cat's change was more puzzling, but he had no strength left to bother with that. He clung to the remnants of his life. Something told him he should, and dumbly he obeyed.

Varnar crawled to where Kirion stood looming over him, back carelessly turned. Long ago Varnar had been given a broach. It was tawdry, tarnished brass with the glitter of glass jewels. But the woman who'd gifted it had owed him a debt. He might not be lovely, but he was strong. He'd saved her child from danger, so she gave him the only gift she had that her man would have allowed. Varnar had kept it, the sole gift freely given and with honest gratitude and kindness that he'd ever received. Laboriously he unfastened it with one hand as he crawled.

Within his rooms and tower Kirion wore boots of soft leather. They came to mid calf, sagging a little in elegant black creases. Down the back they bore insets of patterned gray lizard skin. Varnar fixed his eyes above the boot tops, where Kirion's calf muscle bulged out.

The broach lay open in his hand. It was large enough, a typical ornament of the poor quarter, where size and show were counted as status. The pin behind it was a full four fingers in length. Varnar opened it, and as Aisling and Wind Dancer attacked again, he drove it into his master's leg from behind, deep into the fleshy calf just above the boot top. Kirion's initial yelp was more surprise than pain. Buried in bleeding flesh the pin did no true damage, but the distraction did.

From one side Wind Dancer latched on to Kirion's wildly waving arm. Maddened, Kirion reeled, unable to concentrate on further spells or chant as the brass pin stabbed pain with every movement of his leg. The cat's claws and teeth sliced savagely into one arm. The sorcerer howled inhumanly in pain and fury. He'd wreak such a vengeance on these who defied him as would warn others for a generation. His free hand fell to his sword. It was a pretty toy, but the point was needle sharp. He'd kill both cat and sister. He drew, stepped back and away from the wall to gain room for his thrust, and his heel came down beside Shastro.

The duke lay still, the white fire burning too deep for him to make a sound, but he knew how desperately others battled his enemy. He'd liked Murna. He did not wish to see her die, whoever she really was, Kirion's sister or Shastro's friend. Sharna's beloved face drove him on. Maybe if he redeemed himself a path would open, and he would go where his kin had gone. In his hand he felt the chased hilt of her grace knife. He drove it home, slicing deeply through the soft leather of the sorcerer's boot.

He'd cut crossways, and severed the tendon at the back of Kirion's heel. This time Kirion's scream was genuine agony as well as surprise. It echoed from the walls as he howled, reeling, trying to keep his balance on one foot, the other foot turning under him, as the severed tendon refused to take his weight. Wind Dancer released the mangled arm to spring again.

With the weight gone abruptly from his arm, Kirion waved it frantically in the air trying desperately to save his balance. He was falling. Instinct told him that to fall before these foes was to lose the battle. He fought to remain upright. Wind Dancer sprang high, his teeth bit into the bone in the sorcerer's wrist even as some thirty-five pounds of cat jerked down against the savaged limb. It was enough. The big cat leaped free again as the sorcerer stumbled, his balance gone. Kirion landed hard on the floor beside his puppet duke.

With a bitter smile Shastro raised himself on one elbow, leaned over, and carefully cut Kirion's throat. Then he slumped back to lie beside his fallen sorcerer. Aisling cried out in horror. Kirion's eyes closed. His power was gone. His heart slowed, stopped, and in the room where so many others had died at his command, he followed them.

Wind Dancer had halted, waiting to see what would happen when Kirion fell. He padded back now, sniffed his dead enemy, and spat vigorously through bristling whiskers. Then, turning his back, he pawed the floor as if covering waste. After that he marched over to stand by his human. Wind Dancer had delivered his verdict on events. No one else need comment. By the door Keelan and Hadrann, freed by Kirion's death, began to grin.

Aisling dropped to one knee beside the duke. He was dying. She could not prevent it, and she was not sure she would have tried. He too had been part of the geas. His rule had not been good for the land yet he'd been kind to her. She had liked him. She was grateful only that his death had not been at her hands and that he did not have to die writhing. She laid her hands against his chest, took away the pain, and waited. His eyes opened slowly to study her. The pain had gone, but he could feel the ice of death closing about his heart.

"Kirion's dead." It was a statement, but she answered it.

"He's dead. You killed him."

"Murna? Who are you really?"

"Aisling. Sister to both Keelan and Kirion."

"Why?"

She understood the question. "Why did I fight him? For Karsten. Over-mountain where I studied, a geas was laid on me. Sister against brother for the life of our land. If Kirion had lived he'd have persuaded you to wage war with Estcarp. In that war both our lands would have descended into darkness. Karsten would have been destroyed. When a land is weak enemies gather. Even if we could have defeated Estcarp those others would have come hunting, with Alizon likely to be the first." She took his hand.

"I love Karsten. It's my land. I couldn't let it die if I could save it. So I came back, hid my identity, and waited." Her finger lay over the pulse in his wrist. She could feel it fading. "You loved Kars. In the end you've helped to save it. You liked Murna, Shastro, and she liked you too. You helped to save her—me—as well. What service do you ask for that?" His lips parted slowly, she leaned close to hear his whisper.

"Bury me . . . Sharna . . . Paran."

She took his face in her hands, focused his gaze. "You shall lie with them, I swear it. In the tombs of the rulers of Kars." His eyes met hers, and he smiled. Then the life went out of him. Aisling laid down the head grown heavy.

Over-mountain, Hilarion sighed. It was done. The trap jewel had not been used as it had been crafted to be, but Kirion had been forced to waste his stolen power to protect himself from it, which had led to his death. Hilarion and Escore would settle for that. His good student had completed the task. Lines of power faded; the geas was fulfilled.

In the quiet room, Hadrann lifted Aisling to her feet and held her as she leaned back against him. His voice was gentle.

"In the end Shastro died well. Let him have his tomb and his kin." His arms closed around her. He could afford to be generous. He'd known that in some ways she'd been drawn to the duke. In her there was a need to heal. He knew, for the sake of Karsten, she'd have considered wedding Shastro if the duke had ever asked. Thanks be that he was dead. And greater thanks that Aisling had not been forced to cause that death. The duke had died well enough for Hadrann to praise him honestly.

He drew her away from the bodies. She came alive again, falling to her knees to hug Wind Dancer. "Mighty warrior. That was a battle you waged. I boast the best sword brother one could have."

Wind Dancer purred thunderously, thrusting his head against her stroking hands. Of course he'd fought well and valiantly; no one should harm his human while he stood by. He marched over to the duke and considered. But the man had liked cats, no human like that was all evil. He purred again and looked up at Aisling. His paw came out to pat gently at the duke's pallid cheek. Hadrann chuckled.

"That's that, sister dear. Kirion goes out with the garbage; Shastro gets honorable burial. The cat has spoken." Wind Dancer looked reproving. It was true, but he wasn't sure he liked Hadrann's tone. Aisling smiled.

"That's one thing to say, another to do. Rann, you'll have to talk to your friend." She touched her pendant. "The guards will have heard nothing through that heavy door. They won't enter if we forbid them in the duke and Kirion's names. We can say that the two of them are deep in discussion about Franzo's army and what to do." She darted to a table where small parchments and quills lay. "Kee, Shastro's already signed these passes. Where's his seal?"

"On his finger, I think." At her nod he investigated and returned with it. The pass to permit passage through the Kars gate was completed with their names, the seal impressed into the hot wax. Hadrann picked it up carefully.

"Stay here, Kee. Aisling and I will go and tell Franzo the news. She can make the guards open the gates if we have to do it that way. We should be back with Franzo and a few of his men as witnesses within the hour." He gave Aisling his arm, then impulsively pulled her hard against him. "As for you, my lady warrior. You owe me the oath of Cup and Flame. When all is done here I shall hold you to that."

Aisling grinned up at him, two years of comradeship and love in that gaze. "As you say, so shall it be. But first we must tell my grandmother."

XXII

------◇------

$\mathscr{F}$ranzo came back with them, cloaked, with ten of his best fighters riding unobtrusively around him. Gold had persuaded the gate warden to open the gates for Hadrann and Aisling to leave. That and the signed and sealed pass from the duke and the warden's knowledge that this noble was in the duke's favor and a regular messenger. Hadrann and Aisling had ridden out quietly. The city was often in darkness these days, the streets mostly empty of people save for those with particular business, and the wise among them went in groups or with guards.

Lamp oil and candles were too expensive to waste, and if you stayed in your bed, hunger didn't bite quite so deep. Even without fuel for a fire you might not freeze to death. There'd been many deaths of that kind as winter wore on, most in the low quarter. Other deaths had often followed, as the besieged of Kars suffered in despair. The guards too stayed inside their warmer barracks as much as possible these days.

Small groups of low-quarter dwellers could attack a home safely if it was not well guarded, the alarm was not given, or, if it was, if they moved swiftly enough. If the attack was unheard, the only sign would be a door standing open when morning arrived. After that some in the low quarter might have food and fuel enough to survive a week longer. Such attacks were one reason some low-quarter residents moved in groups. The other was that too many lone walkers had vanished since the siege began to bite down.

Shastro had given up trying to prevent such attacks. Another assault on the low quarter a month after the first had resulted in the retreat of his guards after much skirmishing with little effect. After that he'd settled for peace in the streets, a few hangings, and a lot of nagging at Kirion. To soothe his annoyance at the lack of effectiveness of these measures he'd drunk more and ignored any pleas for aid from the merchant quarter.

Franzo arrived at the gates, his men about him. Hadrann led with Aisling riding at his shoulder. The gate guard grunted at the pass, accepting a coin eagerly. Aisling had unobtrusively settled a "do not notice them" spell about Franzo and his men as they rode toward the gates. Along with the forged pass it served, and the gates swung open. In Kirion's tower the bemused guards stood aside. They were suspicious, but Hadrann had come and gone often.

He made his voice stern, confident. "Let us pass. The duke requires to talk with this man."

The guard eyed him. "I'd like to see a face. Who is he?"

Hadrann snorted. "If the duke wanted all the world to know who he summons, this one wouldn't be cloaked, would he? Let us pass. Or do I mention that we were delayed by some fool who countermanded his duke's orders?" The last man who'd done that had been given to Kirion, who'd made an example of him with glee. The guard hastily stood aside.

Hadrann knocked, Keelan opened the door and sniffed. "You've taken long enough. His Grace is becoming annoyed. Come in quickly." He looked at the guards. "Get about your business."

They stepped back, stiffening into line, eyes frightened. Franzo, still cloaked, entered, followed them to the main room, and stood gazing down on the man who had wronged him. Then he moved to stare down at the dead sorcerer.

"Which of them was responsible?"

"Both," Aisling said in a soft sigh. "If you give power to a man who has never had responsibility, never been taught that he owes a duty to those he rules even as they owe a duty to him, then you have a ruler who takes what he will and thinks that he is the law. But if a dog pisses upon the carpets and bites whoever seeks to stop it, who is to blame?"

"The owner," Franzo said sharply. "That he has not trained the beast to know better."

"Then of these two, the sorcerer was responsible. Whatever Shastro desired, Kirion gave him. He did not teach the man he raised how to rule. Was that man then evil because he thought that as duke all was his and his desires alone were law?"

Franzo eyed her shrewdly. "You are trying to persuade me the duke was more puppet than ruler. Why?"

"I swore to him that he would lie in the Ruler's Tomb. And that his cousins, whom he loved and Kirion murdered, would lie with him there. Hadrann knows where they were buried. We wish to see that they do lie with Shastro as I promised."

Franzo looked down at the bodies and shrugged. "If that's your only request I see no reason to refuse it. He was duke. It sets a bad example to the people if they see a ruler's body ill treated." He looked at her. "And you did say that at the end it was he who killed the sorcerer?"

Remembering that tiny flashing blade she nodded. "Well enough, then. Let him have his tomb and companions. But we're going to need another duke." His back straightened, "And despite what my clan may think, it isn't going to be me!"

Hadrann grinned wearily. "I said to Aisling you wouldn't like the idea, but we do have a candidate. Lord Jarn of Trevalyn keep on the Estcarp border. He's Geavon's grandnephew and well trained in what responsibility and duty mean. Jarn's oldest son is of an age to take over keep rule, but Jarn should have enough years in him barring enemies to care for Kars another thirty years at least—long enough for the land to settle into a solid peace."

Franzo was approving. "Such a man would likely be suitable. The clan would agree if I spoke for him." He looked at them. "What of your kin and the city?"

Hadrann answered that. "My father agrees. I spoke to him about it. Aisling and Keelan's grandfather approves, and he is kin to Geavon. I think right now the city would accept any ruler who had your siege lifted and food and firewood distributed."

A slow wicked smile spread over Franzo's face. "Then that is how it shall be." He pointed a finger at Aisling. "You and your brother shall leave quietly for Trevalyn keep. While you are gone I'll arrange for trader caravans to be waiting. You shall persuade Jarn into this and return with him and all the pomp you can summon. I shall formally lift the siege and accept him as the new duke of Kars. When he gives the order to bury the duke, with city-wide feasting and wine, food and drink will supplied from the ducal storehouses."

By now all three of those he faced were nodding. They could see what would happen. Keelan grinned. "By the time the people wake up to the fact that Kirion and Shastro are dead and they have a new ruler, they also will have had time to think. They will have no siege; goods and traders will be back. The country and Kars will have peace, and if Jarn announces some reform at that time too, no one will complain."

Aisling had been remembering some of the events of the siege. "What about duke's justice. A lot of people died in all this."

Franzo sighed, his face sobering. "I know. War is not a toy for dukes who wish to play at soldiers, but if you punish all who committed crimes, then what of those who acted so their families did not starve? What of those whose acts were self-defense. From what Hadrann tells me many witnesses may well be dead. It's to my mind that Jarn should declare amnesty where the truth cannot be clearly ascertained."

He looked at them ruefully. "And you convince Jarn it's his work. Sorting out all the cries for justice will settle him in fast, and it will accustom the people to his rule. Hadrann, you'd better forge another letter from Shastro to his captain of the guards. Say that Shastro and Kirion are working a great sorcery against the besiegers. It may take a number of days and they cannot be disturbed. You've been delegated to make the decisions until then."

His gaze fell again on the bodies. "And something will have to be done about those too."

"I'll see to it before Keelan and I leave. I can spell them with a holding that will last some days. The bodies won't change." Aisling's voice was quiet.

"Good. Then I'd better gather my men and rejoin the army before some fool out there decides Hadrann played me false and panics."

He tramped out, his men forming up to follow him as he left the palace. Once he was gone, Aisling had the bodies of Shastro and Kirion carried up to the highest room in Kirion's tower. They were placed on the four-poster there, covered decently, and the curtains pulled about them. Then she laid a preservation spell over the bed and its occupants that would hold about a week; she had that much power and knowledge. After that they might have to chose another method.

The forged papers had convinced Shastro's guard captain. Hadrann was busy keeping the city under some sort of calm, not an easy task with most of the population desperate. Aisling and her brother chose to ride to Trevalyn keep; it was a swifter easier method of travel. With them went their three guards. They had no idea of what was happening, but they trusted their employers.

The trip was exhausting. Aisling pushed her mount, using her gift to keep herself warm, balancing that with the need not to draw too deeply on what she had left, but she kept up. They dared not waste time on this. As she rode she mourned the man Shastro could have been. If only Kirion had not murdered Paran and Sharna, she was sure that with them at his side, he'd have been a different man, even a good duke. She remembered a night just before the siege when they had danced. They'd hunted earlier, now she teased him as they swung through the figures of an old country circle dance.

"Ah, sire. You trip this as well as any farmer."

His return smile had been oddly wistful. "I sometimes wonder if I would not have made a good farmer. I like beasts. They never play you false as men do. They love or hate openly."

"Ah, but a farmer weds. He works all day and has a wife and children. How would that have pleased you, my Lord Duke?"

"Very well, perhaps." His eyes darkened in remembrance. "Once I would not have minded being wed. I thought of children too. I would have liked that, with her." He visibly wrenched his mind from that thought. "And you, my dear Murna, will you wed and have a husband, children?"

"If my uncle finds me a man I deem acceptable."

"Ah ha. Choosy are we?"

"Indeed, my Lord Duke. Better no marriage than an unhappy one. I will always have a place with my uncle, and I have a tiny income of my own. That shall content me if no good man comes courting."

Shastro opened his mouth. She saw the thought in his face and hastily distracted him. Yet the shadow of memory was still on Shastro's face. Would he have made a good husband with the cousin he had loved? She thought he might have, with his love and his friend to temper him. The minstrel had begun to sing.

> *Oh, Pagar, duke of Karsten,*
> *He took ten thousand men,*
> *He marched them into the mountains and*
> *None ere came home again.*

Shastro snarled into the sudden hush. "Another song, minstrel. That one I like not to hear."

The minstrel bowed and hastily plucked the strings again. This time the song was approved. He sang at length of Sirion, duke of Kars when the incomers first settled. Apparently the man had all the virtues and then some. Shastro settled back in his seat with a cynical grin as the song wound on. He leaned over to Aisling to speak quietly.

"I doubt the man was any better than Pagar, but distance in time aids forgetting. In the end it doesn't take much before the people remember only that Sirion pleased them."

"That's true, sire."

Shastro sighed softly. "I wonder what they'll sing of me when I'm dead. Will I be a hero too?"

"I think it likely, sire. All dukes tend to be heroes once they're gone."

Shastro chuckled. "True, although Pagar wasn't. But then, I've not lost near as many as he did. Maybe I'll get a better song."

They turned to laughing over court gossip. As they rode now, Aisling remembered that night. It had been so innocent at the time, but in its way foreshadowing what was to come. She wondered, had they been right? Would Kars remember Shastro kindly now he was gone?

Back in the city Hadrann was hiding the death of the two men who'd ruled Kars, each in their own way. If the secret were discovered the people would riot, the guards rebel, and anarchy would descend on Kars. Hadrann had seen to it that small amounts of fuel and food were distributed from Shastro's storehouses without fuss.

It kept the people quiet for a while longer. The guards had been ordered out to patrol more often in greater strength. They had extra rations added to compensate, so they grumbled but obeyed. In the hills five riders hammered on a keep gate and were admitted. Keelan and Aisling, shedding snow from their cloaks, refused more than a mug of hot trennen and urgently demanded the keep lord.

Once closeted with Jarn neither minced words. He listened. It took most of two days, but he was Geavon's kin, born and bred to serve his land, and once he'd heard everything, he understood the necessity.

"Jannor, my heir, is wed. He has a little daughter already, and his wife bears again. If I am assassinated as duke, then Trevalyn is not rulerless. I will come."

He rode out with them, almost every man of his who could sit a horse riding in double file behind. Over them waved the banner of the dukes of Kars, taken quietly by Aisling before she and Keelan had left the city. On Jarn's arrival at the Kars gate, Franzo formally raised siege. By the time it sank into citizen minds that this wasn't their old duke giving the orders at the palace now, they didn't care. Shastro had caused the siege, given them over to fear and death. This new duke had opened the palace warehouse so that they had something to eat and drink again.

With the siege lifted, many of those who'd fled were already returning, bringing with them in some cases coin to aid those they'd been forced to leave behind. Old Lady Varra was in the forefront of these in a horse litter. Her eyes and tongue were busy as she swept her kin up to her suite and saw to it that they settled in. She herself sought out Aisling for a good enjoyable gossip. She'd always been first to know the news, and dead dukes and sieges were grist to her mill.

Trader and merchant caravans were arriving almost daily now as an early spring contributed to the city's relief. The markets were filling with fuel, food, wine, horse fodder, and other essentials. The low quarter watched to see how much of the inflow was portable. They'd lost almost three-quarters of their number and all of such scraps of goods as they had ever owned. They settled very happily to repairing their loss of numbers as well.

Jarn announced that since so many had suffered they should have a chance to rebuild. Taxes would be remitted by one half for all families who had been present during the siege. In addition, if they could prove to the duke a genuine inability to pay, ducal estate would be kept to a minimum for five years and the taxes halved for that period also. For the next five years they would rise by half of the announced reduction. After that they would return to the original level. Those merchants and tradesmen who believed themselves ruined rejoiced.

Jarn saw to the funeral with Aisling's advice. It was long, boring, and pompous. The feasting and flow of wine afterward was phenomenal. In the end Shastro slept in the tomb of the dukes of Kars. He lay richly clad, the tiny grace knife in his clasped hands. At his right lay the disinterred bones of Paran, his kinsman and friend. At his left, Sharna, cousin and beloved. Aisling stayed as the others left. She looked at those who lay in eternal silence now.

"I've done as you wished, my Lord Duke. I hope you all find peace together wherever your spirits wander."

She grinned in rueful amusement. In the way of people, tales had started circulating in Kars ever since the duke's death became known. The population had heard that it was Shastro who'd killed Kirion and been spelled to death in return. The people had made from this their own stories. It looked likely that in a short time Shastro would be remembered as the man who'd died saving Kars from sorcery. Well, everyone needed heroes, and, remembering their discussion on how the people saw their dukes, she thought it would have made Shastro smile.

But Kirion, sorcerer, evil puppet master, was not so easily disposed of. Aisling felt that his body still held danger. Wind Dancer, brought in as a test, had spat again, so vigorously his whiskers shook. He'd performed his waste-covering actions, and his tail quivered angrily. Jarn wasted no time after that.

"Burn him. Fire cleanses. Use any ceremony you like, but it's to be public so all can be satisfied how it was done and that he is truly gone. Have priestesses of Cup and Flame there so the people are certain all was done properly."

Called in, the high priestess from Kars Shrine was adamant. "I do not know the powers with which that fool trafficked, but in some way they hold him even now. Evil resides within him. That binding must be broken." She made suggestions that met with the approval of Aisling and Keelan.

Kirion's funeral pyre was in the city square. It was laid with a base of logs of sun-dried wood. Over them Aisling and the priestess laid herbs. Illbane, wound-scour, feverfew, and the tiny delicate flowers of the goddess-love, which always grew about Gunorra's shrines. Then more firewood, this time drenched in oil. On top of the man-high pyre they laid Kirion's body. Over it Aisling placed a wall-hanging. It was sent from Aiskeep, one Ciara had made so many years ago. Foolish and evil though Kirion had been, Aiskeep was still his birthplace.

When the time came, four came forward to send Kirion home. Aisling, Keelan, Hadrann—now officially betrothed to her—and, bringing applause, gasps of awe, and gentle laughter from the crowd, Wind Dancer, showing his true size and carrying a smaller flaring torch carefully in his mouth. The high priestess moved with them to pour wine across the bier.

"Go to the goddess, Kirion of Aiskeep. In her light be redeemed." Fire was applied, and the pyre blazed up. In the heart of Cup and Flame evil howled and then died. The pyre burned for twenty-four hours, until there was only gray ash. That Aisling scattered to the winds of the hills. She had privately burned all her brother's books, tools, notes, and other items of sorcery.

She rode out of Kars with Hadrann and their three guards a tenday later. Keelan rode between them, insisting it was only proper they should have a chaperone. They rode joyously, laughing, teasing, talking. Mind Dancer, in his carrysack over Aisling's shoulder, was sometimes bounced more than the road justified, but he merely growled softly, accepting that his human had her occasional faults. Once at Aiskeep Hadrann called for the finest lightest grade of paper, ink, and quills.

"Why?" Aisling was curious.

He grinned cheerfully at her. "I think someone over-mountain might be interested in events, don't you?"

"Flames, yes. I'd almost forgotten. I was asked to send a message if the geas was accomplished." She laughed. "Not that one would have been needed. I felt it when Shastro and Kirion died. Hilarion is an adept and many in the valley have more of the Gift than I do. They'd have known at once as well. But write; they may only know we won, not how we succeeded."

Hadrann nodded. "I'm sure Estcarp has spies here and there. They'll know Jarn rules Kars. We may even have someone appear here to collect our account. I'll write twice: once for Hilarion, once for Estcarp if they ever come to claim it. Your grandmother has said she will copy twice more: once for Aiskeep records and once for us to take to Aranskeep."

He finished the accounts after two days' hard work and stood, shaking stiffened fingers. At the window a hawk cried softly, a messenger from Hilarion. He tucked the scroll into a firmly tied ribbon, then bound it gently to the bird's leg. The hawk watched with interest. Hadrann offered refreshment, and stood guard as it ate and drank. Then he watched as it launched from the window. The other finished scroll he laid on the table. Ciara would deal with that.

Once he'd had a brother, one who had loved him and been loved with all the strength of a small boy's heart. That brother had died ill. Now those responsible were dead in turn. It was done. Over. Aisling brought him another brother and love again. In time he would rule Aranskeep and its people. He would not forget his brother nor cease to love him, but life was for the living and roads must be traveled. He and Aisling had their own path to walk. He remembered the feel of her soft lips against his, and his heart warmed.

Below in the main hall Keelan was uncomplicatedly happy with his grandparents. Ciara was demanding the tale of how they had helped the noblewomen and children to escape. She'd heard it once but wanted to hear it again with old Hannion and Harran. Keelan was delighted to oblige. Trovagh listened, nodding approval. The boy would make a good lord to Aiskeep when the time came.

Wind Dancer sat outside in the courtyard by the gate, his human with him. Aisling would wed in the fall. She would go to live in Aranskeep, and he would go with her. Aisling was smiling to herself. She and Hadrann had snatched half a candlemark alone in the midst of the bustle. His kisses had burned. This was no arranged marriage. She went eagerly to the man she loved.

After some time alone she returned inside to add further details to her brother's tale. After that she fell into the bustle of homecoming, riding about the garths of Aiskeep, talking to its people, and telling them all over again, at their demand, of the events of the siege and the deaths of Shastro and Kirion. In Kars life in the city settled down through spring and early summer. Traffic began again on the roads until in late summer a minstrel came riding. Ciara greeted him kindly.

"Welcome are you, man. Stay the night and sing for us."

"Old songs and new as it please you, my Lady." Old songs he did sing while all sang with him. But at the last he stood. "One last song, good folk. A new song lately sung in the court of Kars before none less than my Lord Duke, an' it please you?"

Ciara looked at Trovagh. Both nodded. The minstrel smiled, stepped back, and broke into a quiet tune, gentle and unfamiliar. Then he sang.

> *Kars was well ruled in the year of the Siege*
> *Duke Shastro was lord, of his people their liege.*
> *Shastro the sorrowful, Shastro the kind.*
> *Who knew very well the ruled's heart and mind.*
>
> *Ruled he alone. Foully slain love and kin*
> *By an evil man, Kirion, on him be the sin.*

> *Shastro the love-lost, Shastro the lone,*
> *Shastro who'd wed never, his heart a stone.*

Aisling glanced across at Hadrann. In some way whoever had penned the song had found a portion of truth. She believed, would always believe, that had the duke's love and his love's brother survived, Shastro might have been a different man.

> *Blood-magic power, cruel black the heart,*
> *Blinding the duke, to the sorcerer's part.*
> *But Shastro was clever and Shastro had sight,*
> *Shastro was ruler with aid of the Light.*

Keelan hid a smile. Precious little Light around Shastro, and none at all around Kirion—that part was true. He remembered his own years of bowing to his brother and being bullied. He'd been tricked often enough by Kirion too. Maybe the duke hadn't been quite as much to blame as Keelan had once thought.

> *Sorcerer's will and his evil desire,*
> *Will drag all of Karsten into the Mire.*
> *His throne our dead bodies, terror his sword.*
> *"Not while I live," swore Shastro, Kars' Lord.*

> *Out stood Duke Shastro, his people to aid.*
> *"None die at your bidding, not beggar nor maid."*
> *Shastro the warrior, Shastro the brave,*
> *Shastro who'd fight, his people to save.*

Hadrann listened. It wasn't the way it had been, yet did one ever know for sure. Kirion had tempted and, with none to hold him back, Shastro had fallen. Who was so strong that offered all his desires he could not fall if there were none to aid? The song wound on before the final verses, where the tune took on a triumphant note.

> *Wizard for evil, ruler for Light,*
> *Strive they in battle away from Kars' sight.*
> *Shastro the honest, Shastro the brave,*
> *Giving his life, his people to save.*
>
> *Honor our duke, let evil take wing.*
> *Dying to save us, of Shastro we sing.*
> *Shastro the hero, Light binds his sword.*
> *Did ever a people have such a lord?*

The people of Aiskeep applauded the song. Hadrann added his own approval. Maybe much of the song wasn't quite how it had happened, but Shastro had slain Kirion, that was the truth. Keelan too was clapping. Kirion was dead; he and Aiskeep were free. That was good enough for him. Aisling smiled at the minstrel, her eyes glittering with sudden tears. It had been the death of Shastro's kin that had begun the evil. If they had not died he'd have been content.

Well, let him lie content now. The minstrel was singing the song again at the demand of those who had not heard it properly before. Once Shastro had wondered if the people would sing ballads about him after he was dead. She hoped that wherever his soul might wander now, it was with his love and his best friend, and that wherever they all were, they could somehow hear the song Kars sang. Only she of all who'd known Shastro might also know his motives, and she would say nothing, ever. Let him have his tomb and his song. In the end he'd earned them both.

ABOUT THE AUTHORS

ANDRE NORTON, named a Grand Master by the Science Fiction Writers of America and awarded a Life Achievement World Fantasy Award, is the author of more than one hundred novels of science fiction and fantasy adventure. Beloved by legions of readers the world over, she has thrilled generations with such series as *Beast Master*, *Time Traders*, *The Solar Queen*, *Witch World*, and others. She lives in Murfreesboro, Tennessee. Visit her Web site at *www.andre-norton.org*.

LYN McCONCHIE is the coauthor, with Andre Norton, of *Beast Master's Ark* and *Beast Master's Circus, Ciara's Song*, and other novels. She also writes novels and short stories on her own. A native of New Zealand, she has been awarded the Sir Julius Vogel Award for Best Science Fiction or Fantasy Novel of 2002 by a New Zealander for *Beast Master's Ark*.

Look for

SILVER MAY TARNISH

BY ANDRE NORTON AND LYN McCONCHIE

**Now available in Hardcover
by Tom Doherty Associates**